A Heron Books Publication

THE MASTERPIECES OF

Guy de Maupassant

II

GUY DE MAUPASSANT
1850–1893

Guy de Maupassant

UNE VIE
OR
THE HISTORY OF A HEART
AND
OTHER STORIES

HERON BOOKS · LONDON

CONTENTS

Author's Introductory Note.................................. i

Une Vie 1

Mademoiselle Fifi 268
Moonlight (*Claire de Lune*) 286
Miss Harriet 292
Toine 321
The String (*La Ficelle*)...............................334
A Mesalliance (*une Mésalliance*)......................344
The Umbrella (*La Parapluie*) 354

CONCERNING NOVELS

I HAVE no intention of pleading here for the novel that follows. On the contrary, the ideas that I am going to try to express deal with the criticism of that description of psychological study which is shown in "Pierre and Jean," as well as with novels in general. I am not the only writer to whom one particular reproach is addressed every time he brings out a new book. In the midst of eulogistic phrases, I regularly find the following from the pen of the same critic: "The greatest defect of this book is that it is not, properly speaking, a novel." I might reply in the same terms: "The greatest defect of the writer who does me the honor to review me is that he is not a critic."

What, in fact, are the earmarks of a critic?

It is necessary that, without bias, without preconceived notions, without ideas of any "school" or special regard for any one class of artists, he should comprehend, distinguish, and explain the most opposite tendencies and the most contrary temperaments, and admit and accept the most diverse efforts of art.

Now the critic who after reading "Manon Lescaut," "Paul and Virginia," "Don Quixote," "Les Liaisons Dangereuses," "Werther," "Elective Affinities," "Clarissa Harlowe," "Émile," "Candide," "Cinq-Mars," "René," "Les Trois Mousquetaires," "Mauprat," "Le Père Goriot," "La Cousine Bette," "Colombe," "Le Rouge et le Noir," "Mademoiselle de Maupin," "Notre-Dame de Paris," "Salammbo," "Madame Bovary," "Adolphe," "M. de Camors," "L'Assommoir," "Sapho," etc., still feels impelled to cry, "This is a novel and that is not a novel," seems to me endowed with a perspicacity which strongly resembles incompetency. Generally the critic understands by a novel a narrative more or less true, arranged in the manner of a play in three acts, of which the first contains the exposition, the second the action, and the third the *dénouement*. This method of composition is quite admissible, on condition that we accept all others also.

Are there any rules for the making of a novel, which, if neglected, put the book into another class? If "Don Quixote" is a novel, is "Le Rouge et le Noir?" If "Monte Christo" is a novel, is "L'Assommoir?" Can any satisfactory comparison be drawn between Goethe's "Elective Affinities," Dumas's "The Three Musketeers," Flaubert's "Madame Bovary," Octave Feuillet's "M. de Camors," and Zola's "Germinal?" Which of them is The Novel? What are these famous rules? Where did they originate? Who laid them down? And by what principle, on whose authority, and through what process of reasoning?

And still, apparently, these critics know in some positive and indisputable way how a novel is constituted and what marks it out from other tales which are not novels. This is as much as to say that without being creators themselves they are leagued in a school, and that they, as do the writers of novels, set aside all work planned and executed beyond the pale of their æsthetics. An intelligent critic should, on the contrary, seek out everything that bears the least resemblance to the novels already written, and encourage young authors to essay as far as possible new paths.

Writers in general, Victor Hugo as well as M. Zola, have persistently claimed the absolute and incontrovertible right to compose: *i. e.,* to imagine or observe, according to their individual idea of originality—that is, a special manner of thinking, seeing, understanding, and judging. Well, the critic who assumes that The Novel can be defined in conformity with the ideas which he has based upon the novels he himself prefers, and that certain hard and fast rules of construction can be laid down, will invariably find himself at war with the artistic temperament of a writer who introduces a new style of work. A critic who is really worthy of the name should be an analyst, without either preferences or passions; like a connoisseur of pictures, he ought simply to sum up the artistic value of the object of art presented to him. His intelligence, open to everything, must supersede his individuality so far as to leave him at liberty to discover and praise books which as a man he may not like, but which as a judge he is bound to appreciate at their proper value.

But critics, in the majority of cases, are merely readers; and so it happens that they almost invariably find fault with us on wrong grounds, or praise us unreservedly and without discretion.

The reader who only asks from a book that it shall satisfy the natural bent of his mind wants the novel to respond to his particular taste, and he always praises a book or a passage which appeals to his imagination, whether it be idealistic, gay, licentious, melancholy, dreamy or positive, "striking" or "well written."

The public as a whole consists of diverse groups, whose cry to us authors is: "Comfort me," "Amuse me," "Touch me," "Make me dream," "Make me laugh," "Make me shudder," "Make me weep," "Make me think." Only a few chosen spirits say to the artist: "Give me something good in any shape that suits you best, according to your own temperament."

The artist makes the attempt; and succeeds or fails. The critic should judge the result only in relation to the nature of the attempt; he has no business to trouble himself about tendencies. This has been said a thousand times already; it will always bear repetition.

Therefore, after a succession of literary schools which have given us deformed, superhuman, poetic, pathetic, charming, or splendid pictures of life, a realistic or naturalistic school has arisen, which maintains that it shows us the truth, the whole truth, and nothing but the truth.

All these theories of art must be recognized as of equal interest, and we must judge the books which they produce solely from the point of view of artistic value, with an *a priori* acceptance of the general ideas

iv

which gave them birth. To question the author's right to produce a practical or a realistic work is to attempt to coerce his temperament, to take exception to his originality, to forbid him to use the eyes and brains with which nature has endowed him. To find fault with him for seeing things as beautiful or ugly, as mean or sublime, as gracious or sinister, is to reproach him for not being made on this or that pattern, and for possessing eyes which do not see precisely as do our own.

By all means leave him at liberty to conceive things as he chooses, provided he is an artist. If he is an idealist let us soar to poetic heights to judge him, and then show him that his dream is commonplace and ordinary, not mad or magnificent enough. But if we are judging a materialist, let us show him how the truth of life differs from the picture of it in his book. It needs no argument to prove that schools differing so widely must have adopted diametrically opposite processes in composition.

The novelist who perverts unchangeable truth — however uncompromising and unpleasing it may be — in order to cull from it an exceptional and pleasing plot, must of necessity distort events without respect for probability, molding them to suit himself, arraying or arranging them so as to attract, excite, or affect the reader. The plan of his novel is but a sequence of ingenious combinations, skillfully leading up to the *dénouement*. The incidents are planned and graduated up to the culminating point of the conclusion, the crowning and fateful climax, satisfying the curiosity aroused in the beginning, quenching the interest, and ending the tale so completely that we have no further desire to know what happened the next day to the most interesting characters in it.

The novelist who, on the contrary, purposes giving us a true picture of life must carefully avoid any collection of events which might appear exceptional. His aim is not to tell a story for our amusement, or as an appeal to our feelings, but to make us reflect and understand the mysterious and deeper meaning of events. By seeing and meditating, he has come to regard the world, events, men, and things in a way peculiarly his own, which is the product of the sum total of his study and observation. It is this individual view of the world which he tries to convey to us by reproducing it in a book. To make his view of life as clear to us as it has been to himself, he must bring it before our eyes with scrupulous fidelity. Therefore he must compose his work with such ability, it must be so full of art disguised in simplicity, that it will be impossible to detect and delineate the scheme or to perceive the purpose of the author.

Instead of working up an adventure and constructing it in such a way that it will be interesting to the end, he will take his character or characters at a certain stage of their lives and lead them by natural stages to the next. In this way he will depict either how the minds of mankind are influenced by their environments, or how men's passions and sentiments grow; how they love or hate; how they struggle in every sphere of society; how their interests conflict —social interests, pecuniary interests, family interests, political interests.

The skill of his plot will consist, not in the power to affect or to charm, in a pleasing opening or a thrilling *dénouement*, but in the skillful grouping of small but invariable facts from which the final issue of the work may be gathered. If in the space of three hundred pages he portrays ten years of a life so as to show what its individual and characteristic significance has been in the midst of all the other human beings surrounding it, he should know how to cast out from the innumerable petty events of every-day life all which do not help his purpose, and how to show in a special light all those things which would have remained unseen to the eyes of the less observant, things which give his book weight and value as a whole.

It is conceivable that this mode of construction, so unlike the old method which was evident to everyone, is certain often to mislead the critics, and that all of them will not descry the subtle and secret wires — fine almost to invisibility — which certain modern artists use instead of the one formerly called the "plot."

In short, where the novelist of yesterday preferred to narrate the crises of life, the acute phases of the mind and heart, the novelist of the present day writes the history of the heart, the soul, and the intellect in their normal condition. To attain the effect he strives after, which is the sense of simple reality, and to teach the artistic lesson he attempts to draw therefrom, which is a revelation of the status of present-day mankind in his eyes, he must intrude no facts that are not universal and invariable.

But even when we do take the same point of view as these realistic artists, we may discuss and question their theory, which might be comprehended in these words: "The whole truth and nothing but the truth." As the end they propose is to evolve the philosophy of certain fixed and current facts, they must frequently alter events in favor of probability and to the loss of truth; for "Truth is sometimes opposed to probability."

The realist, if he is an artist, will not try to present us with a commonplace photograph of life, but will endeavor to give us a picture of it more perfect, more striking, more convincing than reality itself. To tell everything is impossible; it would require at least a volume for each day to enumerate the endless insignificant incidents with which our life is filled. A choice must be made — and this is the first blow to the theory of "the whole truth."

Besides, life is made up of the most dissimilar things, the most unexpected, contradictory, and incongruous; it is brutal and without sequence or connection, full of inexplicable, illogical, and contradictory catastrophes, which can only be classed as miscellaneous facts. It is for this reason that the artist, his subject chosen, can select from this life, overcrowded with chances and trifles, only such characteristic details as apply to that subject, and reject all else — everything that is merely incidental.

Here is one instance from among a thousand. The number of persons who daily meet with a fatal accident, throughout the whole world, is very considerable. But how can an author drop a tile on the head of an important character, or fling him under the wheels of a vehicle in the middle of his story, under the plea that accident must play its part?

Again, in real life there is no difference between foreground and distance, and events are sometimes hurried on, and sometimes they are left lingering indefinitely. On the contrary, art consists in the employment of foresight and elaboration, in the arrangement of skillful and ingenious gradations, in setting essential events in a strong light simply by the skill of composition, and in giving all other events that degree of relief, proportionate to their importance, which is necessary to convey a convincing impression of the special truth to be communicated.

"Truth" in such a work consists in the production of a perfect illusion by following the common logic of facts, and not by writing them down headlong as they follow one another. For this reason I maintain that the higher order of Realists should rather call themselves Illusionists.

How childish it truly is to believe in this Reality, since the truth, to each of us, is in his own mind, his own organs. Our individual eyes and ears, taste and smell, create in us as many different truths as there are human beings in the world.

And our brains, duly and differently informed by these organs, apprehend, analyze, and judge as variously as if each of us were a being of an alien race. Each of us, therefore, has simply his own illusion of the world, poetic, sentimental, cheerful, mournful, or vulgar, according to his nature. And the author's only mission is faithfully to reproduce this illusion, with all the elaborations of art which he has learned and has at his command. The illusion of beauty — it is nothing but a conventional term invented by mankind! The illusion of ugliness — it is a matter of varying opinion! The illusion of truth — never unchangeable! The illusion of depravity — how many minds does it fascinate! Those are the great artists who can make other people see their own particular illusion.

We ought not be angry with any one theory, since each is merely the outcome, in generalizations, of a special temperament analyzing itself. Of these theories two have been in particular the subject of discussion, and have been opposed to each other instead of being recognized as on an equal footing; that of the purely analytical novel, and that of the objective novel.

The partisans of analysis require the author to devote himself to the indication of the slightest evolutions of the soul, and of all the most secret springs of action, attaching quite a secondary importance to the act and fact itself. The latter is merely a milestone, or else the goal, the excuse for the book. If they are to be believed, these works, exact and visionary at the same time, in which fancy mingles with observation, should be written in the way a philosopher composes a psychological treatise, should follow causes to their remotest origin, tell the why and wherefore of every impulse, and detect every phase of the soul's movements under the several impulses of interest, passion, or instinct.

The partisans of realism — I do not like the word — striving, on the other hand, to give us an exact picture of all that happens in life, carefully avoid all involved explanations, all discourses on motive, and content themselves with letting persons and events pass before our eyes. They hold the opinion that the psychology of action should be concealed in the book, in the same way as it is in reality hidden from ordinary eyes under the facts of existence. As planned on these lines the novel gains in interest; the narrative contains more movement, more color, more of the action of life.

Instead, therefore, of giving long explanations of the state of mind of an actor in the story, the objective writer tries to find out the action or gesture which that state of mind will inevitably produce in that person, under the circumstances detailed. And he makes him conduct himself from one end of the book to the other in such a way that all his actions and gestures shall be the expression of his innermost nature, his thoughts, his impulses, or his waverings. In this way he conceals psychology instead of discovering it; he uses it as the skeleton of his work, just as the unseen bony framework is the skeleton of the human body. The artist who paints our portraits does not display our bones.

It seems to me that the novel constructed on this principle gains also in sincerity. In the first place it is more probable, for the persons we see moving around us do not lay bare to us the motives from which they act.

We must also recognize the fact that even if by close observation of men and women we can so exactly sound their characters as to prophesy what will be their conduct under almost any circumstances — if we can say conclusively, "Such an one, of such a disposition, in such a case, will do this or that," it does not follow that we could trace out one by one all the secret workings of his mind — which is not our own — all the secret appeals of his instinct — which is not the same as ours — or all the varied promptings of his nature—in which the organs, nerves, blood, and flesh differ from ours.

However great the genius of a gentle, delicate-minded man, innocent of passion and devoted to science and work, he can never so put himself into the personality of a dashing, sensual, and violent man of exuberant vitality, torn by every desire or even vice, as to understand and depict the secret impulses and feelings of an individual so unlike himself, even though he may be able very thoroughly to imagine and relate all the actions of his life.

In a word, the writer of purely psychological bent can do nothing more than put himself in the place of all his puppets in the different situations he has made for them. He cannot possibly change his organs, which are the only links between outward life and ourselves, which govern us by their perceptions, narrow our sensibilities, and create in each of us a soul essentially different from all around us. Our outlook over, and our knowledge of, the world, as well as our ideas of life, we acquire by the help of our senses, and we cannot but transfer them to some extent to all the persons whose secret motives we set ourselves to reveal.

It is therefore always ourselves we display in the body of a king or an assassin, a robber or an honest man, a courtesan, a nun, a young girl, or a vulgar market woman; for we cannot help putting the problem in the personal form: "If *I* were a king, a murderer, a courtesan, a nun, or a market woman, what would *I* do, what would *I* think, how would *I* act?" All we can do is to differentiate our character by altering the age, the sex, the social status, and all the environment of life, of that *ego* which nature has shut up behind the insurmountable barrier of the organs of sense. Skill consists in not displaying this *ego* to the reader, but in concealing it under the different masks which we employ for that purpose.

Yet although, as regards perfect accuracy, pure psychological analysis is not beyond the reach of attack, it can, notwithstanding, produce as great works of art as any other method.

Why not take the *Symbolists* for instance ? Their artistic dream is a worthy one; besides, they have this especially interesting feature that they appreciate and declare the extreme difficulty of art. Really a man must be very bold or very foolish to write at all in these days. Amid so many and various masters of the art, of such many-sided genius, what remains to be done that has not already been done, or what to say that has not been said ? Who among us can boast of having written a page or a sentence which cannot be found — or something closely resembling it — in some other book ? When we read, we who are so saturated with literature that our whole system seems as if it were a sheer compound of words, do we ever come upon a line or a thought which is un-familiar to us, or of which we have not had at least a previous inkling ? He who tries merely to amuse his public by hackneyed methods writes with confi-dence, in his ingenuous mediocrity, works intended only for the ignorant and idle mob.

But those who feel the weight of centuries of past literature, who are displeased with everything because they dream of something better, for whom the bloom is off everything, and who are always struck with the uselessness, the commonplaceness of their own works, grow to look upon literary art as a thing unattainable and mysterious, hardly to be discovered except in a few pages by the greatest masters. A score or so of sentences suddenly thrill us like a revelation; but the words which follow are just like all other words, the rest of the prose is like all other prose.

Men of genius, doubtless, escape this regret and pain because they have within themselves resistless creative power. They do not pass judgment upon themselves. The rest of us, who are no better than plodding, conscientious toilers, can but strive against invincible discouragement by unending effort. Two men have given me by their simple, clear teaching the strength to try again and again: Louis Bouilhet and Gustave Flaubert. If I join my name with theirs here, it is so that their counsel, summed up in a few lines, may be of use to any young writers who may be less self-confident than most of those who make their *début* in print.

Bouilhet, with whom I first became intimate some two years before I attained the friendship of Flaubert, by telling me that a hundred lines or even less, if they are flawless, and contain the essence of the talent and originality of even a second-rate man, are sufficient to establish his reputation as an artist, convinced me that persevering work and a perfect knowledge of the art, might, in some fortunate hour of clearness, power, and enthusiasm, by the fortuitous advent of a subject in complete accord with the tendency of one's mind, lead to the production of a single work, short but as perfect as man can make it. Then I comprehended that the best known writers have scarcely left us more than one such volume; and that essential above all is the good fortune which enables us to discover and see, among the varied mass of matter which is ready for selection, the subject which will absorb all our faculties, all that is good in us, all our artistic powers.

Later on, Flaubert, whom I had sometimes met, took a liking for me. I ventured to show him a few attempts. He kindly read them and replied: "I cannot say whether you have any talent. What you have brought me proves a certain intelligence; but never forget this, young man: talent — as Chateaubriand says — is nothing but long patience. Go and work."

I worked; and I frequently went to see him, feeling that he liked me, for he had begun to call me, jestingly, "his disciple." For seven years I wrote poetry, I wrote stories, I even wrote a villainous play. Nothing of all these remains. The master read it all; then while we breakfasted together the following Sunday he would give me his criticisms, instilling into me two or three principles which sum up the drift of his long and patient exhortations: "If you have any originality," said he, "you must above all things show it; if you have none you must acquire it."

Talent is long patience. Everything you wish to say must be thought over long and attentively, till you can find some aspect of it which no one has yet seen and expressed. To everything there is an unexplored side, because as a rule we never use our eyes except with the remembrance of what others have already thought of the things we see. The smallest thing has something unknown in it; that we must find. To describe a blazing fire, a tree in a plain, it is necessary to stand face to face with that fire or that tree till to us they are totally unlike any other fire or tree. In this way we may become original.

Then having formulated the truth that there are not two grains of sand, two flies, two hands, or two noses absolutely alike in the whole world, he would make me describe in a few sentences some person or object, so as to define it exactly, and distinguish it from all others of the same race or species.

"When you pass a grocer sitting at his doorway," he would say, "a porter smoking his pipe, or a cab stand, let me see that grocer and that porter, their attitude and their whole appearance, with an indication of their whole moral nature, in such a fashion that I could not mistake them for any other grocer or porter; and by one word make me comprehend wherein one cab-horse differs from fifty others in front or behind it."

I have described his ideas of style at greater length elsewhere; they bear a strong relation to the theory of observation I have just laid down. Whatever the thing we want to say there is just one noun to name it, just one verb to give it motion, just one adjective to qualify it. We must seek till we find this noun, this verb, and this adjective, and never be content with getting close to it, never permit ourselves to play tricks, even happy ones, or have recourse to juggling with language to escape a difficulty. The subtlest thing may be expressed and suggested by applying the hint conveyed in Boileau's line: "He taught the power of a word put in its place."

There is no necessity for an eccentric vocabulary to express every shade of thought—no need for the multitude of complicated, outlandish words which are foisted upon us to-day in the name of artistic writing; but every modification of the value of a word by its place in the sentence must be distinguished with the greatest clearness. Give us fewer nouns, verbs, and adjectives, with almost indiscernible shades of meaning, and a greater variety of phrases, more variously put together, ingeniously divided, sonorous and full of cultured rhythm. Let us try to be admirable in style, rather than remarkable for collecting rare words.

It is in truth more difficult to bend a sentence to our will and make it express everything — even what it does not say — to fill it with suggestion, than to invent new expressions or to seek out in old, forgotten books all those which have fallen into disuse and lost their meaning, so that to us they are nothing but a dead language.

The French language, it is true, is a pure stream which affected writers never have sullied and never can sully. Into its clear waters every age has flung pretentious archaisms and euphuisms, but on the surface no trace can be seen of these useless and impotent attempts. The nature of the language is to be clear, logical, and forcible. It does not lend itself to feebleness, obscurity, or corruption.

Those who write without due care for abstract terms, who make rain and hail mar the clear shining of the windowpanes, may throw stones at the simplicity of their brothers of the pen. The stones may certainly hit their brothers, who have a body, but they will never hurt simplicity — which has none.

GUY DE MAUPASSANT.

LA GUILLETTE, ÉTRETAT, *September, 1887.*

UNE VIE

CHAPTER I.

THE START FOR THE "POPLARS"

WHEN Jeanne had finished packing her trunks she went to the window, but the rain had not ceased falling.

The downpour had sounded against the window-panes and the roof all night long. It seemed as if the sky, lowering and saturated with water, had burst, emptying itself upon the earth, diluting it into a sort of hasty-pudding, melting it like sugar. Sudden squalls passed over, filled with a strong heat. The roaring of overflowing gutters filled the deserted streets, in which the houses, like sponges, drank the humidity, which penetrated within them·and made the walls perspire from the cellar to the garret.

Jeanne, who had left the convent the day before, finally free forever, and ready to seize upon all the pleasures of life, feared her father would not start if

1

the weather did not clear, and for the hundredth time since morning she examined the horizon.

Then she perceived that she had forgotten to put her calendar in her traveling bag. She took from the wall the little card which was divided into months, and which bore in the midst of a pretty design the date of the current year, 1819, in figures of gold. Then she crossed off with a pencil the first four columns, erasing each month's name and each day's number, until she came to the second of May, the day of her leaving the convent.

A voice on the other side of the door, called, "Jeanne!" Jeanne answered: "Come in, papa." And her father appeared.

Baron Simon-Jacques Le Perthuis des Vauds was a gentleman of the former century, crazy and good. An enthusiatic disciple of Jean-Jacques Rousseau he had all the tenderness of a lover for nature, the fields, the woods, the animals.

Aristocrat by birth, he hated by instinct the year 1793; but, philosopher by temperament, and liberal by education, he execrated tyranny with an inoffensive and declamatory hatred. His great strength and his great weakness were his good nature, a good nature which had not arms enough to caress, to yield to embrace, a creative good nature, without resistance, from lack of volition, of energy, almost a vice.

A man of theories, he had thought out a whole plan of education for his daughter, desiring to make her happy, good, upright, and tender. She had remained at home up to the age of twelve, when, in spite of her mother's tears, she was placed in the convent of the Sacred Heart.

2

He had kept her rigidly shut up there, cloistered, ignorant of human things. He wanted them to restore her to him chaste, at the age of seventeen, to steep her himself in a sort of bath of poetry; and by the fields, in the midst of the fruitful country, to open her soul, to sharpen her ignorance by the aspect of artless love, of the simple tenderness of animals, of the severe laws of life.

She left the convent now, radiant, full of sap and appetite for happiness, ready for all joys, for all the charming vicissitudes which her mind had already gone through in the idleness of her days, the lengthiness of the nights, the solitude of her hopes.

She seemed a portrait by Paul Veronese, with her fair, shining tresses, which might have been said to have colored her flesh, an aristocratic flesh slightly tinted with pink, shaded with a light down, a sort of pale velvet, just perceptible when the sun kissed it. Her eyes were blue, that opaque blue which is seen in figures of Holland *faïence*. Upon her left nostril she had a little beauty spot, and another at the right upon her chin, where there were a few tiny hairs so like her skin that they could hardly be distinguished. She was tall, with a well-developed chest and an undulating figure. Her clear voice sounded at times too sharp, but her frank laugh spread joy about her. Often, with a familiar gesture, she carried her two hands to her temples as if to smooth her hair.

She ran to her father and kissed him with a hug. "Well, are we going to start?" she asked. He smiled, shook his locks, now already white, which he wore quite long, and stretching his hand toward the window said:

3

"How can we travel in such weather?"

But she begged him, cajoling and tender: "Oh, papa, let us start. It will clear up in the afternoon."

"But your mother will never consent to it."

"Yes, I promise you that she will. I will answer for it."

"If you succeed in persuading your mother, I am willing myself."

Jeanne hastened to the Baronne's room, for she had awaited this day of departure with a growing impatience. Since entering the Sacred Heart she had not left Rouen, her father not permitting any distraction before the age which he had fixed. She was going now to pass the summer on their estate of the "Poplars," an old family château situated on the cliff near Yport, and she anticipated infinite joy in the free life at the edge of the waves. Then it was understood that this manor would be presented to her, and that she should live in it when she was married. And the rain falling ceaselessly without respite since the day before was the first great sorrow of her existence.

But in three minutes she came running out of her mother's room, crying all through the house: "Papa, papa, mamma is willing. So have them harness up."

The deluge was not lessening, it might even be said that it was redoubling, when the barouche was driven to the door. Jeanne was ready to get into the carriage when the Baronne came downstairs supported on one side by her husband, and on the other by a tall chambermaid, strong and strapping as a lad. The latter was a Norman woman of the country of Caux, who appeared at least twenty, although she was eighteen at the most. She was treated in the family as a second daughter, for she was Jeanne's foster-sister. Her name was Rosalie, and her principal function consisted in guiding the steps of her mistress, who had become enormous in the last few years by reason of a hypertrophy of the heart, of which she always complaining.

The Baronne, panting a good deal, reached the steps of the old residence, looked at the court where the water was streaming and murmured: "It is truly not sensible."

Her husband smiling, replied: "It is you who desired it, Madame Adelaide."

As she bore the pompous name of Adelaide, he always preceded it by "Madame" with a respect that seemed a little derisive. Madame continued her progress and climbed painfully into the carriage, all the springs of which bent. The Baron sat at her side, and Jeanne and Rosalie took their places on the opposite seat, with their backs to the horses.

The cook Ludivine brought a lot of cloaks, which were put over the knees, and two baskets, which were concealed beneath the legs of the travelers; then she climbed to the box beside father Simon; and wrapped herself in a great rug which entirely covered her. The porter and his wife came to give their parting salutations as they shut the carriage door, and received the last orders about the trunks which would follow in a wagon, and so they started. Father Simon the coachman, his head bowed, his back bent under the rain, disappeared beneath his box coat with its triple cape, the howling storm beat upon the carriage windows and inundated the highway.

The "berlin," with the two horses at a trot descended rapidly to the quay, skirted the line of great ships whose masts, yards, and rigging rose gloomily in the dripping sky, like leafless trees: then it took the long boulevard of Mount Riboudet.

Soon they crossed the meadows, and from time to time, a drowned willow with its branches falling with the abandonment of a corpse, outlined itself somberly through a sheet of rain. The horses' hoofs clattered and the four wheels made circles of mud.

They were silent: their minds themselves seemed to be wet like the earth. Madame, lolling back, pillowed her head and closed her eyes. The Baron inspected the drenched and monotonous fields with a dejected glance. Rosalie, a parcel on her knees, was dreaming with the animal-like reverie of the common people. But Jeanne, under this tepid downpour, felt herself reviving like a plant which has been shut up and which has just been restored to the air; and the density of her joy sheltered her heart from sorrow, like foliage. Although she did not speak, she wanted to sing, to stretch out her hand in order to fill it with rain-water which she drank: and she enjoyed being carried along at full trot by the horses, looking at the desolation of the landscape and feeling herself protected in the midst of this inundation. And under the pelting rain the gleaming backs of the two animals dripped with streaming water.

The Baronne gradually fell asleep. Her face, framed by six dangling ringlets, gradually disappeared softly supported by the three great billows of her neck whose last undulations were lost in the full ocean of her chest. Her head rising at each breath fell again, her cheeks were puffed, while between her partly opened lips a loud snore passed. Her husband leaned toward her, and gently placed a little leather pocketbook in her hands which were folded upon the amplitude of her stomach.

This touch awakened her: and she gazed at the object with a sort of drowned look, with that stupid expression of interrupted dreams. The pocketbook dropped and opened. Gold coins and bank bills were scattered in the barouche. This completely aroused her, and the gaiety of her daughter was heard in a peal of laughter.

The Baron picked up the money and placing it on her knees said: "This, dear, is all that is left of my farm at Eletot. I sold it to repair the "Poplars," where we shall often live in the future."

She counted six thousand four hundred francs and put them tranquilly in her pocket. It was the ninth farm thus sold out of the thirty-one which their parents had left to them. They nevertheless still possessed about twenty thousand livres of income from lands which, properly managed, would have yielded them thirty thousand francs a year.

As they lived simply, this revenue would have been sufficient if there had not been a bottomless hole always open in the house, good-natured generosity. It dried up the money in their hands as the sun dries up the water in the marshes. It flowed, fled, disappeared. How? Nobody knew. One of them frequently said to the other:

"I don't know how it is, but I have spent a hundred francs to-day, without buying anything much."

7

This faculty of giving was, however, one of the great pleasures of their life. They agreed on this point in a way which was both superb and touching.

Jeanne asked: "Is it handsome, now, my château?"

The Baron answered gaily: "You shall see, little daughter."

But gradually the violence of the storm lessened: then there was only a sort of mist, a fine dust of whirling rain. The vault of clouds seemed to rise and to whiten: and suddenly through a rift, a long slanting ray of sunshine fell upon the meadows, and the clouds having been rent asunder, the blue heights of the firmament appeared: then the tearing increased as a veil is torn: and a beautiful azure sky, clear and fathomless, spread over the world.

A fresh and gentle breath of wind was felt, like a happy sigh of the earth, and when they skirted gardens or woods they heard at times the sprightly song of a bird, drying his wings. Evening came. Everyone in the carriage was asleep except Jeanne. Twice they stopped at inns to rest the horses and give them a little hay and water.

The sun had set. Bells were ringing in the distance. In a little village the people were lighting the lamps; and the sky was also illumined by myriad stars. Lighted houses appeared from place to place, piercing the shadows with a point of fire; and suddenly behind a hill, through the branches of the fir-trees, the moon rose, red, enormous, and, as it were, torpid with sleep.

It was so pleasant that the windows were lowered. Jeanne, exhausted with dreams, surfeited with happy visions, was now reposing. At times the be-numbed feeling occasioned by remaining too long in one position made her open her eyes: then she looked out and saw the trees of a farm pass in the luminous night, or perhaps some cows lying here and there in a field, and which raised their heads.

Then she sought a new posture, and tried to take up an interrupted dream; but the continuous rolling of the carriage filled her ears, fatigued her mind, and she closed her eyes, feeling her spirit overpowered with lassitude as well as her body.

At last they stopped. Some men and women were standing before the carriage door with lan-terns in their hands. They had arrived. Jeanne, suddenly awakened, quickly jumped out. Her father and Rosalie, lighted by a farmer, almost carried the Baronne, who was enfeebled, groaning in distress, and continually repeating in a weak little voice: "Ah! my God, my poor children!" She would not take anything to eat or anything to drink, went to bed and at once fell asleep.

Jeanne and the Baron had supper together. They smiled as they looked at each other, taking hands across the table; and both seized with a childish joy, they began to inspect the restored manor.

It was one of those high and vast Norman resi-dences, comprising both the farmhouse and the château, built of white stone which had turned gray, and spacious enough to hold a tribe. An immense vestibule divided the house in two and crossed it, opening its great doors on two *façades*. A double stairway seemed to bestride this entrance, leaving the center and uniting its two flights of steps at the second floor after the fashion of a bridge. On the ground floor on the right was an inordinately large drawing-room, hung with tapestries representing foliage with birds. All the furniture, upholstered in tapestry, illustrated La Fontaine's Fables: and Jeanne had a shiver of pleasure on seeing again an old chair which she had loved as a child, and which represented the history of the Fox and the Stork.

At one side of the drawing-room were the library filled with old books and two other unused rooms. At the left were the dining-room with new wainscoting, linen-room, the butler's pantry, and a little apartment containing a bath tub.

A hall divided the whole second story. The ten doors of the ten rooms opened from this hall; quite at the back, on the right, was Jeanne's apartment. They entered it. The Baron had just had it newly refurnished, merely having employed the hangings and the furniture remaining unused in the garret. Tapestries of a Flemish origin, and very old, peopled this place with singular personages.

But when she perceived her bed, the young girl uttered cries of joy. At the four corners, four large oaken birds, all black and gleaming with wax, supported the couch and seemed to be its guardians. The sides represented two long garlands of carved flowers and fruits: and four finely fluted columns terminating in Corinthian capitals supported a cornice of Cupids intertwined with roses.

It stood monumental, and yet very graceful, in spite of the wood darkened by time. The coverlet and the hangings of the canopy shone like two firmaments. They were made of rich silk of a deep blue and were starred in places by large lilies. When she had sufficiently admired it, Jeanne, raising her light, examined the tapestries to make out the subject.

A young seigneur and a young lady dressed in green, red, and yellow, in a most strange fashion, were conversing under a blue tree, on which white fruit was growing. A fat rabbit of the same color was nibbling a little green grass.

Just above the figures at a conventional distance, five little round houses with pointed roofs were perceived, and higher up, almost in the sky, a very red windmill. A great deal of conventional ornamentation representing flowers ran through all this. The two other panels much resembled the first, except that out of the houses came four little old men clad in the Flemish fashion, and raising their arms to heaven in token of their extreme astonishment and anger.

But the last hanging represented a drama. Near that rabbit, which was still nibbling, the young man was stretched out seemingly dead. The young lady, looking at him, was piercing her bosom with a sword, and the fruits of the tree had become black. Jeanne gave up trying to understand when she observed in a corner a tiny little beast, which the rabbit, had he lived, could have swallowed like a blade of grass. And yet it was a lion.

Then she recognized the misfortunes of Pyramus and Thisbe, and although she smiled at the simplicity of the designs, she felt happy to be inclosed within this adventure of love, which would continually speak to her thoughts of cherished hopes, and

11

every night this legendary affection would come to hover over her slumbers.

All the rest of the furniture was made in the most diverse styles. They were pieces which each generation leaves in the family, and which make of ancient houses a sort of museum, in which all kinds of things are mingled. A superb Louis XV. commode, bound in shining brass, was flanked by two Louis XV. chairs, still covered with their silken bouquets. A rosewood *secrétaire* stood opposite the chimney-piece, on which was an Empire clock under a glass globe. It was a golden beehive upheld by four marble columns above a garden of gilt flowers. A slender pendulum, hanging from the hive through a long slit, swung eternally a little bee with enameled wings over this flower bed. The dial was of painted *faïence*, and set in the side of the beehive. It began to strike eleven. The Baron kissed his daughter and went to his own room. Then Jeanne, with regret, went to bed.

With a last glance she ran over the room, and then extinguished her candle. But the bed, whose head alone was against the wall, had a little window at its left, through which a flood of moonlight streamed, spreading a flash of brightness on the floor. Reflections were cast upon the walls, pale reflections, feebly caressing the motionless figures of Pyramus and Thisbe. By the other window, opposite her feet, Jeanne perceived a tall tree, all bathed in a soft light. She turned on her side, shut her eyes, then in a little while opened them again.

She seemed to feel still shaken by the jolting of the carriage, whose rolling noise still lingered in her head. She remained quiet at first, hoping that this repose would make her finally go to sleep: but the impatience of her mind soon spread through her whole body. She had twitchings in her legs, and an increasing fever. Then she rose, and barefooted, bare-armed, with her long night robe, which gave her the appearance of a phantom, she crossed the little lake of light spread over the floor, opened her window, and looked out.

The night was so clear that a person could see in it, as in full daylight; and the young girl recognized all that country, beloved of her early childhood. There was first, opposite her, a large barn, yellow as butter, under the nocturnal light. Two giant trees stood before the château, a plane-tree on the north, and a linden on the south. Away at the end of the great stretch of grass, a little grove terminated this domain, sheltered from tempests by five rows of ancient elms, twisted, clipped, eaten away, bent like a roof by the unceasing ocean wind.

This little park was bounded on the right and left by two long avenues of extremely tall poplars, which separated the residence of the owners from the two adjacent farmhouses, one occupied by the Couillard family and the other by the Martin family.

These poplars had given their name to the château. Beyond this inclosure stretched a long uncultivated plain, thick with furze, where the breeze whistled and galloped day and night. Then suddenly the coast fell in a cliff of a hundred meters, steep and white, bathing its foot in the ocean waves.

Jeanne gazed afar over the long mottled surface which seemed to slumber beneath the stars. In this interregnum of the light all the odors of the' earth were spread abroad. A jasmine clambering about the lower windows continually exhaled its penetrating breath, which mingled with the lighter fragrance of the growing leaves. Sluggish breezes passed, bringing the strong savors of the saline air and the vicious moisture of the seaweeds.

The young girl at first gave herself up to the pleasure of breathing: and the repose of the fields calmed her like a cool bath. All the animals which awake when evening comes and conceal their obscure existence in the tranquillity of the nights filled the half shadows with a silent agitation.

Large birds, which uttered no cries, winged the air like shades; hummings of invisible insects touched the ear; silent tracks crossed the grass heavy with dew or the dark surface of the deserted roads. Only the melancholy frogs sent to the moon their short and monotonous notes.

It seemed to Jeanne that her hearing grew larger, filled with the whisperings of this tranquil night, feeling suddenly a thousand roving desires, similar to those nocturnal animals whose quiverings surrounded her. An affinity united her to this living poetry: and in the soft whiteness of the night she felt strange shivers run over her, the throbbing of impalpable hopes, something like a breath of happiness.

And she began to dream of love.

Love! for two years it had filled her with the increasing anxiety of its approach. Now she was free to love; she had nothing more to do but to meet *him*. How would it come to pass? She did not exactly know, and she did not even question. It would be *he*, that was all.

14

She only knew that she would adore *him* with all her soul, and that *he* would cherish her with all *his* strength. They would take walks on evenings like this one, beneath the luminous dust that falls from the stars. They would go hand in hand close together, hearing the beating of their hearts, feeling the warmth of their shoulders, mingling love with the sweet simplicity of the summer nights, so united that by the sole power of their tenderness they would easily penetrate each other's more secret thoughts. And this would continue forever in the serenity of an indescribable affection.

It seemed to her suddenly that she felt *him* there, near her, and a vague shiver of sensuousness ran over her from head to foot. She pressed her arm against her breast, with an unconscious action, as if to clasp her dream, and upon her lips pouting toward the unknown there passed something which almost made her swoon, as if the breath of spring had given her a kiss of love.

All at once she heard some one walking in the night, behind the château. And in an impulse of her perturbed soul, of a transport of faith in the impossible, in providential chances, in divine presentiments, in the romantic convolutions of fate, she thought, "If it only were *he?*" She listened eagerly to the rhythmic step of the approaching person, sure that he was going to stop at the iron gate to ask hospitality. When he had passed, she felt as after some deception. But she understood the exaltation of her hopes, and smiled at her folly.

Then, a little calm, she let her mind float on the current of more reasonable reverie, seeking to penetrate the future, planning her existence. She would live here with *him* in their quiet château which overlooked the sea. She would doubtless have two children, a son for *him* and a daughter for herself. And she would see them running over the grass beneath the plane-tree and the linden, while the father and mother followed them with ravished eyes, exchanging looks full of passion above their heads.

And she remained long, long, musing thus, while the moon completing her voyage across the heavens was disappearing in the ocean. The air became cooler. Toward the Orient the horizon grew lighter. A cock crowed on the farm at the right; another answered from the farm on the left. Their hoarse cries seemed to come from very far away through the partition of the poultry houses; and the stars imperceptibly paling disappeared in the immense vault of the sky.

A little cry of a bird rose somewhere. Twitterings, timid at first, came from the leaves; then they grew bolder, became vibrating, joyous, spreading from branch to branch and from tree to tree. Jeanne suddenly perceived herself to be in a ray of light, and raising her head which she had hidden in her hands, she closed her eyes, dazzled by the splendor of the dawn.

A mountain of empurpled clouds, partly concealed beneath the great avenue of poplars, cast their hues of blood upon the awakened earth. And slowly, bursting asunder the gleaming clouds, touching with fire the trees, the plains, the ocean, all the horizon, the great flaming globe appeared.

Jeanne felt herself becoming mad with happiness. A delirious joy, an infinite tenderness before the splendor of things drowned her fluttering heart. It was her sun! her dawn! the beginning of her life! the rising of her hopes! She stretched her arms toward the shining space, with a desire to embrace the sun; she wanted to speak, to utter something divine, like this opening of the day, but she stood paralyzed in an impotent enthusiasm. Then resting her forehead on her hands, she felt her eyes filling with tears, and she wept deliciously.

When she raised her head the superb glory of the dawning day had disappeared. She felt soothed, a little weary, as if chilled. Without shutting the window she threw herself upon the bed, mused a few minutes more, and fell into such a profound sleep that she did not hear her father's calls at eight o'clock, and only awoke when he came into her room.

He wanted to show her the improvements of the château, of *her* château. The *façade* which looked upon the exterior of the estate was separated from the road by a great court planted with apple-trees. This road, called the parish road, running between the fields of the peasants, joined, half a league away, the great highway from Havre to Fécamp.

A straight avenue came from the wooden fence to the steps of the house. The outbuildings, small structures, made of pebbles, roofed with thatch, lined both sides of the court, along the edge of the two farms.

The covers had been newly made: all the woodwork had been restored, the walls repaired, the rooms rehung with tapestries, and all the interior repainted. And the weather-stained old manor bore, as spots, its new shutters of silver white and the recent plastering, on its great grayish *façade*. The other *façade*, that in which was one of Jeanne's windows, looked upon the distant sea, above the grove and the wall of elms beaten with the wind.

Jeanne and the Baron, arm in arm, inspected everything, not omitting a corner; they walked slowly through the long avenue of poplars which inclosed what was called the park. The grass had sprouted beneath the trees, spreading its green carpet. The grove at the end was charming, with its crooked little paths, separated by partitions of foliage. A hare was suddenly started, which frightened the young girl; then it leaped the embankment and scampered off through the furze toward the cliff.

After breakfast, as Madame, still exhausted, declared that she was going to lie down and rest, the Baron proposed to go down to Yport. They started, just passing through the hamlet of Etouvent, in which the "Poplars" was situated. Three peasants saluted them as if they had always known them. They entered the wooded slope running down to the sea, as it followed a winding valley. Soon the village of Yport appeared. Women who were mending clothes, seated at the threshold of their homes, watched them pass. The sloping road, with a gutter in the middle and heaps of refuse lying about before the doors, exhaled a strong odor of brine.

The brown nets in which at different places gleaming scales remained, like bits of silver, were dripping before the doors of the houses, whence came the sounds of numerous families swarming in one room. A few pigeons were walking along the edge of the gutter, looking for food.

Jeanne looked at all this, which seemed curious and new to her, like a scene in a theater. But suddenly as they turned the angle of a walk, she perceived the sea, of an opaque blue, and smooth, stretching out of sight. They stopped, opposite the beach, to look. Some sails were passing in the distance, white as the wings of birds. At the right and left rose the enormous cliff. A sort of cape stopped the view on one side, while on the other side the coast line was indefinitely prolonged until it became nothing but an imperceptible point.

A harbor and some houses appeared at the foot of one of these cliffs; and very little waves rolled with a light noise upon the shingle, making a fringe of foam upon the water. The boats of the country, hauled upon the slope of round pebbles, lay upon their sides, stretching their round cheeks, varnished with tar, to the sun. A sailor approached to offer some fish, and Jeanne bought a brill, which she wanted to carry home to the "Poplars" herself.

Then the man tendered his services for trips on the sea, repeating his name time and time again to impress it on their memories: Lastique, Joseph Lastique. The Baron promised not to forget him, and they took the road back to the château.

As the big fish tired Jeanne, she passed her father's cane through its gills. Each took one end and they went along gaily climbing the hill, chatting like two children, their foreheads to the wind and their eyes brilliant, while the brill, which gradually fatigued their arms, swept the grass with its fat tail.

19

CHAPTER II.

A CHARMING and free life began for Jeanne, she read, dreamed, and wandered about, all alone, in the neighborhood. She loitered along the ways, her mind in a dream; or perhaps she gamboled down the crooked little valleys whose two sides bore a carpet of furze flower like a sheet of gold. Their sweet and fragrant odor, increased by the heat, intoxicated her like a perfumed wine; and at the distant sounds of the waves rolling on the beach, a billow rocked her spirit.

A lassitude occasionally made her stretch herself on the thick grass of a hillside; and at times, when she suddenly perceived at a turn of the valley, in a funnel of turf, a triangle of blue sea sparkling in the sunshine with a sail at the horizon, there came to her inordinate joys as at the mysterious approach of happiness hovering over her.

A love of solitude seized her in the sweetness of this fresh country and in the calm of the rounded

20

horizons, and she remained so long seated on the hilltops that the wild rabbits bounded by her feet.

She often ran along the cliff, caressed by the soft air of the coast, vibrating with an exquisite enjoyment in moving without fatigue, like the fish in the water or the swallows in the air. She sowed memories everywhere as seeds are cast upon the earth, memories whose roots hold till death. It seemed to her that she cast a little of her heart into all the folds of these valleys.

She began to go in passionately for bathing. She swam almost out of sight, being strong and sturdy and without consciousness of danger. She felt well in this cold, limpid, blue water which bore her up and rocked her to and fro.

When she was far from the shore, she floated on her back, her arms crossed upon her chest, her eyes lost in the profound azure of the sky which the flight of a swallow quickly cleft, or the white silhouette of a sea-bird. No other sound was heard than the distant murmur of surf on the shingle, and a vague noise of the land gliding over the undulations of the waves, but confused and almost imperceptible. And then Jeanne righted herself in the water and, in the distraction of joy, uttered sharp cries as she struck out with both hands.

Sometimes when she ventured too far a boat went out for her. She came back to the château pale with hunger, but light, alert, with a smile on her lips and her eyes beaming with happiness.

The Baron on his side planned great agricultural enterprises, he wanted to make trials, to organize progress, to experiment with new implements, to acclimatize foreign varieties; and he passed part of his days in conversation with peasants who shook their heads, incredulous at his attempts. Often also he went to sea with the sailors of Yport. When he had visited the grottoes, the springs, and the points of the vicinity, he wanted to fish like a simple sailor.

On breezy days when the filled sails made the chubby shells of the boats fly over the waves, and when over each side dragged, almost to the bottom of the sea, the long fleeing cords which schools of mackerel pursued, he held in his hand, which trembled with eagerness, the little line which vibrates as soon as a hooked fish begins to struggle.

By moonlight he would hand in the nets placed the night before. He loved to hear the mast creak, to breathe in the fresh and whistling squalls of the night; and after having tacked a long time, to find the buoys, guiding himself by a peak of rocks, the roof of a belfry, or the Fécamp lighthouse, he delighted to remain motionless beneath the first gleams of the rising sun which made the slimy backs of the large fan-shaped rays and the fat stomachs of the turbots glisten on the deck of the boat.

At each repast he enthusiastically recounted his expeditions, and the Baronne in her turn told how many times she had walked through the great avenues of poplars, the one on the right, toward Couillard farm, the other one not having sufficient sun.

As they had recommended her to have exercise, she took to walking. As soon as the chill of the night had disappeared, she descended, leaning on Rosalie's arm, wrapped in a cloak and two shawls, with her head concealed in a black hood which was still covered by a red scarf.

Then dragging her left foot, which was a little heavier, and which had already traced throughout the whole length of the road, one in going and the other in returning, two dusty trails, where the grass was dead, she began unceasingly to journey in a straight line from the angle of the château to the first shrubs of the grove. She had caused a bench to be placed at each end of this track; and every five minutes she stopped, saying to the poor patient maid who assisted her, "Let us sit down, my girl, I am a little tired."

And on each stop she would leave on one of the benches, now the scarf which covered her head, now one shawl and then the other, then the hood, then the cloak; and all this made at both ends of the avenue two big parcels of clothing which Rosalie would carry on her free arm when they came in to breakfast.

And in the afternoon the Baronne began in a more moderate way, with longer rests, even napping an hour from time to time on a reclining-chair which was rolled out doors for her.

She called this taking her exercise, as she would say, "my medicine."

A physician, consulted ten years previous, had spoken of hypertrophy because she had suffered from suffocation. Since that time this word, of whose significance she had little knowledge, had been established in her head. She obstinately made the Baron, Jeanne, and Rosalie sound her heart, which nobody could no longer feel, so deeply was it covered by the adipose tissue of her chest; but she energetically refused to have herself examined by any new physician, for fear that he would discover other diseases. She spoke of her hypertrophy on all occasions, and so often that it seemed as if this malady was special to her, and belonged to her as something unique, over which no one else had any right.

The Baron would say, "My wife's hypertrophy" and Jeanne, "Mamma's hypertrophy," as they would have mentioned her dress, her hat, or her umbrella.

She had been very pretty in her youth and slender as a reed. After having waltzed at the functions of the empire, she had read "Corinne," which made her cry, and she remained as if marked by that novel.

As her figure grew stouter her soul had taken the most poetical impulses, and when obesity had restricted her to an easy-chair, her thoughts wandered through tender adventures of which she fancied herself the heroine. She had some favorite ones which she always recalled in her reveries, as a music-box, when wound up, interminably repeats the same air. All the languorous novels, in which captives and swallows are mentioned, infallibly filled her eyes with tears: and she liked even certain broad songs of Béranger on account of the regretful sorrows which they expressed.

She often remained motionless for hours, abstracted in these daydreams, and her home, the "Poplars," was infinitely pleasing to her because it furnished a frame for the romances of her soul, recalling to her by the surrounding woods, by the waste-lands and by the neighborhood of the ocean, the books of Sir

Walter Scott, which she had been reading for some months.

On rainy days she remained shut up in her room for the purpose of visiting what she called "her relics." These were all her old letters, letters from her father and mother, letters from the Baron when they were engaged, and still others. She had locked them in a mahogany secretary, with brass spikes at the corners, and she would say in a peculiar voice: "Rosalie, my girl, bring me the drawer with the souvenirs."

The maid would open the secretary, take out the drawer, place it on a chair beside her mistress, who began slowly to read these letters one by one, letting a tear fall upon them from time to time.

Jeanne sometimes took the place of Rosalie, and walked with her mother, who recounted to her the memories of her childhood. The young girl saw herself in the stories of the past, being astonished at the simplicity of their thoughts, at the kinship of their desires; for each heart imagines itself thus to have trembled before all others beneath a crowd of sensations which made the hearts of the first beings beat, and would yet make those of the last men and women palpitate.

Their slow pace followed the slowness of the story which was sometimes interrupted for a few seconds by oppressions; and then Jeanne's mind, leaping over the adventures which had been begun, threw itself toward a future filled with joys, and revelled in hopes. One afternoon as they were resting on a bench, they suddenly perceived at the end of the avenue a stout priest who was coming toward them. He greeted them with a bow while still at a distance, assumed a smiling air, bowed again when he was three feet away, and cried:

"Well, Madame la Baronne, how are you?" It was the curé of the village.

The Baronne, born in the century of philosophers, brought up by a father who was not very orthodox in the days of the Revolution, did not often go to church, although she liked the priests from a sort of religious instinct which women possess. She had entirely forgotten the Abbé Picot, her curé, and blushed as she saw him. She made excuses for not having anticipated his call, but the good man did not seem at all rumpled; he looked at Jeanne, complimented her on her appearance, sat down, placed his three-cornered hat upon his knees, and wiped his brow. He was very stout, very red, and perspired profusely. He drew from his pocket every moment an enormous handkerchief and passed it over his face and his neck, but hardly was the damp linen replaced in the hidden recesses of his robe when new beads of sweat accumulated on his skin and falling upon his soutane, girdled with a sash at the stomach, fixed the flying dust of the roads in little round spots.

He was gay, a true country priest, tolerant, garrulous, and kind. He told stories, spoke of the people of the country and did not seem to notice that his two parishioners had not yet attended service, the Baronne reconciling her indolence with her confused faith, and Jeanne too happy at being freed from the convent, where she had been satiated with pious ceremonies.

The Baron appeared. His pantheistic religion left him indifferent to dogmas. He was friendly with the abbé, whom he recognized at a distance, and kept him to dinner. The priest knew how to please, thanks to that unconscious astuteness which the handling of souls gives to the most mediocre men who are called by the chance of events to exercise a power over their fellows.

The Baronne paid him every attention, attracted perhaps by one of those affinities which draw similar natures together, the ruddy face and short breath of the stout man being pleasing to her puffing obesity.

Toward dessert he had the animation of a curé in a merry mood, that familiar abandon of the ends of joyous repasts. And suddenly he cried as if a happy idea had crossed his mind: "I have a new parishioner whom I must present to you, Monsieur the Vicomte de Lamare."

The Baronne who had at the ends of her fingers all the peerage of the province, inquired:

"Is he of the family of Lamare of l'Eure?"

The priest replied:

"Yes, Madame, it is the son of the Vicomte Jean de Lamare, who died last year."

Then Madame Adelaide, who loved the nobility above everything, asked a lot of questions, and learned that, after paying his father's debts, he had sold the family château and established himself in a little box, on one of the three farms which he possessed in the commune of Etouvent. These estates represented in all five or six thousand livres of income; but the Vicomte was of an economical and wise turn of mind, and counted on living simply for two or three

years in the modest pavilion in order to save enough
to cut some figure in society, to marry to advantage
without contracting debts or mortgaging his farms.

The curé added: "He is a charming fellow; and
so steady and quiet. But there is not much to amuse
him in the country."

The Baron said: "Bring him to see us, Monsieur
l'Abbé, that will distract him from time to time."
And then they spoke of other things.

When they entered the drawing-room, after having
taken coffee, the priest asked permission to take a
stroll in the garden, having the habit of a little exercise after his meals. The Baron accompanied him.
They slowly walked the whole length of the white
façade of the château, to return then upon their steps.
Their shadows, one thin and the other round and
wearing a mushroom hat, came and went, now before
them, now behind them, accordingly as they walked
toward the moon or turned their backs upon it. The
curé chewed a sort of a cigarette which he had
taken from his pocket. He explained its use with
the frankness of country folk:

"It is in order to prevent risings in the stomach,
because my digestion is a little slow."

Then suddenly looking at the sky, in which the
clear moon was journeying, he said: "A man is
never weary of that spectacle." And he went in to
take his leave of the ladies.

CHAPTER III.

MONSIEUR DE LAMARE

THE following Sunday the Baronne and Jeanne went to mass, impelled by a delicate sentiment of deference for their curé. They waited after the service in order to invite him for breakfast on Thursday. He came out of the sacristy with an elegant young man who familiarly gave him his arm. As soon as he perceived the two women, he made a gesture of joyous surprise and cried:

"How fortunate this is! Permit me, Madame la Baronne and Mademoiselle Jeanne, to present your neighbor, Monsieur the Vicomte de Lamare."

The Vicomte bowed, spoke of his long desire to make the acquaintance of these ladies, and began to converse easily, as a man of society who had seen life. He possessed one of those happy faces about which women dream and which are disagreeable to all men. His black curly hair shaded his smooth and sunburned brow and two large eyebrows, regular as

29

if they were artificial, rendered deep and tender his dark eyes, whose whites seemed a little tinged with blue.

His long and close eyelashes lent to his glance that passionate eloquence which creates a havoc in the drawing-room of the haughty dame, and makes the girl in a cap carrying a basket in the streets turn around. The languorous charm of those eyes made everyone believe in the depth of his thoughts and gave importance to his slightest words. A thick beard, glossy and fine, concealed a chin which was a trifle too heavy. They separated after many compliments.

Two days later Monsieur de Lamare made his first call. He arrived as they were trying a rustic bench placed that very morning beneath the tall plane-tree opposite the drawing-room windows. The Baron wanted to have another placed under the windows of the lindens as a pendant, the Baronne, who disliked symmetry, did not wish it. The Vicomte, being consulted, was of the Baronne's opinion. Then he spoke of the country, which he declared very picturesque, having discovered many delightful views in his lonely walks.

From time to time, as if by chance, his eyes met Jeanne's; and she felt a singular sensation at this brusque glance, and quickly turned away from a look in which a caressing admiration and an awakened sympathy appeared.

Monsieur de Lamare, the father, who had died the preceding year, had known very well an intimate friend of Monsieur des Cultaux, the Baronne's father: and the discovery of this acquaintance started an interminable conversation about alliances, dates, and relationships. The Baronne accomplished great feats of memory, settling the ancestry and descendants of other families, wandering in the complicated labyrinth of genealogies without ever getting lost.

"Tell me, Vicomte, have you heard speak of the Saunoy family of Varfleur? The oldest son Gontran married a young de Coursil, a Coursil-Courville, and the younger son, one of my cousins, Mademoiselle de la Roche-Aubert, who was related to the Crisange family. Now Monsieur de Crisange was the intimate friend of my father and must also have known yours."

"Yes, Madame. Isn't it that Monsieur de Crisange who emigrated and whose son was ruined?"

"Precisely. He had asked for the hand of my aunt in marriage after the death of her husband, Comte d'Eretry; but she did not want him because he took snuff. Do you know, by the way, what became of the Viloises? They left Touraine toward 1813, after reverses of fortune, to settle in Auvergne, and I haven't heard of them since."

"I believe, Madame, that the old marquis was killed by a fall from his horse, leaving one daughter who was married to an Englishman, and another who was married to a certain Bassolle, a rich merchant, who they say had seduced her."

And the names learned in childhood, and retained since then in the conversations of old retainers, came back to her. And the marriage of these equal families took in their minds the importance of great public events. They spoke of people whom they had never seen as if they were well acquainted with them; and the other people, in other districts, spoke of them in the same way; and they felt acquainted at a distance, almost friends, almost relations, by the mere fact of belonging to the same class, the same caste, and of being of equal birth.

The Baron, sufficiently savage in nature and with an education which made him differ from the beliefs and principles of people of his set, knew little of the families of the neighborhood. He questioned the Vicomte about them.

Monsieur de Lamare answered: "Oh, there are not many of the nobility in the district," in the same tone in which he would have declared that there were not many rabbits on the hillsides; and he gave particulars. Only three families lived within a sufficiently short radius: the Marquis de Coutelier, a sort of chief of the Norman aristocracy; the Vicomte and Vicomtesse de Briseville, persons of excellent family but keeping themselves rather isolated; and, finally the Comte de Fourville, a kind of a bogey who was said to be killing his wife with sorrow, and who lived as a hunter in his château of "La Vrillitte," built near a pond. Some parvenus, who associated with each other, had bought estates here and there. The Vicomte did not know them.

He took his leave, and his last glance was for Jeanne, as if he addressed to her a special farewell, more cordial and more sweet. The Baronne found him charming, and above all, very good form. The Baron remarked: "Yes, certainly, he is a very well brought up young man."

They invited him to dinner the following Sunday. He came quite regularly after that. He arrived, most often, about four o'clock in the afternoon, joining the

Baronne in "her avenue" and offering her his arm to take "her exercise." When Jeanne had not gone out, she supported the Baronne on the other side, and all three walked slowly from one of the great roads to the other, going and returning ceaselessly. He spoke little to the young girl, but his eyes, which seemed of black velvet, often met Jeanne's eyes, which might have been made of blue agate. Very often they both went down to Yport with the Baron.

As they were on the beach one evening, father Lastique approached them, and without taking from his mouth his pipe, the absence of which would have astonished people more than the disappearance of his nose, he said:

"With the wind, Monsieur le Baron, we ought to be able to get to Étretat and back to-morrow without any trouble."

Jeanne clasped her hands: "Oh! papa, if you would!" The Baron turned toward Monsieur de Lamare:

"Are you inclined, Vicomte? We will go and take luncheon down there." And the expedition was at once decided upon.

Jeanne was up at dawn. She waited for her father who was slower in dressing, and they started to walk in the dew, crossing first the plain, and then the woods all musical with the song of birds. The Vicomte and father Lastique were seated on a capstan.

Two other sailors assisted in the start. The men placing their shoulders against the sides of the boat pushed with all their strength. They advanced with difficulty over the beach. Lastique slipped some guard rollers of wood beneath the keel; then, taking up his position again, uttered in a drawling voice his interminable "Oh, yeo, ho!" intended to regulate the general effort.

But when they came to the slope the boat started, all of a sudden, and slid down upon the round pebbles with a great sound like a torn sail. It stopped short at the foam of the little waves and all took their places on board; then the two sailors who stayed on shore shoved the boat off.

A light but steady breeze, blowing from off shore, skimmed and wrinkled the surface of the water. The sail was hoisted, it bellied a little, and the boat gently started, hardly rocked by the sea.

They stood off at first. Toward the horizon the blending sky mingled with the ocean. Toward the shore, the high, steep cliff cast a broad shadow at its foot, and the sunny slopes of turf indented it at certain spots. Behind them in the distance the brown sails were leaving the white beach of Fécamp, and, before them a rock of strange shape, rounded and flooded with light, looked like an enormous elephant burying its trunk in the waves. It was the little harbor of Étretat. Jeanne, holding the weatherboard with one hand, a little dizzy with the rocking of the waves, looked far away; and it seemed to her that only three things were truly beautiful in creation: light, space, and water.

No one spoke. Father Lastique, who held the tiller and the sheet, took a nip occasionally from a bottle hidden under the seat, and unceasingly smoked his stump of a pipe which seemed inextinguishable. There continually rose from it a slender thread of blue smoke, while another similar one escaped from the corner of his mouth. Yet no one ever saw the sailor light his bowl of clay, blacker than ebony, or fill it with tobacco. Sometimes he took it in one hand, removed it from his lips, and from the same corner from whence issued the smoke, he squirted into the sea a long jet of brown saliva.

The Baron seated forward, watched the sail, taking the place of a sailor. Jeanne and the Vicomte sat side by side, both a little disturbed. An unknown force made their eyes meet when they raised them at the same moment, as if an affinity had impelled them; for there already floated between them that subtile and vague tenderness which springs up so quickly between two young people, when the young man is not ugly and the girl is pretty. They felt happy near each other, perhaps because they were thinking of one another.

The sun climbed as if to view from a higher plane the vast sea stretched beneath it. But the sea was coquettish and clothed herself in a light mist which veiled her from its rays. It was a transparent fog, very low and gilded, which did not really conceal anything, but rendered the distance softer. The orb darted its flames to melt this shining cloud; when it was in all its strength the vapor evaporated, disappeared, and the ocean, smooth as a mirror, began to glisten in the light.

Jeanne murmured with emotion: "How beautiful it is!" The Vicomte assented. The serene brilliancy of this morning awakened an echo in their hearts.

Suddenly the great arcades of Étretat were perceived, like two arms of the cliff extended into the water, high enough to serve as an arch for ships; while a point of rock, white and sharp, rose in front. They touched the shore, and while the Baron, disembarking first, held the boat to the bank by its painter, the Vicomte took Jeanne in his arms in order to put her ashore without letting her wet her feet. Then they went up the hard beach together, side by side, both moved by this close entwining, and they suddenly heard father Lastique say to the Baron:

"It is my opinion that they would make a fine couple, those two."

The luncheon in a little tavern near the shore was charming. Old ocean, benumbing voice and mind, had made them silent; the table made them talkative and garrulous as schoolboys on a vacation. The simplest things gave them endless merriment.

Father Lastique, seating himself at a table, carefully hid in his cap his still smoking pipe; and they laughed at that. A fly, no doubt attracted by his red nose, kept alighting on it; and when he brushed it off, with a hand too slow to catch it, it would post itself on a muslin curtain, which many of its fellows had already specked, and seemed carefully to watch the sailor's highly colored proboscis, for it would soon again fly back to it.

At each of the flights of this insect they shouted with laughter; and when the old man bothered by this tickling, muttered: "It is deucedly persistent," Jeanne and the Vicomte laughed till the tears came into their eyes, stifling their outbursts with their napkins.

When coffee had been served Jeanne said: "What if we were to take a little walk?"

The Vicomte rose, but the Baron preferred to bask in the sun on the beach, saying: "Go on, my children, you will find me here in an hour."

They passed in a straight line the few cottages of the place; and after going beyond a little château, which resembled a big farmhouse, they found themselves in an open valley extending before them.

The motion of the sea had wearied them, disturbing their ordinary equilibrium, the strong saline air had made them hungry, then the luncheon had appeased them, and the merriment had weakened them. They now felt moved with a wild desire to run madly through the fields, and Jeanne felt her ears ringing, full of emotion from so many new and rapid sensations.

A scorching sun was shining on them. On both sides of the road the ripened harvest bent under the heat. The locusts called, numerous as the blades of grass, uttering everywhere in the wheat, in the rye, in the furze of the slopes, their thin and deafening cry.

No other voice was heard beneath the torrid sky, of a glittering blue, shading to yellow, as if it were about to turn red, after the manner of metals too near a fireplace.

Having observed a little grove further on, toward the right, they went to it. Inclosed between two slopes a narrow path stretched beneath tall trees impenetrable to the sun. A kind of moist coolness impressed them, that dampness which makes the skin shiver and penetrates the lungs. The grass had disappeared for want of light and free air, but a covering of moss hid the soil.

"Come, we can sit down over there," said Jeanne. Two old trees had died, and taking advantage of the opening made in the foliage a flood of light descended there, warmed the earth, awakened the germs of the grass, of the dandelions and the convolvuli, made the little white flowers, fine as a mist, bloom, and the fox-gloves abound. Butterflies, bees, hornets innumerable, gnats which resembled the skeletons of flies, a thousand flying insects, some red and spotted, some of greenish hues, others black, with horns, peopled this hot and luminous recess, hidden in the cold shadows of the heavy foliage.

They sat down, their heads in the shade and their feet in the sun. They gazed at all this swarming tiny life which a ray of light caused to appear, and Jeanne, affected, kept repeating:

"How delightful it is! How delicious the country seems. There are moments when I would like to be a fly, or a butterfly, and hide myself in the flowers."

They spoke of themselves, their habits and tastes, in that low, intimate tone in which confidences are told. He said that he was already disgusted with the world, tired of its futile life; it was always the same thing; nothing true, nothing sincere was to be met. The world! she would have liked to know it; but she was convinced beforehand that it was not worth the country. And the nearer their hearts grew to each other, the more ceremoniously they called each other "Monsieur" and "Mademoiselle," the more smiling and simultaneous became their glances; and it seemed to them that a new good entered into them, a keener sympathy, an interest in a thousand things about which they had never concerned themselves.

They returned, but the Baron had set out on foot for the "Maiden's Chamber" a grotto in a ridge of the cliff; and they waited for him at the inn. He did not appear until five o'clock in the afternoon, after a long walk on the hillsides. They re-embarked. The boat went gently, the wind blowing from behind with hardly any motion, and not seeming to advance. The breeze came in slow and warmish puffs which bellied the sail for a second, then let it fall, limp, along the mast. The opaque sea appeared dead; and the sun worn with its labors in following its rounded path softly descended the horizon. The torpor of the ocean again made everyone silent.

Jeanne finally said: "How I love traveling!"

The Vicomte replied: "Yes, but it is lonely to travel by yourself; there must be at least two so that you can exchange impressions."

She reflected: "It is true—, but I like to go alone—it is delightful to travel all alone."

He looked at her steadily. "It is possible for two to dream together," he said.

She dropped her eyes. Was it a confession? Perhaps. She gazed at the horizon as if she would look still further off; then in a slow voice, she said: "I should like to go to Italy—and to Greece—ah! yes, to Greece—and to Corsica; it must be so wild and beautiful!" But he preferred Switzerland on account of the châlets and the lakes.

She rejoined: "No, I should like entirely new countries, like Corsica, or countries which are very old and full of memories, like Greece. It must be so pleasant to find the traces of peoples whose history we have known since our childhood, and to see the places where great things have been accomplished."

The Vicomte, less wrought-up, declared: "As for me, England attracts me strongly; it is a historic country."

Thus they ran over the universe, discussing the agreeable features of each country, from the poles to the equator, going into ecstasies over imaginary landscapes and the odd customs of certain peoples like the Chinese and the Laplanders. But they arrived at the conclusion that the most beautiful country in the world was France, with its temperate climate, cool in summer and mild in winter, its rich fields, its green forests, its great calm rivers, and that cultivation of the fine arts which had existed nowhere else since the great centuries of Athens.

Then they were silent. The sun, sinking lower, seemed to bleed; and a broad luminous track, a dazzling path, ran over the water from the ocean's limit to the wake of the boat. The last slants of wind died away; every ruffle was smoothed and the motionless sail was red. A limitless calm seemed to benumb space, to spread silence around this meeting of the elements; while, offering her gleaming bosom, the sea, a monstrous bride, awaited her fiery lover now descending to her. Hastening to his fall, he empurpled her with the desire of their embrace. Now he joined her; and little by little, she devoured him. Then coolness spread from the horizon; a shiver wrinkled the moving bosom of the waters, as if the engulfing of the orb had cast upon the world a sigh of assuagement.

Twilight was short: the darkness spread, studded with stars. Father Lastique took the oars: and they all observed that the sea was phosphorescent. Jeanne and the Vicomte, side by side, watched the moving gleams which the boat left behind it. They thought but little any longer, vaguely gazing, breathing in the evening with a delicious comfortableness; and as Jeanne had one hand resting upon the seat a finger of her neighbor as if by chance touched her skin: she did not move, surprised, happy, and confused at this contact which was so light.

When she retired that evening, she felt strangely affected and so softened that everything made her wish to cry. She looked at her clock, thought that the little bee beat like a heart, a friend's heart; that it would be the witness of all her life, that it would accompany her joys and her sorrows with this lively and regular ticking; and she stopped the gilded insect to imprint a kiss upon its wings. She would have kissed no matter what. She remembered hiding in the bottom of the drawer an old doll of bygone days: she hunted for it, found it with the joy a person feels on meeting dear old friends; and pressing it to her breast, she covered with warm kisses the painted cheeks and the curled tow hair of the toy.

And while she held it in her arms she dreamed. Was he really the husband, promised by a thousand secret voices, whom an all-wise Providence had thus thrown in her way? Was he really the being created for her, to whom she would devote her existence? Were they the two predestined ones whose united affections should entwine, indissolubly mingling and engendering love?

41

She no long~~ felt those tumultuous impulses of her whole being, those mad raptures, those profound uprisings which she thought to be passion. It seemed to her, nevertheless, that she was beginning to love him, for she felt at times quite weak in thinking of him; and she thought of him continually. His presence moved her heart. She blushed and turned pale when she met his glance and shivered when she heard his voice.

She slept very little that night. Then from day to day the disturbing desire to love overwhelmed her more and more. She questioned herself continually, questioned the daisies, too, and the clouds, and coins tossed in the air. One evening, her father said to her: "Make yourself pretty, to-morrow morning."

She asked: "Why, papa?"

He answered: "It is a secret."

And when she came down the next morning, all fresh in a bright costume, she found the drawing-room table covered with boxes of bonbons, and on a chair an enormous bouquet. A carriage entered the court. On it might be read the words: "Lerat-Fécamp, pastry-cook. Wedding Breakfasts"; and Ludivine, assisted by a scullion, drew from the trap opening behind the vehicle, big flat baskets which had an appetizing smell.

The Vicomte de Lamare appeared. His pantaloons were tight and strapped down under his small polished boots indicating the smallness of his feet. His long frock-coat, fitted to his figure, let the lace of his shirt frill show at the chest; and a rich cravat, with many folds, made him hold high his fine dark head,

which bore the stamp of race. His air was unusual,
an air which special dress lends to the best-known
countenances. Jeanne, astounded, looked at him as
if she had not yet seen him; she thought him supremely the gentleman, a great seigneur from head to
foot.

He bowed smilingly, saying: "Well, my little
dame, are you ready?"

She stammered: "Why, what is it?"

"You will know presently," said the Baron.

The barouche, which had been made ready, drove
up. Madame Adelaide came down from her room in
full dress on Rosalie's arm, who seemed so much impressed by Monsieur Lamare's elegance that the Baron
muttered:

"I say, Vicomte, I believe that our maid finds you
to her taste." The Vicomte blushed to his ears, pretended not to have heard, and taking up the huge
bouquet, offered it to Jeanne. She took it, more
astonished than ever.

All four got into the carriage; and the cook Ludivine, who brought the Baronne a cup of cold broth
to keep her strength up, declared: "Truly, Madame,
people would say it was a wedding."

They alighted from the carriage, as they entered
Yport, and as they advanced through the village, the
sailors in their new clothes, whose folds showed, left
their houses, bowed, pressed the Baron's hand, and
began to follow as if behind a procession. The Vicomte had offered Jeanne his arm and walked at the
head with her.

When they arrived in front of the church, they
halted, and the great silver cross appeared, held

straight by a choir-boy preceding another red and white urchin, who carried the holy-water urn in which the sprinkler was dipping.

Then three old choristers passed, one of whom was lame, then the serpent, then the curé, wearing upon his fat stomach the gilded stole with its cross. He said good morning with a smile and a nod; then, with his eyes half closed, his lips moving in prayer, his cap pulled down nearly to his nose, he followed his surpliced staff toward the sea.

On the shore there was a crowd waiting about a new boat, which was garlanded with flowers. Its mast, sail, and rigging were covered with long ribbons flapping in the breeze, and the name "Jeanne" appeared on the stern in letters of gold.

Father Lastique, master of this boat, which had been built with the Baron's money, advanced in front of the procession. All the men, with one accord, took off their hats; and a rank of devotees, clad in large black cloaks falling in great folds from their shoulders, knelt in a circle at the sight of the cross.

The curé, between the two choir-boys, stood at one end of the boat, while, at the other end, the three old choristers in their soiled white vestments, with stubby chins, a serious air, and their eyes on their book of chants, sang out of tune at the top of their lungs in the bright morning.

The still and transparent sea appeared to be taking part in the baptism of the boat, hardly moving, only a slight sound as of a rake scratching the shingle, its tiny waves a finger high. And the big white sea-gulls with widespread wings swept in curves through the sky, withdrawing and returning in rounded flight above the kneeling crowd, as if they too desired to see what was going on.

But the chanting ceased after an Amen howled for five minutes; and the priest in a puffy voice clucked some Latin words of which only the sonorous terminations were distinguishable. He next walked around the boat sprinkling it with holy water, then he began to mutter the "Oremus," stationing himself now a plank's length in front of the godfather and godmother who stood motionless, hand in hand.

The young man had the expression of a handsome lad, but the young girl, choked by a sudden emotion, faltering, began to tremble so violently that her teeth chattered. The dream which had haunted her for some time had just taken the appearance of a reality, set in a sort of hallucination. They had spoken of a wedding, a priest was there, surpliced men were chanting prayers; was she not getting married? Was there a nervous shaking of his fingers, had the obsession of her heart run the length of her veins to the heart of her companion? Did he understand, did he divine—was he, like her, seized with a sort of intoxication of love? Or, indeed, did he know by experience that no woman could resist him?

She suddenly perceived that he pressed her hand, gently at first, but harder and harder, almost hard enough to break it. And without his face moving, without anybody perceiving it, he said, yes, he certainly did, and very distinctly: "Oh, Jeanne, if you were willing, this might be our betrothal!" She bowed her head with a very slow motion, which perhaps signified "Yes." And the priest who was

45

still sprinkling holy water, scattered several drops upon their fingers.

It was finished. The women rose. The return was a stampede. The cross, between the hands of the choir-boy, had lost its dignity; it quickly vanished, ·oscillating from right to left, or perhaps dipping forward, ready to fall on anyone's nose. The curé, who no longer prayed, was hurrying behind; chanters and the serpent had disappeared by a side street the more quickly to doff their vestments, and the sailors hastened away in groups. The same thought, which filled their heads like the smell of a kitchen, lengthened their legs and made their mouths water. A good luncheon awaited them at the "Poplars."

The great table was spread in the court under the apple-trees. Sixty people took places at it; sailors and peasants. The Baronne, in the center, had the two curés at her sides, the one from Yport and the one from the village. The Baron, opposite, was flanked by the mayor and his wife, the latter a thin countrywoman already old, who kept making little bows on all sides. She had a narrow face, squeezed into her big Normandy cap, a veritable hen's head with a white crest, with round eyes which always seemed astonished; and she ate with quick little bites as if she were pecking her plate with her nose.

Jeanne, beside the Vicomte, was swimming in happiness. She no longer saw, or knew anything, and she was silent, her head turned with joy.

She asked him: "What is your home name?"

"Julien," he replied; "did you not know?"

But she did not reply, thinking: "How often I shall repeat that name."

When the meal was finished they left the court to the sailors and went to the other side of the château. The Baronne began to take her exercise leaning on the Baron, escorted by the two priests. Jeanne and Julien went to the grove, and entered one of the little bushy roads; and suddenly he seized her hands:

"Tell me," said he, "will you be my wife?"

She again bowed her head; and as he stammered: "Answer, I beg of you!" she raised her eyes toward him, very gently, and he read his answer in their glance.

CHAPTER IV.

Marriage and Revelation

The Baron came into Jeanne's room one morning before she was up, and sitting by the foot of the bed, said:

"Monsieur the Vicomte de Lamare has asked us for your hand." She wanted to hide her face under the bed-clothes.

Her father continued: "We have postponed our answer for a little while." She gasped, choking with emotion.

At the end of a minute the Baron, who was smiling, added:

"We did not wish to do anything without speaking to you about it. Your mother and I are not opposed to this marriage, without desiring neverthe-less to urge you to it. You are very much richer than he, but when the happiness of a life is con-cerned, we should not think too much about money. He has no parents; so that if you marry him, it would be a son entering our family, while with another, it would be you, our daughter, going among strangers. The boy pleases us. Does he please you?"

She stammered, red to her hair, and replied: "I am willing, papa."

And her father, looking to the bottom of her eyes, and still smiling, murmured: "I thought as much, Mademoiselle."

She remained in a sort of intoxication of emotion until evening, without knowing what she was doing, taking one object for another mechanically, her legs limp from fatigue without having walked. Toward six o'clock as she was sitting with her mother under the plane-tree, the Vicomte appeared.

Jeanne's heart began beating wildly. The young man approached without seeming disturbed. When he was very near, he took the Baronne's fingers and kissed them; then raising the trembling hand of the young girl, he gave it a long kiss, tender and grateful.

The radiant period of betrothal commenced. They talked alone in the corner of the drawing-room, or on the slope at the end of the grove before the stretch of wild land. Sometimes they walked in the Baronne's avenue, he speaking of the future, she with her eyes cast down upon the Baronne's dusty foot-prints.

The thing once decided upon, they wanted to hasten matters. It was therefore agreed that the ceremony should take place in six weeks, on the fifteenth of August; and that the young couple should start at once on their wedding trip. Jeanne was consulted about the country which she would like to visit, and chose Corsica, where people could be more alone than in the Italian cities.

They awaited the moment fixed for their union without a too lively impatience, but wrapped in a delicious tenderness, tasting the exquisite charm of insignificant caresses, of clasped fingers, of passionate looks so long that their souls seemed to mingle; and vaguely tormented by the wavering desire for a long embrace.

It was resolved not to invite anybody to the wedding except Mademoiselle Lison, the Baronne's sister, who lived as a lady boarder in a convent at Versailles. After the death of their father, the Baronne wanted to keep her sister with her; but the old maid, possessed of the idea that she was in everybody's way, that she was useless and troublesome, retired into one of those religious houses which rent apartments to people who are sorrowful and isolated in life.

She came to spend a month or two with the family from time to time. She was a small woman who spoke little, always retiring, appearing only at meal-time, and going back again to her room, where she remained shut up continually.

She had a placid and aged air, although she was only forty-two, with gentle and sad eyes, and had never counted for anything in the family. When quite little, as she was neither pretty nor naughty she was not much petted, and she stayed in corners, tranquil and sweet. Later she was always sacrificed. As a young girl nobody noticed her.

She was something like a shadow or a familiar object, a living piece of furniture, which people are accustomed to see every day, but about which they do not disturb themselves.

Her sister, from the habit learned in the paternal mansion, considered her a strange being, quite insignificant. They treated her with an easy familiarity which concealed a sort of good-natured contempt.

She was called Lise, and seemed hurt by this childish and jaunty appellation. When it was seen that she would not marry, they had changed the name Lise to Lison. From Jeanne's birth she had become Aunt Lison, a humble relative, neat, frightfully timid, even with her sister and her brother-in-law, who, for all that, were fond of her, but with a vague sort of affection, made up of indifference, unconscious compassion, and natural benevolence.

Sometimes, when the Baronne was speaking of the far-off things of her youth, she said, in order to fix the date: "That was at the time of Lison's inconsiderate act."

This was never explained further; and that "inconsiderate act" remained as if hidden in a fog. One evening Lise, then twenty years old, had thrown herself into the water without anyone knowing why. Nothing in her life, in her deportment, gave warning of that folly. She had been fished out half dead, and her parents raising their indignant hands, instead of seeking the mysterious cause of the deed, were contented to speak of the "inconsiderate act" as they spoke of the accident to the horse Coco, which had broken his leg a little before this in a rut and had to be killed.

Since then Lise, afterward Lison, was considered as of a very weak mind. The gentle contempt which she had inspired in her nearest relatives spread slowly through the hearts of all the persons who surrounded her. Little Jeanne herself, with that natural divination of children, paid no attention to her, never went up to kiss her in her bed, nor entered her room. Good Rosalie, who gave this room a few necessary attentions, seemed the only one to know where it was situated.

When Aunt Lison entered the dining-room for breakfast, the "Little One" went, from force of habit and held her forehead to be kissed, and that was all. If anyone wanted to speak to her, a servant was sent to look for her; and when she was not· there, no one worried about her, no one ever had the notion of ever being disturbed at her absence and of saying: "Here, I haven't seen Lison this morning."

She held no stated place; she was one of those beings who live unknown even to their kindred, as unexplored entities, and whose death makes no gap or void in a house — one of those beings who do not know how to enter into the existence, nor into the habits, nor into the love of those who live at their side. When "Aunt Lison" was uttered, these two words aroused, so to speak, no affection in anyone's spirit. It was as if anyone had said "the coffee-pot," or "the sugar bowl."

She always walked with quick, silent steps; never made any noise, never ran against anything, seemed to communicate to objects the quality of making no sound. Her hands seemed made of a kind of wadding, she handled so lightly and delicately anything she touched.

Aunt Lison arrived toward the middle of July, quite upset by the idea of this marriage. She brought a lot of presents which, coming from her, were almost unobserved. From the day after her arrival no one noticed that she was there. But an extraordinary emotion was stirring within her, and she hardly took her eyes off the engaged couple. She busied herself with the wedding outfit with a singular energy, a feverish activity, working like a simple seamstress in her room where no one ever came to see her.

Every morning she presented the Baronne with handkerchiefs which she had hemmed herself, with towels on which she had embroidered the crests, asking: "Is that right, Adelaide?" And the Baronne, while carelessly examining the object, would reply: "Don't give yourself so much trouble, my poor Lison." One evening, toward the end of the month, after a day of sultry heat, the moon rose in one of those clear warm nights, which disturb, soften, exalt, and seem to arouse all the secret poetry of our souls.

The soft breath of the fields entered the quiet drawing-room where the Baronne and her husband were languidly playing a game of cards in the round spot of light which the lamp-shade marked upon the table. Aunt Lison, seated between them, was knitting; and the young people, leaning at the open window, looked out into the garden which was full of light. The linden and the plane-trees cast their shadows on the great lawn, which stretched away, pale and gleaming, to the dark grove.

Irresistibly drawn by the tender charm of this night, by this misty light of the trees and shrubs, Jeanne turned toward her parents and said:

"Father, we are going to take a stroll on the grass there, in front of the château."

53

The Baron replied without stopping his playing: "Go, my children," and continued the game.

They went out and began to walk slowly over the great white lawn as far as the little grove at the bottom. Time advanced without their thinking of returning. The Baronne, wearied, wanted to go up to her room. "We must call the lovers," she said. The Baron with a glance, ran over the great luminous garden where the two shadows were slowly wandering, rejoined:

"Leave them alone, it is so pleasant out of doors! Lison will wait for them, won't you, Lison?"

The old maid raised her restless eyes and answered in her timid voice: "Certainly, I will wait for them."

The Baron assisted his wife to rise, and, tired himself by the heat of the day, said: "I am going to bed, too." And he departed with the Baronne.

Then Aunt Lison rose in her turn and, placing her unfinished work on the arm of the chair, her wool and her long needle, she went to lean at the window and enjoy the charming night. The engaged pair walked endlessly across the lawn from the grove to the steps, from the steps to the grove. They held each other's hands and did not speak, as if they had gone out of themselves, all mingled with the visible poetry which was exhaled from the earth.

Jeanne suddenly perceived in the square of the window the silhouette of the old maid which the lamplight outlined. "Well," she said, "there is Aunt Lison, looking at us."

The Vicomte raised his head, and, with that indifferent voice which speaks without thought, replied: "Yes, Aunt Lison is looking at us."

And they continued to dream, to walk slowly, to make love.

But the dew was palpable, and they shivered a little from the coolness. "Let us go in," said Jeanne. And they went in.

As they entered the drawing-room, Aunt Lison had begun her knitting again; she had her forehead bent over her work, and her thin fingers trembled a little as if they had been very tired.

Jeanne approached her:

"Aunt, everyone is going to retire, now," she said.

The old maid turned away her eyes; they were red as if she had been weeping. The lovers paid no attention to this; but the young man suddenly perceived the fine shoes of the young girl covered with dew. He was seized with anxiety and tenderly inquired: "Aren't your dear little feet cold?" And suddenly the aunt's fingers were seized with such a trembling that she dropped her work; the ball of yarn rolled far over the floor, and quickly hiding her face in her hands, she began to weep with great convulsive sobs.

The two lovers looked at her in astonishment, without moving. Jeanne quickly went to her, put aside her arms, agitated, and asked: "What is the matter, what is the matter, Aunt Lison?"

Then the poor woman, stammering, with her voice all drowned in tears and her body shriveled with grief replied: "It is because he asked you — 'Aren't your dear l-l-l-little f-feet c-c-cold?' No one ever said anything like that to me, never — never —"

Jeanne, surprised, touched with pity, nevertheless felt like laughing at the thought of a lover lavishing tenderness on Aunt Lison; and the Vicomte turned aside in order to conceal his mirth. But the aunt suddenly rose, left her yarn on the floor and her knitting on the chair, and went without a light up the dark stairway, groping to her room.

Left alone, the two young people gazed at each other, amused and softened. Jeanne murmured: "Poor aunt! A little crazy, this evening." They held each other's hands without deciding to separate, and gently, very gently, they exchanged their first kiss before the empty chair which Aunt Lison had just quitted.

They gave no thought the next day to the tears of the old maid. The two weeks which preceded the wedding left Jeanne calm and tranquil enough, as if she were worn out with sweet emotions. She had no time for reflection upon the decisive day itself. She only felt a great sensation of emptiness throughout her whole body, as if her flesh, her blood, her bones, were all melted together under her skin; and she perceived, as she touched various objects, that her fingers trembled a good deal.

She did not regain her self-possession until in the choir of the church during the ceremony.

Married! So she was married! The succession of things, of movements, of events, accomplished since dawn, seemed to her a dream, a true dream. There are those moments in which all about us seems changed; even gestures have a new significance; there are even hours which do not seem in their ordinary place.

She felt bewildered, astonished, above all. The day before, nothing had been altered in her existence; the constant hope of her life was only becoming a little nearer, almost tangible. She had gone to sleep a young girl, she was a woman now. She had crossed this barrier which seemed to conceal the future with its joys, its happiness so long dreamed of. She felt, as it were, an open door before her; she was about to enter into the "Hoped-For."

The ceremony was ended. They passed into the almost vacant sacristy; for no one had been invited; then they went out. As they appeared at the door of the church a formidable uproar startled the bride, and made the Baronne utter a loud cry: it was a salvo of guns fired by the peasants, and even as far as the "Poplars" was the firing continued.

A collation was served for the family, for the curé of the manor and the one from Yport, and for the husband and the witnesses selected from among the principal farmers of the neighborhood. Then a turn was taken in the garden to await dinner. The Baron, the Baronne, Aunt Lison, the mayor, and Abbé Picot began to stroll through the mother's avenue, while in the opposite avenue the other priest was reading his breviary and walking with long strides. From the other side of the château was heard the gaiety of the peasants, who were drinking cider beneath the apple-trees. All the countryside in its Sunday best thronged the court. The lads and girls chased each other about.

Jeanne and Julien crossed through the grove, climbed the slope, and, both silent, began to look at the sea. It was a trifle cool, although it was the middle of August; the north wind was blowing and the great sun was shining austerely in the blue sky.

The young people, in order to find shelter, crossed the heath, turning to the right, desiring to reach the undulating and wooded valley which descends toward Yport. As soon as they had gained the coppice no breath of wind touched them, and they left the road to take a narrow path buried in the foliage. They could hardly walk forward, and she felt an arm sliding gently about her waist.

She said nothing, her heart quickening, her breath broken. Low branches caressed their heads; they often had to stoop in order to pass. She gathered a leaf; two ladybirds, like two frail little red shells, were hidden beneath it. Then she said, quite innocently, and a little reassured: "Look, a household."

Julien placed his mouth to her ear and said: "This evening you will be my wife." Although she had learned many things in her sojourn in the country, she had thus far thought only of the poetry of love and was surprised. His wife? Was she not that already?

Then he began to kiss her with little rapid kisses on the temple and on the neck, where the first tresses began to grow. Thrilled each time by this man's kisses to which she was not accustomed, she instinctively withdrew her head the other way in order to avoid this caress, which she nevertheless found delightful. But they suddenly found themselves at the edge of the wood. She stopped, confused to be so far away.

"What would people think? Let us return," she said.

He withdrew his arm from her waist, and, both turning, they faced each other, so near that they felt each other's breath upon their faces, and they gazed at each other. They gazed with one of those sharp, fixed, searching looks in which two souls mingle. They looked into each other's eyes, into that impenetrable "unknown" of each being; they sounded each other in a silent and prolonged interrogation. What would they be to one another? What would this life prove which they were beginning together? What joys, happinesses, or disillusions were there for each other in that long, indissoluble *tête-à-tête* of marriage? And it seemed to them both that they had not yet seen each other.

And suddenly Julien, placing his two hands upon his wife's shoulders, planted full on her mouth a long kiss, such as she had never received. It descended, that kiss, and penetrated her veins and her marrow, giving her such a shock that she wildly pushed Julien away with both arms, and almost fell backward.

"Let us go away from here, let us go away from here," she stammered.

He did not reply, but he took her hands and held them in his own. They did not exchange a word until they reached the house. The rest of the afternoon seemed long.

All gathered at the table at nightfall. The dinner was simple and sufficiently short, contrary to Norman customs. A sort of stiffness paralyzed the guests. Only the two priests, the mayor, and the four farmers showed a little of that heavy gaiety which generally accompanies weddings. The laughter seemed lifeless. A witticism of the mayor reanimated it.

It was about nine o'clock; they were about to take coffee. Outside, beneath the apple-trees of the first court, the dancing in the open air began. Through the open window the festivity might be observed. The bits of candle hung on the branches gave the leaves tints of *vert-de-gris*. Rustic dancers swung round, singing a wild air which two violins and a clarinet feebly accompanied, mounted on a large kitchen table used as a stage. The tumultuous song of the peasants at times entirely drowned the sound of the instruments; and the slender sound, torn by the unbridled voices, seemed to fall from the sky in shreds, in little pieces of scattered notes.

Two big casks surrounded by flaming torches furnished drink for the crowd. Two servants were occupied in continually washing glasses and bowls in a tub, to hold them, still dripping with water, under the spigots from which flowed a stream of red wine or of pure cider. And the dancers, the thirsty dancers, the older ones tranquil, the girls perspiring, crowded around, stretching out their arms to seize in their turn any glass whatever and pouring at a toss into their throats, throwing back their heads, the liquid which they preferred.

On a table there were bread, butter, cheese, and sausage. Everyone took a bite from time to time, and beneath the roof of illuminated leaves, this wholesome and lively festival gave the dull guests in the dining-room the desire to dance too, to drink from those big barrels, and to eat a slice of bread and butter with a raw onion.

The mayor, who was keeping time with his knife, cried:

"Heavens, that is fun, it is like the wedding of Ganache."

A ripple of subdued laughter ran around the assembly. But Abbé Picot, the natural enemy of civil authority, replied: "You mean the marriage at Cana." The other did not accept the correction.

"No, Monsieur the Curé, I mean what I say. When I say Ganache, it is Ganache."

They rose and passed into the drawing-room. Then they mingled a little with the merry crowd, and soon the guests retired.

The Baron and Baronne had a sort of a quarrel in a low tone. Madame Adelaide, more breathless than ever, appeared to refuse what her husband asked; finally she said: "No, my friend, I cannot. I would not know how to go about it."

The father, then, brusquely leaving her, approached Jeanne: "Will you take a walk with me, my daughter?" he asked.

Filled with emotion, she answered:

"As you like, papa." They went out.

As soon as they were outside, on the side toward the sea, a little breeze fanned them—one of the cold breezes of summer which already smack of autumn. Clouds were scudding through the sky, now veiling, now revealing the stars. The Baron pressed his daughter's arm against him, tenderly clasping her hand. They walked for a few minutes. He seemed undecided, disturbed. Finally he made up his mind.

"Darling," said he, "I am going to fill a difficult part, which ought to be taken by your mother. But as she refuses it, I must take her place. I am not sure of what you know of the things of existence.

There are mysteries which are carefully hidden from children, from girls especially, from girls who must be kept pure in mind, irreproachably pure, up to the time when we place them in the arms of the man who is to take charge of their happiness. It belongs to him to lift that veil thrown over the sweet secret of life. But if no hint has been given to them, they sometimes revolt before the slightly brutal reality hidden behind their dreams. Hurt in their soul, hurt even in their body, they refuse to their husbands that which the law accords to him as an absolute right. I cannot tell you more, my darling; but do not forget that you belong wholly to your husband."

What did she know exactly? What did she guess? She began to tremble, oppressed with melancholy overwhelming and painful as a presentiment. They went back into the house. A surprise stopped them at the drawing-room door. Madame Adelaide was sobbing on Julien's breast. Her obstreperous tears, driven as by a bellows, seemed to spring at the same time from her nose, mouth, and eyes; and the young man, confused and awkward, held the mother, who had cast herself into his arms to implore him to cherish her beloved, her darling, her adored daughter.

The Baron hastened forward.

"Oh, no scene, please; no weakening, I beg of you"; and taking his wife, he seated her in an easy-chair, while she wiped away her tears. He then turned toward Jeanne:

"Come, little one, kiss your mother quickly and go to bed."

Ready to cry too, she kissed her parents rapidly and fled. Aunt Lison had already retired to her room.

The Baron and his wife were left alone with Julien. They were alone there, so constrained that not a word came to them, the two men in evening dress, standing up, with averted eyes, and Madame Adelaide reclining on her chair with the remnants of sobs in her throat. The embarrassment becoming intolerable, the Baron began to speak of the trip which the young people were to take in a few days.

Jeanne, in her room, let herself be undressed by Rosalie who wept like a fountain, her hands wandering at hazard, so that she could not find hooks or pins. She seemed assuredly much more moved than her mistress. But Jeanne paid little attention to her maid's tears; it seemed to her that she had entered another world, had gone upon another earth, separated from all that she had cherished. Everything seemed overturned in her life and in her thoughts; even this strange idea came to her: "Did she love her husband?" He suddenly seemed to her like a stranger whom she hardly knew. Three months before, she did not know that he existed, and now she was his wife. Why was this? Why fall into marriage as into a hole open under your feet?

When she was in her night costume, she slipped into bed; and the sheets, a little cool, made her skin shiver, increasing that sensation of cold, of solitude, of sadness, which had weighed upon her soul for two hours. Rosalie fled, still sobbing, and Jeanne waited. She waited, anxious, her heart oppressed, for that certain something, divined and announced in confused terms by her father, that mysterious revelation of the great secret of love.

Without her having heard anyone climb the stairs, there were three light knocks on her door. She trembled horribly and did not answer. The knocking was renewed, then the lock grated. She hid her head under the covers as if a robber had entered the room. Footsteps sounded softly upon the floor, and suddenly some one touched her bed. She gave a nervous start and uttered a little cry, and uncovering her head, she saw Julien standing before her, smiling as he looked at her.

"Oh! how you frightened me!" she said.

He replied: "Then you did not expect me?"

She did not reply. He was in evening dress, with the serene face of a happy husband, and she felt horribly ashamed to be in bed thus before this man, so gallant in his attire. They did not know what to say, or what to do, not daring even to look at each other, at this serious and decisive hour on which the intimate happiness of their whole lives depended.

He felt vaguely perhaps, what danger this battle offered, and what a supple self-possession and what artful tenderness were necessary, not to offend any of the subtle modesties, the infinite delicacies of a virginal soul nourished on dreams. Then, very gently he took her hand and kissed it, and kneeling at the bedside, as at an altar, he murmured in a voice as light as a breath: "Won't you love me?" She, suddenly reassured, raised her head upon the pillow among the lace, and smiled. "I love you already, my friend."

He put his wife's fine little fingers in his mouth, and, in a voice muffled by the act, he said: "Will you prove to me that you love me?"

She answered, troubled anew, without exactly understanding what she was saying, remembering the words of her father: "I am yours, my friend." He covered her wrist with warm kisses, and raising himself slowly, he drew near to her face, which she began to conceal again.

Suddenly throwing one arm forward, he infolded his wife through the covers, while slipping his other arm under the pillow, he raised it with her head, and very softly asked: "Then you will make a little place for me beside you?"

She was filled with an instinctive fear, and stammered: "Oh, not yet, please."

He seemed disappointed, a little ruffled, and he rejoined in a tone still suppliant, but a little more brusque: "Why later, since it must be?" She was angry with him for saying that; but, submissive and resigned, she repeated for the second time: "I am yours, my friend."

Then he disappeared suddenly in the dressing-room; and she distinctly heard his motions, with the rustling of garments being taken off, a sound of coins in his pocket, the successive falling of his shoes.

And suddenly, in his underwear and socks, he quickly crossed the floor to place his watch on the mantelpiece. Then he returned, running, to the small adjoining room, moved about a little while longer, and Jeanne turned rapidly to the other side, shutting her eyes. When she felt that he had arrived, she made a leap as if to throw herself on the floor, but there quickly glided against her leg another leg cool and soft; and, her face in her hands, bewildered, ready to cry out with fear and terror, she cowered to the back of the bed.

Then he clasped her in his arms, although she turned her back upon him, and he voraciously kissed her neck, the floating laces of her night headdress, and the embroidered collar of her night-robe. She did not move, stiffened with a horrible anxiety, feeling a strong hand which sought her bosom hidden between her elbows. She gasped, overwhelmed by this brutal touch; and she desired, more than ever, to escape, to run through the house, to shut herself up somewhere far from this man. He no longer stirred. She felt his warmth on her back.

Then her fright was again allayed, and she suddenly thought that she would only have to turn and embrace him.

Finally he seemed to grow impatient, and, in a grieved voice, he said: "Then you won't be my little wife?"

She murmured through her fingers: "Am I not that now?"

He answered with a shade of bad humor: "No, my dear, come, do not make game of me."

She felt moved by the discontent in his voice, and she suddenly turned toward him to ask his forgiveness. He madly clasped her in his arms, as if starving for her, and he covered with rapid, biting, frantic kisses her whole face and the top of her throat, smothering her with caresses. She had opened her hands and remained inert under his efforts, no longer knowing what she was doing, or what he was doing, in a bewilderment which prevented her from understanding anything. But she felt a sharp, sudden pain; and she began to groan, twisting in his arms while he possessed her.

What happened then? She had little recollection of it for she had lost her head; it seemed to her only that he showered upon her lips a storm of little, grateful kisses. Then he spoke to her and she answered him. Then he made other attempts, which she resisted with fright, and as she struggled, she felt on her bosom that thick hair which she had already felt upon her leg, and she recoiled from the shock. Wearied, finally, of soliciting her without success, he remained motionless upon his back.

Then she began to think. She said to herself, despondent to the bottom of her heart, in the disillusion of an intoxication which she had dreamed to be so different, of a dear expectation destroyed, of a dead bliss: "So this is what he calls being his wife!"

And she remained a long while thus, disconsolate, her glances wandering over the tapestries of the wall, over the ancient legend of love which adorned the room.

But as Julien no longer spoke, no longer moved, she slowly turned her face toward him, and perceived that he was asleep. Asleep, with his mouth partly open and a calm countenance. Asleep! She could not believe it, feeling indignant, more outraged by this sleep than by his brutality, treated like the first comer.

Could he sleep on such a night? What had passed between them was, then, nothing more to him? Oh! she would rather have been struck, treated violently again, bruised with odious caresses until she had lost consciousness. She remained quiet, leaning on her elbow, bending toward him, listening to the light breath passing between his lips, which at times became something like a snore.

Day dawned dull at first, then clear, then pink, then brilliant. Julien opened his eyes, yawned, stretched his arms, looked at his wife, smiled, and asked: "Did you sleep well, darling?"

She perceived that he used the *tu* now, and replied with the more formal *vous*: "Oh, yes. And you?"

He said: "I, oh! very well." And, turning toward her, kissed her, and then tranquilly began to talk. He developed plans for their life, with notions of economy, and that word, often recurring, astonished Jeanne. She listened to him without fully seizing the meaning of the words, looked at him, and thought of a thousand things which passed over the surface of her mind.

Eight o'clock struck. "Come, we must get up," said he, "we should be ridiculous to stay in bed late," and he rose first. When he had finished dressing, he jauntily assisted his wife in all the small details of her toilette, not permitting Rosalie to be summoned.

As they were going out, he stopped her. "You know," said he, "that we may use the *tu* now, between ourselves. But before your parents we would better wait awhile. It will be quite natural when we come back from our wedding journey."

She did not appear until the breakfast hour. And the day ran on just as ordinarily as if nothing new had happened. There was simply one man the more in the house.

CHAPTER V.

Corsica and a New Life

FOUR days later the berlin arrived which was to take them to Marseilles. After the pang of the first night, Jeanne had become accustomed to the contact of Julien, to his kisses, his tender caresses, although her repugnance for their more intimate relations had not decreased. She thought him handsome, she loved him; and again she felt herself happy and gay.

The good-byes were short and without sorrow. The Baronne alone seemed affected; and as the carriage was about to start, she placed a purse, heavy as lead, in her daughter's hand. "It is for your little expenses as a young wife," she said. Jeanne thrust it into her pocket, and the horses dashed off.

Toward evening Julien said to her: "How much did your mother give you in that purse?" She had thought no more about it, but now she emptied it on her lap. There was a flood of gold, two thousand francs. She clapped her hands: "I will do all sorts of foolish things with it," she said, as she gathered up the money.

After a week's journey, through terrible heat, they arrived at Marseilles. The next day the "Roi-Louis," a little packet which was going to Naples touching at Ajaccio, took them toward Corsica. Corsica! the *maquis*, the bandits! the mountains! the birth-place of Napoleon! It seemed to Jeanne that she had gone out of reality, to enter, wide awake, into a dream. Side by side on the deck of the ship, they watched the cliffs of Provence glide by. The mo-tionless sea, of a deep azure, as if congealed and hardened in the glowing light of the sun, stretched away under an infinite sky of a lighter blue almost exaggerated.

Said Jeanne: "Do you remember our sail in father Lastique's boat?" Instead of answering he gave her a quick kiss on the ear.

The paddles struck the water, disturbing its heavy slumber; and astern, in a long, foamy trail, a great wavering track where the water in commotion frothed like champagne, the narrow wake of the boat stretched as far as the eye could reach.

Suddenly, off the bow, only a few fathoms away, an enormous fish, a dolphin, leaped out of the water, plunged back into it headfirst, and disappeared. Jeanne, quite frightened, uttered a cry, and threw herself on Julien's breast. Then she began to laugh at her terror, and watched attentively to see if the fish would not reappear. In a few seconds it leaped again, like a great mechanical toy. Then it fell back and sprang again; then there were two, then three, then six, who seemed to gambol around the heavy boat, as an escort to their huge brother, the wooden fish with the iron fins. They passed at the left, returned on the right of the ship, and now all together, now in succession, as in play, or in a gay pursuit, they threw themselves into the air with leaps which described a curve, and then dived back, one after the other.

Jeanne clapped her hands, jumping for joy, delighted at each apparition of these huge and supple swimmers. Her heart bounded with them in a mad and childish pleasure. Suddenly they disappeared. Once or twice they were seen very far off toward the open sea; then they vanished, and Jeanne felt, for a few seconds, sorry at the departure.

The evening came, a calm, radiant evening, full of light, of happy peacefulness. Not a shiver in the air or on the water, and the illimitable repose of the ocean and of the sky spread itself over enervated souls where likewise there was no shiver.

The great sun sank softly beneath the horizon, toward invisible Africa, Africa, the burning land whose ardors they already seemed to feel; but a sort of cool caress, which yet was not a breeze, lightly touched their faces when the orb had disappeared.

They did not wish to seek their stateroom, where there were all the horrible odors of a packet-boat; so they both stretched themselves on the deck, side by side, wrapped in their cloaks. Julien went to sleep at once; but Jeanne remained with her eyes open, agitated by the unknown features of the journey. The monotonous sound of the wheels lulled her; and she looked above her at the legions of stars, so bright with a sharp light, scintillating and, as it were, moist in the pure sky of the south.

Toward morning, nevertheless, she slumbered. Noises and voices awoke her. The sailors, with their song, were making the ship's toilette. She shook her husband, who was motionless in sleep, and they rose. She drank in with exultation the savor of the salt mist, which penetrated to the end of her fingers. The sea was everywhere. Nevertheless, off the bow, something gray, confused still in the growing dawn, a sort of accumulation of strange, pointed, jagged clouds, seemed to float on the waves. Then it appeared more distinct; the forms were more sharply outlined on the brightening sky; a long line of angular and fantastic mountains rose: it was Corsica, enveloped in a sort of light veil.

The sun rose behind, outlining all the projections of the peaks in black shadows; then all the summits were illumined while the rest of the island remained enshrouded in vapor.

The captain, a little dried-up, sunburned, short, shriveled man, shrunk by the harsh salt winds, appeared upon the deck, and in a voice hoarse with thirty years of command, worn by orders shouted in storms, said to Jeanne: "Do you smell it?"

There was, in fact, a strange and peculiar odor of plants and wild shrubs. The captain resumed:

"It is Corsica which smells like that, Madame; it is her own pretty woman's odor. After twenty years' absence I would recognize it five miles away. I belong there. The one I revere, far away at St. Helena, is always speaking, they say, of the odor of his native country. He is of my family." And the captain, raising his hat, saluted Corsica, saluting at the same time, across the ocean, the great imprisoned Emperor, who was of his family. Jeanne was so touched that she almost wept.

Then the sailor stretched his arm toward the horizon: "The Sanguinaires!" said he. Julien, standing near his wife, held her by the waist, and they both looked far off to discover the indicated point. They finally descried some pyramid-shaped rocks, which the vessel soon rounded in order to enter an immense and tranquil gulf, surrounded by a number of lofty peaks whose lower slopes seemed covered with moss.

The captain pointed out this verdure: "That is the *maquis*," said he. In proportion as they advanced, the circle of mountains seemed to close in behind the ship, which slowly sailed in an azure lake so transparent that they could at times see the bottom. Suddenly the city appeared, all white, at the end of the gulf, beside the billows, at the foot of the mountains.

Some little Italian boats were anchored in the harbor. Four or five lighters came prowling about the "Roi-Louis" to seek passengers for the shore. Julien, who was collecting their luggage, asked his wife in a low tone: "It is enough to give the steward twenty sous, isn't it?" For a week he had been asking that same question, and every time it annoyed her. She answered with a little impatience: "When a person is not sure of giving enough, he gives too much."

He continually disputed with the managers and waiters of the hotel, with coachmen, with the sellers of no matter what, and when, by force of quibbling, he had obtained a slight reduction, he said to Jeanne, rubbing his hands: "I don't like to be robbed."

She trembled when bills were presented, sure in advance of the remarks which he would make on each item, humiliated by this haggling, blushing to the roots of her hair under the contemptuous look of the servants who followed her husband with their glance while holding his insufficient fee in the palm of their hand. He had a discussion with the boatman who put them ashore.

The first tree which she saw was a palm! They went to a great empty hotel, at the angle of a big square, and had breakfast served. When they had finished eating, just as Jeanne was rising to go for a stroll through the city, Julien, taking her in his arms, murmured tenderly in her ear: "Suppose we lie down a little while, sweetheart?"

She was taken by surprise: "Go to bed? But I am not tired."

He embraced her. "I need you. Do you understand? It's two days — !"

She grew purple, abashed, and stammered: "Oh! Now? But what will people think? How can you ask for a bedroom in full daylight? Oh! Julien, I beg of you."

But he interrupted her: "I don't care what the hotel people may say and think. You will see how little that bothers me." And he rang the bell. She said no more, her eyes downcast, revolted, nevertheless, in her soul and her flesh, before this incessant desire of her husband, obeying only with disgust, resigned but humiliated, seeing in this some-

74

thing bestial, degrading, in fine an obscenity. Her senses were still sleeping, and her husband treated her now as if she shared his ardors.

When the waiter arrived, Julien asked him to show them to their room. The man, a true Corsican, hairy to his eyes, did not understand, saying that the apartment would be prepared for the night. Julien impatiently explained: "No, now, at once. We are tired with the voyage and we want to rest."

Then a grin appeared in the valet's beard and Jeanne wanted to escape. When they came downstairs again, an hour later, she dared no longer pass in front of the people whom she met, persuaded that they would laugh and whisper behind her back. She was angry at heart with Julien for not understanding this, for not having these little modesties, these delicacies of instinct; and she felt a barrier between them, perceiving for the first time that two persons never penetrate to each other's soul, and that, entwined at times but not mingled, the moral nature and the individuality of each one of us remain eternally alone through life.

Then an itinerary was arranged for their trip, and in order not to come back over any difficult road, they decided to hire their horses. They engaged, therefore, two small Corsican stallions with restless eyes, thin and tireless, and set out one morning at daybreak. A guide, mounted on a mule, accompanied them and carried the provisions, for inns are unknown in that wild country.

The road at first followed the gulf, to plunge later into a shallow valley going toward the great peaks.

Often they crossed torrents which were almost dry: an appearance of a stream still flowed beneath the stones, like a slinking animal, and made a timid gurgle!

The uncultivated country seemed all naked. The hillsides were covered with tall grass, yellow at this hot season. At times they met a mountaineer, either on foot, or on a small horse, or astride a donkey about the size of a dog. All carried a loaded gun on the shoulder — old, rusty weapons, but formidable in their hands.

The sharp perfume of the aromatic plants with which the island is covered seemed to thicken the air; and the road kept gently ascending amidst the long folds of the mountains. The summits of pink or blue granite gave tints of fairyland to the vast landscape; and over the lower slopes forests of huge chestnut-trees had the air of green bushes, so gigantic are the undulations of the upheaved earth in this country.

Sometimes the guide, pointing toward the steep heights, would mention a name. Jeanne and Julien looked, saw nothing, then finally discovered something gray, like a mass of rock fallen from the summit. It was a village, a little hamlet, hanging there, clinging like a bird's nest, almost invisible on the immense mountain.

This long journey at a slow walk wearied Jeanne. "Let us canter a little," said she. And she urged her horse. Then, as she did not hear her husband galloping near her, she turned around, and began to laugh heartily at seeing him careering along, pale, holding his horse's mane, and bounding up and down most strangely. His beauty, his face — fit for a "handsome cavalier"—made his awkwardness and his fear even more ridiculous. They then began to trot gently.

The road now stretched between two interminable coppices which covered the whole of the slopes like a mantle. This was the *maquis*, the impenetrable *maquis*, formed of green oaks, junipers, arbutus, mastic, alatern, heather, laurel, thyme, myrtle, and box mingling like tresses with entwining clematis, monstrous ferns, honeysuckles, laburnum, rosemary, lavender, and briers, covering the sides of the mountains with a tangled fleece.

They were hungry. The guide rejoined them and conducted them to one of those charming springs so frequent in mountainous countries, a slender thread of water coming from a hole in the rock and flowing in a tiny canal formed by a chestnut-leaf placed there by some passerby to lead the slight current to the mouth. Jeanne felt so happy that she could hardly restrain herself from uttering cries of joy. They started again, and began to descend, passing round the Gulf of Sagone.

Toward evening they went through Cargese, the Greek village, founded in former times by a colony of fugitives driven from their native land. Tall and lovely girls, with straight backs, long hands, fine figures, singularly graceful, formed a group about a fountain. Julien having greeted them with a "Good evening," they replied in a musical voice in the harmonious language of their abandoned country.

Arriving at Piana, they had to ask for hospitality, as in ancient times and lost regions. Jeanne shivered with pleasure while waiting for the door, at which

77

Julien had knocked, to be opened. Oh! this was indeed traveling! with all the unforeseen happenings of unexplored ways. They were making application to a young household, and were received as the Patriarchs might have received guests sent by God. They slept on a corn mattress, in an old worm-eaten house. All its woodwork was punctured with holes, and threaded by long borer worms which are devourers of wood. It rustled, seeming to live and breathe.

They departed at sunrise, but soon halted in front of a forest, a true forest of purple granite. It was one of those peaks, columns, or towers, a startling shape modeled by time, the wind, and sea-mist.

Three hundred meters high, slender, round, twisted, crooked, misshapen, unexpected, fantastic, these surprising rocks appeared to be trees, plants, animals, monuments, men, robed monks, horned devils, huge birds, a collection of monstrosities, a nightmare's menagerie, petrified by the fiat of some whimsical god. Jeanne no longer spoke; her heart was oppressed, and she took Julien's hand, clasping it tightly, overwhelmed with the need of loving, before all this natural beauty.

Suddenly rising out of this chaos, they discovered a new gulf entirely girdled with a blood-colored wall of red granite. These scarlet rocks were reflected in the blue water. Jeanne stammered: "Oh! Julien!" not being able to find other words, softened with admiration, her throat choking; and two tears fell from her eyes. He looked at her astonished, and asked: "What's the matter, little one?"

She wiped her cheeks, smiled, and in a slightly trembling voice, she said: "It is nothing—I am nervous—I don't know—I was affected. I am so happy that the least thing upsets my heart."

He did not understand these womanly weaknesses, the shocks of these vibrating beings, perturbed by a mere nothing, whom an enthusiasm will move like a catastrophe, whom an impalpable sensation revolutionizes, maddens with joy, or plunges into despair. These tears seemed ridiculous to him, and, wholly occupied with the dangerous road, he said: "You must watch your horse."

By an almost impassable road they descended to the bottom of this gulf, then turned to the right to climb the somber valley of Ota. But the path proved horrible. Julien proposed trying it on foot. She asked nothing better, delighted to walk and to be alone with him after her recent emotion.

The guide went ahead with the mule and the horses, and they walked on slowly. The mountain opened, cleft from top to bottom. The path buried itself in this breach. It followed the bottom, between two prodigious walls; and a great torrent ran through this crevasse. The air was chill, the granite seemed black, and, far above, all that could be seen of the blue sky seemed astonished and bewildered. A sudden sound made Jeanne start. She raised her eyes: an enormous bird flew from a hole, it was an eagle. Its opened wings seemed to seek the two sides of the shaft and it mounted into the azure and disappeared.

Further off, the crack in the mountain divided: the path climbed between the two ravines in zigzags. Jeanne, light and sportive, went first, making the pebbles roll under her feet, intrepid, leaning over abysses. He followed her, a little out of breath, keeping his eyes on the ground for fear of a vertigo.

Suddenly the sun inundated them: they felt as if they had just come out of hell. They were thirsty, a damp trail guided them across a chaos of rocks to a tiny little spring running through a hollow stick put there for the use of the goatherds. A carpet of moss covered the soil round about. Jeanne kneeled to drink, and Julien did the same.

As she was enjoying the coolness of the water, he took her waist and tried to steal her place at the end of the little wooden conduit. She resisted: their lips touched, met, and parted. In the chances of the struggle, they seized in turn the slender end of the tube and bit it in order not to let it go. And the thread of cold water, taken and left continually, broke and renewed itself, splashed their faces, necks, clothes, and hands. Little drops like pearls glistened in their hair. And kisses flowed with the stream.

Suddenly Jeanne had an inspiration of love. She filled her mouth with the clear liquid, and, her cheeks swollen like leather bottles, made Julien understand that she wanted to give him a drink. He held his mouth, smiling, his head thrown back, his arms open; and he drank a draught from this fountain of living flesh which filled him with a wild desire. Jeanne leaned upon him with an unwonted tenderness; her heart palpitated; her eyes seemed softened, moist with water. She murmured low: "Julien—I—I love you," and drew him to her.

They were a long time in reaching the top of the mountain, she was so breathless and overpowered

with lassitude, and it was evening when they reached
Evisa and found the house of a relative of their
guide, Paoli Palabretti. He was a man of tall figure,
a little bent, with the melancholy air of a consump-
tive. He conducted them to their room, a gloomy
room with walls of naked stone, but handsome for
a country where all elegance is unknown, and he
expressed, in his Corsican dialect,—a mixture of
French and Italian,—his pleasure at receiving them.
A clear voice interrupted him, and a small dark
woman, with big black eyes warmed by the sun,
with a slender form, her teeth showing from her
habit of laughing continually, rushed forward, kissed
Jeanne, shook Julien's hand and said: "Good day,
Madame; good day, Monsieur; are you well?"

She removed the hats and shawls, doing everything
with one arm, for she carried the other in a sling, then
she drove everybody out, saying to her husband:

"Take them for a stroll till dinner."

Monsieur Palabretti immediately obeyed, placed
himself between the two young people and took them
to see the village. He dragged his steps and his
words, coughing frequently and repeating every five
minutes: "It is the cold air of the valley which has
affected my lungs.'

He guided them by a hidden path under enormous chestnut-trees. Suddenly he stopped, and, with
a monotonous accent, said: "It was here that my
cousin, Jean Rinaldi, was killed by Mathieu Lori. I
was there, quite near Jean, when Mathieu appeared
at ten paces from us. 'Jean,' he cried, 'don't go to Al-
bertacce; don't go there, Jean, or I will kill you, I
tell you.' I took Jean's arm, and said: 'Don't go there,

Jean, he'll do it.' It was on account of a girl whom both were following, Paulina Sinacoupi. But Jean replied: 'I'll go, Mathieu; you can't prevent me.' Then Mathieu lowered his gun, before I could aim mine, and fired. Jean gave a great leap with both feet, like children skipping rope, yes, Monsieur, and fell full upon me, so that my gun escaped me and rolled as far as that chestnut there. Jean opened his mouth wide but did not speak a word, he was dead."

The young people, stupefied, looked at the tranquil witness of this crime. Jeanne asked: "And the assassin?"

Paoli Palabretti had a long fit of coughing, then he continued: "He reached the mountains. My brother killed him, the next year. You know my brother, Philippi Palabretti, the bandit."

Jeanne shivered: "Your brother a bandit?"

The placid Corsican had a gleam of pride in his eyes. "Yes, Madame, he was a celebrity, he was. He laid low six gendarmes. He was killed with Nicolas Morali, when they were surrounded in Niolo, after a six days' battle, and when they were almost dying with hunger."

Then he added with a resigned air: "It is the way of the country," in the same tone in which he said: "The air of the valley is cold." Then they returned for dinner, and the little Corsican woman treated them as if she had known them for twenty years.

But an uneasiness haunted Jeanne. Would she again find in the arms of Julien that strange and impetuous shock of the senses which she had felt on the moss at the fountain? When they were alone in their room she trembled lest she should be still insensible under his kisses. But she was quickly reassured: it was her first night of love.

The next morning, at the hour of starting, she did not like to leave this humble house in which it seemed to her that a new happiness had begun for her. She drew her host's little wife into her room, and while asserting that she would not ask her to accept a present, she insisted that she must be permitted, after her return, to send her from Paris some souvenir, to which she attached an almost superstitious idea.

The young Corsican woman resisted a long while, not wanting to accept anything. Finally she consented: "Well," said she, "you may send me a small pistol, quite a small one."

Jeanne opened her eyes wide. The other added in a low tone, almost in her ear, as a person confides a sweet and intimate secret: "It is to kill my brother-in-law." And smiling she quickly unrolled the bandages which enveloped her unused arm, and showed her round white flesh, pierced quite through with a stiletto, the wound having almost healed, leaving a scar.

"If I had not been as strong as he, he would have killed me. My husband is not jealous, he knows me; and then he is ill, you know, and that calms his blood. Besides, I am an honest woman, Madame; but my brother-in-law believes everything that anyone tells him. He is jealous for my husband, and he will certainly make another attempt. Then if I should have the pistol, I should be tranquil, and sure of avenging myself."

Jeanne promised to send her the weapon, kissed her new friend tenderly and continued her journey. The rest of the trip was only a dream, endless embraces and intoxicating kisses. She saw nothing, neither landscapes, nor places where she stopped. She saw nothing but Julien.

Arriving at Bastia, the guide had to be paid. Julien rummaged in his pockets. Finding nothing, he said to Jeanne: "As you are not using your mother's two thousand francs, give them to me to carry for you. They will be safer in my belt; and it will prevent my having to make change." And she handed him the purse.

They reached Leghorn, visited Florence, Genoa, and all the Corniche district. One morning, when the mistral was blowing, they arrived at Marseilles. Two months had flown since their departure from the "Poplars." It was now the 15th of October. Jeanne, affected by the cold wind which seemed to come from far-off Normandy, felt sad. Julien had for some time seemed changed, tired, indifferent: and she was afraid without knowing of what she was afraid.

She delayed their homeward journey four days more, not being able to make up her mind to leave this country of the sun. It seemed to her that she had just reached the acme of happiness.

Finally they started. They were to make in Paris all the purchases for their definite installation at the "Poplars"; and Jeanne was anticipating delight at taking home marvels, thanks to her mother's gift; but the first thing of which she thought was the pistol promised to the young Corsican woman of Evisa.

The day after their arrival she said to Julien: "My dear, will you please give me back mamma's money because I want to make some purchases."

He turned toward her with a displeased expression of face: "How much do you need?"

She was surprised and stammered: "Why, as much as you like."

He replied: "I am going to give you one hundred francs; be careful not to waste it."

She did not know what to say, abashed and confused. Finally she hesitatingly said: "But I gave you that money to—"

He did not let her finish: "Yes, certainly. Whether it be in your pocket or in mine makes no difference, now that we have the same purse. I don't refuse it to you, do I, since I am giving you a hundred francs?"

She took the five twenty-franc pieces without adding a word; but she dared not ask for more, and bought nothing but the pistol.

A week later they started on the return to the "Poplars."

CHAPTER VI.

DISENCHANTMENT

BEFORE the white fence with brick pillars the family and the servants stood waiting. The post carriage stopped, and there were long embraces. The Baronne wept. Jeanne, affected, wiped away two tears; her father walked up and down nervously. Then, while the luggage was removed, the journey was recounted before the drawing-room fire. Words flowed abundantly from Jeanne's lips; and all was told in half an hour, except, perhaps, some little details, forgotten in this rapid recital.

Then the young woman went to open her parcels. Rosalie, much affected herself, assisted. When this was finished, when the linen, the dresses, the toilette articles had been put in place, the little maid left her mistress; and Jeanne, a trifle tired, sat down. She wondered what she should do now, seeking an occupation for her mind, an employment for her hands. She had no desire to go down to the drawing-room with her mother who was dozing; and she thought of a walk; but the country seemed so dull that simply from looking at it through the window she felt a weight of melancholy.

Then she perceived that she had not anything to do, never more anything to do. All her youth in the convent had been preoccupied with the future, busy with dreams. The continual agitation of her hopes filled, at that time, her hours without her feeling them pass. Then hardly had she left those austere walls where her illusions had bloomed, when her expectation of love was immediately realized. The man hoped for, met, loved, married in a few weeks, as people marry on these sudden determinations, took her to his arms without permitting her to reflect upon anything.

But now the sweet reality of the first days had become the daily reality, which closed the doors to the undefined hopes, to the charming disquietudes of love. Yes, waiting was finished. There was nothing more to do, neither to-day nor to-morrow nor ever. She felt all that vaguely, with disillusion, with a sinking of her dreams. She rose and pressed her forehead to the cold window-pane. Then, after looking for some time at the sky where somber clouds were rolling, she decided to go out.

Were they the same fields, the same grass, the same trees as in the month of May? What had become of the sunny gaiety of the leaves and the green poetry of the lawn where the dandelions flamed, or the poppies bled, or the daisies blossomed, or the fantastic yellow butterflies hovered as if at the end of invisible strings? And that intoxication of the air charged with life, with aromas, and with fecundating atoms existed no longer.

The avenues, washed out by the continual downpours of autumn, stretched away, covered with a thick carpet of dead leaves, beneath the shivering thinness of the almost naked poplars. The slender branches trembled in the wind, still stirring some slight foliage ready to drop into space. And continually, all day long, like an incessant rain sad enough to make one weep, these last leaves, all yellow now, like big golden sous, became detached, turned, whirled, and fell.

She went as far as the grove. It was as sorrowful as the room of a dying man. The green wall which separated and hid the pretty walks was scattered. The entangled shrubs, like a lace-work of fine wood, struck their thin branches against each other; and the murmur of fallen and dried leaves, which the breeze stirred, moved, and piled up in heaps, seemed the last sigh of dying agony. Some little birds hopped from place to place looking for a shelter.

Protected, nevertheless, by the thick curtain of elms, placed as an advance guard against the sea winds, the linden and the plane-tree, still covered with their summer attire, seemed clad, one in red velvet and the other in orange silk, tinted thus by the first cold days according to the nature of their sap.

Jeanne went and came with slow steps in the Baronne's avenue, along the line of the Couillard farm. Something weighed upon her, like a presentiment of the long weariness of the monotonous life which was beginning for her.

Then she seated herself on the slope where Julien had for the first time spoken to her of love; and she remained there, musing, almost without ·thinking, with a pining heart, with a longing to go to sleep in order to forget the sadness of this day.

Suddenly she perceived a sea-gull, soaring through the sky, borne upon the breeze; and she called to mind that eagle, which she had seen, there in Corsica, in the gloomy vale of Ota. She felt in her heart the sharp shock which is given by the memory of something sweet but forever finished; and she suddenly seemed to see the radiant island with its wild perfume, its sun which ripened the oranges and the citrons, its pink-topped mountains, its azure gulfs, and its ravines where torrents rushed.

Then the damp and harsh landscape which surrounded her, with the dismal falling of the leaves and the gray clouds driven before the wind, enveloped her in such a depth of desolation that she went back into the house in order to avoid sobbing outright.

Her mother, torpid before the fireplace, was napping, accustomed to the melancholy of the days, not feeling it any longer. The Baron and Julien had gone for a walk that they might talk over their affairs. And night came, casting a gloomy shadow through the vast drawing-room, which was lighted by the flickering reflections of the fire. Without, through the windows, a remnant of daylight still made visible the unkempt nature of the end of the year, and the grayish sky looked as if it, had been rubbed in mud.

The Baron soon appeared, followed by Julien. When he entered the darkened room, he rang, crying: "Quick, quick, some lights! It is gloomy here." And he sat down before the fireplace. While his damp feet smoked near the coals, and the mud, dried by the heat, fell from his boot-soles, he rubbed his hands gaily. "I believe," he said, "that it is going to freeze; the sky is lighting to the north; there is a full moon this evening, and the frost will bite hard to-night."

Then turning toward his daughter, he said: "Well, little one, are you contented to be back in your own country, your own house, with the old folk?"

This simple question upset Jeanne. She threw herself into her father's arms, her eyes filled with tears, and kissed him nervously, as if to ask his pardon; for, in spite of the efforts of her heart to be gay, she felt overwhelmed with sadness. She thought of all the joy of which she had promised herself on returning to her parents; and she was astonished at this coldness which paralyzed her tenderness. She felt like one who has thought a good deal, while far away, of people beloved — people mixed up with one's daily life — and who feels, upon finding them again, a sort of check on the affections until such time as the bonds of the former common life are renewed.

The dinner was long; there was little conversation. Julien seemed to have forgotten his wife. In the drawing-room, afterward, she let herself doze by the fire; opposite, the Baronne slept outright. Jeanne, awaked a moment later by the voice of the two men who were engaged in a discussion, wondered, as she tried to rouse her energies, if she also were going to be seized by that dull lethargy which nothing interrupts.

The flames of the fireplace, soft and reddish through the day, became lively, bright, and crackling. They threw sudden gleams on the faded chair-covers, on "the fox and the stork," on "the melancholy heron," and "the grasshopper and the ant."

The Baron drew near, smiling and holding his open hands to the live brands: "Ah, ah! the fire burns well, this evening. It is freezing, my children." Then he placed his hands on Jeanne's shoulder, and pointing at the fire: "You see, daughter, this is the best thing in the world; the home hearth, the hearth with one's own gathered round. Nothing equals that. But it is bedtime; you ought to be very tired, children."

When Jeanne had gone up to her room, she wondered how two returnings to the same place, which she thought she loved, could be so different. Why did she feel as if bruised, why should this house, this dear country, all that which up to the present time made her heart thrill, seem to-day so heartbreaking?

But her glance suddenly fell on the clock. The little bee still swung from left to right, and from right to left, with the same rapid and continuous motion, above the vermilion flowers. Suddenly Jeanne felt an impulse of affection, moved even to tears before this little machine which seemed alive, which sang to her the hour and palpitated like a heart. She certainly had not been so moved in kissing her father and mother. The heart has mysteries which no reasoning can penetrate.

For the first time since her marriage she was alone in bed, Julien, under the pretext of fatigue, having taken another chamber. It had been arranged, for that matter, that each should have his or her own. She was a long time getting to sleep, astonished at no longer feeling anyone at her side, unaccustomed to sleeping alone and annoyed by the harsh north wind which beat against the roof. She was awakened in the morning by a great light which bathed the foot of her bed. The window-panes, thick with frost, were reddened as if the whole horizon was on fire.

Wrapping herself in a large dressing-gown, she ran to the window and opened it. An icy breeze, healthful and sharp, made her skin tingle with a piercing cold which brought the tears to her eyes; and in the midst of a purple sky a great sun appeared behind the trees, shining and puffed like the face of a drunken man.

The earth, covered with white frost, hard and dry now, creaked beneath the tread of the farm-people. In that single night, all the unstripped branches of the poplar trees had been denuded; and behind the waste land appeared the great, greenish line of the waves all strewn with white trails.

The plane-tree and the linden were quickly stripped by the blasts. At each passing of the icy wind the clouds of leaves detached by the sudden frost were scattered in the air like a flight of birds. Jeanne dressed herself, went out, and, for something to do, started to see the farmers.

The Martins welcomed the mistress of the house, and kissed her on both cheeks; then they urged her to drink a little glass of cordial, and then she went to the other farm. The Couillards opened their arms to her; the mistress of the house pecked her on the ears, and she had to drink a little glass of black currant wine. After this she went back to breakfast.

The day passed like the preceding one, cold instead of damp. And the other days of the week resembled these two; and all the weeks of the month resembled the first week. Little by little, however, her longing for far-off countries grew weaker. Habit placed a coating of resignation over her life like the chalky deposit which limestone springs leave upon objects. And a certain interest in the thousand insignificant things of daily existence, a care for the simple and trifling regular occupations, sprang up again in her heart.

There developed in her a species of meditative melancholy, a vague disenchantment with life. What did she require? What did she desire? She knew not. No worldly need possessed her: no thirst for pleasures, no inclination even toward possible joys; what were they, for that matter? Just as the old armchairs of the drawing-room faded in time, everything gradually lost its color in her eyes, everything lost its ancient character, or took on a pale and dull hue.

Her relations with Julien had completely changed. He seemed quite another person since the return from their wedding journey, like an actor who has played his part and reassumes his ordinary character. He hardly noticed her, or even spoke to her; all trace of love had suddenly disappeared, and the nights were few when he entered her room.

He had taken charge of the fortune and of the house, altered the leases, harassed the peasants, curtailed the expenses, and, having put on the bearing of a gentleman farmer, had lost the polish and the elegance of the betrothed young man. He never discarded an old velvet hunting-coat adorned with brass buttons, which he had found in his wardrobe, although it was stained with spots; and influenced by the negligence of those who have no longer the desire of pleasing, he had ceased to shave himself, so that his long badly-trimmed beard disfigured him incredibly. His hands were no longer cared for; and after each meal he drank four or five glasses of brandy.

Jeanne having tried tender reproaches, he had answered her so shortly: "Let me alone, won't you?" that she did not venture any more advice. She had resigned herself to these changes in a way which astonished herself. He had become a stranger to her, a stranger whose soul and heart were closed to her. She often thought about it, wondering how it came that after having thus met, loved, and married in a glow of tenderness, they should suddenly find themselves almost as unknown to each other as if they had never slept side by side.

And how was it that she did not suffer more from his abandonment? Was life like this? Had they deceived themselves? Was there nothing more for her in the future? If Julien had remained handsome, well-groomed, and seductive as of old, she might have suffered much more.

It was decided that after New Year, her father and mother would go to their house in Rouen for a few months. The young couple were to spend the winter at the "Poplars," so as to get familiar with the surroundings in which they would have to spend their whole life. Besides, they had neighbors to visit — the Brisevilles, the Couteliers, and the Fourvilles, to whom Julien intended to present his wife. They could not visit them as yet, as a new coat of arms had to be painted on the family carriage. Under no consideration would Julien go out in it until the arms of the De Lamares were mingled with those of the Perthuis des Vauds.

There was but one man in the country who could paint heraldic designs. His name was Bataille, and for years he had gone from castle to castle, painting the coats of arms of the Norman nobility on their respective vehicles. He had had a nasty affair, they said, but the very fact that he mingled with aristocracy had made the people forget it long ago.

One morning in December, Bataille arrived at the "Poplars," his paint-box on his back. He was ushered in the dining-room and served as a gentleman. His constant relations with aristocracy and his knowledge of heraldry had ennobled him somewhat, and the aristocrats willingly shook hands with him, treating him almost as an equal.

While Bataille breakfasted, the Baron and Julien made different sketches, and the Baronne, who always took a deep interest in such things, gave her advice; even Jeanne took part in the discussion.

After breakfast, Bataille was conducted to the coach-house and the cover was taken off the carriage. Bataille examined it, stated gravely what dimensions he thought he would need for his drawing, and after further exchange of ideas, he set to work.

Although it was very cold, the Baronne had a seat brought in so as to watch him work and as her feet were getting cold, she also asked for a foot-warmer. She sat there, talking to Bataille, asking him about the recent births, marriages, and deaths. Julien sat near his mother-in-law, listening and smoking his pipe, watching at the same time the progress in the painting.

Old Simon passed on his way to the garden, and he too stopped in to examine the work. The event having been noised about the two farms, the good wives soon made their appearance and standing on each side of the Baronne, they admired and commented upon Bataille's work.

The painting was not completed until about eleven o'clock the next morning, when the coach was brought out to judge better of the effect. Everybody was present and pronounced it a work of art. Bataille was complimented and went on his way again, with his paint-box on his back. The Baron, his wife, Jeanne, and Julien all agreed that Bataille was a clever man, and might have become a great artist.

Julien's economy had introduced several new rules at the "Poplars." The old coachman had become the gardener; Julien having decided to drive himself. He had sold the coach horses so as not to be obliged to feed them. As some one was needed for the stable, he had made a groom out of Marius, the little cowkeeper. Then he devised a plan to procure a pair of horses without having to buy them. He introduced a clause in the lease of the Couillards and Martins, compelling each of them to furnish him with a horse on a certain day of the month designated by him, and in return he exempted them from the poultry tax.

So the Couillards brought an immense, shaggy, yellow-haired horse, while the Martins sent a small, white horse with long hair. The curious pair was duly harnessed and Marius, completely swallowed up in one of Simon's liveries, brought the coach in front of the door.

Julien looked quite well. He looked a little like his old self, but his long beard made him look common in spite of all.

The Baronne came down leaning on her husband's arm, who assisted her in and propped her up with cushions. Then Jeanne appeared. She laughed at the strange pair of horses. The white one was the yellow one's grandson, she said; but when she saw Marius with his high hat coming down well over his ears and nose, his hands entirely hidden in the sleeves of his coat, the tails of which almost entirely covered him, when she saw him throw his head backward so as to be able to see under his big hat and raise his feet so high when he walked that he looked as if he intended to jump a creek, she was seized with convulsive, uncontrollable laughter.

The Baron turned to look at Marius, and the sight was too much for him; he, too, burst out laughing.

"Look, look at Marius" he said to his wife; "look, is he not funny?"

The Baronne leaned out of the window, and when she saw Marius, she was seized with such a fit of laughter that the coach shook on its springs. Julien, who thought everything was satisfactory, was pale with anger. He turned to them and said:

"What is the matter with you all? You must be crazy to laugh like that."

Jeanne was convulsed, unable to stop. She sat on the steps and so did the Baron, and inside of the coach the Baronne was choking with laughter. Suddenly Marius understood what they were laughing at, and he too laughed heartily under his big hat, shaking the tails of his coat like a pair of wings.

Julien was exasperated. He gave the boy such a powerful slap, that it sent his big hat off his head. Then turning to his father-in-law he said angrily:

"It seems to me that it is not your place to laugh. If you had not squandered your money as you did, we would not be in such straitened circumstances. Whose fault is it if you are ruined?"

This threw a chill on everyone and the laughter ceased immediately. Jeanne was on the verge of tears. She quietly took a seat near her mother, and the Baron sat opposite them stunned and ill at ease. Julien took his place on the seat and hoisted Marius up next to him. The poor child was in tears and his cheek was swelling rapidly.

The three occupants of the carriage were silent and sad. They preferred to be silent, knowing full well that the same sad thoughts engrossed them and they could not have spoken without touching on the painful subject.

The ride was a sad and dreary one. The irregular trot of the ill-mated horses jolted the carriage along the road, scaring the chickens, and the dogs barked furiously at the strange vehicle.

At last they reached a broad avenue surrounded with pines. The carriage jogged up and down on the uneven road, throwing it all on one side, making the Baronne scream with fright. They reached a white gate and Marius got down to open it. An immense lawn leading to a large, dreary building with shutters tightly closed met the visitors' view.

The door opened and an old servant, partly paralyzed, clad in a striped waistcoat which barely hid his apron, came down to meet the visitors, walking sideways in short, spasmodic steps. He took the visitors' names and ushered them into a spacious reception-room, opened the shutters and left them. They sat down and inspected the room. The furniture, clock, and candle-sticks were all covered with cloths. The air was icy, damp, and moldy; penetrating the lungs, chilling the heart.

Hurried footsteps in the rooms above denoted an unusual haste. Other steps were heard in answer to a bell; the host and hostess were evidently dressing in a hurry. The Baronne, who had taken a chill, was sneezing repeatedly, and Jeanne sat near her gloomy and despondent. Julien was walking up and down, while the Baron stood with his back to the mantelpiece, a frown on his brow.

At last the door opened and the Viscount and Viscountess de Briseville entered. They were both short and thin; they both looked ceremonious and embarrassed in their state clothes. The Viscountess was attired in a flowered silk dress and a gorgeous cap adorned her glossy curls. She spoke rapidly, in a thin, shrill voice. The Viscount was tightly encased in a gorgeous frock-coat, and bent the knee as he bowed, looking very pompous. He was shiny from head to foot. It would have been hard to guess their age and they both had the neat appearance of things that have been put away carefully for months.

After exchanging the usual compliments there was a general hush; then the conversation picked up a little. They all hoped the amicable relations existing between them would continue, as it was such a source of enjoyment to visit one's neighbors when one lived in the country all the year through.

The icy air penetrated them through and through and the Baronne coughed and sneezed alternately. At last, the Baron gave the signal to depart. The De Brisevilles would not hear of it.

"So soon? Do stay a little longer"; but Jeanne stood up to take leave, although Julien, who thought the visit too short, was making signs to her to keep her seat.

The hostess tried to ring the bell to call the carriage, but the bell was out of order, so the host rushed out and came back presently to say that the horses had been unharnessed, so everybody sat down again and waited. There was another lull in the conversation and for want of a subject, they talked of the weather. Jeanne asked the De Brisevilles how they occupied their time. She could not help shuddering as she spoke. The question seemed to surprise them. Oh, they had plenty to do, they wrote regularly to their several titled relatives; besides, they found a great deal to talk about and never wanted for occupation.

At last the coach came to the door, but Marius had disappeared. No doubt the boy thought he would not be wanted until evening, and had taken a walk. Julien was furious. He gave orders to send him on, and after numerous bows on either side, they started for the "Poplars."

As soon as the coach door was closed, Jeanne and her father began to laugh and imitate the De Brisevilles. They had somewhat recovered from Julien's brutality and they imitated the Viscount and the Viscountess, mimicking their voices, their gestures, and mannerisms. Their antics did not quite please the Baronne; she felt a little hurt.

"You ought not to ridicule them," she said. "They are very nice people and belong to an excellent family." Jeanne and her father stopped so as not to annoy her, but after a while they started again; they could not resist the temptation. The Baronne smiled complacently; still, she was not entirely pleased.

"You should not make fun of people in our class," she said.

Suddenly the carriage stopped, and they heard Julien call to some one behind. Jeanne and the Baron looked out of the window and beheld a singular object which seemed to roll toward them. It was Marius, running for dear life to catch up with the coach. The poor boy had a hard time of it. The tails of his long coat, tangled up in his legs, impeded his movements. One of his hands held on to his hat which completely obstructed his view, while the other flapped up and down like the paddle of a mill; falling into mud puddles, stumbling against stones, he at last caught up with the carriage. Julien caught him by the collar and brought him up on the seat beside him. Dropping the reins, he showered blow after blow upon his head, until his hat sank down to his shoulders. The boy was screaming and squirming to get away, but Julien held him with one hand, while he struck him with the other.

"Father, oh, father!" said Jeanne.

The Baronne was indignant. She took hold of the Baron's arm and said: "Jacques, why do you not stop him?"

The Baron lowered the front window and catching hold of Julien's arm: "Stop beating that child," he said.

"Just look at the state his livery is in," answered Julien. "The beast is mud from head to foot."

"It makes no difference; you should not be so brutal."

"Mind your own business and leave me alone," said Julien angrily. He raised his hand to strike the boy again, but the Baron caught him:

"If you do not stop hitting that child, I will come out and make you," he said. Julien cooled down, shrugged his shoulders, and whipped up the horses. The two women were livid; they neither moved nor spoke.

At dinner that night, Julien was charming, as if nothing had happened. In their serene kindness of heart, they were pleased to see him pleasant once more and gladly shared his mirth. Jeanne again spoke of the De Brisevilles and Julien himself made fun of them, but he added quickly:

"Nevertheless, they are very nice people."

They paid no other visit; being afraid to revive the Marius question. They agreed to simply send cards at New Year's, and wait until spring to resume their visits. At Christmas, they invited the village priest and the mayor and his wife and invited them again at New Year's. After that, it was the same monotonous life day after day.

The Baron and Baronne were to leave on the ninth of January. Jeanne tried to persuade them to stay, but Julien's coldness decided them and they resolved to go. They were to go the next day, and as it was a beautiful night, Jeanne and her father visited Yport. They had not been there since her return from Corsica. They passed through the same woods where she and Julien had walked the day of their marriage. It was there she had received his first caress. It was there she had hung upon his arm and mingled her soul with him whose helpmate she had become for life. In that same path she had shuddered at the first presentiment of the love of which she knew nothing, until their lips had met at the spring in the vale of Ota. The woods were bare and desolate now. The trees and bushes were leafless. Everything was under the spell of winter, that master supreme.

They reached the village. The streets were quiet and deserted. In front of the doors the big nets were stretched to dry, while an odor of seaweeds filled the nostrils. The eternal swish, swish of the sea could be heard in the distance. On the beach the fishing-boats, lying on their sides, looked like immense dead fishes. It was getting dark, and the fishermen came in groups, walking clumsily with their big boots and bulky clothing, a bottle of liquor in one hand and a lantern in the other.

Jeanne and her father watched them as they busied themselves with their boats. They were getting ready to go to sea. They moved with that Norman slowness which is characteristic of that race, putting in the nets and buoys, a big loaf of bread, a crock of butter, and lastly, the glass and bottle.

When everything was ready, the boats, pushed into the water, slid noisily over the pebbles and danced gracefully on the waves, the lantern on the mast telling the course. One by one all the boats disappeared. The fishermen's wives, gaunt and ruddy, clad in thin, black dresses, watched the last boat disappear, and walked noisily back through the village, rousing the villagers with their shrill voices.

Jeanne and the Baron had watched the fishermen disappear, thinking how the poor wretches risked their lives each night for a mere existence. So poor were they that meat was an unknown delicacy to them.

"How beautiful, yet how terrible this sea is," said the Baron. "Is it not magnificent, Jeannette?"

"Yes," she answered with a sickly smile, "but I prefer the Mediterranean."

"The Mediterranean! A bucket of water; as tame as a river. Look at this one. Think of those men who have now disappeared, giving their lives into its keeping. See those mountains of waves, how terribly beautiful they are!"

"That is true," said Jeanne sighing; but her thoughts had gone back to that far-off country, where her dreams of love were buried.

Instead of coming back through the woods they came back slowly by the road. Neither of them spoke; their hearts were full of sadness at the approaching separation. As they passed the farms, a sweet odor of fresh-crushed apples and newly-made cider permeated the air. A faint light in the distance indicated the humble dwellings setting far back from the road. Jeanne's soul communed with those invisible things. Those lights scattered here and there made her feel lonelier than ever, and her heart bled for those beings, separated from those they loved and weaned from the things they loved best and longed for in vain.

"Life is not all sunshine," she said resignedly.

"It cannot be helped, dearie," said the Baron with a sigh.

The next day, the Baron and his wife left the "Poplars" and Jeanne and her husband were left to themselves.

CHAPTER VII.

JEANNE'S DISCOVERY

CARDS had been introduced by Julien as a pastime, and each day after breakfast they played several games, while Julien smoked and drank numerous glasses of cognac. After that Jeanne went up to her room, took a seat near the window, picked up some embroidery, and while the wind and rain beat against the windows, she would dream and dream. She had nothing else to do, in fact; Julien attended to everything, so as to satisfy his cravings for authority and economy. He was parsimonious to the extreme and even reduced the food allowance to bare necessity. The baker used to bring a little Norman cake every morning for Jeanne's breakfast, and Julien suppressed it as a useless expense. Poor Jeanne was reduced to toast thereafter. She said nothing, so as to avoid all explanations and quarrels, but she suffered tortures. Her husband's avarice seemed to her a base, despicable thing, which she could not understand. She had been raised in

106

an entirely different way. Her mother often said:
"Money is made to spend."

Julien was the contrary; he was never so happy
as when he had saved a few cents or made a good
bargain. He often said to Jeanne: "Will you ever
learn the worth of money?"

Some days, Jeanne would drift into her old dreams
of long ago. She would stop working, and her gaze
would wander far away; but as soon as she heard
Julien's voice giving some orders to Simon or some
one else, she was instantly brought back to reality.
She would pick up her work with a sigh, and often
a tear dropped on her hands. "Alas, that is all
over!" she would say.

Rosalie, who was always so light-hearted, was
fearfully changed. Her cheeks once round and rosy,
were now hollow and pale. "Are you sick?" Jeanne
often asked her, but she always answered: "No,
Madame," and she would run away blushing. Instead of tripping along as she always did, she dragged
her feet painfully after her. The peddlers' wares had
no more attraction for her; she seemed to have lost
interest in everything.

The end of January came and the old house looked
desolate, buried in its mantle of snow. Julien spent
his time in the grove behind the house, watching for
the last of the emigrating birds. Sometimes, a shot
rang out in the wintry stillness and a flock of crows
would fly away screeching.

At times, Jeanne was so overcome with sadness
that she would go out on the veranda and listen to
the distant sounds of life brought from afar on the
deathly stillness. After that she heard nothing but

the dismal swish of the sea, and then silence—eternal silence.

One dismal morning, Jeanne was warming her feet in front of the fire in her room, and Rosalie, more changed than ever, was making the bed. Suddenly she heard a deep sigh behind her, and without turning her head she asked: "What is the matter with you?"

But Rosalie answered as usual: "Nothing, Madame." Her voice sounded weak and far off to Jeanne, but she was thinking of other things, so she did not pay any attention to it. Finally, she noticed that the girl was very quiet.

"Rosalie!" she called. No answer. Then, thinking that she had gone out, she called louder: "Rosalie!"

Not receiving any answer for the second time, she reached for the bell, when suddenly she heard very near her a piteous moan. She rushed to Rosalie, who lay helpless on the floor, fixing upon her mistress a look of agony, while she stifled a cry of pain between her tightly closed teeth. "What ails you? Tell me," said Jeanne, moved to pity, but the girl answered nothing. Jeanne heard queer sounds, and she noticed that something moved under the girl's dress. Then she heard a long, plaintive cry; the first cry of pain of a creature entering life. Jeanne understood at last. She ran to the head of the stairs and called:

"Julien! Julien!"

"What do you want?" he answered from below.

"It is Rosalie who—" She could not say any more.

108

Julien ran up, two steps at a time, and entered the room. When he saw the little morsel of humanity squirming and crying on the floor beside Rosalie, his face became positively wicked.

"This does not concern you," he said, pushing Jeanne out of the room. "Send Ludivine and Simon to me."

Jeanne went down to the kitchen trembling and feeling faint. She did not dare go up again. Presently, she saw a servant run out and come back with the widow Dentu, the village midwife; then she heard steps up and down the stairs, as if they were carrying some one, and then Julien came down to tell her that she could go back to her room.

She went up, resuming her position in front of the fire and shivered from head to foot, as if she had just witnessed a terrible accident.

"How is she?" she asked her husband.

Julien seemed preoccupied and nervous, and walked up and down with a frown on his face. He did not answer at first, but stopping abruptly in front of Jeanne he asked:

"What do you intend to do with this girl?" Jeanne did not understand him.

"How, what do you mean?" she asked.

"We certainly cannot keep an illegitimate child in the house," said Julien.

Jeanne was perplexed, and after a long silence she said: "But we might put him out to board, dear."

Julien interrupted her roughly: "And who will pay the expenses? You, perhaps?"

Jeanne reflected for a long time, trying to solve the problem. "The father will take care of it," she said at last, "and if he marries Rosalie, everything will be satisfactory."

Julien was furious. "The father—the father!" he said impatiently, "do you know who is the father? No? Well, then—"

"He certainly would not have the heart to abandon this girl," said Jeanne, excitedly. "He would be a coward! We will find out his name, and when we do, we will go and see him and force him to an explanation."

Julien cooled down a little and resumed his walk up and down. "My dear, she will not tell his name either to you or to me," he said. "Supposing he does not want to marry her, we cannot keep this girl and her illegitimate offspring in our house! Do you understand now?"

"This man is a coward, whoever he is," Jeanne repeated obstinately, "but we will find him and will show no mercy." Julien blushed furiously at this, and added quite irritated:

"Yes, but—in the meantime—" Jeanne did not know what to say or do.

"What do you propose?" she asked Julien.

"Oh, if I had my say, I would simply give her some money and turn them both out."

Jeanne was indignant. "Never! This girl is my foster-sister. We have been raised together and I love her. She has sinned, it is true, but I will not put her out for that, and if need be, I will raise her child."

Julien could control himself no longer. "Yes, we will make a fine reputation for ourselves. Everybody will say that we harbor vice, that we keep a fallen woman under our roof, and they will sneer at us and turn their backs on us. No one will want to know us. What are you thinking of, anyway? You must be crazy!" But Jeanne remained calm and answered:

"I will never consent to having her put out. If you do not want to keep her, my mother will take her, and we will find out who the father of her child is sooner or later."

Julien was exasperated. He went out slamming the door saying: "Women are a stupid lot, anyway."

In the afternoon, Jeanne went up to Rosalie's room. The widow Dentu sat rocking the newborn babe. As soon as she caught sight of her mistress, Rosalie burst into tears and hid her face in the sheets sobbing piteously. Jeanne wanted to kiss her, but she resisted all her efforts. At last the nurse uncovered her face and Jeanne kissed her, while Rosalie, still crying softly, resisted no more.

A sickly fire was burning, and the room was very cold. The baby cried piteously, but Jeanne did not dare speak of him for fear Rosalie would take another fit of crying; she simply took the girl's hand and repeated abstractedly:

"Never mind, dear, everything will be all right."

The poor girl cast furtive glances at the crying baby in the arms of the nurse. The startled look on her face told volumes of love, and she cried softly to herself, smothering her sobs. Jeanne kissed her once more and whispered:

"Have no fear, dear, we will take good care of him," and as Rosalie again burst into tears, she left the room hurriedly.

She went up to see her every day after that, and every day Rosalie would burst into tears as soon as she saw her mistress. It was finally agreed to send the baby to a neighbor's to board.

Julien scarcely spoke to his wife, as if he had some grudge against her for not sending Rosalie away. He reopened the subject one day, but Jeanne took a letter from her pocket which she had received from her mother, telling her to send Rosalie to her immediately, if they did not want her at the "Poplars."

"Your mother is as bad as you are," said Julien angrily, but he dropped the subject.

In a fortnight, the girl was able to resume her duties around the house, and Jeanne, one morning, made her sit in front of her, took hold of her hands, and looking her straight in the eyes said:

"Come, Rosalie, tell me all."

"What, Madame?"

"Who is the father of this child?"

The poor girl shed burning tears and tried to disengage herself, but Jeanne kissed her, saying:

"My dear girl, do not be afraid and tell me his name. You have been weak, I know, but you are not the first one to whom this has happened, and if the father of your child marries you everything will be forgotten. We can take him into our employ and he will be with you always."

Jeanne's words tortured Rosalie, who made frantic efforts to disengage herself. Jeanne continued:

"I know how you feel. No one sympathizes with you any more than I do. I understand that you should feel ashamed, but you see I am not angry. If

112

I ask you for the man's name it is for your own
good. I see by your tears that he intends to abandon you, but I will prevent him from doing so.
Julien will find him and we will force him to marry
you; then, as he will be in our employ, we will
make it our business to see that he makes you
happy."

Rosalie made a final effort to free herself and
having succeeded, she ran out of the room as if
crazy.

That night, at dinner, Jeanne said to Julien: "I
tried every means to make Rosalie reveal to me the
name of her child's father, but I have not succeeded.
Do try and find out, so that we can force him to
marry her."

Julien turned on her angrily: "I will not hear any
more about this affair. You insisted on keeping her;
well, keep her, but leave me out of it entirely."

His temper was wretched since the birth of Rosalie's baby. He was always irritable, and never
spoke to Jeanne without raising his voice. She, on
the contrary, spoke softly to him and tried every
means to avoid quarrels and discussions. Very often
she cried herself to sleep. Although he was constantly irritable and ill tempered, Julien had resumed
his old habits. He was all attention to his wife, and
scarcely three days ever passed that he did not visit
her before retiring. He became very pleasant all of a
sudden and Jeanne felt a little happier. She was
filled with new hopes, though at times she suffered
greatly, but she never complained.

Rosalie had quite recovered, and she looked brighter,
but she had a haunted look in her eyes, as if be-

sieged by some unknown fear. Twice Jeanne tried to question her, but both times she eluded her.

The weather was wretched. Neither man nor beast ventured out. The farmhouses looked horribly dismal behind their curtain of tall trees completely enveloped in their mantle of snow; the smoking chimneys alone revealed signs of life.

Jeanne awaited anxiously the return of spring. She attributed her illness to the severe weather. At times she was unable to eat, having a profound disgust for food of any kind; then again, she would eat ravenously. She was nauseated, her pulse beat rapidly. Her nerves were completely unstrung, and she was in a state of constant agitation which was almost unbearable.

One bitter cold night, Julien left the dinner table complaining of the cold. The room was extremely cold (it was never warm enough, he stinted so on the fuel), and he said to Jeanne, rubbing his hands:

"This is a good night to cuddle up, isn't it, little one?" He laughed good-naturedly — that happy laugh of old — and Jeanne put her arms around his neck and kissed him; but she felt so miserable, so strangely nervous, that she whispered to him, her lips close to his, that she preferred to be alone. In a few words, she told him what she felt; she told him her fears and hopes.

"Never mind, darling," she added; "I shall feel better to-morrow, I hope."

"Just as you say," answered Julien. "If you are sick, you had better take care of yourself."

Jeanne went to bed early, and Julien sent a servant to build a fire in his room (an extraordinary thing

for him to do), and when he was informed that it
was burning, he kissed his wife on the forehead and
went to his room.

The big house seemed thoroughly penetrated with
the intense cold, and Jeanne lay in bed shivering,
unable to get warm. She got up twice to put fresh
logs on the fire, and she piled all the clothing she
could find upon the bed, but she could not get warm.
Her teeth chattered, her heart thumped furiously, then
again it seemed to stop and she felt a terrible oppres-
sion, as if dying for the want of air. She was chilled
through. A terrible anguish seized her. She had
never felt that way before and she thought: "Perhaps I am dying!"

Crazed with terror, she reached for the bell and
rang for Rosalie. She waited, but received no answer. She rang again and again, but Rosalie did
not come. She was sleeping, no doubt, that heavy
sleep which nothing can disturb, and Jeanne, on the
point of fainting, ran upstairs in her bare feet. She
reached the landing, and finding Rosalie's door open,
called:

"Rosalie!" No answer. She advanced into the
room, and having encountered the bed, passed her
hands over it and found it was empty and cold, as if
it had not been disturbed. She was dumfounded!
"Out in such weather!" she said to herself, but as
her heart thumped more furiously than ever, as her
head reeled and her limbs gave way beneath her, she
went down again with the intention of waking
Julien. She was fully convinced that she was going
to die and her only desire was to see him before she
lost her senses altogether.

She entered Julien's room, and by the pale light of the candle she saw Rosalie lying at the side of her husband. She gave a horrible scream, which made them both sit up, and then she stood still for a minute, as if turned to stone. Then suddenly she ran to her room again. Julien had called her, and when she heard his voice a horrible fear seized her. How could she listen to him? How could she look into his eyes and hear him try to deceive her? No, she could not. The thought gave her new vigor and she ran faster than ever. Down the stairs she went, clad only in a nightdress and barefooted. She ran on, regardless of danger, possessed only by an imperious desire to go, to escape from everything, to hear nothing; to know nothing! When she reached the bottom of the stairs, she sat down on the last step, confused and numb.

Julien had dressed himself hurriedly, and as he reached the landing she got up and started again.

"Listen, Jeanne," he cried; but Jeanne ran on. No, she would not listen; she would not let him touch her. She ran to the dining-room and, seeing no better place of concealment, crouched down under the table. Julien came in after her, holding the light above his head and calling:

"Jeanne! Jeanne!"

She bounded past him and into the kitchen. She ran around it like a creature at bay, looking for some escape, and as Julien almost caught her, she quickly opened the garden door and flew out into the night. On, on she sped, sometimes sinking into the snow up to the knees, past the garden, across the ditch and started for the moor. She did not feel the cold;

although barely covered she felt nothing. In fact, the contact of the frozen snow under her feet gave her new courage. To escape was her only thought.

There was no moon, but the stars shone brightly in the clear, cold sky, lighting her path, aiding her flight in the silence of the night. Faster she ran, holding her breath, seeing nothing; absolutely senseless. Suddenly she reached the edge of the cliffs, and instinctively she stopped short. She sat down on the very edge of the cliffs, her head in her hands and her hair flying to the winds, absolutely devoid of thought or feeling. She sat there a long time in the same position. All at once, she shook from head to foot with convulsive shivers, and then her reason came back to her, clearer and keener than ever. Visions passed before her eyes. The sail in Père Lastique's boat, their conversation full of those sweet nothings, the first dawning of love she had felt for him, and then the christening of the boat. She even went back further. To the day of her arrival at the "Poplars" and now, now, everything was over! Her life was crushed. There was no more joy for her; only the torture of Julien's deceit and eternal sorrow awaited her! Better die; then all would be over!

Suddenly Julien's voice rang out in the still night air:

"Here are footprints; quick, quick, this way!"

Oh, she could not, would not see him again. Below her the great sea moaned, and the waves beating against the cliffs seemed to beckon to her to come. She stood ready to spring, the last word of the dying upon her lips, that sweet word which the young soldier on the battlefield murmurs with his dying breath: "Mother!"

At that moment, the vision of her mother in tears passed before her eyes. She could see her father kneeling beside her corpse, and in that one minute of agony she lived through the sorrow and despair which would be theirs if they were to lose her. She fell back powerless into the snow, and when Julien came up to her, followed by Simon and Marius, when they pulled her away, so near the edge was she, she resisted no more; she let them do what they pleased with her. She felt them carry her, put her into bed and rub her with hot cloths and then—nothing!

Then a long nightmare—was it a nightmare? She thought she was in her own room in bed, that it was broad daylight, but she could not get up and she wondered why. She thought she heard a slight noise like something scratching. She looked and saw a little gray mouse walking on her bed; then a second and a third walked toward her. She was not afraid, she simply wanted to catch them, but was unable to do so. Then a score, a hundred, a thousand came on every side; she could feel them climbing all over her. She struggled to catch one, but she could not. She screamed and wanted to run. It seemed to her that some one was holding her, but she saw no one. How long she lay in that state she never knew.

At last came the awakening. She slowly opened her eyes, and was not surprised to see her mother sitting near her bed. A big man whom she had never seen sat near her mother talking.

"See, she is conscious again," he was saying. Her mother burst into tears.

"Be calm, Madame, I implore you," said the big man. "I give you my word that she is out of danger; but above all things, do not make her speak. Let her sleep."

It seemed to Jeanne that she lay there for a long time in a state of semi-consciousness, and that she was unable to think. She did not want to think. A vague vision of the truth flashed through her mind, and she was afraid to face reality.

When she woke up one morning, her eyes fell on Julien sitting near her bed and instantly she remembered everything. A terrible pain shot through her heart, and again the desire to go seized her. She threw the bedclothes aside and jumped out, but her limbs refused to carry her. Julien ran toward her, but she screamed and writhed. She shrank from him in mortal fear that he would touch her. Aunt Lison and the widow Dentu came running up, followed by the Baron and Baronne, the latter all out of breath, a look of dismay upon her face. They put her back to bed and she immediately closed her eyes, slyly simulating sleep. She did not want to speak; she wanted to think in peace.

Her mother and Aunt Lison pressed around her. They questioned her anxiously. "Do you hear us, Jeanne?" they asked; but she did not answer. She lay there as if she did not hear.

Dusk came, and she saw the nurse take her place beside her bed. She drank without a word what the nurse brought her, and lay back on her pillow again. She did not sleep; she just thought. She tried to reason, to connect certain things with others which she seemed to have forgotten. Little by little the mist cleared, and it all came back to her. She dwelt obstinately on each fact. Her mother, father, and Aunt Lison were here, so she must have been very sick. Did they know anything? What had Julien told them? And Rosalie—where was she? What was she going to do? What could she do? A sudden idea came to her. She would go back to Rouen and live with her father and mother as before; she would be a widow, that was all. She listened attentively to all that was said around her, understanding perfectly, but simulating indifference, gloating slyly on her returned reason and patiently waiting for her chance.

That same night she at last found herself alone with her mother, and she whispered: "Dear mother!" Her voice seemed so changed, she hardly recognized it.

The Baronne was enraptured. She caught her daughter in her arms and asked: "My darling girl! My dear little Jeanne! Do you really know me?"

"Yes, mother darling, but you must not cry. We have a great deal to talk about. Did Julien tell you why I ran away that night?"

"Yes, darling, you have been dangerously ill."

"I know, mother dear, but I had the fever afterward. Did he tell you what brought on this fever and why I ran away?" persisted Jeanne.

"No, darling."

"Well, it is because I found Rosalie in his room." The Baronne thought she was getting delirious again and tried to soothe her:

"There, my pet, you are tired. Try and sleep, darling," she said; but Jeanne added obstinately:

"You think I am delirious, mother dear, but I am not, I am perfectly rational. I am not raving as I did when I had the fever. The night I ran away, I felt very sick and I went to his room to wake him. Rosalie was there with him. I lost my head, and ran out into the snow to throw myself from the cliffs."

"Yes, dearie," the Baronne repeated, "you have been very sick."

"I tell you, mother dear, that I found Rosalie with Julien, and I will not live with him any more. You will take me to Rouen with you and father, won't you?" The Baronne was afraid to contradict her; the doctor having recommended her to be careful on that point.

"Yes, darling," she answered.

But Jeanne got impatient: "I see that you do not believe me, mother dear. Bring father to me; he will understand." The Baronne got up with difficulty, and, with the help of her two canes, went out dragging her feet painfully after her. She came back in a few minutes leaning on her husband's arm.

They both sat down near the bed and Jeanne told them everything. Slowly, in clear, precise tones, she told of Julien's temper, of his avarice, and, lastly, of his infidelity. The Baron saw that she was rational, but he did not know what to say or do. He took her hands in his and said tenderly:

"Listen, darling, we must be prudent and not go too fast. Try and bear it until we see what can be done. Promise me you will."

121

"I promise, father, but I will not stay here when I am well." Then she asked very low:

"Where is Rosalie?"

"You will not see her any more," replied the Baron.

But Jeanne insisted: "Where is she? Tell me." The Baron acknowledged that she had not left the house, but he assured her she would.

When they left the room, the Baron's anger knew no bounds. He was deeply hurt at the treatment his child had received. He went straight to Julien and said to him bluntly: "Sir, I have come to demand an explanation of your conduct toward my daughter. You have been unfaithful to her, and with one of the servants, which is still worse."

Julien feigned surprise. He denied the accusation, swore by everything that was sacred that he was innocent; besides, what proofs had they? Was not Jeanne out of her mind? Did she not have brain fever? Did she not, in her delirious madness, run out in the snow, clad only in her night clothes? It was precisely on that same night that she pretended having seen Rosalie in his room. He talked loud and angrily and threatened to sue them. The Baron was confused. He begged Julien's pardon, and offered him his loyal hand which Julien refused to take.

When Jeanne heard what Julien had said she did not get angry. She said very quietly:

"He lies, father dear; but we will prove his guilt some day."

For two days Jeanne was quiet. On the third morning, she asked to see Rosalie, but the Baron refused, saying that she had gone. Jeanne insisted that they go for her. She had worked herself up to such a pitch that she began to cry, almost screaming between her sobs:

"I want to see Rosalie. I must see her!" At that moment, the doctor came in and the Baron told him all, asking his advice as to what to do.

The doctor took Jeanne's hand between his and said in low tones: "Be calm, Madame. Any excitement might prove fatal. Your life, as well as that of the little creature within you, is at stake."

Jeanne was stunned, and all at once she thought she felt something move within her. She lay very quiet, paying no attention to what was said around her. She was deep in thought. She did not sleep that night. The one thought which possessed her was that a little child was coming into the world. Her child; Julien's child. She trembled with fear when she thought that it might resemble Julien.

One morning, she called for her father: "Father dear, I must know everything. Absolutely everything, do you hear? No, do not contradict me, especially now, it would be dangerous. You will go and get the priest. If he is here Rosalie will tell the truth. You will bring him up here and you and mother will come here also. Be very careful that Julien suspects nothing, otherwise all would be lost."

An hour later, the priest was ushered into her room. He sat down all out of breath, puffing laboriously, rubbing his forehead with his big colored handkerchief. As soon as he had caught his breath, he began to joke.

"Well, Baronne, I see that you are not getting thin. I think we make a very good pair." Then, turning to Jeanne, he said: "What is this I hear, young woman, we are going to have a christening soon? Ah! ah! And not of a boat this time." Then he added gravely: "It will be a defender for the country." Then, reflecting for a minute: "Unless it is a good wife and mother, like you, Madame," he said, bowing to the Baronne.

The door opened, and Rosalie, pushed by the Baron, stood in the doorway. She did not want to come in and struggled desperately. The Baron got impatient and gave her a vigorous push which sent her into the middle of the room. She stood still for a moment, covering her face with her hands and sobbing as if her heart would break.

Jeanne raised herself in bed, and her face became as pale as death when she saw Rosalie. Her heart beat so fast she could not breathe. She was suffocated with emotion. At last, she spoke with effort: "I do not—need—to question you. The guilty look of shame—on your face—is enough—" and, after a pause: "But I must know all—all. I have asked the reverend father to be present, so that you would tell the truth. It is to be a confession; do you understand?"

Rosalie stood motionless, clutching her hands tightly. The Baron, who could scarcely control his anger, took hold of her arm and pushed her to her knees, saying:

"Will you speak? Answer!" Rosalie kneeled against the bed, hiding her face in her hands. Then the priest spoke to her: "Come, Rosalie, do what you are told and answer. We are not going to hurt you, we simply want to know the actual facts."

"Is it not true," said Jeanne, leaning over the edge of the bed, "that when I went into Julien's room that night, I saw you there with him?"

"Yes, Madame," groaned Rosalie, still covering her face.

The Baronne burst into tears, mingling her sobs with those of Rosalie.

"How long had this been going on?" asked Jeanne with a searching look.

"Since—since he came here." Jeanne did not understand.

"Since he came here—then—since last spring?"

"Yes, Madame."

"Since the first day he came here?" Jeanne repeated.

"Yes, Madame."

Jeanne pressed her with questions and spoke rapidly:

"Tell me how it happened. How did he ask you? What did he say? How did you yield? How could you give yourself to him?"

Rosalie uncovered her face at last, suddenly seized with a feverish desire to speak—to tell all: "I don't know. It was the day he came here to dinner for the first time. He had hidden himself in the garret, and he came to my room after everyone was in bed. I did not dare scream for fear to make a scene, so he stayed in my room all night. I did not know what I was doing. I let him do what he liked with me, because I liked him!"

"Then—your child—it is his?" Jeanne cried in anguish.

"Yes, Madame," said Rosalie, sobbing piteously.

There was a terrible hush. Alone, the sobs of
Rosalie and the Baronne disturbed the silence.
Jeanne was overwhelmed with grief. Her eyes
filled with tears and dropped silently on her cheeks.
Her servant's child belonged to the same father as
her own! Her anger was appeased now. The only
feeling which penetrated her was a dull, endless despair which nothing could allay.

"After we came back from — from our journey,
when did he renew his relations with you?" asked
Jeanne, in a changed, choked voice.

"The — first night," answered Rosalie. The
words went through Jeanne's heart like a knife. So,
the very first night of their return to the "Poplars,"
Julien had left her to go with this girl! That was
the reason he was so cold toward her! She knew
enough now; she did not want to know any more.

"Go away! Leave me!" screamed Jeanne. Rosalie did not move. The poor girl was paralyzed with
fear.

"Make her go, take her away," said Jeanne to
her father. The priest, who had not spoken all
through the scene, thought the time had come to
preach a little sermon.

"You have done a terrible wrong," he said addressing Rosalie. "I am afraid God will never forgive you. Think of it, hell is your doom if you do
not reform! For the sake of your child, your conduct must be blameless hereafter. No doubt the
Baronne will do something for you, and we will find
you a husband." He would have gone on indefinitely, but the Baron had caught Rosalie by the shoulders and thrown her out of the room like a bundle

of rags. When he came back into the room, he was as pale as death; paler than Jeanne, even.

The priest continued: "They are all the same around here, they never marry until they have had a child! Never, Madame. It is horrible, I know, but what can we do? Human nature is weak, and we must be indulgent. It seems a custom here," he said smiling. Then becoming indignant: "Even the children! Did I not find two of them in the cemetery last year? I told the parents, and do you know what they answered me? 'It is not our fault, your reverence, we do not teach them such things.' There you are; your servant did like the rest of them."

"It is not the girl I blame," said the Baron, trembling with anger. "It is he, the cowardly villain, and I will take my daughter away from him." He took big strides across the room, getting angrier every minute. "He is a cowardly, miserable villain, to have deceived my daughter, and I will tell him so. I—will kill him!" The priest slowly absorbed a pinch of snuff, and deliberated on the best means of conciliation.

"Come," he said, "between you and me, he did what all the men do. Do you know many husbands who are faithful? You, for instance," he added, with a malicious twinkle in his eye, "have done the same thing, no doubt." The Baron stopped short and looked at the priest. "Yes," he continued, "you have done like the rest of them. I tell you they all do it. You did not love your wife any the less, did you?"

The Baron stood still; completely upset. He certainly had done the same thing, every time he had

had a chance, especially if the servants were pretty. Was he a villain for that? Why did he judge Julien so severely, when he had never thought his own conduct reprehensible?

The Baronne, still in tears, smiled faintly at the recollection of her husband's escapades. Hers was a sweet, sentimental nature, easily moved to pity, quick to forgive; love affairs, for her, were part of everyone's existence.

Jeanne lay back, staring before her, thinking of Rosalie's confession. Those words came back to her, filling her soul with anguish: "I let him do what he liked with me, because I liked him." She too had liked him, and for that sole reason, she had given herself to him; bound her life to his. She had fallen into his net, and her reward was misery, sorrow, and despair! Why? Because, like Rosalie, she had "liked him."

The door was pushed open with violence and Julien came in, looking ferocious. He had met Rosalie on the stairs crying and he had come up, guessing that something was going on; fearful that she had spoken. At sight of the priest, he stood motionless:

"What is the matter?" he asked in an unsteady voice, but trying to appear calm. The Baron, who a minute ago was so violent, said nothing. He thought of the priest's argument and of his own conduct. The Baronne sobbed louder than ever. Jeanne had raised herself and was staring at Julien, who made her suffer so cruelly.

"The matter is," she stammered, "that we are no longer in ignorance. We know everything—

everything, do you hear? Your villainy, your cowardly conduct since — since the day you entered this house, has been revealed to us. Rosalie's child is yours, like — like mine. They will be brothers." Unable to control herself at the thought, Jeanne fell back sobbing frantically.

Julien was dumfounded. He did not know what to do or say. The priest again came to the rescue:

"Come, my dear Madame, be reasonable. Do not take things so to heart." He approached the bed and laid his hand on Jeanne's forehead. The touch of his hand soothed her, a hand accustomed to comfort and absolve and endowed with a mysterious power to calm. The priest continued:

"We must forgive, Madame. You are in great trouble, it is true, but God in his mercy has sent you a great happiness, to compensate for your sorrow. Your child will be a comfort to you, and it is in his name that I implore you to forgive your husband. That child will be a bond between you; a pledge of his future faithfulness. Could you live forever disunited from the father of your child?" Jeanne did not answer. Bruised and weary of soul and body, she had no strength left; even for anger or forgiveness.

"Forgive, Jeanne, dear," said the Baronne, who was incapable of resentment.

The priest took Julien's hand and placed it on that of his wife, giving them a gentle tap as if to join them, and resuming his jovial air:

"There, believe me, it is better so."

Their hands, united for a moment, almost immediately fell apart. Julien did not dare kiss Jeanne, so he kissed the Baronne on the forehead, and taking

the Baron's arm, he suggested that they go out and
have a smoke. The Baron was so glad that everything had been arranged satisfactorily that he had
forgotten all his anger toward Julien.

After they had left, Jeanne exhausted, fell asleep,
while the priest and the Baronne talked in whispers.
The priest disclosed his plans, and the Baronne
assented to everything.

"So then, it is understood, you give the Barville
farm to Rosalie," the priest was saying, "and I am
to find her a husband. Oh, it will not be hard to
find; with twenty thousand francs she will have
plenty of suitors; the only trouble will be to find the
right one."

The Baronne smiled; she was happy now, though
her face still showed traces of tears.

"But remember," she said, "the Barville farm is
worth at least twenty thousand francs, and it must
be in the name of the child; the parents to have the
use of it during their lifetime."

The priest got up to take leave, shaking hands
with the Baronne, saying: "Do not disturb yourself,
Baronne. I know what it is, every step counts."

On his way out he met Aunt Lison coming to see
Jeanne. As usual she suspected nothing, knew nothing, and was told nothing.

CHAPTER VIII.

MATERNITY AND A MARRIAGE

ROSALIE had left the "Poplars," and had been replaced by a big, strong peasant woman, who helped the Baronne when she took her daily walk, in her own favorite path, where traces of her heavy foot showed plainer each day.

Jeanne was going through the painful period of pregnancy. She awaited her child without pleasure; without interest. Still bowed down with her recent sorrows, she was in constant fear of some new misfortune. Spring had come. It was still quite chilly, but in the ditches, under the dead leaves, the cowslips were coming up.

Jeanne, who was always ailing, leaned on her father's arm, while Aunt Lison, anxious and agitated at the coming event, at this unknown mystery which she was never to know, walked on the other side holding Jeanne's hand. They would walk in this manner for hours, scarcely speaking a word, while

Julien, who had taken a sudden fancy for riding lately, spent his time riding through the country. The Baron, his wife, and Julien paid a visit to the De Fourvilles, with whom Julien seemed to be well acquainted, a thing quite inexplicable. Another ceremonious visit was exchanged with the De Brisevilles in their old, dull château, and then nothing more disturbed the dull routine of their life.

One afternoon about four o'clock, a man and a woman came in on horseback, and Julien, who had seen them, came into Jeanne's room and said excitedly: "Quick, quick, go down. It is the De Fourvilles who have come to see how you are. Say that I am out, but will be back soon. I am going to dress." Jeanne was surprised. She went down to receive the visitors.

A pretty young woman, with a sad, pale face, large, luminous eyes, and hair of a dull blonde, presented her husband to Jeanne. M. de Fourville was a sort of giant, with a large, red mustache.

"We have met your husband several times and we heard from him that you were not well, so we did not want to put off our visit any longer. We just came in as neighbors, to see how you are. As you see, we came without ceremony, on horseback. We had the pleasure of a visit from your mother and the Baron the other day." She spoke with ease and in a familiar tone, but she was extremely ladylike and refined. Jeanne was bewitched and loved her right away.

"This is a friend," she thought.

The Count de Fourville was the opposite of his wife. He seemed out of place in a parlor and ill at ease. After sitting down, he laid his hat on a chair beside him and after hesitating for a while what to do with his hands, he crossed them as if in prayer. Just then, Julien came in. He looked so handsome that Jeanne did not know him. He had shaved, dressed and looked as handsome as he did before her marriage. He shook hands with the Count and kissed the hand of the Countess, who blushed slightly. Julien was transformed. He had regained his old amiability, and his large, luminous eyes had become caressing and tender again. His hair, which a moment ago was rough and dull, was now smooth and shiny.

As the De Fourvilles were taking leave, the Countess said to Julien:

"My dear Viscount, will you ride with me Thursday?"

"I should be delighted, Madame," said Julien, bowing low.

The Countess took Jeanne's hand in hers, and smiling sweetly said:

"When you are well, we three shall take long rides together; it will be lovely!" and picking up her riding-habit, she jumped lightly into the saddle, while her husband followed her on his big Norman horse, after having bowed awkwardly. When they had disappeared, Julien said to Jeanne:

"What charming people! They are the right kind of people to know."

"The little Countess is delightful! I feel that I shall love her; but the husband looks like a boor! Where did you meet them?" Jeanne was happy, she did not know why.

"I met them at the De Brisevilles," said Julien rubbing his hands. "The husband is an inveterate hunter. He is a little bit rough, but a real noble-man."

At dinner they were both cheerful; as if some sudden happiness had come into their lives.

Nothing else happened until the end of July. One night, they were sitting under a tree under which a rustic table had been built, and Julien sat in front of a decanter of cognac, when suddenly Jeanne screamed and became very pale. A sharp pain went through her and after a few minutes, another followed, more lasting than the first. With great difficulty, she was helped, almost carried by her husband and father to her room. She groaned involuntarily, wanted to sit down every minute, as if unable to carry the intoler-able weight of her body. The time of childbirth had not come and they feared an accident; so they dis-patched old Simon for the doctor. He arrived at midnight, and saw at a glance what was happening. Jeanne had been put to bed. The pains had ceased somewhat, but a terrible anguish filled her soul; like a presentiment of death. The room was full of peo-ple. The Baronne sat in an armchair breathing la-boriously. The Baron had lost his head, and went from one to the other, bringing different articles which were not needed and consulted the doctor every min-ute. Julien walked up and down, frowning, but calm.

At the foot of the bed stood the widow Dentu, a blank expression upon her face, as if nothing could move her. She was nurse, midwife, and watcher of the dead all in one. With the same indifference, she received the newborn babe into her arms, heard his first cry, bathed and soothed him, and when anybody died, she was there to hear their last word and receive their dying breath. It was she who prepared them for burial and watched them night after night. Ludivine the cook and Aunt Lison discreetly hid themselves behind the door.

From time to time Jeanne moaned piteously. At daybreak, she was seized with horrible pains, and she thought of Rosalie who had scarcely suffered at all, and whose illegitimate child had come into the world without effort. She compared herself with her, and in her misery she cursed God whom she had thought just; cursed the unjust preferences of fate which made her suffer. At times, her suffering was so great that all thought and feeling left her; she had strength for nothing, not even to suffer. When she was quiet for a few minutes, she could not keep her eyes off Julien. Anguish filled her heart when she remembered how he had acted the day Rosalie had given birth to her child; she remembered his looks, his gestures, and now she could see on his face the same look of annoyance, the same indifference as for the other — that look of carelessness, irritation, and egotism, the look of a man with a new burden on his shoulders. Suddenly, she was seized with violent spasms.

"I am dying," she thought, and a terrible hate filled her soul for this man, who was the cause of this horrible suffering. She was filled with an invincible desire to curse him; to curse the unknown child who was killing her! She struggled desperately for a few minutes, and then the pain ceased; her suffering was over.

The doctor and nurse were bending over her, and she saw them take away something. Then she heard the same plaintive cry that she had once before heard; it filled her heart, her soul, her whole being with rapture and, unconsciously, she opened her arms. A feeling of peace and joy filled her soul. She was happy, oh, so happy! She was a mother! She asked to see her baby. He had no hair, no nails, having been born too soon, but when they gave him to her her joy knew no bounds; she felt that she was saved. She would know sorrow no more. That little child was her safeguard against despair.

Hereafter, she would have but one thought—her child. She loved him desperately, fanatically; all the more so because she had been deceived in her love. She wanted his cradle always near her bed and when she was able to get up, she would sit for hours rocking him. She became jealous of the nurse, and when the little one cried for the breast, she felt an insane desire to snatch him away and tear the peasant woman's breast with her nails. She insisted on making every article of clothing he wore. She embroidered and tucked beautiful garments for him; his wardrobe was a mass of lace and ribbons. She paid no attention to what was said around her, but she often interrupted people's conversation to make them admire a new cap, a fancy bib, or ribbon. She handled every article lovingly and holding them up with pride she would say:

"How beautiful he will be with that on!"

The Baron and Baronne would smile tenderly, but Julien, whose habits were disturbed, who was unconsciously jealous of the child who had taken his place as master of the house, repeated impatiently, angrily:

"What a nuisance she is with her baby!"

Jeanne had become so passionately fond of her child, that she spent whole nights near his cradle, watching him sleep. She took no rest; she became weak and thin and coughed incessantly. The doctor ordered that the child be placed in the nurse's room every night. Jeanne cried, begged her not to take him away, but she pleaded in vain. Each night, the nurse took him with her and Jeanne would stand outside of the door, barefooted, and listen if he slept without waking; worrying for fear he should want for anything.

One night, Julien who had dined at the De Fourvilles, came home very late, and found Jeanne in her habitual place at the nurse's door. The day after, they locked her in her room to compel her to go to bed.

The christening took place at the end of August. The Baron was godfather and Aunt Lison the godmother. They named him Pierre Simon Paul; Paul for use. The early part of September, Aunt Lison left just as silently as she had come.

One evening after dinner, the priest called. He seemed embarrassed, as if something was on his mind, and after several useless efforts to broach the subject, he finally asked the Baronne and her husband to give him a few minutes in private. The three left together and walked slowly up and down the poplar path, talking rapidly; while Julien, suspicious and irritable, wondered what the secret could be. When the priest left, he insisted on accompanying him to the rectory.

It was chilly, almost cold, and the family went indoors. They were dozing when Julien came back. He stood in the doorway, flushed and angry. He did not stop to think that Jeanne was there, and addressing his father and mother-in-law he yelled:

"You must be crazy to give that girl twenty thousand francs!" They were all so surprised they could say nothing. He continued yelling louder: "You must be raving mad! Do you want to leave us penniless?" The Baron, who had somewhat recovered from the shock, tried to stop him:

"Hush," he said, "Jeanne is here."

"What do I care," said Julien exasperated, "she must know all about it. It is a downright robbery!" Jeanne stunned, looked from one to the other.

"What is it all about?" she stammered. Julien turned to her and he told her the plan to marry Rosalie and to settle the Barville farm, which was worth twenty thousand francs, on the child.

"Your parents are mad, my dear," he repeated. "Raving mad! Twenty thousand francs! Twenty thousand francs for an illegitimate offspring! They have completely lost their heads!" Jeanne listened, cool and calm, surprised at herself, indifferent at everything which did not concern her child. The Baron, suffocated with anger and stamping his foot, said:

"Control yourself. It is positively revolting! Whose fault is it if we have to take care of this girl? Whose child is it? And now you want to abandon it! For shame!"

Julien was taken aback at the Baron's violence. He continued in a calmer tone: "Fifteen hundred francs would have been sufficient. They all have children before their marriage here. It does not matter whom it belongs to, and the very fact that you give her a dowry will make people suspect the truth. You ought at least to have thought of our name; of our position." He spoke severely, like a man who is sure of himself and knows what he is talking about.

The Baron was abashed; he could find nothing to say to such an argument and Julien quickly took advantage of his position: "It is a good thing that nothing has been settled as yet. I know the man who wants to marry Rosalie. He is a good fellow and everything can be arranged satisfactorily. I will see him." He went out immediately, afraid to renew the discussion; jubilant at everyone's silence, which he took for acquiescence.

As soon as he had disappeared, the Baron, who had gotten over his surprise of the moment, exclaimed:

"Oh, this is too much!" Jeanne glanced at her father's upset face and burst into hearty laughter— that clear laughter of the past, when she heard something funny.

"Did you hear how he said 'twenty thousand francs!' father?"

The Baronne, who was just as quickly moved to mirth as to tears, joined Jeanne and shook with laughter when she remembered her son-in-law's angry face, his violent words and actions, his positive refusal to give to the girl he had seduced money which did not belong to him! She was happy, too, at Jeanne's good humor and she laughed until the tears ran down her cheeks. The Baron joined in also, and the three of them, forgetting everything else, enjoyed a good laugh, as in their days of happiness. When they had calmed themselves a little, Jeanne said:

"Is it not strange, nothing affects me now? He seems like a stranger to me. I cannot imagine that I am his wife. You see, I actually laugh at his — his rudeness!" And those three, still smiling involuntarily, kissed each other tenderly.

Two days later, as Julien was leaving for his usual ride, a tall, well-built fellow of about twenty-five years, clad in a peasant's blue blouse, brand-new and stiff, sneaked in as if he had waited for his chance since morning. He walked along the Couillard fence, and in a roundabout way he at last reached the tree where the Baron and the two women were still sitting. He took off his cap and bowed awkwardly, and when he got near enough he stammered:

"It's me, Desiré Lecoq." The name conveying nothing to him, the Baron asked:

"What is it you wish?" Seeing the necessity of an explanation, the peasant became more and more muddled. He twisted his cap between his hands and at last said:

"His reverence spoke to me about that affair—" He stopped, afraid to say too much or compromise himself. The Baron, who did not understand, continued:

"What affair? What are you talking about?" The peasant determined to explain at last.

"That affair about Rosalie," he said in a low voice. Jeanne, who had guessed what it was about, immediately left with her baby in her arms.

140

"Come nearer," said the Baron, and he showed him the seat which Jeanne had just vacated. The peasant sat down and murmured awkwardly: "You're very kind." Then he stopped, as if he had nothing more to say. After a long silence, he raised his eyes to the sky and said:

"We're having beautiful weather for this time of year. It'll be good for the crops," and he again lapsed into silence. The Baron got impatient and he bluntly asked the peasant:

"Then you are to marry Rosalie?" The peasant, taken aback at such a blunt question, fearing to commit himself, answered in the evasive way which is characteristic of the Norman peasant:

"That depends, maybe yes and maybe no." The Baron, irritated at the peasant's evasiveness, said:

"Confound it, answer me. Do you take her, yes or no?" The man was perplexed and stared at his feet.

"If I get what his reverence promises, I'll take her; but if I get what Mr. Julien says, I won't."

"What did Mr. Julien say?"

"Mr. Julien said that I would get fifteen hundred francs, and his reverence said that I would get twenty thousand. I'll take her for twenty thousand, but not for fifteen hundred."

The Baronne was highly amused at the peasant's craftiness, and she smothered a laugh. The peasant, who did not understand why she laughed, was not altogether pleased and he gave her a black look from the corner of his eye.

The Baron, who did not like this haggling, cut the matter short, saying:

"I told his reverence that I would give you the Barville farm for use during your lifetime, the same to revert to the child after your death. I never go back on my word. The farm is worth twenty thousand francs. Do you accept or not?" The peasant grinned humbly and became suddenly talkative.

"Oh, then, if that's the case, I don't say no. When his reverence spoke to me I was willing right away. 'It will please his lordship,' I said to myself, 'and I won't lose anything by it'; but when Mr. Julien came to me, he only wanted to give me fifteen hundred, and I said to myself: 'You'd better find out what's what'; not that I did not have confidence, but I wanted to know. Business is business, your lordship." The Baron stopped him, saying:

"When will you be ready to marry her?" The peasant became timid and embarrassed again.

"Won't we draw up a paper first?" he said hesitatingly. The Baron lost his temper altogether.

"Confound it, you will have the marriage contract, it is the best paper you can have." But the peasant insisted.

"Yes, but I could draw a paper just the same, it wouldn't do any harm."

"Look here," said the Baron, getting up, "answer yes or no, right now. If you do not want to accept, say so; I have another suitor for her." The crafty Norman, fearing competition, held out his hand to the Baron, as is their custom when they conclude a bargain and said:

"Shake; it's done."

The Baron took his hand and called: "Ludivine, bring us a bottle of wine."

The cook having brought the wine, they drank to the prospective wedding and the peasant departed with a lighter step.

Nothing was said to Julien about the affair. The contract was drawn up in secret, and one Monday morning, the wedding took place. A neighbor carried the baby behind the bride and bridegroom, as a sure sign of prosperity. No one was surprised; they simply envied Lecoq for his good fortune. He was born lucky, they said, winking slyly, but without a bit of malice, however.

There was a terrible scene when Julien heard of it, which hastened the departure of the Baron and Baronne. Jeanne was not so sad this time; Paul having become an inexhaustible source of happiness —in fact her sole object in life.

CHAPTER IX.

DISCOVERY AND DEATH

JEANNE had completely recovered, and Julien proposed that they return the De Fourvilles' visit, and also that they call on the Marquis de Coutelier. He had bought a phaeton at auction, because it needed but one horse, and in that manner they would be able to go out twice a month.

One clear morning in December, the big bay horse was hitched to the new phaeton and Jeanne and Julien started on their visit to the De Fourvilles. The castle of "La Vrillette" was surrounded on one side by an immense fish-pond and on the other by pine woods. To gain access to the castle, it was necessary to pass over an antique drawbridge and thence through a massive iron portcullis of the Louis XIII. period. The castle itself was of the same period. Julien described every part of the building to Jeanne, as one who was well acquainted with it.

"Just look at that entrance; is it not magnificent? Look at that building, how imposing it is! The

entire length of the other side faces the pond; a
broad veranda leading to it. Four boats are anchored
there; two for the Count and two for the Countess.
To the right, where you see those poplars, is the end
of the pond, and the river begins there. It goes
straight to Fécamp. The Count loves to hunt on this
pond; it is full of waterfowl. This is what I call a
real castle!"

The door had opened and the pale Countess appeared. She came to meet the visitors, clad in a
soft, trailing gown, looking like a real lady of the
manor; a fit picture for the beautiful frame. She
ushered them into the reception-room, an immense
room with eight windows in it; four of which faced
the water.

The Countess took Jeanne's hand in hers as if she
had known her all her life. She made her sit down,
and sat near her on a low seat. Julien, who for the
past five months had regained his old amiability,
smiled and talked familiarly. The Countess and he
talked of their rides. She made fun of his riding,
calling him the "stumbling cavalier," while he named
her "the queen of Centaurs." A shot rang under the
windows; it was the Count hunting. His wife called
him, and immediately, they heard a noise of oars on
the water, then of a boat bumping against the stone
wall and the Count appeared, followed by two dogs,
wet and tawny like himself, who stretched themselves
on the mat outside the door. He seemed more at
ease in his own home and looked pleased to see
Jeanne and Julien. He ordered some more logs
thrown on the fire and some Madeira and cake
brought.

"You will dine with us, of course?" he exclaimed suddenly. Jeanne, who never forgot her baby for a minute, declined; but he insisted and as she obstinately refused, Julien made a gesture of impatience. Lest she should rouse his ugly and quarrelsome temper, and although she was in tortures at the thought of not seeing Paul until morning, she accepted at last.

They spent a delightful afternoon. They visited the springs, then they went boating. The Count rowed, his dogs sitting on each side of him, their noses up in the air. Jeanne sat alone, and from time to time she dipped her hands in the water, and enjoyed the chill that went through her at the contact of it. Julien and the Countess sat in the rear, smiling at each other, that eternal smile of people who are supremely happy. Dusk had come. The setting sun was fast disappearing behind the giant pines and the red sky made one feel cold to look at it.

They returned to the reception-room, where an immense fire was burning. The heat was quite acceptable and made them all feel jovial. The Count, who felt happy, caught his wife in his robust arms and, raising her as he would a baby, kissed her noisily on both cheeks. Jeanne smiled at the big, good-natured giant whom everybody called a bore and thought: "How mistaken we are sometimes." Involuntarily, she turned to look at Julien, and the expression on his face scared her. He stood in the doorway, horribly pale and staring at the Count.

"Are you sick? What is the matter with you?" asked Jeanne.

"Oh, it's nothing," he answered angrily. "I have caught cold. Leave me alone."

When they went to dinner, the Count asked permission to let his dogs come in. They sat on each side of him, wagging their tails frantically and squirming with contentment. The Count gave them a morsel from time to time and patted their silky ears.

After dinner, as Jeanne and Julien were getting ready to go, Count de Fourville begged them to stay a while longer and see him fish by torchlight. He stationed them on the veranda and he got into a boat, followed by a valet carrying a lighted torch and a landing-net. The light of the torch threw strange shadows on the trees, and the Count, standing in the boat, looked like a fantastic giant. He raised the net which he held and his arms looked as if they were reaching for the stars. He lowered them, and the trio on the veranda heard a splash; then the reflection of his shadow was repeated on the wall of the castle.

"Gilberte," shouted the Count, "I have caught eight!" A moment after the Count came up the steps, followed by the valet with the torch, and threw his net on the veranda.

Jeanne and Julian at last took leave, after they had been wrapped up in shawls and blankets loaned to them by their friends. Jeanne said to Julien:

"What a good fellow that giant is!"

"Yes, but he does not know how to behave before strangers," answered Julien.

A week later, they went to visit the De Couteliers, who were considered the very best family in the county. Their new castle of Reminil, built during the reign of Louis XIV., was hidden in a magnificent park surrounded with stone walls. On the hill, the ruins of the old castle could be seen. Valets in magnificent liveries ushered the visitors into a spacious, stately room, in the middle of which was a sort of pedestal on which stood an immense Sèvres vase. In the base of this vase was a frame containing an autograph letter of the king, begging the Marquis Leopold-Hervé-Joseph-Germer de Varneville de Rollebosc de Coutelier to accept this present from his sovereign.

Jeanne and Julien were admiring this royal present, when the Marquis and his wife entered. The Marquise's hair was powdered. She was amiable through habit, and her desire to be condescending gave her an affected manner. The Marquis was stout, his white hair was brushed up on top of his head, his voice, his gestures, in fact his whole attitude was haughty, as if to impress the visitors with the full weight of his importance. They were people who were slaves to etiquette. Their thoughts and actions were always correct. They kept up a constant conversation, without waiting for the answers. They smiled indifferently, as if accomplishing a duty, imposed by their rank, in receiving with politeness the smaller gentry of the neighborhood.

Jeanne and Julien tried their best to make a good impression, but they were ill at ease. They were afraid to stay too long, and yet they did not know how to take leave. The Marchioness herself put an end to the visit; she simply stopped the conversation abruptly, like a queen politely dismissing a subject.

Going home Julien said: "If it is agreeable to you, we will limit our visits to the De Fourvilles; they are quite sufficient for me." Jeanne agreed with him.

December was a very slow month. It was the same indoor life as last year, but Jeanne was not lonesome, she had Paul to think about. Julien always seemed discontented and anxious when he looked at the baby. Sometimes, when Jeanne held him in her arms and, with that burst of frenzied tenderness which seizes all mothers occasionally, would kiss and fondle him, and would hold him toward Julien, saying: "Why do you not kiss him? You do not seem to love him!" Julien, very much against his will, would lean over and touch the baby's forehead with his lips, keeping at a distance, as if fearing to meet his little clenched hands, and would leave abruptly, as if the sight of him filled him with aversion.

The mayor, the doctor, and the priest were invited to dinner from time to time. So were the De Fourvilles, with whom they were getting more and more intimate. The Count De Fourville seemed to love Paul. When he came to visit at the "Poplars," he would hold him on his lap all the time; sometimes for the whole afternoon. He handled him gently, afraid of hurting him with his big hands, would tickle his nose with his mustache, and at times would kiss him passionately. His constant suffering was that his union had not been blessed with children.

March came, clear and bright; almost like spring. Countess Gilberte again spoke of going on long rides together. Jeanne, who was a little tired of the long, monotonous days and nights, eagerly assented. For a whole week she amused herself making her riding-habit. Then the excursions began. They always rode two by two, the Countess and Julien

ahead, and the Count and Jeanne a hundred feet behind. These two conversed quietly like two old
friends. Their simple and upright natures sympa-
thized with each other, and for that reason they had
become fast friends. The other two spoke in whispers, and at times laughed immoderately. Then
again, their eyes met, as if saying things they could
not speak of, and they would gallop away, as if suddenly possessed with an insane desire to escape; to
get out of view. Sometimes, Gilberte's irritated voice
would sound from afar, and the Count would turn to
Jeanne with a smile and say: "My wife is not always in a good humor."

One night coming home, the Countess was more
irritable than ever. She excited her mare and then
abruptly checked her.

"Be careful for goodness' sake," Julien repeated
several times, "your horse will run away."

"What do I care! Mind your own business," she
answered. Her words sounded clear and harsh on
the still air. The excited mare reared and foamed at
the mouth and the Count became uneasy.

"Be careful, Gilberte!" he shouted to her. But
the Countess, as in a spirit of defiance, gave the
mare a brutal blow with her riding-whip between
the two ears. The furious animal reared again, stood
up on her hind legs, and started down the road at a
terrific pace. Through meadows and plowed fields
she flew, so fast that horse and rider were scarcely
discernible. Julien seemed paralyzed with terror. He
stood still, calling faintly: "Madame! Madame!"

The Count bent over his big Norman horse, and
exciting him with his voice and spurs, disappeared

150

in pursuit of his wife. Jeanne watched him disappear in the distance. Then Julien approached Jeanne and said in an angry tone: "She is crazy to-day, I think!"

Slowly they retraced their steps and went in search of their friends. About fifteen minutes after, they saw them coming back and soon joined them. The Count was red and all in a perspiration, but he looked happy; he laughed gaily and held triumphantly, in his firm grasp, the bridle of his wife's horse. Gilberte's face was very pale and contracted; she leaned on her husband's shoulder as if ready to faint. From that day, Jeanne knew that the Count was madly in love with his wife.

During the following month, the Countess was brighter than she had ever been. She came oftener to the "Poplars," and was always gay and laughed incessantly. In a sudden impulse, she would kiss Jeanne, as if some mysterious happiness had come into her life. Her husband, happy to see her happy, scarcely could keep his eyes from her, and every minute, he tried to touch her hand, her gown. One evening he said to Jeanne:

"I am supremely happy just now. Gilberte never was like that before; her temper is perfect, she never gets irritable or angry any more. I was in doubt whether she loved me, but now I know she does."

Julien also was changed. He was brighter, more amiable; as if the friendship existing between the two families had brought peace and happiness among them.

It was an early and peculiarly warm spring that year, and Jeanne felt strangely agitated. Sometimes, at the sight of a little flower, she would suddenly become languid. She spent hours in sweet, dreamy melancholy. Her soul was sweetly stirred by recollections of her first days of love; not that her love for Julien had revived, oh, no, that was all over forever; but her whole being was strangely moved, as if some invisible thing tenderly called her. She liked to be alone; to abandon herself to the warm rays of the sun. One morning, she was in her usual dreamy state, when a vision passed before her eyes — a vision of that spot in the woods near Étretat, where for the first time the young man, who loved her then, had spoken sweet words of love. It was there she had dreamed of a radiant future and the realization of all her hopes. She wished to see this spot once more; to make a sort of sentimental pilgrimage, as if the sight of it would bring some change into her life.

Julien had gone since morning: she knew not where. She had the little white horse saddled and she started on her pilgrimage. It was a beautiful, quiet day, one of those days when the grass, the trees, everything is still, as if all nature slept. Jeanne rode slowly along, the little white horse walking at his ease. She was happy with her dreams. She went down the valley leading to the sea, and through the arch in the cliffs which is called the door of Étretat, and thence to the woods, to look for the spot her heart so longed to see. She wandered through different paths, but was unable to find it. All of a sudden, as she was crossing a wide path, she saw in the distance, two saddle horses tied to a tree.

She recognized them immediately; they were Julien's and Gilberte's. She was a little tired of her solitude and the unexpected meeting pleased her.

She urged her horse on so as to join them. When she reached the spot where the two horses were standing, very patiently, as if accustomed to long periods of waiting, she called. She received no answer. A woman's glove and two riding-whips were lying on the grass.

"They have been here," she thought "and have gone a little further off." She waited fifteen, twenty minutes, wondering where they could be. She had alighted and was leaning against a tree. Two little birds flew down and came very near to where she was standing. She was so quiet that they had not seen her. The male hopped around his mate, bowing and chirping, and Jeanne watched them and thought: "I forgot, it is springtime."

Then another thought, a sort of suspicion came to her. She looked again at the glove, at the riding-whips, and at the deserted horses, and abruptly she jumped into the saddle and rode away. She urged her horse into a gallop coming back, and on the way she thought and argued with herself, connecting one fact with the other. Why had she not guessed sooner? How could she have been so blind? Why had she not guessed the motive of Julien's long rides, of his renewed coquetry, his amiability, and good temper? She remembered now Gilberte's changeable temper; her sudden bursts of tenderness, her inexplicable nervousness, and, lately, the sudden change in her which made her husband so happy!

She checked her horse, for the quick pace disturbed her and she had to think — think seriously. After a few minutes, she had regained her habitual composure. No jealousy or hatred filled her heart, only disdain. She did not even think of Julien, nothing that he could do surprised her, but the treachery of the Countess, her friend, was revolting to her. Was there nothing but perfidy and falsehood in this world? However, she resolved to hide her feelings. Hereafter, she would close her heart to everything but Paul and her parents, and stand everything else as quietly as she could.

As soon as she got home, she took Paul with her to her room, and for a whole hour she kissed him without stopping. Julien came in for dinner. He was extremely good-natured, positively charming.

"Aren't your parents coming this year?" he asked Jeanne.

Jeanne was so thankful to him for that remark, that she almost forgot the discovery in the wood. An irresistible desire to see her parents, whom she loved best after Paul, seized her, and she spent the whole evening writing them; telling them to hasten their visit.

They named the twentieth of May for the day of their arrival, and it was only the seventh. Jeanne waited impatiently for the time to come; not only for the desire to see them again, but she felt the need of opening her heart to them, of talking once more with good, honest people, whose actions, thoughts, and desires were pure and blameless. She schooled herself to dissimulate, and greeted the Countess smilingly, with outstretched hands. What she felt now was a sensation of isolation, a complete void, and a profound disdain for all men. It increased with each day, and when the gossip of the neighborhood was brought to her, she was filled with disgust.

Couillard's daughter had just had a baby and was to be married soon. The Martins' servant and a little girl fifteen years old, a neighbor, were in the same condition. A poor, lame widow, nicknamed "Dirt" because she was so filthy, was also in that condition. Each day some new gossip was brought to her. The precocious, warm spring seemed to incite the creatures as well as the plants. Jeanne, whose heart was broken, whose senses were dead, whose sentimental nature was filled only with exalted dreams, wondered and rebelled at their beastliness. If she despised Gilberte, it was not because she had taken her husband from her, but for the very fact that she too had fallen into the mire. She was not of that race which is dominated by low instincts, she was of a different stamp. How could she have fallen in the same manner as these brutes?

The day she expected her parents, Julien revived her feelings of repulsion, by telling her laughingly, as a natural thing, that the day before, which was not baking day, the baker had heard a noise in the oven. He had expected to find a stray cat in it; but he found his wife instead, who "was not baking bread." "He stopped up the opening," Julien continued, "and they almost smothered to death. Her little boy had seen them go in and he warned the neighbors. It reads like one of La Fontaine's fables!"

When the carriage stopped in front of the door and she saw her father's face at the window, Jeanne felt an emotion, a sudden burst of affection for her parents, such as she had never felt before; but when she saw her mother, she was thunderstruck; she almost fainted. The Baronne had aged ten years during the last six months. Her bloated, flabby cheeks had become purple. Her eyes were dull, she breathed with difficulty and she could not get around without being supported on each side. It was painful to look at her. The Baron, who saw her every day and who was constantly with her, had not noticed the change, and when she complained of her increasing heaviness, he would answer:

"But, my dear, I have always seen you that way."

After Jeanne had accompanied them to their room, she went to her own to cry. Then she went to her father, her eyes still wet with tears:

"Oh, father, how changed mother is!" she said. "Tell me, what is the matter with her?" He seemed surprised.

"Do you think so?" he answered. "I think you are mistaken. I have never been away from her and I cannot see any difference. She is just the same as she always was."

That night, Julien said to his wife: "Your mother looks terrible. I think she is pretty sick." Jeanne burst into tears.

"There, now, I did not say that she was lost. You always exaggerate things. She is much changed, that is all; it is quite natural for a woman of her age."

A week after, Jeanne had gotten over the shock and she was accustomed to her mother's looks. Perhaps she tried to drive away her fears and apprehensions concerning her. The Baronne could scarcely walk; she went out a half hour each day, and when she had walked through "her" path once, she would ask to sit down on "her" bench. Sometimes she could not even go the whole length of the path; she would stop in the middle and say: "Let us stop here; I can go no further to-day."

She seldom laughed now, she simply smiled at the things which last year would have made her shake with laughter. Her eyesight was good, however, it was about the only thing left to her, and she spent days reading over "Corinne" or Lamartine's "Meditations." Very often, she would ask for her "souvenir drawer" and having emptied on her lap the old letters dear to her heart, she would put them back one by one, after having silently perused them. When she was alone, really alone, she would kiss certain ones secretly, reverently, as one would a lock of hair belonging to some dear one. Sometimes, Jeanne would find her crying bitterly and she would ask: "What is the matter, mother dear?"

The Baronne would sigh deeply and answer:

"My relics have affected me. I have revived things dear to my heart and which are now over! You think of people whom you had almost forgotten; you imagine you see them, hear them, and it affects you terribly! You will know that feeling later."

When the Baron came in unexpectedly, and assisted at one of these melancholy scenes, he would say:

"Jeanne, darling, believe me, burn all your letters — your mother's, mine, every one of them. There is nothing sadder when you are old than to revive recollections of your youth." But Jeanne kept her letters. Although she differed from her mother in every other way, she had the same dreamy, sentimental nature and she too prepared her "souvenir drawer."

The Baron had been called away on business. The Baronne seemed very much better, and Jeanne, forgetting Gilberte's treachery and Julien's love affairs, was almost happy. The weather was beautiful. The fields were full of flowers, and the beautiful sea, now peaceful and calm, shone with splendor under the sun's rays.

One morning, Jeanne took Paul in her arms and walked through the fields, looking one minute at her son and the other minute at the flowers. She began to dream of her son's future. What would he be? She wished he would become a great man; then, again, she preferred him to remain humble and obscure, so that he would always be near her, always full of tenderness and love for her. She loved him with her selfish mother's heart, she wished he would remain her son, nothing more; but at times she reasoned with herself and wished he would become a great man. She sat on the grass to contemplate him, as if she had never seen him. She wondered when she thought of him as a full-fledged man; when he would have a beard, would walk with a firm step, and speak in a sonorous voice. She was deep in thought, when she heard some one calling her. She looked up and saw Marius running toward her. She immediately thought of visitors and was displeased at being disturbed. Marius was coming at full speed. When he got near enough he shouted:

"Madame, the Baronne is very sick." Jeanne felt as if some ice-water had been thrown down her back. She was bewildered and she ran toward the house as fast as she could. She could see a group of people standing under the plane-tree. When she

reached the spot, they made way for her, and she saw
her mother, stretched out on the ground, her head resting on pillows. Her face was black, her eyes were
closed, and her chest was perfectly still; she who for
the last twenty years was always panting was now
motionless. The nurse took Paul from Jeanne's arms
and went away. Jeanne, with a wild look on her
face, asked:

"What has happened? How did she fall? Quick,
go for the doctor!" As she turned she saw the
priest, who had been summoned by some one, no
one knew by whom. He offered his services, rubbed
vinegar on the Baronne's face and hands, but to no
avail.

"She ought to be put to bed," said the priest.

Couillard, the farmer, was there as well as Simon
and Ludivine, and together with the priest they tried
to carry the Baronne to her room; but her head fell
back limply, and her dress tore under her weight.
Jeanne screamed with terror and they laid her down
on the ground. An armchair was then brought from
the parlor and they sat the Baronne in it. Slowly
they proceeded, up the veranda, the stairs, and finally
they reached her room. They laid her on the bed,
and as Ludivine was struggling to get the Baronne's
clothes off, the widow Dentu made her appearance,
just as mysteriously as the priest had, "as if they
had smelled death," the servants declared.

Joseph Couillard went in haste for the doctor, and
as the priest was getting ready to go for the holy
oils, the widow Dentu whispered to him:

"Do not disturb yourself, your reverence; it is no
use; she is dead!"

The priest gave absolution. "At any rate, it will do no harm," he thought.

For two hours they waited and watched that purple and lifeless body. Jeanne was distracted; wild with anguish. She kneeled near the bed sobbing bitterly.

At last the doctor appeared and it seemed to her that hope and consolation had entered with him. She described to him, the best way she could, what she knew of the accident:

"She was taking her daily walk, she felt good—very good. She even ate some soup and two eggs at breakfast. Suddenly she fell—and her face got black—just as you see it now—and she has not moved since. We have tried everything to revive her—everything—" She stopped when she saw the widow Dentu make discreet signs to the doctor, but even then she refused to understand, and she asked anxiously of the doctor:

"Is it very serious? Do you really think it is serious?" At last the doctor answered:

"Have courage, Madame, I am afraid that—that it is the end!" Poor Jeanne raised her arms and fell on her mother's body. At that moment, Julien came in. He had been taken unawares, and had not had time to prepare either his face or his demeanor. He looked annoyed, but his face showed no apparent sorrow.

"I expected it," he said; "I knew she would not last long." He pulled out his handkerchief, pretended to wipe his eyes, crossed himself devoutly, kneeled and muttered something. After a few minutes, he got up and tried to raise Jeanne, but he was unable to do so. She held her mother's body tightly clasped in her arms and was covering it with kisses. She whispered endearing words to her. She looked as if she had lost her reason, and they actually had to tear her away.

An hour after, when Jeanne returned to her mother's room, she had lost all hope. The apartment had been turned into a house of mourning. Julien and the priest stood near the window talking in whispers, while the widow Dentu was comfortably settled in an armchair, feeling perfectly at home and already dozing, like one accustomed to long periods of waking.

Night had set in. The priest went toward Jeanne, and, taking her hand in his, he tried to comfort her. He whispered unctuous words of consolation. He spoke of the deceased in laudable terms, with the assumed sorrow of those to whom death brings money, and offered to spend the night in prayers near the corpse. Jeanne tearfully refused; she wanted to be alone, absolutely alone with her mother.

"It is impossible," said Julien. "I will stay with you." Jeanne, who was unable to speak, motioned "no" with her head.

"It is my mother," she said at last. "I must be left alone with her."

The doctor whispered: "Let her do as she likes; the nurse can stay in the next room." The priest and Julien, who thought of their beds, gladly consented. The priest kneeled in prayer for a few minutes, and left the room, saying:

"She was a saint!" He said this in the same tone as he would have said: "*Dominus vobiscum.*"

Julien approached Jeanne, and said in his usual voice: "Do you wish anything?"

Jeanne, who did not know he was addressing himself to her, did not answer.

"You would do well to eat something," he continued; "it will strengthen you."

"Send for father right away," Jeanne answered distracted. Julien went out to send a messenger to Rouen. Jeanne remained in a kind of stupor, as if waiting for the hour when she would be alone, to give way to her increasing despair. The widow Dentu walked noiselessly around the room, arranging different objects. She lighted a candle which she placed on a table at the head of the bed, but Jeanne saw nothing; she did not seem to understand. She was waiting to be alone.

Julien came back. He had just had his dinner, and he asked Jeanne for the second time: "Won't you have something?"

Jeanne motioned "no" with her head. Julien sat down, looking more resigned than sad and kept silent. From time to time the widow Dentu, who was dozing, would snore a little, then she would wake suddenly. At last Julien got up and, approaching Jeanne, said: "Do you wish to be left all alone now?"

Jeanne involuntarily took his hand and answered: "Yes, leave me."

He kissed her on the forehead and murmured: "I will come in and see you once in a while," and he went out. The widow Dentu also went out, rolling her chair into the next room.

Jeanne left alone, closed the door, then opened both windows wide. A sweet scent of new-mown hay penetrated the room and caressed her face. The sensation hurt her; it seemed a mockery, and she came back to the bed, took one of her mother's hands in hers and looked at her closely. She was not swollen any more; she seemed to sleep peacefully, and in the pale reflection of the candle, she looked almost lifelike and seemed animated. Jeanne looked at her greedily. A multitude of recollections came back to her. She remembered her mother's visits to the convent; the way she used to hand her the bag of cakes, a multitude of facts, details, words, and familiar gestures; the way she wrinkled up her eyes when she laughed, and the way she sighed when she sat down all out of breath. She stood contemplating her in a sort of dull stupor, repeating:

"She is dead!" Suddenly, the horror of it all struck her. This corpse was her mother, her dear mother, and she would never speak or laugh again; she would never sit opposite her father at the table and would never again say: "Good morning, Jeannette." She was dead! They would nail her up in a box and put her in the ground and then — all would be over; she would never see her again!

Was it possible? Was her mother to be taken away from her? That dear face so familiar, the first one she had ever beheld and loved, the dear one which had been first in her heart was no more? Only a few hours were left to her to contemplate this motionless face, and then nothing would be left her but a recollection! She fell on her knees, seized with a horrible despair. She buried her face in the bed, wringing her hands, and in a heartrending voice wailed: "Oh, mamma, my poor mamma!"

She felt her reason give way, like the night she had run out into the snow; she rose and went to the window to breathe the pure air and cool her brow.

The peaceful stillness of the night and the sweet scent of fresh-cut grass quieted her a little, and she cried softly. She came back and sat down near the bed, and again took one of her mother's hands in hers, as if she were only sick. A large insect, attracted by the light, was flying from one end of the room to the other. Jeanne watched it for a while and then forgot all about it. Then she was attracted by the tick of the clock and another slight almost imperceptible sound. It was her mother's watch, which was still going, attached to her dress, which had been carelessly thrown on a chair at the foot of the bed. The link between her mother and this little watch which had not stopped ticking made her sorrow keener than ever. She looked at the time. It was scarcely half past ten o'clock. She was seized with horror at the thought of spending a whole night in that room.

Then her thoughts drifted to other things; recollections of her life — Rosalie, Gilberte — her bitter deceptions. Was there nothing but misery, sorrow, and death? Everything was deceit, falsehood, suffering, and tears! Where could she find peace and happiness? In another sphere, perhaps, when the soul was delivered from its earthly cares. The soul! She pondered on this fathomless mystery. Where was the soul of this cold and motionless body? Where was her mother's soul? Very far away perhaps, in some unknown place, but where? Perhaps very near; in this room, perhaps, hovering around the inanimate body lying on the bed. Suddenly, Jeanne thought she felt an invisible breath, like a spirit hovering around her, and she was seized with terror. She was so terrified that she did not dare move, breathe, or look behind her. Her heart beat as if it would burst.

All at once, the insect resumed its mad flight around the room. Jeanne shook with fright, but suddenly she felt reassured on recognizing the noise and she got up and looked behind her. Her gaze fell on her mother's writing-desk. A sweet and peculiar thought took possession of her. She would read the old letters dear to her mother's heart; as if she were reading a pious book. She would be accomplishing a sacred duty; a filial action which would please her mother in the other world. It was the correspondence of her grandparents, which she had never read.

She got up, opened the desk, took from the bottom drawer several packages of yellow, faded paper neatly tied together. In a sort of subtle, sentimental feeling, she deposited them all on the bed, on her mother's body, and started to read. The first one was addressed to "My darling"; the second, "My dear little one"; then "My dear child"—"My darling girl"—"My dear Adelaide"—accordingly. They were full of passionate tenderness, full of a thousand details so insignificant to strangers. "Father had the influenza; Hortense had burned herself; Croquerat the cat had died; mother had lost her prayer-book coming back from church; she thinks it was stolen from her." They also spoke of the people unknown to Jeanne, but whose names she remembered having heard when a child.

She was sweetly affected by these details, as if suddenly she had been transported in the midst of her mother's past life; in the inmost recesses of her heart. She read the letters aloud, as if to comfort and console her dead mother. One by one, she laid them at the foot of the bed after reading them, thinking: "They shall be put in the coffin like flowers."

She opened another package in a different handwriting. She read: "I cannot live without your love. I love you to madness." No signature; nothing more. She did not understand. She turned the paper in her hands; it was addressed to "The Baronne Le Perthuis des Vauds." She opened another one and read: "Come to-night as soon as he goes out; we will have an hour. I adore you." Then another: "I have spent a delirious night, vainly wishing for you. You were in my arms, your lips to mine, and then I felt like jumping out of the window when I thought that at the same hour you slept at his side." Jeanne was confused; she did not understand. To whom were these words of love addressed? For whom were they intended?

She continued to read. It was the same always — burning epistles of love, ending with recommendations to be prudent, and at the end these words: "Be sure and burn this." At last, she came across a commonplace note accepting an invitation to dinner. It was in the same handwriting and signed: "Paul d'Ennemare." It was he the Baron called "my old friend Paul" and whose wife had been the Baronne's best friend.

Suddenly, a suspicion entered her mind, and it

immediately became a certainty. This man had been her mother's lover! She sprang to her feet, and threw the love letters from her as if recoiling from a reptile, and burst into bitter tears. Giving way to profound despair, she sank limply to the floor. She sobbed bitterly, hiding her face in her hands, so that her groans would not be heard.

She might have remained in that position all night, but a step sounded in the next room and it roused her. Perhaps it was her father. Those letters strewn all over the bed and floor, he would only need to read one and he would know everything! She gathered quickly all the old letters, those of her grandparents, those of the lover, those she had not read as well as those which were still tied up, and threw them in the fireplace; then, taking the candle, she set fire to them. When there was nothing left but a handful of ashes she resumed her seat near the window; she did not dare go near her mother. She hid her face in her hands and moaned: "Oh, my poor mamma, my poor mamma!"

Then a terrible thought came to her. Supposing her mother was not dead; if she were only asleep and should awake, would not the knowledge of the horrible secret affect her love for her? Could she kiss her with the same devotion, the same sacred affection? No! it was impossible. This thought filled her with anguish.

The night was waning, the stars had almost disappeared and the moon was fast disappearing into the sea. Jeanne's thoughts reverted to the night she had arrived at the "Poplars." She had sat at the window all that night, but under different circumstances. How changed everything was; how different the future seemed!

It was daylight now,—a beautiful day, and Jeanne wondered how it could be possible that, with such a radiant dawn, there could be no joy or peace on this earth. The noise of some one opening the door startled her. It was Julien.

"Well, are you very tired?" he asked.

"No," she answered, almost pleased to see him.

"You had better go and take a rest now," he said. Jeanne slowly, sadly, kissed her mother and went to her room. That night the Baron arrived. He cried bitterly. The funeral was to take place the next day.

When Jeanne had kissed her mother's forehead for the last time, when she had seen them nail her up in the coffin, she stepped aside, for the visitors were coming. Gilberte came first, and throwing her arms around Jeanne, she kissed her, sobbing bitterly. Several women, clad in deep mourning, whom Jeanne did not know, were coming in. The Marchioness de Coutelier and the Viscountess de Briseville both kissed her. Suddenly, she saw Aunt Lison glide toward her and she pressed her to her heart, which almost made the old maid faint. Julien entered, in deep mourning, and he looked well. He whispered to his wife, asking for some advice; then he added:

"All the nobility are here. It will be perfect." And bowing to the ladies he left.

Aunt Lison and Gilberte remained near Jeanne during the ceremony. The Countess kissed her continually and repeated: "You poor darling!"

When the Count came for his wife, he was crying bitterly, as if he had lost his own mother.

CHAPTER X.

THE ABBÉ AND RETRIBUTION

Gloomy, indeed, were the days that followed, for the house seemed empty through the absence of the loved one laid to rest, and the sight of the things she had handled during lifetime fell like a weight on the hearts of those who remained. There was the glass which the maid had forgotten to put away, her armchair, her parasol in the hall! And in every room they found things she had left there: her scissors, a glove, a book whose leaves were worn by constant use, and a dozen other trifles which assumed a painful significance because they brought to mind many of her little habits.

Her voice, also, haunted them; they fancied they could hear it and would gladly have gone anywhere to escape the frightful obsession of these things.

Then, too, Jeanne was crushed by her discovery. The thought of it weighed on her mind; her mangled heart refused to heal. And her loneliness was increased by the knowledge of that terrible secret; her last confidence and last belief had disappeared together.

The Baron, after a while, went away; he needed a change of air and scenery, and hoped to shake off the depression into which he was sinking more and more. And the life of the big house, whose masters thus left one by one, went on calmly and regularly.

·Then Paul was taken sick, and Jeanne, almost frantic with anxiety, remained at his bedside for twelve nights, scarcely taking any food.

He recovered. But she remained terrified at the thought that she might have lost him. Then what would she have done? What would have become of her? And presently a longing for another child crept into her soul. Her old dream of seeing two little children playing around her, a girl and a boy, thrilled her whole heart with an intense desire, which gradually possessed her entirely.

But since the affair with Rosalie, she had lived apart from Julien, and it seemed almost impossible to effect a reunion under the existing circumstances. Then her husband had another attachment; of that she was certain, and the mere thought of again receiving him made her shudder with disgust.

Still, she was ready to set aside her repulsion in her desire for a child; but she had no idea of how to bring about a reconciliation. She would have preferred to die rather than let him know her intentions, for apparently he had ceased to care for her.

Perhaps Jeanne would have given up her fondest wish; but now, every night in dreams she saw a little girl playing under the plane-tree with Paul, so that sometimes she felt an almost irresistible impulse to arise and seek her husband without a word. Twice she crept softly to his door, but halted before she turned the knob, and fled, overcome with a burning sense of shame.

The Baron was away; her mother was dead; she had nobody to consult, nobody to whom she could confide her intimate secrets. So she resolved to go to Abbé Picot, and to tell him, under the seal of confession, the difficult plans she harbored.

She found him in his little garden planted with fruit-trees, reading his breviary. After uttering a few commonplaces, she blushed and stammered: "I want to confess myself, Monsieur l'Abbé."

The priest looked up in surprise, and adjusting his spectacles so as to examine her more closely, he laughed and said: "I hardly think you have very great sins on your conscience." In spite of her intense embarrassment she managed to reply: "No — not exactly — but, you see I want your advice in a matter so — so very delicate, that I cannot speak of it — in this way."

He dropped his jocund manner instantly and assumed a sacerdotal expression: "Well, then, my child, I will listen to you in the confessional. Let us go into the church."

But all at once Jeanne felt as if she could not possibly broach such shameful matters in the sacred peace of the empty tabernacle, and catching hold of his arm, she pulled him back.

"No — Monsieur le Curé — if — if you do not mind — I would rather tell you what I came for here. We can go and sit in the arbor."

They walked slowly toward the little bower and sat down. Jeanne was trying to find her opening words.

"My father," she began, as if she were confessing her sins, then she hesitated, repeated again, "My father—" and stopped short, overcome with confusion. The abbé folded his hands and waited. Finally, seeing how embarrassed she was, he spoke to her encouragingly: "Well, my child, you seem to be afraid? Come now, out with it."

At last she mustered sufficient courage (like a coward seized with a fit of daring), and stammered hurriedly: "Father, I want another child."

As he did not quite understand her, he made no reply. Seeing this, she tried to make her meaning clear, and stammering painfully she continued:

"You see, I am quite alone in the world now; my father and my husband do not agree; my mother is dead, and"—she spoke almost inaudibly—"the other day, I came near losing my boy! What would have become of me then?" She paused. The abbé considered her with a dazed expression.

"Well," he said, "come to the point."

Then she repeated: "I want another child."

He smiled, for he was used to the broad pleasantries of the peasants; they did not mind what they said before him. He answered with a knowing toss of the head: "Well, I think that rests with you."

She raised her candid eyes to him and stammered: "Yes—but you know—since the affair with—with the maid—we—my husband and myself—live apart."

Accustomed as he was to the lax morals of the country, the priest was surprised at this revelation;

and suddenly he thought he guessed the young wife's real desire.

He looked at her sideways, filled with kindliness and pity for her distress. "Yes," he said, "I see, I see. It is perfectly natural that your — your widowhood should be obnoxious to you. You are young and healthy, it is perfectly natural."

And the loose nature of the country priest asserted itself again in a smile, while the abbé gently patted Jeanne's hand and resumed: "And it is quite allowable, too; the Commandments say so. You are married? Well then, it is not for planting potatoes, is it?"

At first she did not catch the drift of his words, but when their meaning dawned upon her, she flushed painfully and her eyes brimmed with tears: "Oh! Monsieur le Curé, what do you mean? What do you think? Oh! I swear to you —" And great sobs stifled her voice.

The abbé was very much surprised. He tried to comfort her: "There now — there — I did not want to hurt your feelings. I was only joking, you know. It is of no consequence when a woman is virtuous. But rely on me, rely entirely upon me. I will see Monsieur Julien."

A week passed. Jeanne lived in a fever of anxiety. One evening at dinner, Julien looked at her in a peculiar way, with an expression of the mouth he always wore when he was in a playful mood. He even treated her with slightly sarcastic gallantry, and when, after dinner, they were walking along her mother's avenue, he bent toward her and whispered: "So we have made up, have we?"

She did not answer. She was studying a straight line on the ground; it was scarcely visible for the grass had grown over it. It was the trace of her mother's foot, as faint as a recollection. Her husband went on unheedingly: "I am very glad of it. I was only afraid it would displease you."

The sun had set behind the trees, the evening air was mild. Jeanne felt as if she wanted to cry and throw her arms around some one, to pour her troubles into a sympathetic ear. A sob rose in her throat, and opening her arms she sank on her husband's breast.

She cried and sobbed while he looked down at her in amazement, for she had buried her face in his coat and he could only see the wavy mass of her hair. Imagining that she loved him still, he condescendingly kissed her head. They returned without a word. And he went upstairs with her into her bedchamber.

Their interrupted relations were resumed. He fulfilled his part with the sense of performing a duty not altogether unpleasant; she submitted to what she considered a painful and repulsive necessity, resolving in her heart to cease all intercourse forever, as soon as she became a mother.

Soon, however, she noticed that Julien's manner had changed. He no longer acted with the perfect security of a husband, but rather with the discretion of a lover. It surprised her and she resolved to watch. Then she discovered that he always remained perfectly self-possessed.

Once, her lips on his, she whispered: "Why are you not quite the same as you used to be?"

174

"Because I do not want any more children," he replied sneeringly.

She started. "Why not?" she queried. Almost speechless with astonishment he answered: "What? Are you insane? Another child? I should say not! Isn't one enough to upset the whole house and to cost money? A baby? No, thank you!"

Throwing her arms around his neck, she implored him in a kiss: "Oh! Julien, please let me have another child." But he grew as angry as if she had hurt him: "Really, you must have lost your mind, Jeanne. Leave me alone with your silly notions."

She was silent, but in her heart she resolved to force him by artifice to give her the longed-for happiness. So she tried to prolong their kisses, played the comedy of passion, called to her aid every subterfuge; but all in vain, for he retained always complete mastery over himself.

Seeing the futility of her efforts and goaded to desperation by her wish for a baby girl, she resolved to face anything and dare all. She went back to Abbé Picot. He had just finished his breakfast and was crimson, for he always had palpitation of the heart after meals. As soon as he saw Jeanne he exclaimed: "Well?"—for he was eager to learn the result of his arbitration.

Without any of her former modest hesitation she immediately replied: "My husband does not wish another child." Greatly interested, the priest turned around, ready to root in those connubial mysteries which so often made the confessional pleasant to him. "How's that?" he inquired. Despite her resolve and determination she could not help feeling

175

intensely uncomfortable. "Why—he—he refuses to let me become a mother."

The abbé understood, for he knew these things. Still he questioned her closely. He reflected a while, and then, in a quiet voice, as if he were discussing the prospective crop, he proposed, with great detail, a plan which she was to follow.

"There is only one thing to do, my child," he said, "make him believe that you are pregnant. Then he will not be so careful."

She flushed to the roots of her hair, but she had steeled herself against the ordeal and inquired determinedly: "And if he does not believe me?"

The abbé was familiar with the ways of men: "Tell the news to everybody," he said, "and after a while, your husband will believe it himself." Then, in order to excuse himself for using such a stratagem, he added: "It is your right to do so, for the Church only tolerates these relations for the purpose of procreation."

Jeanne followed his artful advice and, two weeks later, announced to Julien that she thought she was to become a mother. He started and exclaimed: "It cannot be possible!"

She insisted and told him the reason for her suspicion. But he only replied: "Bah! wait a little while. We will see."

Every day he queried: "Well?" But she always replied: "No, not yet. I should be very much surprised if I were not *enceinte*." He fumed, exclaimed, was unwilling to believe it, and went about repeating: "I cannot understand it; I do not see how it happened; it is impossible."

After a month or so she announced the news to everyone, excepting Countess Gilberte, on account of a certain complicated and delicate feeling of modesty. Since the first warning, Julien had ceased to visit his wife; but after a while, he became resigned to the inevitable. Though he declared angrily: "Here's one who came without being asked," he renewed their relations. What the priest had expected, happened. She became *enceinte.*

Then, in an ecstasy of joy, she closed her door to Julien forever, and, in an impulse of gratitude toward the vague divinity she worshiped, vowed henceforth to remain eternally chaste.

She was almost happy again, and was surprised herself at the promptness with which her grief at her mother's death had subsided. She had thought she could never be reconciled to it; and now hardly two months had elapsed and already the wound was healing. There only remained a sort of tender sadness, like a veil spread over her life. She thought that no other events would be able to hurt her now. Her children would grow up and cherish her; and she could spend her old age in peace, without giving a thought to her husband.

Toward the end of September, Abbé Picot, wearing a new cassock, made a ceremonious visit to introduce his successor, Abbé Tolbiac, a very young priest of solemn demeanor, whose sunken eyes, surrounded with deep circles, revealed his violent character.

The old curé had been elected dean of Goderville. Jeanne felt a genuine sadness to have him leave. His face was linked with all the events of her young womanhood. He had married her, christened her boy, and buried her mother.

She could not picture Etouvent without the genial face of the Abbé Picot, as he went from one farm to another, and she liked the old man, because he was so jolly and natural.

In spite of his advancement the abbé did not seem happy. "It is very hard for me, very hard indeed, Madame la Comtesse," he said. "I have been here for the past eighteen years. The parish is poor and does not bring in much. The men are not religious and the women are flighty. The girls come to me to get married only after they are in trouble, and the orange blossom is not worth much around here; but nevertheless, I have been happy."

At this the new curé reddened and showed signs of impatience. Then he said abruptly: "All that will have to change now." He looked like a sullen child, so thin and delicate did he appear in his worn but immaculate cassock.

Abbé Picot glanced at him sideways, a trick he had when he felt particularly jocular, and resumed: "You see, abbé, in order to prevent it, you would have to chain your flock, and even that wouldn't help you much."

In a cutting tone the little priest replied: "Well, we shall see." The old curé smiled and took a pinch of tobacco. "Age will moderate you, abbé, and so will experience; you will only keep the worshipers away from the church, that's all. In these parts, the peasants are religious but obstinate; so take care. You see, when a girl with a rather large waistband comes to hear me preach, I only think, 'She is bring-

178

ing me a new parishioner'—and try to get her married. You cannot stop them from being naughty, you know, but you can go to the man and see that he does not forsake the mother. Marry them, abbé, marry them, and do not trouble about the rest."

The new priest answered with asperity: "We think differently, so it is useless to continue the discussion."

Abbé Picot began again to lament the loss of the village, the ocean he could see from the windows of the rectory and the funnel-shaped valleys in which he read his breviary, while he watched the white sails in the distance. Then the two priests rose to take leave, and the old man kissed Jeanne, who felt her tears very near.

A week later, Abbé Tolbiac called again. He spoke of the reforms he had inaugurated, like a prince who has taken possession of a realm. Then he requested the Viscountess not to miss the Sunday service and to take communion on each Church holiday. "You and I," he explained, "are at the head of this place; we must govern and set the example; and we must act jointly, so that we may be powerful and respected. When the Church and the castle go hand in hand, the cottages will fear and obey."

Jeanne's religion was all sentiment. She possessed that dreamy faith which a woman never relinquishes, and if she kept up her religious duties at all, it was because she had formed the habit at the convent. The breezy philosophy of her father had long ago upset her convictions. Abbé Picot was satisfied with the little she gave him, and never chided her for it. But his successor, when he failed to see her at the service on the previous Sunday, hurried to the château, anxious and severe.

As she did not want to break with the rectory, she promised to attend church, but resolved inwardly to be less punctilious after the first few weeks.

However, little by little, she got into the habit of going to church, and unconsciously submitted to the influence of the frail and domineering priest. He pleased her mystic nature by his exaltation and ardor. He knew how to awaken the religious poesy that lies dormant in the soul of woman. His unimpeachable austerity, his contempt of the world and its pleasures, his disgust for human ambitions, his love for God, his youthful and arrogant inexperience, his direct speech, his inflexible will, gave Jeanne the impression of what martyrs must have been; and she, the disillusioned sufferer, was attracted by the rigid fanaticism of this child-priest.

He talked to her of Christ, and told her that the pious joys of religion would calm all her sufferings; and she would kneel in the confessional and feel small and weak before this priest who looked like a boy.

But soon the whole place despised him. Inflexibly severe toward himself, he was absolutely intolerant toward others. One thing above all excited his wrath and indignation: love. He vilified it in the pulpit, using the crudest terms, and thundered against the sin of concupiscence, trembling with rage at the scenes his mind evoked in these furies.

The men and the girls exchanged sly glances across the aisle; and the old peasants, who liked to joke about certain things, criticized the attitude of the little priest while they walked home from church with their wives and sons.

The whole place was in a turmoil. Everybody grumbled about his severity at confession and told of the severe penances he inflicted. When he obdurately refused to absolve maidens whose virtue was not intact, his flock began to deride him, and everybody laughed when at the communion services on holidays, some girls remained on their benches instead of going to the holy table with the rest.

So like a gamekeeper, who wants to trap a poacher, he began to spy on lovers, in a vain effort to frustrate them. He chased them from the ditches, from behind the barns on moonlit nights and from the clumps of rushes that grew on the slope of the tiny hills. Once, he came across a couple who did not separate when he hove in sight; they were walking along a stony ravine, and kissing each other at every step. He shouted to them: "Will you stop that, you blockheads!"

But the youth only turned around and shouted back: "Mind your own business, M'sieu l'Curé; this doesn't concern you."

Then the abbé picked up some stones and threw them at the culprits as if they were dogs. They fled laughingly; and the following Sunday he denounced them by name, from the pulpit. Then all the men of the place stopped going to church.

The curé dined at the château every Thursday, but he often came during the week to have a talk with his penitent. She had become as exalted as he; they discussed immaterial things and brought up aged and complicated religious controversies. They would walk along the Baronne's alley talking of Christ and the Apostles, of the Virgin and of the Fathers of the Church, as if they had known them.

Once in a while they stopped to ask each other some ponderous question on which they then digressed mystically, Jeanne losing herself in poetical arguments that ascended toward heaven like rockets, while the priest, whose mind was more logical, argued like a mathematician trying to demonstrate the quadrature of the circle.

Julien treated the new curé with great respect, repeating all the time: "I like that priest, he does not knuckle." And he went to confession and took communion whenever he was requested to do so, thus giving a splendid example.

Now he spent almost every day with the De Fourvilles, hunting with the husband, who had grown very fond of him, and riding with the Countess in spite of wind and weather. The Count remarked: "They are really crazy about riding, but it does my wife a great deal of good."

Jeanne's father came home about the middle of November. He had changed, had grown older, and seemed bent by a sorrow which had taken a firm hold of his mind. His fondness for his daughter had increased, as if a few months of desperate loneliness had increased his longing for affection and love.

Jeanne refrained from mentioning her ideas, her intimacy with Abbé Tolbiac, and her religious ardor; but the first time he met the priest the Baron took a vehement dislike to him. And when in the evening his daughter inquired: "How do you like him?"

he answered: "That man is an inquisitor! I think he must be very dangerous."

Then, when he learned through the peasants how severe and violent the young priest was, and how he seemed to exert a persecution against natural laws and inborn instincts, his dislike grew to hatred. He himself was one of those old philosophers who worship nature, and are moved by the mere sight of its manifestations; he practiced a sort of pantheism and rebelled against the Catholic conception of the Almighty, which meant to him a Lord possessing all the craftiness of a Jesuit and the baleful power of a tyrant,— a God, who in his idea, belittled creation, fatal, limitless, all-powerful creation, creation which is life, light, earth, sun, plant, rock, man, air, beast, star, God, and insect all in one, and creates because it *is* creation, stronger than will and above argument.

Creation, in his idea, contained all germs, thought and life developed through it as flowers and fruits grow on trees, producing without aim, reason, or limit and in every conceivable shape, according to the necessities of chance and the proximity of the suns which heat the universe. To him reproduction was the great universal law, the sacred, respectable, divine act by which the obscure and continuous purpose of the Universal Being is accomplished.

Going from farm to farm, he started a violent campaign against the intolerant, persecuting priest. Jeanne was grieved at this turn of affairs, implored her father to desist, and supplicated the Lord, but the Baron always replied: "These men must be fought. It is our right and our duty. They are not human." Shaking his long, white hair he would repeat again: "They are not human, they do not understand anything. They are acting under a false impression; they are against nature." He uttered the words: "Against nature," as if he were uttering a curse.

The priest was well aware of this enmity. But as he wished to continue controlling Jeanne and the château, he bided his time, feeling sure that the final victory would be his.

Then, too, he was haunted by a fixed idea; chance had revealed to him the intimacy of Julien and Gilberte, and he desired to stop it at any cost. One day, he went to Jeanne, and after a lengthy, mystical conversation, asked her to unite with him in stamping out an evil existing in her own family and to help him to rescue two imperiled souls. She failed to comprehend what he desired of her and questioned him. But he replied: "The hour has not come, I will see you again," and left abruptly.

The winter was nearly over. It had been a green winter, mild and damp. The abbé returned a few days later and spoke to Jeanne in veiled terms of an infamous *liaison* which existed between two people whose conduct should be above suspicion. It behooved those who were aware of the facts to stop it by all possible means, he said. Then he entered upon lofty considerations, and, taking hold of Jeanne's hand, entreated her to let the scales drop from her eyes, to understand what was going on around her and to help him in his mission.

This time she guessed the truth, but was silent because she was terrified at the thought of all the

misery it would bring into her peaceful home. So
she professed she did not understand him. Seeing
this, he spoke without restraint.

"I have a painful duty to perform, Madame la
Comtesse, but I cannot shrink from it. My mission
on earth compels me to enlighten you about something which you are called upon to stop. Your husband entertains a criminal friendship for Madame de
Fourville." Jeanne, helpless and resigned, dropped
her head upon her breast.

The priest continued: "Now, what do you intend
to do?"

"What can I do, Monsieur l'Abbé?" she stammered.

"Put yourself in the way of this culpable passion,"
he answered roughly.

Jeanne burst into tears, and in a despairing voice
said: "He has already deceived me with a maid; he
will not listen to me; he no longer loves me, he
maltreats me as soon as I manifest a wish that does
not suit him. What can I do?"

The abbé did not answer her question, but cried:
"Then you are abetting it, you are resigned, you are
accessory! Adultery exists under your roof and you
tolerate it! The crime takes place under your very
eyes and you turn your glance away? Are you a
wife? a Christian? a mother?"

"What do you wish me to do?" she sobbed.

"Anything, rather than to permit such an infamy.
Anything, I say. Leave your husband. Flee from
this polluted house."

"But I have no money, Monsieur l'Abbé; and I
have no courage, either; and then, how can I leave

him without proofs? I haven't even the right to do so."

Trembling with indignation, the priest rose: "You are actuated by cowardice, Madame; I thought you different. You are unworthy of God's mercy!"

Jeanne fell on her knees: "Oh! do not forsake me, please advise me!"

"Open Monsieur de Fourville's eyes. It is he who should break up the *liaison*," he uttered in a brief tone.

This suggestion filled her with terror: "Oh! he would kill them, Monsieur l'Abbé, and I would have denounced them! Oh! no, anything but that!"

Then, in his anger he raised his hand as if to curse her: "Remain in your shame and your crime; for you are more sinful than they. You are the complacent wife! I have nothing more to do in this house."

And he left her, his whole body trembling with wrath. Jeanne followed him out of the room, ready to yield and beginning to make promises. But the priest in his indignation strode away rapidly, viciously waving his big blue umbrella. Suddenly he perceived Julien standing near the fence, superintending some workmen; he turned to the left to walk across the Couillards' farm, and repeated, "Leave me, Madame, I have nothing more to say to you."

Right in his path, in the middle of the yard, a group of children from the farm and neighboring houses, had crowded around the kennel of Mirza. They were watching something with keen interest and mute, concentrated eagerness. In their midst, the Baron, with his hands clasped behind his back, was also watching. He looked like a schoolmaster. But when he caught sight of the priest, he walked away to avoid meeting him.

Jeanne was saying: "Give me a few days, Monsieur l'Abbé, and come back again. I will think it over and tell you what I can do and what I have prepared, and we can consult."

They reached the children, and the abbé took a few steps forward to see what attracted them so. It was Mirza who was in litter. Five puppies were already crawling around the mother who licked them tenderly, and just as the priest bent over her, another little dog appeared. All the urchins began to clap their hands and shouted delightedly: "There's another one, there's another one!" It was all like play to them, natural play in which there was nothing impure whatever. They watched the birth of the puppies just as they would have watched apples fall from a tree.

At first the abbé was stunned. Then he was seized with an ungovernable fit of rage, so that he took his big umbrella and rained blows on the heads of the assembled children. The astonished urchins scampered away as fast as their legs would carry them; and suddenly he was left alone with the dog who was trying to get on its feet. He did not give it a chance to rise and began beating it with all his might. The beast, unable to escape, for it was chained to the kennel, groaned in agony under his blows. The umbrella broke. Having lost his weapon, he stamped on her, bruising, crushing her with frenzy. Then with his heel he finished the mangled and bleeding body that continued to twitch convulsively, while the newborn puppies, blind and awkward, were already seeking nourishment.

Jeanne had fled; but suddenly the priest felt a hand on his throat, his hat was knocked off, and the exasperated Baron dragged him to the fence and threw him in the road. When M. le Perthuis turned around, his daughter was on her knees by the little dogs, sobbing and gathering them up in her skirt. He strode toward her angrily, gesticulating and exclaiming: "That's like him, the godly man! Do you see what he is now?"

The farm-hands ran up, everybody came to see the butchered dog; and Mother Couillard exclaimed: "How is it possible to be such a brute?"

But Jeanne picked up the seven puppies and declared she would bring them up. She tried to give them some milk, but three died the following day. Then Père Simon searched broadcast for a nursing bitch. He did not find what he wanted and so brought home a cat, saying that she would do as well. Then they killed three more puppies and gave the last one to the newly-found mother of a different race. She adopted it immediately and tended it with great care.

The puppy was weaned two weeks later, so as not to exhaust its adopted parent and Jeanne decided to bring it up on the bottle, herself. She called it Toto, but her father used his authority to change its name and christened it "Slaughter."

The priest did not call again, but the following Sunday, from the pulpit, he hurled curses and imprecations against the château, saying that it was necessary to uproot evil growths, thundering against the

Baron (whom it greatly amused), and alluding in veiled terms to Julien's new attachment. The latter was exasperated by the priest's attack, but smothered his anger for fear of creating a scandal.

Henceforth in every sermon, the abbé continued to announce that he would be avenged, and that the hand of God would descend on all his enemies. Julien wrote a respectful but firm letter to the archbishop. Abbé Tolbiac was threatened with dismissal, and so he was silenced. After that, he could be seen taking long, solitary walks in the country, wearing an exalted expression. Gilberte and Julien saw him every day when they were out riding, a black spot in a field or on the edge of the cliff, or walking and reading his breviary in some dale. Then they would turn their horses' heads so as to avoid him.

Spring had come, and with it greater passion. Every day found the Countess and Julien together, sometimes here, sometimes there, under any shelter the wood afforded. As the foliage of the trees was still thin and the grass damp, and as it was impossible for them to hide in the brushwood, they often took possession of the traveling hut of a shepherd, which had been left on the top of the hill of Vaucotte since fall.

This moving house, perched on high wheels, had been abandoned in this spot, situated about five hundred yards from the cliff. There, they feared no detection, for they could see across the plain, and the horses, tied to the shafts of the hut, waited patiently for them to reappear.

But one day, as they were coming out of their refuge, they caught sight of the abbé sitting among the rushes that grew on the hill. "We will have to leave the horses in the ravine," said Julien, "because they might reveal our hiding-place from the distance." And henceforth they tied them in a path hidden by bushes.

One evening, as they were returning together to "La Vrillette," where they were to dine with the Count, they met the curé of Etouvent coming from the château. He stepped aside to let them pass and raised his hat without a look. A feeling of anxiety crept over them, which, however, soon disappeared.

One afternoon Jeanne was sitting in front of the fire (it was the beginning of May and very chilly) when she suddenly perceived the Comte de Fourville walking hurriedly toward the château. Immediately she thought that some dreadful misfortune had happened.

She went forward at once to receive him, but when she saw his face, she thought he had gone mad. He had on a large fur cap, which he only wore at home, and his hunting coat. He was so pale that his reddish mustache, which generally harmonized with his ruddy complexion, looked like fire. His eyes rolled wildly in their sockets.

"My wife is here, isn't she?" he stammered.

Jeanne lost her head and replied: "No, I have not seen her to-day."

He sat down as if his knees had given way under him, took off his cap and mechanically mopped his brow several times with his handkerchief. Then he jumped up and walked toward Jeanne with outstretched hands and parted lips, ready to speak, about to make some frightful revelation. But suddenly he stopped, and, looking at her steadily, stammered in a sort of delirium: "But it's your husband — and you too—" Then he dashed out toward the ocean.

Jeanne ran after him with a beating heart, calling to him and pleading with him: "He has discovered it! What will he do? Oh! I hope he will not find them!" she thought.

But she could not catch up with him, and he turned a deaf ear to her pleadings. He ran on without hesitating, sure of his goal. He leaped over the ditches and across the rushes until he finally reached the cliff. Jeanne, standing on the slope, watched him a long while; then, when she lost sight of him, she retraced her steps with a heavy heart.

He had turned to the right and started to run. The choppy sea was white with foam; big black clouds drifted across the sky and drenched the coast with rain. The wind whistled and moaned, bending the new crops and the rushes, and carrying inland large, white birds that looked like huge snowflakes.

The rain stung the Count's face, soaked his cheeks and his mustache, which hung down straight, and filled his ears with noise and his heart with tumult. In front of him lay the valley of Vaucotte. Nothing was to be seen but the hut of a shepherd standing in a deserted pasture. Two horses were tied to the shafts of the rolling house. What was to be feared in such a storm?

As soon as he perceived the horses, the Count got down on his hands and knees and began to crawl toward the hut, looking, with his heavy body covered with mud and his fur cap, like some huge monster. He crept up to the lonely cabin so that he would not be discovered through the cracks in the boards.

The horses, catching sight of him, became restive, and he deliberately cut their bridles with the open knife he held in his hand. Just then a gust of wind swept down upon the hut and the animals galloped away, stung by the hail that beat on the sloping roof of the wooden house, which swayed and shook on its high wheels.

Then the Count got upon his knees, and putting his eye to the crack of the door he peered inside. He did not move; it seemed as if he were waiting. Some time passed; then he got up; he was covered with mud from head to foot.

With a mad gesture he shot the bolt which fastened the door from the outside, and taking hold of the shafts shook the cabin as if he wished to smash it into a thousand pieces. Then all at once he hitched himself to it, bent his tall figure in a desperate effort, and with the strength of an ox dragged the rolling house and its occupants toward the steep embankment. From within came cries and raps, for Julien and the Countess did not know what had happened to their hut.

When the Count arrived at the top of the slope, he let go of the shafts and sent the light cabin rolling down the incline. An old tramp who was lying in a ditch saw the thing pass over his head, and heard horrified screams proceed from within.

All of a sudden the wooden box lost one of its wheels, turned over on one side, and continued its course like an uprooted house falling down the side

of a mountain. Arriving at the edge of the last ravine, it shot into the air and fell to the bottom, where
it shivered like an eggshell.

As soon as it reached the ground, the old tramp,
who had watched its course, climbed down through
the rushes to where it lay. But his innate prudence
forbade him to approach the wrecked hut and he
went to the nearest farm to report the accident.

The farm-hands ran to the scene at once; they
lifted the boards and found two bodies badly crushed
and bleeding. The man's head was open and his
whole face was knocked in. The woman's jaw was
hanging, it had been dislocated by the fall, and their
mangled limbs were as soft as if no bones were under the flesh. They were recognized in spite of their
disfigurement, and everyone began to conjecture on
the cause of the disaster.

"What were they doing in that hut?" said a
woman. Then the old tramp told that they had
apparently sought refuge from the storm, and that the
high winds had probably sent it rolling down the
embankment. And he added that he himself was
just going to enter it, when he saw the horses tied
to the shafts and concluded that it was already occupied.

"If it had not been for that," he added, with a
pleased expression, "it would have been my turn."

"Wouldn't it perhaps have been better?" said a
voice.

The old man flew into a terrible passion: "Why
would it have been better? Because I am poor and
they were rich? Look at them, now —" And
trembling with rage, dripping with water, the ragged

193

beggar, with unkempt beard and long hair falling from under his battered hat, pointed to the bodies with his crooked stick. "We are all equal in death," he declared.

More peasants had gathered around, and they stood looking at the corpses with expressions of cowardice, egotism, anxiety, and craftiness. They all consulted about what was to be done, and decided, in the hope of a reward, to take the bodies back to the château.

Two wagons were hitched up. Then a new difficulty was encountered. Some wanted to lay a few bundles of straw in the bottom of the wagons, while the rest, out of respect for the dead, thought they had better use mattresses.

"But they will be terribly stained," cried the woman who had spoken before, "and will have to be washed in Javelle water."

Then a fat farmer, with a round, jolly face, declared: "Then they will have to pay for them. The more they are worth, the more they will have to pay." His argument proved decisive.

So the two carts on high wheels and without springs started out at a trot, one going to the right and the other to the left, with the remains of the two lovers jolting within.

As soon as he saw the cabin leap down the incline, the Count fled as fast as his legs would carry him, pushing through the bushes, leaping over ditches, and crossing roads. He returned to the château at sunset, without knowing how he got there.

The frightened servants were waiting for him and told him that the two horses had come back riderless.

Julien's animal had followed the other home. M. de
Fourville staggered. "Something must have happened to them," he said in a choked voice. "Everybody must go out to look for them."

He started out again himself; but as soon as he
was out of sight, he hid beneath a bush to watch
the return of her whom he still loved with a savage
passion, and who would be brought home dead or
dying, maimed and disfigured for the rest of her
days.

Soon a cart drove past him, carrying something
peculiar. It stopped in front of the château and entered. Yes, that was it, it was she; but a frightful
anguish nailed him to the ground, a horrible fear of
the truth kept him motionless and made him start
like a hare at the slightest noise.

He waited for an hour or two. The cart had not
left. He imagined his wife was dying, and the
thought of seeing her, of meeting her glance, filled
him with such horror that all of a sudden he grew
afraid of discovery, of being compelled to witness
her agony. He fled into the wood. Then he reflected that perhaps she needed help and that possibly no one could assist her and darted homeward
again.

As he came back, he met the gardener and
shouted: "Well?" The man did not dare to answer him. M. de Fourville almost howled: "Is she
dead?" And the man replied: "Yes, Monsieur le
Comte." He felt immense relief. Perfect calmness
had abruptly entered his blood and his straining muscles, and with a firm step he walked up the wide
stoop.

195

The other cart had reached the "Poplars." Jeanne saw it as it hove in sight, saw the mattress, guessed that a body was lying on it and understood what had occurred. Her fright and horror were so intense that she dropped to the floor unconscious.

When she came to, her father was holding her head and bathing her forehead with vinegar. "Do you know?" he asked hesitatingly. "Yes, father," she whispered. But when she wished to arise, terrible pains prevented her.

That very night she gave birth to a dead baby; a girl.

She saw nothing of Julien's funeral, she knew nothing of it. After a day or two, she noticed that Aunt Lison had come back; and in her feverish nightmares she obstinately tried to remember when the old maid left the "Poplars" and under what circumstances she went.

She could not arrive at any satisfactory explanation, however, even in her lucid moments; she only remembered that she had seen her after her mother's death.

CHAPTER XI.

The Development of Paul

For three months, Jeanne kept to her room, having become so pale and weak that everyone thought she was lost. But little by little her strength returned. Her father and Aunt Lison were with her all the time and had installed themselves at the "Poplars." The shock she had experienced left her with a nervous malady; she fainted at the slightest noise and fell into long spells of unconsciousness, brought on by the most insignificant occurrences.

She never asked about Julien's death. What did it matter to her? Had she not sufficient knowledge already? Everybody thought that it was an accident, but she knew better; the secret which tormented her she locked in her breast, that is, the knowledge of the adultery and the vision of the Count's short and stormy visit on the day of the catastrophe.

Strange to say, her soul was haunted by tender reminiscences of the short-lived love she had borne her husband. Every once in a while she would start at some abrupt and unexpected recollections; she saw him as he had been during their brief engagement and as he had been during their honeymoon, the only time she ever experienced passion, under the burning sun of Corsica. All his faults diminished, all his harshness disappeared, even his betrayals faded away in the distance now his grave was closed.

Jeanne was invaded by a sort of gratitude for the man who had held her in his arms; she forgave him her past sufferings to remember only the happy moments of their married life. Then, as time passed on and one month followed after the other, throwing a veil over her sorrows and reminiscences, she gave herself up entirely to the education of her boy.

He grew to be the idol, the one absorbing thought of his mother, grandfather, and aunt, and he reigned over them like a despot. A kind of jealousy even existed between these three slaves, for Jeanne felt nervous when she saw him hug his grandfather after the latter had jolted him on his knee, and Aunt Lison, whom the child, like everybody else, sorely neglected, and whom he would sometimes treat like a servant, though he could hardly lisp, would shut herself up in her room and cry over the insignificant demonstrations of affection she had to beg from him, while the boy seemed dearly to love his mother and grandfather.

Two years passed without being marked by any events. At the beginning of the third winter, they decided to move to Rouen till the spring; so the whole family packed up and left the "Poplars." But when they arrived in the damp, deserted house, Paul had bronchitis so badly that it was feared it might develop into pleurisy. So his relatives declared he could not thrive in any other place but the country, and as soon as he recovered, they moved back to the "Poplars."

Then began a series of happy and monotonous years. Always gathered around the boy, sometimes in the nursery, sometimes in the drawing-room, sometimes in the garden, they would go into raptures over his lispings, his funny sayings, his gestures. His mother lovingly called him "Paulet," and as he could not articulate the word, he pronounced it "Poulet," a name which never failed to arouse storms of laughter. It clung to him, too, and he was never called anything else.

As he grew very rapidly, one of the absorbing pastimes of his three relatives, whom the Baron called "his three mothers," was to measure his growth.

The door of the drawing-room had been marked by scratches made by a penknife, which indicated from month to month his accessions in height. This scale was called "Poulet's scale," and it held an important place in their daily life.

After a little while a new individual appeared on the scene, and played an important part in the family. It was Slaughter, who, now that Jeanne was so absorbed by her boy, had been sorely neglected. He was always chained to his kennel in front of the barn, and lived the life of a hermit, tended and fed by Ludivine.

One morning Paul noticed the dog and cried to be allowed to pat him. They led him up to the

beast with dire misgivings. But the dog received the
boy with great demonstrations of affection, and the
little fellow also took a great fancy to the dumb
brute and screamed when they had to part. So
Slaughter was unchained and henceforth allowed to
live in the house.

The two became inseparable. They romped together, curled up side by side on the rug, and soon
Slaughter was permitted to sleep on the bed of his
little companion, who would not consent to be without him for a moment. Jeanne discouraged the friendship on account of the fleas; and Aunt Lison could
not forgive the dog for having taken such a large
part of the boy's affection, which rightfully belonged
to her.

Once in a while, the family visited the De Brisevilles and the Couteliers. But only the mayor and
the physician came to the old château regularly.

Since the killing of Mirza and the horrible end of
Julien and Gilberte, Jeanne, whose suspicions had
been aroused against the priest, had not entered the
church; she felt irritated that God could have such
ministers.

From time to time, in direct terms, Abbé Tolbiac
anathematized the château, declaring it to be haunted
by the Evil Spirit, the Spirit of Eternal Rebellion, the
Spirit of Error and Falsehood, the Spirit of Un-
righteousness, the Spirit of Impurity and Corruption.
Those were the expressions he applied to the Baron.

In fact, his church was deserted; and when he
walked through the fields where the peasants were
plowing, they did not even stop to speak to him,
nor did they turn around to bow. They thought he

possessed witchcraft, because he had cast the evil spirit out of a woman.

He knew the words to set aside the spells that were cast over cattle and people, for he considered these same spells in the light of merry tricks of Satan. He laid his hands on the cow that gave blue milk or whose tail was twisted and, by only pronouncing a few unknown words, he could recover lost objects.

His narrow and fanatical mind delved with passion into the study of religious books, which dealt with the apparitions of the Devil, the different manifestations of his power, his varied and occult influences, the resources he possessed and his ordinary pranks. And, as he imagined that he especially was called upon to fight this mysterious and fatal Power, he had learned all the exorcisms given in clerical manuals.

He thought that the Spirit of the Evil One lurked in the dark and the Latin sentence, *" Sicut leo rugiens circuit quœrens quem devoret,''* was always on his lips.

A fear spread among the peasants, a sort of terror of his hidden strength. Even his colleagues, ignorant country priests that they were, who believed in Beelzebub as in God, and whom the minute prescriptions of the rites to be followed in case Satan should manifest himself confused, so that they confounded religion with magic, considered Abbé Tolbiac somewhat of a sorcerer; and they respected him as much, perhaps, for the power they ascribed to him, as for the unassailable strictness of his life. The Abbé no longer bowed to Jeanne when they met.

This state of affairs worried Aunt Lison greatly, for in her timid, old maid's soul, she could not comprehend how it was possible to stay away from Church. She no doubt was pious and confessed herself and took communion; but nobody knew of it or tried to find it out.

When she was alone with Paul, she would speak to him of God. He listened quite eagerly when she told him the miraculous stories of the beginning of the world, but when she said that he must love the Lord dearly, he sometimes answered her: "Auntie, where is he?" Then, pointing her finger toward heaven, she would reply, "He is up there, Poulet, but you must not say so." For she was in mortal dread of the Baron. But one day, Poulet declared: "The Lord is everywhere, but not in church." The boy had told his grandfather of auntie's mysterious revelations.

Paul was now nearly ten years old; and his mother looked as if she were forty. He was strong, turbulent, always ready to climb a tree but reluctant to learn his lessons. When his studies annoyed him, he would simply drop them. Every time his grandfather kept him in front of a book longer than usual, Jeanne would say, "Now let him play. We must not tire him, he is too young." She always fancied that he was about one year old. She hardly could realize that he could walk, run about, and speak already like a little man; and she lived in a constant fear that the boy would fall, or take cold, or play too much, or eat more than he could digest or less than his strength required.

When he was twelve years old, a great difficulty arose: his first communion. One morning, Lise came to Jeanne and told her that it was impossible to allow

the boy to go any longer without religious instruc-
tion, and without fulfilling his primary duties. She
argued in every manner, and invoked a hundred reasons,
of which the predominating one was the opinion of
their acquaintances. Jeanne hesitated, saying that
there was time enough to consider the step.

But, a month later, while calling on the Vicomtesse de Briseville, this lady asked her casually if it
was not this year that Paul would make his first communion, Jeanne, taken by surprise, answered: "Yes,
Madame." This reply settled the question, and without telling her father of her decision, she asked Lise
to take the child to Sunday-school.

All went well during one month; but one evening, Poulet came home with a hoarse voice. The
next day he had a cough. His anxious mother questioned him, and learned that the curé had made him
stand at the door of the church, in a draft, during
the lesson, because he had misbehaved. After that
she kept him home and taught him his catechism
herself. But in spite of Lison's entreaties, Abbé Tolbiac refused to admit him among the communicants,
because, he said, the boy was insufficiently prepared.
It was the same the following year. Then the Baron
grew angry, and declared that it was not necessary
to believe in that tomfoolery, and in the absurd idea
of transubstantiation, to become an upright man. So
they decided to bring him up as a Christian, but not
as an orthodox Catholic, so that when he attained his
majority, he could choose his own faith.

A little later, Jeanne called on the De Brisevilles; but
they did not return her visit. Knowing the careful
attention her neighbors paid to etiquette, she was

surprised at this omission; but the Marquise de Coutelier soon revealed to her, with much haughtiness,
the reason for their abstention.

The Marquise considered herself by right of her
husband's position, his authentic title, and their great
wealth, a sort of queen of Norman aristocracy. She
governed like a real queen, too, was haughty or gracious according to the occasion, and admonished, cor-
rected, or congratulated as she saw fit. Jeanne having
called on her, the lady, after making a few freezing
remarks, said dryly: "Society is divided into two
classes: the people who believe in God and those
who do not. The former, even the most humble, we
consider our friends, while the others are nothing at
all to us."

Jeanne at once felt the attack and replied: "But
is it not possible to believe in God without going to
church?"

"No, Madame; good Catholics go to worship God
in His church just as they go to visit people in their
homes," replied the Marquise.

Jeanne, who felt hurt, answered: "God is everywhere, Madame. I, who in the bottom of my heart
believe in His kindness, do not feel His presence when
certain priests come between Him and me."

The Marquise rose: "The priests carry the banner
of the Church, Madame; whoever does not follow the
banner is opposed to it, and is consequently opposed
to us."

Jeanne had also risen: "Madame, you may believe
in a partisan God. I believe in the God of righteousness." Then she simply bowed and took leave.

The peasants, among themselves, also blamed her

for her laxity concerning Paul's communion. Though they did not attend the services, did not take communion, or only approached the holy table on Easter day according to the formal injunction of the Church, it was different with the children. All of them would have shrunk from the audacity of bringing a child up godlessly, for, after all, religion is religion.

Jeanne was fully aware of this disapproval, and waxed indignant at the hypocrisy, the universal fear of censure, and the cowardice which reside in the hearts of men, and which, when they come to the surface, appear under such respectable masks.

The Baron took Paul's education in hand and began to teach him Latin. "Above all things, you must not tire him," his mother repeated again and again. Her father had forbidden her to enter the room where Paul studied, because she interrupted them continually to inquire: "Are your feet cold, Poulet?" or "Have you a headache, Poulet?" She would interrupt the teacher to say: "Don't make him talk so much, you will injure his throat." So she had to be content to linger near the class-room.

As soon as Paul had finished his lessons, he would go into the garden with his aunt and his mother. They had all taken a great fancy to gardening; and the three planted young trees in the spring, sowed seeds whose growth they watched with delight, trimmed the shrubbery, and cut flowers to make bouquets.

Paul's greatest pleasure was the cultivation of various salads. He owned four large beds in which he grew romaines, lettuces, escaroles, and almost all the known species of these edible leaves. He dug and watered and planted and weeded with the help of his "mothers," who worked like scrub-women. For hours at a time they kneeled in the salad-bed, staining their dresses and their hands to insert the roots of young plants in the holes they dug in the ground with their fingers.

Paul was nearly fifteen years old and was growing tall; the measure in the drawing-room marked sixty-three inches, but he was a child in mind, ignorant and foolish, and spoiled by the two women and his old grandfather, who was not of his time.

Finally, one evening, the Baron mentioned college. Jeanne began at once to cry and Aunt Lison concealed herself in a dark corner of the room.

"Why should he need so much education?" replied the mother. "We will make a country squire of him, a gentleman farmer. He will look after his property like a great many other noblemen. He will live happy and grow old in this house, where his parents have lived before him, and will probably die here. What more could he wish for?"

But the old man shook his head. "What would you say if he should come to you when he is twenty-five years old and say: 'Mother, I am nothing, I know nothing, through your fault, through your maternal selfishness. I feel unable to work, to become some one, and still I was not made for the obscure, humble, and sad life to which your short-sighted affection has condemned me.'"

But Jeanne only wiped away her tears, and turning to the boy: "Tell me, Poulet," she said, "you will never reproach me for having loved you too much, will you?"

"No, mamma," replied the tall lad with astonishment.

"Will you swear it?"

"Yes, mamma."

"You would rather remain here, wouldn't you?"

"Yes, mamma."

But the grandfather spoke firmly: "Jeanne," he said, "you have no right to dispose of his life. What you are doing is cowardly and almost criminal; you are sacrificing your son to your own happiness."

She buried her face in her hands and sobbed convulsively: "I have been so miserable — so miserable! Now that I am getting a little happiness out of life, you want to take my boy away. What will become of me — all alone now?" she stammered through her tears.

Her father rose, went over to her, and taking her into his arms he whispered: "Do you forget me, Jeanne?" She threw her arms around his neck and kissed him tenderly, then making an effort to control her voice she replied: "Yes. Perhaps — you are right — father. Of course, I was foolish, but I have suffered a great deal. I am quite willing that he should go to college, now."

Without knowing exactly what his fate was to be, Poulet also began to whimper. So his "three mothers" kissed him and petted him and encouraged him. When they retired to their rooms, their hearts were heavy, and all, including the Baron who had contained himself, soaked their pillows with tears that night. They decided that they would send the young man to the college at Havre at the begin-

ning of the winter term; so during the whole summer he was more petted and spoiled than ever.

His mother often shrank at the thought of the
approaching separation. She bought him enough
clothes to last him during a ten-years' voyage; and
then, one morning in October, the two women and
the old man started out with him in the family coach
drawn by two horses.

During a previous trip, they had selected his place
in the dormitory and his desk in the class-room.
Jeanne and Aunt Lison spent the whole day arranging his effects in his little bureau drawers. As the
latter could not contain more than a quarter of his
clothes, his mother went to the principal and requested him to give her another one.

An official was called in, and said that such a
quantity of underwear and effects would only be an
encumbrance and would never be used; and referring
to the rules of the college, he declined to furnish
another bureau. Jeanne was so disappointed that she
decided to rent a room in a nearby hostelry for the
purpose of storing the clothes, and gave the proprie-
tor instructions to take the boy anything he might
require. After that, they took a stroll on the pier to
watch the vessels go out to sea.

Twilight descended mournfully over the city, and
one by one the lights began to twinkle in the darkness. They had dinner in a restaurant, but none of
them cared to eat. They looked at each other with
moist eyes, while the waiter brought their order, and
took away the food untouched. Then they started
to walk to the school. Children of all sizes were
arriving from all parts, accompanied either by rela-

tives or servants. A great many of them were crying. In the large, dimly lighted courtyard, muffled sobs could be heard all over.

Jeanne and Poulet hugged each other for a long while. Aunt Lison hung back, with her face buried in her handkerchief; she was forgotten, as always. But the Baron, who was beginning to give way to his feelings, hastened the parting. The coach was waiting in front of the door; Aunt Lison, Jeanne, and the Baron got in, and it started on its homeward journey through the night. Every little while a stifled sob floated through the darkness.

Jeanne spent the next day in tears. The day after, she had the phaeton harnessed and drove to Havre. Poulet seemed already to have made up his mind to the separation. For the first time in his life he had companions, and his desire to play with them was so strong that he could hardly keep on his chair in the parlor.

Jeanne went to see him every two days and took him out on Sunday. During the study hours, she remained in the parlor, for she did not have the strength or the courage to leave the school. Finally, the principal was obliged to ask her to make her visits less frequent, but she paid no attention to his request.

Then he warned her that if she continued to interfere with her son's recreations and studies, he would be compelled to send the boy home; he also dropped the Baron a line to that effect. So they kept a strict watch on her at the " Poplars," and she was not allowed to go to the college. She looked forward to each vacation with more anxiety than her boy.

A perpetual restlessness dwelt in her soul. She began to take long walks in the country, her only companion being the dog, Slaughter. She would sometimes stay out all day, sitting on the cliff during a whole afternoon to watch the surf, or walking to Yport, through the same forest paths she had trodden when a girl. How distant it all seemed, how distant seemed the times when, as a young girl, she walked along the country lanes dreaming and building castles in the air.

Every time she saw her son, it seemed to her that they had been separated ten years. He was growing more like a man from month to month; and from month to month Jeanne was becoming an old woman. Her father appeared to be her brother, and Aunt Lison, who did not age, because at twenty-five she was already faded, looked like her elder sister.

Poulet was not working very hard; he succeeded in pulling through the first two years, but the third and fourth were less successful and when he was twenty years old he was in the class of rhetoric.

He had grown to be a tall, blonde fellow, with the semblance of a mustache and it was he who now came to the "Poplars" every Sunday. He had taken riding lessons since he was a boy, and so he simply hired a horse and rode over in two hours.

Jeanne started out early in the morning to meet him, taking Lison and the Baron along. The latter was growing more and more bent, and walked like an enfeebled old man, with his hands behind his back, so as to keep himself from pitching forward.

They strolled leisurely along the road and sat down on the bank whenever they felt tired, keeping their eyes on the end of the lane for the young horseman. As soon as he appeared, looking like a black speck on a white line, the three old people waved their handkerchiefs. Then he started his horse on a gallop and dashed up to them like a hurricane, a feat which always made his mother and his aunt tremble with fear and elicited enthusiastic approbation from his impotent grandfather.

Though Paul was a head taller than his mother, she always treated him like a little boy, and would make such remarks as: "I hope your feet are not cold, Poulet?" When he walked out on the stoop after breakfast to smoke a cigarette, she would open the window and say: "Please don't go out without your hat, you will take cold."

And she trembled with anxiety when he started back to the city at nightfall. "Now do not ride rashly, Poulet, I beg of you; think of your poor mother who would die if anything should happen to you."

One Saturday morning she received a note from Poulet, stating that he would not be able to see them the following day, because some friends had arranged an outing and had asked him to join them. Her whole Sunday was spent in torturing anxiety, as if she were under an impending misfortune; and on Thursday, she started for Havre, because she could not bear the suspense any longer.

Paul appeared changed to her, though she could not define in what way. He was livelier and spoke in a deeper voice. All of a sudden, as if it were the most natural thing in the world, he said: "Well, mamma, since you came to-day, I will not spend

211

Sunday at the 'Poplars because we are going on another outing."

His words produced a shock in her, and she felt as forlorn as if he had told her he was going to some distant country. Then, when she had recovered her composure sufficiently to speak, she exclaimed:

"Oh! Poulet, what is the matter with you? Tell me, what is it?"

But he only laughed, and kissing her he said: "Why, nothing, mamma. I am going to enjoy myself with friends, that's all."

She could not find a reply and while she was driving home alone in the carriage, curious thoughts came to her. This was not her Poulet, her little Poulet of bygone days. For the first time, she noticed that he was a man, that he had drifted away from her and wished to live his own life without being hampered by the old people at home. He seemed to have changed in a day. What! Was this her son, her little boy who used to make her dig holes in the earth for him to plant salads, this tall, bearded man, whose will had manifested itself so strongly?

During three months, Paul appeared at the "Poplars" only once in a while, and always plainly showed his desire to leave as soon as possible. Each evening he tried to find an excuse for going away an hour earlier. Jeanne was alarmed, but the Baron tried to console her by saying: "Leave him alone, dear, the boy must sow his wild oats."

But one morning a poorly dressed man inquired with a strong German accent for "Madame la Vicomtesse." After much bowing and scraping, he drew forth from his pocket a soiled wallet saying: "I have a little paper for you," and he handed her a piece of greasy paper. She read it, reread it, looked at the Jew, reread it again and inquired:

"What does this mean?"

The man replied with an obsequious bow: "I will explain. Your son, he needed a little money, and as I knew that you are a good mother, I lent him a little something for his needs."

Jeanne was trembling. "But why did he go to you, why didn't he come to me?"

Then the Jew entered into a lengthy explanation about a gambling debt that had to be settled the following day before noon, adding that Paul was a minor and that nobody would lend him money and that "his honor would have been compromised," had he not been obliging enough to advance the young man a little sum.

Jeanne made a motion to call the Baron, but she could not rise from her chair, so severe had the shock been to her nerves. Finally she asked the usurer if he would be kind enough to ring the bell.

Fearing some trap the man hesitated, and stammered: "If I am intruding, I can come another day." Jeanne shook her head. He rang the bell; and without speaking a word, both waited for the Baron.

When the latter arrived, he took in the situation at a glance. The draft was for fifteen hundred francs. He laid down a thousand, and looking the Jew in the eyes: "Never come here again," he said. The man thanked, bowed, and disappeared.

The mother and grandfather started at once for Havre; but when they went to the college, they were

informed that Paul had not put in appearance there
for a month. The principal had received four letters
signed by Jeanne, telling of the boy's sickness and
then giving news of his recovery. Each letter was
accompanied by a physician's certificate; of course all
were forgeries. They were so stunned by this revelation that they remained looking at each other
blankly, forgetting, in their bewilderment, to leave.

The principal felt disconsolate over the whole occurrence and took them to the police station. Afterward Jeanne and her father went to a hotel. Next
day, Paul was found with a woman of bad repute.
His grandfather and his mother brought him back to
the "Poplars" without once addressing a word to
him, Jeanne was crying in her handkerchief. Paul
gazed at the country indifferently.

In a week they discovered that during the last
three months of his college course, he had incurred
debts amounting to fifteen thousand francs. The
creditors had remained away at first, for they knew
that in a few months he would attain his majority.
No explanation took place. His mother and grandfather thought they could reclaim him with kindness.
They cooked delicacies for him, they petted and
humored him.

It was in the spring; they rented a boat for him
at Yport in spite of Jeanne's apprehensiveness, so that
he could go sailing whenever he chose. But they
prohibited horseback riding, for they were afraid he
would return to Havre. He spent the summer in
idleness, and was irritable and even brutal at times.
The Baron worried over his neglected education, and
though Jeanne was disconsolate at the idea of giving

214

him up, she could not but realize that something had to be done with the boy.

One evening, he stayed away. They heard that he had gone sailing with two fishermen. His crazed mother ran bareheaded to Yport in search of him. A few men remained on the wharf to await the return of the boat. A small light gleamed in the distance and drew near. Paul had left the fishermen, after they had rowed him to Havre.

This time the police failed to discover a trace of him. The woman who had hidden him once before had disappeared also, having paid her rent and sold her belongings. In Paul's room, at the "Poplars," they found two letters written by this creature, who seemed madly in love with him. She spoke of a trip to England, having found, she said, the necessary funds. The three inhabitants of the château, silent and gloomy, lived in a sort of moral hell. Jeanne's gray hair had almost turned white. She often wondered why fate had dealt so hard with her.

She received a note from Abbé Tolbiac, saying:

"Madame, the hand of God has descended upon you. You refused to give Him your son; He has now taken him from you and thrown him in the arms of a prostitute. Will your eyes not open at this heavenly warning? The mercy of God is infinite. Perhaps He will forgive you if you come and kneel at His feet. I am His humblest servant, and will open the door for you whenever you knock."

She kept the letter a long while on her knees, unfolded. Perhaps what this priest said was true. And her conscience was rent by religious uncertainties. Could God be as jealous and vindictive as men? If He were not jealous, nobody would fear

Him, nobody would worship Him. So as to bettei manifest Himself to His creatures, He no doubt assumed their feelings and sentiments. And the cowardly doubt which draws sufferers to the Church entered her soul.

At nightfall, one day, she stole to the rectory, and kneeled at the feet of the lean abbé to implore his absolution.

The priest promised her half-pardon, because, he said, the Lord could not grant all His mercies to a house which sheltered such a man as the Baron. "You will soon experience the effects of God's divine mercy," he added. Indeed, two days later, she received a letter from her son; and in her troubled state, she considered it as the first manifestation of the Lord's interference.

"Mother, do not worry. I am in London and am well, but need money badly. We haven't got a cent and some days we have to go without food. The woman who is with me and whom I love with all my soul has spent all she possessed to remain with me: it was five thousand francs; you will understand me when I say that for the sake of my honor I must pay her back before anything else. I would be greatly indebted to you if you would advance me about fifteen thousand francs of papa's inheritance as I will soon attain my majority. You will help me a great deal.

"Good-bye, mother dear, I send you and grandfather and Aunt Lison my best love and hope to see you soon.

"Your son,

"VICOMTE PAUL DE LAMARE."

He had written! So, after all, he had not forgotten her! She did not reflect that he asked for money. She would send him some if he was in need of it. What did the money matter, as long as he had written! And she ran in tears to the Baron to show him the letter. They called Aunt Lison, and read over, word for word, the sentences Paul had written, and discussed their purport.

Jeanne, flying from complete despair to a sort of hopeful intoxication, took her son's part: "As long as he has written to us, he will surely come back."

"Nevertheless, he left us for that woman. He must think more of her than he does of us, since he did not even hesitate," replied the Baron calmly.

A sudden and horrible pang thrilled Jeanne's heart; and immediately her hatred rose against this creature who had stolen her son's love — an unappeasable, savage, maternal jealousy. Till now, all her thoughts had been for Paul. She had hardly reflected that this creature was responsible for his waywardness.

But the Baron's remark had suddenly evoked the rival and revealed her fatal power, and Jeanne felt that between this woman and herself a battle for supremacy had begun. She also felt as if she would rather lose her son entirely than share him with his mistress.

All her joy had vanished. They forwarded fifteen thousand francs and heard nothing more of him for five months.

Then an attorney presented himself to settle up the details of Julien's legacy. Jeanne and her father rendered their accounts without a murmur, and even gave up the interest of the fortune, which rightfully belonged to the mother as long as she lived.

Paul returned to Paris and came into one hundred and twenty thousand francs. Then, in six months, he wrote four letters, giving them, in curt terms,

217

news of his health, and ending up with cool protestations of affection.

"I am working," he wrote; "I have found a position at the Bourse. Some day I hope to be able to visit the 'Poplars,' dear mother."

He never wrote a word about his mistress; and this silence meant more than if he filled four pages about her. Under her son's icy words, Jeanne felt the influence of the courtesan, that ever watchful and implacable foe of mothers. The three hermits consulted about what could be undertaken to save Paul, but they could not reach any decision. A journey to Paris? What good would it do? "Time will wear out his love; he will come back to us of his own accord," said the Baron. But nevertheless their life was pitiable.

Jeanne and Lison stole to church together, unknown to the Baron. A long time elapsed before they received any news, and then, one morning, they were startled by a desperate letter.

"Mother dear, I am lost, I can only blow my brains out unless you come to my rescue. A speculation from which I hoped to derive large profits has fallen through; I owe forty-five thousand francs. If I do not pay up, it means ruin, dishonor, and the blighting of my future. I am lost. I repeat that I will blow out my brains rather than survive this disgrace. I would have done it already had it not been for the encouragement of a woman whom I never mention in my letters and who is my Providence. I kiss you with all my heart, dear mother, perhaps for the last time. Good-bye.

"PAUL."

Bundles of commercial data, forwarded with this letter gave detailed explanation of the catastrophe.

The Baron replied by return mail that all would be settled; then he left for Havre to inform himself of the extent of the disaster. He also mortgaged his estates for the sum that was sent Paul. The young man wrote three letters full of enthusiastic thanks and passionate expressions of affection and announced his imminent arrival at the "Poplars." But he never came.

A whole year elapsed. Jeanne and the Baron had decided to go to Paris to make one last attempt to bring him home, when they learned through a note that he was again in London organizing a company to control a steamship line under the name of "Paul Delamare and Co."

"There is a fortune in it for me," he wrote. "I do not run any risk. You can easily comprehend its advantages. When I see you again, I will have made my mark in life. There is nothing like business to pull a man through, nowadays."

Three months later the steamship company was declared bankrupt, and the manager was being prosecuted for irregularities in the books of the concern. Jeanne had an attack of hysterics that lasted several hours; then, she took to her bed. The Baron left again for Havre, consulted attorneys, lawyers, sheriffs and found out that the deficit of the Delamare company amounted to two hundred and thirty-five thousand francs.

So he mortgaged his property again. The château and the two farms were heavily involved. One evening, as he was attending to the last formalities in the office of his lawyer, he was stricken with an attack of apoplexy. Jeanne was hastily summoned to her father's side, but he died before she could reach him. She brought his body back to the "Poplars," and her sorrow was so great that it approached torpor more than despair. Abbé Tolbiac refused to allow a Church burial, in spite of the desperate entreaties of the two women. So the Baron was interred at nightfall, without any religious ceremony whatever.

Paul heard the news through one of his liquidators. He was still hiding in England. He wrote to excuse himself for having remained away, saying that he had heard of the death too late to be present. "In fact," he said, "now that you have pulled me out of that scrape, mother dear, I will return and see you soon." Jeanne lived in such a state of dejection that it seemed as if her mind must give way.

Near the end of the winter, Aunt Lison, who was sixty-eight years old, took a cold which degenerated into pneumonia; and she quietly passed away, whispering: "My poor little Jeanne, I will ask the Lord to take pity on you."

Jeanne followed her remains to the cemetery, saw the earth fall on the coffin, and as she sank to the ground with a desire to die, to end her torments, a strong peasant woman lifted her in her arms and carried her off as if she were a child.

Arriving at the château, Jeanne, who had spent five sleepless nights with Lison, suffered herself to be undressed by this unknown country woman, who treated her with great gentleness and authority; and then she sank into a slumber caused by exhaustion and suffering.

In the middle of the night, she awoke. A glow-lamp flickered on the mantelpiece. A woman was

sleeping in an armchair. She did not recognize her
and leaned over the edge of the bed to have a
better view of her features, illumined by the flickering light of the wick that floated on the oil in the
tumbler.

It seemed to her, though, that she had seen her
face before. But when? But where? The woman
was slumbering peacefully, with her head on her
shoulder and her cap on the floor by her side. She
was heavily built, high-colored, square, and powerful.
Her large hands fell on either side of the chair. She
had grayish hair. Jeanne, in the bewilderment of
mind which follows after the feverish slumber caused
by great trouble, looked at the woman steadily.

Of course she had seen her face! Had it been in
former days? Had it been recently? She could not
tell, and the puzzle excited and troubled her. She
crept out of bed noiselessly to take a look at the
sleeper, and approached her on tiptoe. It was the
woman who had carried her from the cemetery and
had put her to bed. She remembered this much con-
fusedly. But had she met her before, at another
period of her life? Or was it only that she imagined
she recognized her; and how had she come into her
room? Why?

The woman opened her lids, saw Jeanne, and
rose hastily. They faced each other and were so
close that their bosoms touched. The stranger grumbled: "What! you are up! You will catch cold.
Go right back to bed, now!"

"Who are you?" Jeanne asked.

But the woman opened her arms and lifting her
bodily from the floor, she carried her to the bed.

She laid her gently on the sheets and leaning over her, she began to cry and kiss her cheeks, her eyes, her hair, wetting the pillow with her tears. "My poor mistress, Mam'zelle Jeanne, don't you remember me?" she exclaimed.

Jeanne cried: "Rosalie," and throwing her arms around the woman's neck, she hugged and kissed her. For a moment both sobbed as if their hearts would break, clinging to each other's neck, unable to separate. Rosalie was the first to regain her composure: "Come, now, you must be good," she said, "and not take cold." She smoothed the covers, tucked them in, and then arranged the pillow under her former mistress's head. Jeanne continued to sob, for old recollections had arisen. Finally she inquired: "How did you come back, Rosalie?"

"Do you think that I would have left you all alone now?" the woman replied.

"Light a candle so that I can look at you," said Jeanne. And after Rosalie had placed the light near the bed, the women gazed at each other without a word. Then Jeanne took the hand of her maid and said: "Rosalie, I should never have recognized you, for you have changed very much, but less than I have."

Rosalie gazed at the faded, white-haired woman, whom she had left young and beautiful, and replied: "Yes, you have changed, Madame Jeanne, and more than is necessary. But just think that we have not seen each other for twenty-four years."

They paused for a while to reflect. Then finally Jeanne stammered: "At least I hope you have been happy?"

But Rosalie, fearing to awaken some pang in her mistress's heart, stuttered: "Why, yes — yes — Madame. I needn't complain,— no, no! I have been happier than you. There was only one thing I regretted, and that was to have left this place—" She paused abruptly, frightened at what she had said unthinkingly. But Jeanne replied gently: "Well, Rosalie, one cannot always do as one wishes. You are also a widow, I think?" Then in a trembling voice she added: "Have you other — other children?"

"No, Madame."

"And your — your son — what has become of him? Are you satisfied with him?"

"Yes, Madame, he's a good boy and a worker. He got married six months ago and is going to take my farm, now that I have come back to stay with you."

"You will stay with me, then, Rosalie?" whispered Jeanne, trembling with emotion.

"Of course, Madame, I have made all my arrangements," she replied abruptly.

Then they were silent for a while. In spite of herself, Jeanne kept comparing their respective lives, without bitterness, however, for now she was resigned to the cruelties of fate.

"Was your husband kind to you?" she inquired.

"Oh! he was a good man, Madame, a hard worker who managed to save some money. He died of consumption."

Then Jeanne sat up in bed and desired to hear everything. "Tell me all about your life, Rosalie, it will do me good, to-day," she said.

223

The woman drew up a chair and began to speak of herself, of her house, her surroundings, entering with spirit into the details dear to country people, describing her farm, laughing over some recollections and raising her voice as she went on, after the fashion of a woman used to issuing commands. Finally she declared:

"Oh, I possess a snug little fortune, and need have no fear for the future." Then she grew embarrassed again and continued in a lower voice: "Nevertheless, I owe all this to you, Madame; and I do not expect any wages. No, indeed! No, indeed! And if you do not like it, I will go away again!"

"You do not imagine that you are going to work for me for nothing, do you?" Jeanne replied.

"Yes, indeed, Madame. Money — you to give me money! Why, I have nearly as much as yourself. Do you even know what is left after all your loans and mortgages and interests that have never been paid and that increase from term to term? Do you know? No, you do not. Well, I tell you that you haven't even an income of ten thousand francs. Not ten thousand francs, do you know that? But I will look after all that now, and quick, too." She spoke in loud tones, indignant at the way these things had been neglected and at the ruin that threatened Jeanne. While she spoke, a faint smile of emotion spread over her mistress's face.

"You must not laugh at all this, Madame, because without money one is nobody," she cried.

Jeanne took her hands in hers and held them a long while; then she said slowly — she was always possessed by the one thought: "Oh! I have had no luck in my life. Everything has gone wrong for me. Fate has been very cruel."

Rosalie shook her head: "You should not speak that way, Madame, no, you should not. You were unhappily married, that is all. It really doesn't do, anyhow, to get married the way you did, without thoroughly knowing your suitor."

After that, they continued to speak of themselves like two old friends. And they were still talking when the sun rose.

CHAPTER XII.

A New Home

IN EIGHT days Rosalie had taken the management of the household affairs into her own hands. Jeanne was resigned to everything and obeyed her passively. Feeble and weak on her legs, like her mother used to be, she took short walks leaning on Rosalie's arm. The maid chided her, comforted her with tender and abrupt words, and treated her altogether like a sick child.

They always spoke of old times, Jeanne with tears in her voice and Rosalie in the even and impassive tones of a peasant. The old servant referred several times to the interests which were due; then she insisted that the papers which Jeanne concealed from her out of shame for Paul should be turned over to her at once.

For a week, Rosalie went to Fécamp every day, to seek information from a notary she knew, regarding transactions she did not understand. Then, one evening, after she had tucked her mistress in bed, she sat down by her side and said abruptly: "Now that you are in bed, Madame, let's talk business."

And she explained the whole situation to Jeanne. After everything was settled, there would remain an income of from seven to eight thousand francs. Not a sou more.

"It can't be helped, Rosalie! I feel as if I shall not make very old bones, anyway; it will be sufficient for me," Jeanne replied.

But this angered Rosalie: "Maybe it will be, Madame; but how about M. Paul? Don't you intend to leave him anything?"

Jeanne shivered: "Please never mention him to me. The thought of him makes me suffer too much."

"On the contrary, I must speak to you about him; you see. Madame Jeanne, you are not at all reasonable. He is wayward now, but he will not always be so; he will get married some day and have children. He will have to have money to support them, won't he? Listen to me attentively. You must sell the 'Poplars'!"

Jeanne sat up in bed with a start "Sell the 'Poplars'! Oh! never! never!" But Rosalie was not to be deterred. "I tell you that you will sell the place, Madame, because you must."

And she explained her plans, calculations, and arguments. If they sold the "Poplars" and the two adjoining farms to a purchaser she had found, they would be able to retain the property situated at Saint-Léomard, which, if all the mortgages were paid up, would yield an income of eight thousand three hundred francs. Thirteen hundred francs would be laid aside each year for repairs and the management of the farms; there would be seven thousand francs left from which five thousand francs would be deducted for living expenses; the remainder would constitute an emergency fund.

"All the rest is lost," she added; "there is not a cent left. And I will keep the key to the bank, too, and as for M. Paul, he won't get another penny, not one; he would make away with your last cent."

Jeanne, who was crying silently, murmured: "Yes, but suppose he has not enough money to buy food?"

"Well, if he is hungry, let him come back home. There will always be a bed and enough to eat for him. Do you think he would have committed all those follies if you had not given him any money in the beginning?"

"But he had debts and would have been dishonered for life."

"When all your money is gone, will that prevent him from making them? You paid once, that is all right; but you will not pay again, I tell you that. Now, good night, Madame."

And she went out of the room. After she left, Jeanne did not close her eyes, for the thought of selling the "Poplars" and leaving the house where she had spent her life almost crazed her.

The next morning, when Rosalie entered the room, she said: "I will never be able to leave here, Rosalie."

The servant grew angry: "It will have to be, though, Madame. The notary is coming in a little while with the man who wants to buy the château. If you do not sell it, you will not have a penny left in the world in four years."

Jeanne was annihilated and kept repeating: "I never can; I never will be able to."

An hour later, the postman brought her a letter from Paul, in which he asked for a loan of ten thousand francs. Terrified, Jeanne consulted Rosalie, who threw up her hands and exclaimed:

"There, what did I tell you, Madame? You both would have been ruined if I hadn't come back." And Jeanne, giving way to her servant's wish, wrote to her son as follows:

"MY DEAR BOY: I can do nothing more for you. You have ruined me. As it is, I am obliged to sell the 'Poplars.' But never forget that you will find a home with your old mother to whom you have brought so much suffering.   JEANNE."

When the notary came with M. Jeoffrin, a retired sugar-refiner, she received the gentlemen personally and showed them all over the place.

A month later, she had signed the selling contract, and at the same time had acquired a little house near Goderville on the road to Montvilliers, in the hamlet of Batteville.

She walked till dusk in her mother's alley, distressed in heart and mind and addressed a desperate farewell to the trees, the horizon, the moldy bench under the plane-tree, to all the things she knew so well, to the arbor, to the little hill in front of the meadow where she had sat so often, and from where she had watched the Comte de Fourville on that terrible day of Julien's death, to an old headless tree where she used to lean, to all the familiar garden. Rosalie had to come out and lead her away.

A tall peasant about twenty-five years old was waiting in front of the door. He greeted Jeanne in a friendly tone, as if he had known her for years. "Good day, Madame Jeanne are you well? Mother told me to look after the moving. I would like to know what you want to take, because I will do it little by little, so as not to interfere with my farm work." It was her servant's son, Julien's child, and Paul's brother.

It seemed to Jeanne as if her heart would stop beating, and still she felt as if she could have kissed the young man. She looked him over keenly, to see if she could discover any likeness between him and her husband or her son.

He was red, vigorous, blue-eyed, and fair-haired, like his mother. And still he looked like Julien. In what way? She could scarcely tell, but something about his whole face reminded her of his father.

The young man continued: "If you could show me the things now, I would be very much obliged to you."

But Jeanne had not decided what she wished to take with her, as her new house was so small, so she asked him to call again at the end of the week. Then the thought of moving gave her a new preoccupation and put a little distraction into her monotonous life.

She went from room to room in quest of furniture that was linked in her mind with events: friendly objects which were part of her life and almost of her being, which she had known since childhood and to which clung memories of joys and sorrows; they were like dates in her life's history, mute companions of her joyful and sad hours, which had aged with her and had become worn and tattered.

She chose the pieces one by one; oftentimes hesitating as to what she wanted to take, changing her mind every minute, or wavering between the choice of two chairs or an old writing desk or work-table.

She opened all the drawers in an attempt to remember events of the past. Finally, after she had said: "Yes, I will take this," the object was carried down and placed in the dining-room. She wanted to keep her entire bedroom set, the bed, the clock, the hangings, everything in fact.

She took a few tapestry parlor-chairs, the ones that had amused her as a child; the "fox and the stork," the "fox and the raven," the "ant and the grasshopper," and the "melancholy heron." Then, as she had visited all the corners of the house she was soon to leave, she went up one day to the garret.

She paused in astonishment at the threshold; a multitude of things greeted her eyes, some broken, some only soiled and put away because they were no longer attractive and had been replaced. Jeanne perceived a number of things which were familiar to her and which had disappeared long ago without attracting her attention. Trifles which had surrounded her for fifteen years, whose existence she had never noticed before, but which, now that she had seen them alongside of other familiar objects, she remembered distinctly, were suddenly invested with the importance of forgotten witnesses and long-lost friends. They gave her the impression of being like some people whom one meets frequently without ever discovering their inner thoughts, and who one night, without warning, begin to talk about themselves, and to our utmost amazement reveal their unsuspected souls.

She went from one thing to the other, palpitating with emotion and whispering to herself: "Why, I cracked this china cup, one night, a few days before I was married. Oh! here is mother's little lantern, and the cane that father broke the day he tried to open the wooden gate that was warped by the rain."

There were also a great many things she did not recognize, for they had belonged to her grandparents, things which seemed out of place and out of date, whose history was unknown, nobody having seen those who had chosen, purchased, possessed, and loved them, nobody having known the hands which had touched them fondly, or the eyes that had gazed at them with delight.

Jeanne found pleasure in fingering and examining these dust-covered relics, and stayed a long while in the wonderful attic, under the pale light which crept through the glass panes in the roof. She made a careful examination of some three-legged chairs, to see whether she could remember anything about them, and also of a brass bed-warmer, a dented foot-warmer which seemed familiar, and of a quantity of broken kitchen furnishings.

Then she made a list of the things she wished to take away, and went downstairs to send Rosalie after them. The indignant servant refused to carry down "that trash." But Jeanne, though she had no will left at all, remained firm for once and her order had to be obeyed.

One morning, Denis Lecoq, the young farmer, Julien's son, drove up with a cart to take away the first load. Rosalie accompanied him so as to direct the unloading and the arrangement of the furniture.

Left alone, Jeanne began to wander through the rooms of the château in a fit of agonizing despondency, kissing through sheer love the things she had to leave behind, the large white birds in the drawing-room tapestries, the old candlesticks, in fact, everything she came across. She rushed from one room into the other, her eyes brimming with tears and her brain in a whirl. Then she went out to say farewell to the ocean.

It was near the end of September, and a gray, leaden sky hung over the earth; the yellowish surf stretched far out of sight. Jeanne stood for a long while on the cliff, rolling gloomy thoughts in her mind. Then, as darkness settled, she went back to the château, having experienced more suffering during that day than during any of her previous trials.

Rosalie had returned and was waiting for her; she was delighted with the new dwelling, and declared that it was a great deal more cheerful than this big barn which wasn't even built by the road. Jeanne cried during the whole evening.

Since the peasants had heard that the château was sold, they only showed Jeanne the respect which was absolutely due her. Among themselves they called her "the mad woman," without knowing exactly why, but no doubt because they guessed, with their brutish instinct, her constant sickly sentimentality, her exaggerated ideas, and the disturbance of her poor, suffering soul.

The day before her departure, she stepped by chance into the stables. A low growl caught her ear. It was Slaughter, whom she had not thought of for months. Blind and paralyzed, arrived at a really extraordinary age for a dog, he existed precariously on his straw bed, cared for by Ludivine who had not forgotten him. Jeanne took him in her arms and kissed him, and then carried him into the house. He was heavy, and could hardly stand on his stiff, spread legs, and he barked like those toy dogs which are children's delight.

Finally, the last day dawned. Jeanne had slept in Julien's former bedroom, because her own was empty of furniture. She got out of bed exhausted and out of breath as if she had been running. The wagon containing the trunks and the rest of the furniture was already standing in the yard. A two-wheeled cart was hitched to the back, for the mistress and maid.

Old Simon and Ludivine were to stay until the new owner arrived, and then they were going to live with some relatives, for Jeanne had provided a small pension for them. Besides, they had put aside some money. They were very old now, and had grown garrulous and useless. Marius, having taken a wife, had left long ago.

At about eight o'clock, it began to rain; it was a sort of fine and icy drizzle, driven by a slight ocean breeze. They were obliged to spread covers over the top of the cart. Already the leaves were falling from the trees.

Two cups of coffee stood on the kitchen table. Jeanne sat down in front of hers and sipped it slowly; then, after a while, she rose and said: "Let us go." She put on her hat, her shawl, and while Rosalie drew on her mistress's rubbers she said: "Do you remember, Rosalie, how it rained when we left Rouen to come here?"

234

She had a sort of spasm, put her hands to her heart and fell backward in a faint. For a full hour Jeanne seemed to be dead; then she opened her eyes and was seized with convulsions that were accompanied by torrents of tears.

After she grew a little calmer, she felt so weak that she could not get up. But Rosalie, who feared that other attacks would occur if their departure was deferred, called in her son. They took hold of Jeanne, carried her into the cart and laid her on the wooden bench covered with oil cloth; then the maid wrapped up her mistress's legs, laid a heavy cloak over her shoulders, opened an umbrella, and cried: "Now, hurry up, Denis; we must be off."

The young man climbed up by the side of his mother and sitting on one leg, because there was no room, he started the horse on a brisk trot that jolted the passengers at every turn of the wheels. When they got to the end of the village, they saw some one who was walking back and forth in the road; it was Abbé Tolbiac who seemed to be watching for them.

He stopped to let the cart pass. He held up his cassock with one hand, for fear of soiling its edge with mud, and his thin, black-stockinged legs ended in immense muddy pumps.

Jeanne dropped her eyes so as to avoid his glance, but Rosalie, who was aware of everything, became enraged. "Loafer, loafer!" she murmured, and taking hold of Denis's hand, she muttered: "Son, give him a splashing."

Just as they overtook the priest, the young man let the wheels of his cart sink into the deep tracks of the road, and a stream of mud spurted up and drenched the clergyman from head to foot.

Radiant at this, Rosalie turned around and shook her fist at him, while the priest pulled out his handkerchief to dry his clothes. They had been on their way about five minutes, when Jeanne suddenly exclaimed: "We have forgotten Slaughter."

They had to stop, and Denis, clambering down from his seat, ran back to fetch the creature, while his mother held the reins. The young man reappeared after a while with the dog in his arms, and set the shapeless and scabby brute between the two women.

CHAPTER XIII.

THE QUEST FOR PAUL

Two hours later, the wagon stopped in front of a little brick house built in the midst of a pear-orchard, alongside of the road. Four arbors covered with clematis and honeysuckle formed the corners of the garden, which was divided into little vegetable plots separated by narrow paths bordered with fruit-trees.

A very high hedge inclosed the whole property, which was separated by a field from the neighboring farm. On the road, about a hundred feet away, was a blacksmith's shop. The nearest dwellings were situated a kilometer from the house. The view extended over the Plaine de Caux, dotted with farms inclosed by double lines of tall trees which bordered the apple-orchards.

When they arrived, Jeanne wished to rest, but Rosalie would not permit it, for fear she would relapse into her musings. The carpenter from Goderville was there, ready to help them with the installation; so while waiting for the second cart-load they began at once to arrange the furniture they had brought.

It proved a difficult task and required much concerted argument and reflection. After an hour or so, the cart appeared again at the gate and had to be unloaded in the rain. When night came, the house was in a frightful condition, filled from top to bottom with things piled up high; and that night Jeanne, who was exhausted, dropped asleep as soon as she laid her head on the pillow.

During the following days, she was kept so busy that she did not have time to pause for reflection. She even took a certain amount of pleasure in arranging her new dwelling, because the idea that her son would return to her some day never left her.

The tapestries which had hung in her former bedroom were used in the dining-room, which was at the same time a parlor; and she gave especial care to the furnishing of one of the two rooms on the upper floor, giving it in her mind the designation of "Poulet's apartment."

She reserved the second room for herself, and let Rosalie have the one above, next to the attic. The little house was really attractive, and during the first few weeks Jeanne liked it, though she felt that something was missing, though what it was she could not tell.

One morning, the clerk of the notary in Fécamp brought her three thousand six hundred francs, the price of the furniture left at the "Poplars," which had been valued by an upholsterer. On receiving this money, Jeanne felt a tremor of joy, and as soon as the

man left, she put on her hat to go to Goderville for
the purpose of sending this unexpected sum to Paul.

But as she was walking hurriedly toward the
town, she met Rosalie coming back from market.
The servant at once felt suspicious, though she did
not immediately guess the truth; but when she found
it out, for Jeanne could not hide a thing from her
now, she set her basket on the ground and began to
scold in loud tones, with her fists on her hips. Then,
taking hold of her mistress with one arm and carrying the basket on the other, she continued her way
homeward. As soon as they reached the house, she
insisted that her mistress should turn the money over
to her, which Jeanne did, but not without holding
back the six hundred francs.

But Rosalie, whose suspicions were thoroughly
aroused, saw through her scheme at once and forced
her to hand over the entire amount. The servant,
however, consented to let the small sum be sent to
Paul. The latter wrote to thank his mother a few
days afterward:

"You did me a great favor, mother dear, for we
were in great distress."

But Jeanne could not get used to Batteville; it
seemed as if she could not breathe there as she was
wont to and she felt more than ever before alone,
forsaken, and lost. She would go out for a walk,
would reach the hamlet of Verneuil, would come
back by Trois-Mares and, arriving home, would feel
as if she must start out again because she had forgotten to go just where she desired to walk.

It was the same way every day, and she could
not comprehend the reason of this strange feeling.

But one night, she unconsciously spoke a sentence which revealed to her the secret of her restlessness. In sitting down to dinner, she exclaimed: "Oh! how I would like to see the ocean."

What she longed for was the ocean, which had been her neighbor during twenty-five years, the ocean with its salt air, its furies, its roaring voice, its invigorating breezes, the ocean which she perceived every morning from her room at the "Poplars," whose breath she inhaled night and day, the ocean which was so near, and which she had learned to love like a human creature without being conscious of it.

Slaughter, too, was very restless. Since the night of his arrival, he had chosen to lie at the bottom of the kitchen dresser and would not budge from his selected nook. He lay there all day long, almost motionless, only turning once in a while, with a little grunt.

But at night he would get up and drag himself into the garden, knocking blindly against the walls. Then, when he had stayed out sufficiently, he would walk back, sit himself down in front of the warm stove, and as soon as his mistress had retired, would begin to howl.

He howled all night long in a pitiable and dreary voice; once in a while he would stop for an hour or so, and then begin again in a different key. They chained him to a barrel in front of the house. Then he howled under the windows. And as he was crippled and almost dying, they let him come back into the kitchen.

Sleep became impossible for Jeanne, who was kept awake by the scratching and whining of her old

friend in his unceasing attempts to familiarize himself
with his new home, which he knew well was not
his own. Nothing could quiet him. Asleep during
the day, as if the knowledge of his blindness and his
infirmities prevented him from moving when all
other beings are about, he began to prowl about as
soon as darkness set in, as if he did not dare live or
move except at night when all beings are sightless.
One morning, he was found dead. It was a great
relief to everyone.

Winter was almost over; and Jeanne was invaded
by an unconquerable despondency. It was not one
of those acute sorrows that wear out the very fiber
of the soul, but rather a gloomy and depressing sadness.

No distractions came to her. Nobody bothered
about her. The road in front of her door stretched
to the right and to the left, quite empty most of the
time. Once in a while, a wagon was driven past the
house by a red-faced peasant, whose blouse, inflated
with wind, looked like a blue balloon; sometimes it
was a slow cart that she saw, or two people in the
distance, a man and a woman, who seemed at first
like specks on the horizon and who grew till they
approached the house and then diminished again till
they looked like two insects, far away, at the end of
the white road, which stretched out of sight, disappearing and reappearing according to the undulations
of the ground.

When the grass began to grow, a little girl in
short skirts passed in front of the house every day,
guarding two lean cows which grazed along the
ditches of the road. At night she returned in the

same drowsy manner, taking a step after her cattle, about every ten minutes.

Every night Jeanne dreamed that she still lived at the "Poplars." She was back home with her father and mother and sometimes with Aunt Lison. She lived her former life over again, and often imagined she was supporting Madame Adelaide as the latter strolled up and down her alley. And each of Jeanne's awakenings was followed by tears.

She always thought of Paul and wondered: "What is he doing? What does he look like, now? Does he sometimes think of me?" While wandering slowly through the fields, she would turn in her mind thoughts that tortured her; but she suffered mostly through the hatred she bore the woman who had stolen her son. This hatred, alone, kept her from taking any action toward bringing him back, from going to see him.

She imagined his mistress opening the door for her and saying: "What is it you wish here, Madame?" Her maternal dignity rebelled at the possibilities of such a meeting, and the lofty pride of a pure woman, who had led a blameless life, exasperated her against the cowardice of the man enslaved by physical passion, a passion which debases the heart. Humanity seemed disgusting to her, when she thought of all the foul secrets of the senses, of the caresses that pollute, of all the mysteries of carnal relations.

Spring and summer passed. But when fall, with its long, rainy days, its gray sky and dark clouds returned, she felt such a disgust with everything that she decided to make one last effort to reclaim Poulet. The young man's passion had probably worn itself out by this time, she thought. So she wrote him an imploring letter:

"MY DEAR CHILD: I entreat you to come back to me. Remember that I am ill and old and all alone year in and year out, with a servant. I now live in a small house near the road and am very unhappy. But if you were home, all that would be changed. I have no one but you in the whole world and we have not seen each other for seven years!

"You will never know how unhappy I have been or how I have longed for you. You were my life, my dream, my one hope, my one love, I needed you and you have forsaken me. Oh! come back, my little Poulet, come back to me, come back to your old mother who stretches forth her arms to you. JEANNE."

A few days later, he answered her as follows:

"MY DEAR MOTHER: Indeed I would like to come back home, but I haven't a penny. Send me some money and I will come. In fact, I wanted to see you so as to speak to you of a plan which would allow me to do as you wish.

"The affection and unselfishness of the woman who has been my companion in the dark days through which I am struggling are absolutely unlimited. It is impossible for me to remain any longer without acknowledging publicly her faithful and devoted love. Besides, she has very good manners, which you will be sure to appreciate. She has a good education and is very well read. And you can't imagine what she has always been to me. I would be a brute if I did not show her some gratitude. So I have come to ask you to consent to our marriage. You would forgive my follies and we would all live together in your new house.

"If you knew her, you would give your consent immediately. I assure you that she is perfect and is really very refined. I am sure you would like her. As for me, I could not live without her.

"I am impatiently awaiting your reply, and we both send you our love. "Your son,

"VICOMTE PAUL DE LAMARE."

Jeanne was stunned. She sat motionless awhile with the letter lying unfolded on her lap. She guessed the scheme of the woman who had kept her son away for so many years biding her time, watching for the day when the old and despairing mother, unable to resist the desire to hold her boy in her arms, would weaken and consent to anything.

And she felt a pang to think of the obdurate preference of her son for this creature. She kept repeating: "He does not love me. He does not love me." When Rosalie entered the room, Jeanne stammered: "Now he wants to marry her."

Rosalie started: "Oh! Madame! you can't allow that! M. Paul is not going to marry that creature."

And Jeanne, crushed though she was, rebelled: "Never! Rosalie! Never! And as he does not care to come, I will go and bring him back and we will see which of us will win!" And she wrote immediately to notify Paul of her arrival and to make arrangements to see him away from the home he shared with this woman.

Then, while she waited for an answer, she began to prepare for her trip. Rosalie packed her underwear and clothes in an old trunk. But as she was folding an old country dress, she exclaimed: "Why, you haven't got a thing to wear! I won't allow you to go like that. You would make everybody feel ashamed; and the Parisian ladies would look upon you as a servant."

Jeanne let her have her way, and both women went to Goderville to choose a green checked material which was given to the dressmaker of the town to be made up. Then they went for information to M. Roussel, the notary, who spent two weeks in

Paris once a year. Jeanne had not seen the capital for twenty-eight years.

He gave her advice concerning the best manner of avoiding accidents in the crowded thoroughfares, and of avoiding robbery, and told her that she had better sew her money in her clothes and only keep the necessary change in her purse. He spoke about moderate-priced restaurants and mentioned a few patronized by women; and he said that at the Hotel de Normandie, near the depot, where he always stopped while in the city, Jeanne might use his name if she desired to.

The trains which were so talked about had already been in operation for six years between Paris and Havre. But Jeanne, absorbed in her sorrows, had never seen those great steam carriages which wrought such a revolution in her section of the country.

Paul had not answered his mother's letter. She waited a week, then two, going every morning to meet the postman to ask him in quavering tones: "Haven't you a letter for me, Père Malandain?" And the man, whose voice was roughened by all kinds of weather, always replied: "Nothing to-day, my good lady."

Surely it was that woman who prevented Paul from writing! So Jeanne resolved to delay her departure no longer. She wanted Rosalie to go with her, but the maid refused, so as not to increase the expenses of the journey.

She would not permit her mistress to take more than three hundred francs with her: "If you need more," she said, "you can write me, and I will go to the notary and ask him to send it to you. If I give you more, now, M. Paul will take it away from you."

One December morning, they got into Denis Lecoq's cart and drove to the station. First they bought the tickets, and then, when everything had been settled and the trunk was registered, they waited by the iron tracks, trying to understand the mechanism of the road, and so absorbed in the contemplation that for a while they forgot the sad reasons for Jeanne's trip.

Finally, a distant whistle made them look around, and they perceived a big, black machine drawing near. It rushed up with a frightful noise and passed in front of the two women, hauling along a chain of little, rolling houses. A trainman opened a door and Jeanne, after kissing Rosalie, got into one of the little houses. Rosalie stood on the platform and shouted: "Good-bye, Madame; a pleasant journey; come back soon!"

"Good-bye, Rosalie," replied Jeanne.

A whistle blew again and the whole chain of carriages moved out of the station, at first very slowly, then more rapidly and, finally, attained terrific speed. In Jeanne's *coupé*, two gentlemen had installed themselves in opposite corners.

Jeanne watched the country, the farms, the trees, the villages pass before her eyes with lightning rapidity, and felt as if she had entered upon a new life, and was going to some unknown world, totally different from the monotonous surroundings of her childhood. When the train arrived at Paris, it was getting dark. A man took charge of Jeanne's baggage, and she followed him nervously through the crowd, almost running, for fear she might lose sight of him.

When she arrived in the office of the hotel she quickly stated that she had been recommended there by M. Roussel. The woman at the desk, a ponderous mass of flesh, inquired: "Who is M. Roussel?" Jeanne, slightly taken back, replied: "Why, he is the notary of Goderville, who comes every year."

The fat woman responded: "That is possible. I do not know him. Do you wish a room?"

"Yes, Madame."

So a porter picked up her trunk and went upstairs in front of her to a room. Jeanne's heart was heavy. She sat down in front of a little table and asked for a cup of bouillon and a piece of chicken. She had not eaten anything since dawn. She ate her meal drearily by the light of a candle, thinking of a thousand things; she remembered her trip through Paris when returning from her honeymoon, and some of Julien's traits of character that had cropped out at that time. But she was young and confident and hopeful then. Now she felt old, embarrassed, and even frightened, and weak and nervous concerning the most trivial occurrence.

When she finished her meal she stood at the window and looked at the crowded street below. She wanted to go out, but she did not dare to do so. She would surely lose her way, she thought. So she went to bed, first putting out the candle.

But the noise, and the feeling of being in a strange place, and the excitement of the journey, kept her awake. The noise of the street quieted down little by little, without bringing her rest, for the semi-stillness of large cities made her uneasy. She was used to the calm, deep sleep of the country which pervades everything, men, beasts, and plants; and now all around her she felt a singular and mysterious restlessness.

Voices, almost inaudible, reached her ears through the walls of the hotel. Sometimes the floor cracked, a door slammed, or a bell rang.

All of a sudden, at about two o'clock in the morning, just as she was falling asleep, a woman screamed in the next room; Jeanne sat up abruptly in bed; then she thought she heard a man's laugh. Then, as day began to dawn, thoughts of Paul invaded her, and she dressed as soon as light appeared in the sky.

He lived in the Rue du Sauvage, in the city. She thought she would walk to his house, so as to obey the rules of strict economy that Rosalie had set down for her. The weather was fine; the cold air stung her face; busy people ran hither and thither.

Jeanne walked along as quickly as possible, following a street that had been shown her and at the end of which she was to turn to the right, then to the left; then, when she reached a square, she was to ask her way again. She did not find the square, and asked a baker, who gave her different directions. She started off again, made a mistake, wandered about, followed more directions and, finally, was hopelessly lost.

Almost crazed with fright, she wandered around aimlessly. She was going to hail a cab, when she suddenly came in sight of the Seine. Then she wandered along the quay.

After an hour or so, she entered the Rue du Sauvage, which was a very narrow and dark little street. She stopped in front of the door, so agitated that she could not take a step. Poulet then, was here, in this very house.

She felt her hands and knees tremble; but she went in, traversed a corridor, saw the *concierge's* office and, holding forth a coin, said: "Will you go upstairs and tell M. Paul de Lamare, that an old lady, a friend of his mother, would like to speak to him?"

"He does not live here any more, Madame," the man replied. A tremor ran through Jeanne.

"Where does he live now?" she stammered.

"I don't know," he said.

She felt as if she were going to fall and for a while she could not utter a sound. Then, with a violent effort, her reason came back to her and she murmured:

"When did he leave?"

The man replied volubly: "About two weeks ago. They just left one night and never came back. They owed money all around; so you can understand why they didn't leave their address."

Jeanne saw lights before her, big streams of fire, as if some one had touched off a cannon in front of her eyes. But she was sustained by a fixed idea that kept her up and made her appear calm and collected. She wanted to know everything and to find Poulet.

"Then he didn't say anything when he left?" she continued.

"Oh! no, nothing whatever; they just left so as not to pay, that's all."

"But doesn't somebody come for his letters?"

"Oftener than I would give them. But then, you know, they hardly received ten a year. I took them one, though, just two days before they left."

That was probably Jeanne's letter. "Listen," she said hurriedly, "I am his mother and I have come for him. Here are ten francs. If you should have any news or any information, come and see me at the Hotel de Normandie in the Rue du Havre, and I will pay you well."

"Depend on me, Madame," the man replied.

Then Jeanne left. She did not care now where she went. Still she walked rapidly as if she was striving to keep an important engagement. She ran along, knocking now and then against people carrying bundles; she crossed streets without paying any heed to the carriages and was insulted by their drivers; she stumbled across the gutters and continued on her journey, absolutely forgetful of her surroundings.

All of a sudden she found herself in a garden; she felt so tired that she sank down on a bench.

She must have stayed there a long while, crying softly to herself, for passers-by stopped to look at her. Then she felt cold and rose to go; she was so broken and weak that her legs almost refused to carry her.

She wanted to stop to take some food but dared not enter a restaurant because she felt that her sorrow was plainly visible to all. She would stop in front of an entrance and peep in, and when she saw the people sitting at the tables within, she would flee saying to herself: "I will go into the next one."

But she did not enter into the next restaurant any more than into the preceding one.

Finally, she bought a small roll in a bakery and began to eat it in the street. She was very thirsty, but as she did not know where to go to quench her thirst, she denied herself.

Jeanne passed under an archway and entered into another garden surrounded by arches. She recognized it as the Palais-Royal. As the sun and the exercise had warmed her, she sat down again for an hour or two. A crowd was in the garden, one of those fashionable, bowing, smiling crowds, whose women are beautiful, whose men are wealthy, persons who only live for show and pleasure. Jeanne, feeling out of place in the midst of the gay throng, rose to go; but suddenly she had the idea that Paul might be among these people and she began to mingle with them, scanning each face eagerly.

People turned around to look after her, others laughed and pointed her out. She noticed it and fled, for she knew that her appearance, and the checked dress chosen by Rosalie and made by the village dressmaker, excited their derision.

She did not even dare to ask her way from passers-by. But at last she addressed one and found her hotel again. She passed the remainder of the day on a chair at the foot of her bed. Then she ate some soup and a little meat like on the previous evening and then she retired; but she performed each one of these acts mechanically, out of force of habit.

The following day she went to the police station to ask the authorities to help her in her search for her son. Nothing definite could be promised; but the matter would be kept in mind, they said.

Then she wandered through the streets, always hoping to meet Paul. And she felt more alone, more lost, and more miserable in the midst of the busy crowd than in the deserted fields.

When, at night, she went back to the hotel, she was informed that a man had asked for her on behalf of M. Paul, and that he would come back the next day. A rush of blood mounted to her heart, and she never closed her eyes that night. Supposing it were he? Yes, surely it was Paul, though from the details she had gathered she did not recognize him.

About nine o'clock in the morning, she heard a rap on her door and cried: "Come in!" ready to fly to her son with open arms. But instead of Paul, a stranger entered. And after he had excused himself for having intruded upon her, he explained that he had come to collect one of Paul's debts. While he talked, Jeanne felt that in spite of herself she was crying, and she strove to wipe away the tears with her finger tips as soon as they appeared in her eyes.

The man had been told of her arrival by the *concierge* of the Rue du Sauvage and, as he was not able to find the young man, he addressed himself to his mother. Then he handed her a paper that she took mechanically. She read a cipher, 90 francs, pulled out her purse and paid the man.

That day she did not go out. The following morning some other creditors appeared. She gave them all she had, only keeping a few francs and wrote to Rosalie telling her of the situation.

She spent her days wandering about waiting for a reply. She did not know what to do with herself nor how to kill the time that hung heavily on her hands, for she had nobody to speak a kind word to her, nobody who knew of her misery. She strolled around aimlessly, haunted by an increasing desire to return to her little house built by the solitary roadside.

A few days before, she could not endure it, on account of the immense sadness with which it filled her, but now, on the contrary, she felt as if she would not be able to exist anywhere else but in that dreary little home.

At last, one evening, she found a letter and two hundred francs. Rosalie wrote:

"MADAME JEANNE: Come back quickly, for I shall not send you any more money. As regards M. Paul, I will go for him myself as soon as we get news from him.

"I send you my respectful greetings.

"Your servant,   ROSALIE."

So one snowy and very cold morning, Jeanne returned to Batteville.

CHAPTER XIV.

LIGHT AT EVENTIDE

AFTER she reached home, she did not go out, but remained in the house, awaiting events. Every morning she arose at the same hour, looked out of the window at the weather and then went downstairs to sit in front of the fire. She would sit there days at a time, motionless, with her eyes riveted on the bright flames, letting her pitiable thoughts wander far away, and going over the mournful events of her unhappy life.

Little by little, darkness would settle in the little room, without Jeanne stirring once; though, from time to time, she would throw some wood on the dying embers. Then Rosalie would bring in the lamp and exclaim: "Why, Madame Jeanne, you must move about a little, or else you will have no appetite again this evening."

Jeanne was pursued by fixed ideas which tortured her, and was possessed by forebodings which assumed undue importance in her sick mind. Again and again she lived over the past, the old, old past, with its first important events,— her honeymoon in far-away Corsica. From the embers of the fire rose before her eyes long-forgotten landscapes of the beautiful isle; and she remembered every detail of the trip,— all the faces she had met there. Jean Ravoli, the guide, haunted her; sometimes she thought she could hear his voice.

Then she reviewed the happy years of her son's childhood, the time when he used to make her do gardening, when she kneeled on the soft ground beside Aunt Lison, both of them seeking to please the child and trying to out-do each other in their skillful handling of the plants.

And her lips would murmur low: "Poulet, my little Poulet," as if he were beside her; and then, her dream ending with the word, she would try for hours to write on space, with her pointed finger, the letters which composed the name. She traced them slowly before the fire, imagining at first that she could see them, and then, fancying that she was mistaken, she would begin all over again, starting with P and writing out the entire word. At last, growing exhausted from the exertion, she mixed the letters, formed other words, and finally stopped, almost crazed with nervousness. She possessed all the manias of solitary beings. If the place of the smallest thing in the room was changed, it irritated her beyond measure.

Rosalie insisted on her taking exercise, and made her walk up and down on the road in front of the house; but at the end of twenty minutes, Jeanne would declare: "I cannot go any further, Rosalie," and would sit down on the edge of the ditch. Soon, all motion became unbearable to her, and she kept to her bed as much as possible. But one habit had clung to her since childhood: it was to arise immediately after she had taken her coffee. Besides, she cared for her morning cup in an exaggerated manner, and had she been deprived of it, she would have felt its loss more keenly than anything else.

Every morning Jeanne waited for Rosalie's appearance with an almost sensual impatience; and as soon as the full cup had been placed on the little table beside her bed, she would sit up and drain it with relish. Then, throwing off the bedclothes, she would begin to dress.

But little by little she grew accustomed to linger in bed a few minutes after she had finished the coffee; and from day to day she prolonged this habit until Rosalie would angrily re-enter the room and dress her almost by force. In fact, she no longer possessed even an appearance of will-power, and every time the servant asked her advice or her opinion she would reply: "Do as you like about it, Rosalie."

She believed so firmly that she was pursued by ill-luck that she grew to be as fatalistic as an Oriental. She was so used to seeing her hopes shattered and her dreams crushed that she did not dare to undertake a single thing, and hesitated for days at a time before performing the simplest action, because she felt sure that she would always choose the wrong road, and that everything she touched would turn out badly.

Every moment of the day she would say: "I have had no luck in my life." Then Rosalie would exclaim: "What would you say if you had to earn your living, if you had to get up every morning of your life at six o'clock to go out by the day? There are a great many women, though, who are compelled to do it and when they grow too old to work, have to die in the poorhouse."

"But remember that I am quite alone in the world, Rosalie, and that my son has forsaken me," replied Jeanne.

Then the maid would answer, angrily: "Well, what of it! Think of all the sons that are in the army, and of those who go and establish themselves in America!" To her, America was some undefined land where people went to make their fortunes, and never returned.

"There always comes a time when people must separate, because the old and the young are not made to live together," she continued. Then, in a ferocious tone she continued: "And what would you say if he were dead?"

After that, Jeanne would keep silent.

During the first days of spring, when the air was mild, she gained a little in health, but she only used her renewed activity to plunge deeper and deeper into her dreary thoughts.

When one morning she went up to the attic to search for something, she came across a case filled with old calendars which had been put away, as it is the custom of some old country folk to do. She took them and carried them downstairs. They were of all sizes, some small and some large. She began to assort them on the dining-room table. All at once, she laid her hand on the first one that she had brought with her to the "Poplars."

She gazed at it for a long time; she had scratched the days since the morning of her departure from Rouen after she had left the convent. And she began to cry. The tears coursed slowly and silently down her cheeks; they were tears of an old, unhappy woman who was looking at her wrecked life laid out in front of her on the table.

Suddenly an idea came to her, and grew to be a terrible, ceaseless obsession. She wanted to remember each day of her life.

So she tacked the yellow calendars on the walls, over the tapestries, and spent hours before each one, trying to think: "What happened during that month?"

As she had underlined the memorable dates of her life, she was able to reconstitute whole months, putting together one by one, grouping, linking all the little events that had preceded or followed an important period.

By sheer obstinacy, concentrated will, and effort of mind, she succeeded in re-establishing in their entirety the first two years she spent at the "Poplars," and the memories of her life flocked back to her with surprising lucidity and relief.

But the years that followed seemed cloudy and undefined, and encroached one upon the other; and sometimes she remained hours at a time, bending over a calendar, straining her mind to remember the past; but somehow she could not even recall if that calendar was the proper one to peruse in her search for missing recollections.

Then, when the sap of the trees stirred under the rays of the sun, when the crops began to grow in

the fields and the trees to bud, when the apple-trees
in the orchards blossomed like pink snowballs and
perfumed the plain, a great agitation took hold of
Jeanne.

She could not keep in one place and went back
and forth twenty times a day. In her restlessness
she would go for long walks, from which she would
return exhausted and miserable.

The sight of a daisy growing in the grass, a sun-
beam playing amid the leaves, a pool of water reflecting the azure of the sky, troubled her, mellowed
her, because they brought back long-forgotten sensations, like echoes of her girlhood emotions.

At the time when her future was still clad in
mystery and brightness, she had had the same feelings, had experienced the same intoxication which
accompanies the first days of spring. In her heart
she still felt the old charm of it all; but at the same
time she suffered from it, as if the eternal joy, penetrating as it did her shriveled skin, her thinning
blood, her crushed soul, could only produce a painful
and weakened sensation. It also seemed as if all her
surroundings had slightly changed. The sun was not
so warm as in her youth, the sky was a paler blue,
the grass a paler green, and the flowers were less
perfumed and less colored and did not intoxicate her
as in former days.

Sometimes, nevertheless, such a sensation of
warmth pervaded her being that she would give way
to hope, expectation, and dreams of the future; for,
when the world is so beautiful, it is possible to hope,
in spite of the cruelty of fate.

She walked and walked hours at a time, as if she

were impelled to do so by the excitement that filled her soul. Often she would stop suddenly and sit down by the roadside to think of something sad. Why had she not been loved like other women? Why had she been deprived of the most simple joys of a calm and placid existence?

She forgot sometimes — for a moment — that she was old, that there was nothing left for her, except a few solitary and weary years in this world; that her road had been traveled; and she made happy plans like she used to do when she was a girl. But it was not long before the sensation of reality over-whelmed her; and she would get up feeling crippled, as if her loins were bent by a heavy load. Then she would wander toward her little house, murmuring: "Oh! you old fool! you old fool!"

Rosalie kept repeating to her: "Do be quiet, Madame, what makes you move about so much?"

"Well, I am like Slaughter was, in his last days," Jeanne replied sadly.

One morning the maid brought in her coffee a little earlier than usual, and, setting the cup on the table, said: "Drink it quickly, Madame; Denis is at the door waiting for us. We are going to the 'Poplars' because I have some business to attend to there."

Jeanne felt so agitated that she thought she would faint; and she dressed herself tremblingly, frightened and charmed at the idea of seeing her old home again. A radiant sky hung over the world; and the old nag, feeling its oats, broke into a gallop once in a while. When they neared Etouvent, Jeanne felt her breath coming shorter, and when she caught sight of the brick pillars of the gate, she said to herself two or three times in low tones: "Oh! oh! oh!" just as one exclaims involuntarily at things that revolutionize all our feelings.

They unharnessed the horse at Couillards'; and while Rosalie and her son attended to their business, the farmers proposed that Jeanne should take a look at the château, as its inhabitants were absent; so they handed the keys to her.

She started out alone, and when she found herself in front of the old mansion, by the wing overlooking the sea, she paused to consider it. Nothing was changed on the outside. That day the walls of the grayish manor were illuminated with sunshine. But all the shutters were closed.

A piece of dried twig fell on Jeanne's dress, and when she lifted her eyes, she saw that it came from the plane-tree. She went up to the big tree and stroked its smooth, pale trunk as if it were a creature. She knocked her foot against a piece of rotten wood in the grass: it was the last fragment of the bench on which she had sat so often with her parents, of the bench that had been placed there on Julien's first visit.

Then she went to the storm-door of the vestibule; she unlocked it with difficulty, for the heavy key was rusted and would not turn; but having opened a window, she remained transfixed in front of the familiar and beloved horizon, the arbor, the meadow, the trees, and the ocean, flecked with brown sails that seemed motionless in the distance.

Then she began to wander all through the empty dwelling. She looked for familiar spots on the walls.

She stopped in front of a little hole that her father had bored in the plaster, for, in remembrance of his youth, the Baron often found amusement in fencing with his cane, and knocking the wall in this place.

In her mother's room, she found, back of the door, in a dark corner, a fine gold hairpin she had stuck there years ago (she recalled it all now), and had looked for many a time. Nobody had discovered it. She took it and kissed it like a relic.

She went all over the house, recognizing as she went, the almost invisible traces in the hangings which had not been renewed, and saw again the strange faces that our imagination often makes out of the figures on stuffs, marble, and smoky ceilings.

She walked noiselessly, all alone in the immense, silent château; to her it was somewhat like a cemetery, for was not all her life buried within its walls?

She entered the drawing-room. The shutters were closed and the apartment was quite dark. But her eyes soon became accustomed to the obscurity, and little by little she discovered the wide tapestries decorated with birds. Two armchairs had remained in front of the fireplace as if their occupants had just risen from them; and even the smell of the place, the smell which it had retained, its vague, but easily distinguishable odor, penetrated Jeanne's nostrils and filled her with recollections.

She stood transfixed, with her eyes riveted on the chairs, trying to fill her lungs with that breath of the past. And suddenly, in an abrupt hallucination engendered by her fixed idea, she thought she saw distinctly her father and mother warming their feet before the fire. Terrified, she fell back against the door, which she grasped to prevent a fall, while her eyes remained glued on the fireplace.

But the vision had disappeared. For a few minutes, she was horrified; then she slowly regained her composure and determined to leave the room at once, for she feared that if she did not, she would lose her mind. Then, by mere chance, her glance fell on the door; she perceived Poulet's scale.

The light marks cut the wood at unequal intervals; and then there were ciphers, too, that indicated the ages, the months, and the growth of her son. Sometimes it was the Baron's large handwriting, then her own, a trifle smaller, and then Aunt Lison's uncertain script. And it seemed to Jeanne that the child of long ago was before her now, with his blond curls which he pressed against the wall when they measured him. The Baron would exclaim: "Jeanne, he has grown a quarter of an inch in six weeks."

And she began kissing the marks in a frenzy of love.

But a voice was calling her. It was Rosalie, who was shouting: "Madame Jeanne, Madame Jeanne, breakfast is waiting for you."

And Jeanne came out of the château in great excitement. She could hardly understand what they said to her. She ate the things put before her, listened to their talk without understanding its meaning, spoke to the farmers who inquired concerning her health, let herself be kissed, kissed in return the cheeks which were offered to her, and finally got into the cart and was driven away.

When she lost sight of the high roof of the château, hidden among the trees, she felt as though her heartstrings would snap, for she knew that she had said good-bye forever to her old home. So they returned to Batteville.

As she was about to enter the house, she noticed something white under the door; it was a letter which the postman had put there during her absence. She saw at once that it was from Paul and opened it with trembling hands. He wrote:

"MY DEAR MOTHER: I did not write sooner because I did not want to bring you to Paris on a useless errand, as I had the intention of coming myself to see you. At the present time I am experiencing great difficulties. My wife is dying from the birth of a little daughter, who came into the world three days ago; I haven't a penny. I do not know what to do with the child, who just now is being cared for and brought up on the bottle by the janitress, but I am afraid I may lose her.

"Couldn't you take her? I really do not know what to do and I have no money to send her to board in the country. Please answer by return mail.   Your loving son,

"PAUL."

Jeanne sank on a chair, hardly able, in her agitation, to call Rosalie. After the maid had appeared, both women read the letter over and gazed at each other a long while, mutely. Then Rosalie said:

"I will go and fetch the child, Madame; we cannot leave it there."

Jeanne replied: "Very well, Rosalie."

Then they paused again; finally the servant said: "Put on your hat, Madame, and let us go to the notary in Goderville. If that woman is going to die,

M. Paul must marry her, for the child's sake, you know."

Without a word, Jeanne put on her hat. A deep and unavowed joy filled her heart, a wicked joy, which she sought to hide in every possible way, one of those abominable joys that make us blush, but that we feel keenly far down in the mysterious recesses of our soul: her son's mistress was dying.

The notary gave Rosalie much detailed information, which he had to repeat several times; then, when she was sure of herself she said: "Now, fear nothing, I will take charge of everything." She left for Paris the same night.

Jeanne spent two days in extreme mental agitation and was incapable even of collecting her thoughts. But on the third morning, she received a short note from Rosalie announcing the latter's arrival on the evening train.

At about three in the afternoon, Jeanne had a neighbor's cart drive her to the Beuzeville station, and there she waited for the servant.

She stood on the platform with her eyes riveted on the rails which stretched out of sight and closed at the end of the horizon. Once in a while she looked at the clock. Ten minutes more. Five minutes more. Two minutes more. Now it was time for the train. Still nothing appeared on the distant tracks.

But all of a sudden, she perceived a white speck, it was smoke, and then a black patch that grew and grew and rushed along at high speed. At last, the heavy locomotive slowed up, passed in front of Jeanne, and stopped. Several doors opened; people got out, peasants wearing blouses, farmers' wives with baskets, *bourgeois* in soft hats. Finally, Jeanne caught sight of Rosalie, carrying what seemed to be a white bundle.

She wanted to go to meet her, but she did not dare take a step, for her knees shook beneath her. Rosalie saw her mistress and came up with her usual calmness of expression: "Good day, Madame," she said, "I am back and not without trouble, either."

"Well?" Jeanne stammered.

"Well, she died last night," replied Rosalie. "They were married, and here's the child." And she held up the infant which was buried in its white clothes.

Jeanne took it mechanically and both women left the station and got into the carriage.

"M. Paul will come as soon as the funeral is over. Probably to-morrow, on the same train," Rosalie continued.

Jeanne murmured: "Paul—" and then was silent.

The sun was setting in the distance and bathing with golden light the green fields, flecked here and there with the red blood of the poppies and the azure tints of the cornflowers.

An infinite peace lay over the calm earth in which the seeds were germinating. The cart was bowling along at a good pace, and the peasant who drove it kept exciting the horse with his tongue. Jeanne kept her eyes straight on the sky, watching the arched flight of the swallows. Then, suddenly, a feeling of warmth penetrated her lap; it was the warmth of the little creature she held on her knees.

An infinite emotion invaded her. She uncovered the face of the child, for she had not looked at it yet; her son's daughter. And as the frail creature opened its blue eyes under the glaring light, and puckered its mouth, Jeanne kissed it rapturously, smothering it against her breast.

But Rosalie, happy and grumbling, stopped her: "Come, come, Madame Jeanne, stop; you will make her cry."

Then, as if answering one of her own thoughts, she added: "You see, life is never quite as bad or as pleasant as one imagines it is."

MADEMOISELLE FIFI

THE Major Graf* von Farlsberg, the Prussian commandant, was reading his newspaper, lying back in a great armchair, with his booted feet on the beautiful marble fireplace, where his spurs had made two holes, which grew deeper every day, during the three months that he had been in the château of Urville.

A cup of coffee was smoking on a small, inlaid table, which was stained with liquors, burnt by cigars, notched by the penknife of the victorious officer, who occasionally would stop while sharpening a pencil, to jot down figures, or to make a drawing on it, just as it took his fancy.

When he had read his letters and the German newspapers, which his baggage-master had brought him, he got up, and after throwing three or four enormous pieces of green wood on to the fire — for these gentlemen were gradually cutting down the park in order to keep themselves warm — he went

* Count.

268

to the window. The rain was descending in torrents, a regular Normandy rain, which looked as if it were being poured out by some furious hand, a slanting rain, which was as thick as a curtain, and which formed a kind of wall with oblique stripes, and which deluged everything, a regular rain, such as one frequently experiences in the neighborhood of Rouen, which is the watering-pot of France.

For a long time the officer looked at the sodden turf, and at the swollen Andelle beyond it, which was overflowing its banks, and he was drumming a waltz from the Rhine on the window-panes, with his fingers, when a noise made him turn round; it was his second in command, Captain Baron von Kelweinstein.

The major was a giant, with broad shoulders, and a long, fair beard, which hung like a cloth on to his chest. His whole, solemn person suggested the idea of a military peacock, a peacock who was carrying his tail spread out on to his breast. He had cold, gentle, blue eyes, and the scar from a sword-cut, which he had received in the war with Austria; he was said to be an honorable man, as well as a brave officer.

The captain, a short, red-faced man, who was tightly girthed in at the waist, had his red hair cropped quite close to his head, and in certain lights almost looked as if he had been rubbed over with phosphorus. He had lost two front teeth one night, though he could not quite remember how. This defect made him speak so that he could not always be understood, and he had a bald patch on the top of his head, which made him look rather like a monk, with a fringe of curly, bright, golden hair round the circle of bare skin.

The commandant shook hands with him, and drank his cup of coffee (the sixth that morning) at a draught, while he listened to his subordinate's report of what had occurred; and then they both went to the window, and declared that it was a very unpleasant outlook. The major, who was a quiet man, with a wife at home, could accommodate himself to everything; but the captain, who was rather fast, being in the habit of frequenting low resorts, and much given to women, was mad at having been shut up for three months in the compulsory chastity of that wretched hole.

There was a knock at the door, and when the commandant said, "Come in," one of their automatic soldiers appeared, and by his mere presence announced that breakfast was ready. In the dining-room, they met three other officers of lower rank: a lieutenant, Otto von Grossling, and two sub-lieutenants, Fritz Scheunebarg, and Count von Eyrick, a very short, fair-haired man, who was proud and brutal toward men, harsh toward prisoners, and very violent.

Since he had been in France, his comrades had called him nothing but "Mademoiselle Fifi." They had given him that nickname on account of his dandified style and small waist, which looked as if he wore stays, from his pale face, on which his budding mustache scarcely showed, and on account of the habit he had acquired of employing the French expression, *fi, fi donc,* which he pronounced with a slight whistle, when he wished to express his sovereign contempt for persons or things.

The dining-room of the château was a magnificent long room, whose fine old mirrors, now cracked by pistol bullets, and Flemish tapestry, now cut to ribbons and hanging in rags in places, from sword-cuts, told too well what Mademoiselle Fifi's occupation was during his spare time.

There were three family portraits on the walls; a steel-clad knight, a cardinal, and a judge, who were all smoking long porcelain pipes, which had been inserted into holes in the canvas, while a lady in a long, pointed waist proudly exhibited an enormous pair of mustaches, drawn with a piece of charcoal.

The officers ate their breakfast almost in silence in that mutilated room, which looked dull in the rain, and melancholy under its vanquished appearance, although its old, oak floor had become as solid as the stone floor of a public-house.

When they had finished eating, and were smoking and drinking, they began, as usual, to talk about the dull life they were leading. The bottles of brandy and of liquors passed from hand to hand, and all sat back in their chairs, taking repeated sips from their glasses, and scarcely removing the long, bent stems, which terminated in china bowls painted in a manner to delight a Hottentot, from their mouths.

As soon as their glasses were empty, they filled them again, with a gesture of resigned weariness, but Mademoiselle Fifi emptied his every minute, and a soldier immediately gave him another. They were enveloped in a cloud of strong tobacco smoke; they

seemed to be sunk in a state of drowsy, stupid intoxication, in that dull state of drunkenness of men
who have nothing to do, when suddenly, the baron
sat up, and said: "By heavens! This cannot go on;
we must think of something to do." And on hearing this, Lieutenant Otto and Sub-lieutenant Fritz, who
pre-eminently possessed the grave, heavy German
countenance, said: "What, captain?"

He thought for a few moments, and then replied:
"What? Well, we must get up some entertainment,
if the commandant will allow us."

"What sort of an entertainment, captain?" the
major asked, taking his pipe out of his mouth.

"I will arrange all that, commandant," the baron
said. "I will send *Le Devoir* to Rouen, who will
bring us some ladies. I know where they can be
found. We will have supper here, as all the mate-
rials are at hand, and, at least, we shall have a jolly
evening."

Graf von Farlsberg shrugged his shoulders with a
smile: "You must surely be mad, my friend."

But all the other officers got up, surrounded their
chief, and said: "Let the captain have his own
way, commandant; it is terribly dull here."

And the major ended by yielding. "Very well,"
he replied, and the baron immediately sent for *Le
Devoir*.

The latter was an old corporal who had never
been seen to smile, but who carried out all the orders
of his superiors to the letter, no matter what they
might be. He stood there, with an impassive face,
while he received the baron's instructions, and then
went out; five minutes later a large wagon belonging

to the military train, covered with a miller's tilt, galloped off as fast as four horses could take it, under the pouring rain, and the officers all seemed to awaken from their lethargy, their looks brightened, and they began to talk.

Although it was raining as hard as ever, the major declared that it was not so dull, and Lieutenant von Grossling said with conviction, that the sky was clearing up, while Mademoiselle Fifi did not seem to be able to keep in his place. He got up, and sat down again, and his bright eyes seemed to be looking for something to destroy. Suddenly, looking at the lady with the mustaches, the young fellow pulled out his revolver, and said : "You shall not see it." And without leaving his seat he aimed, and with two successive bullets cut out both the eyes of the portrait.

"Let us make a mine!" he then exclaimed, and the conversation was suddenly interrupted, as if they had found some fresh and powerful subject of interest. The mine was his invention, his method of destruction, and his favorite amusement.

When he left the château, the lawful owner, Count Fernand d'Amoys d'Urville, had not had time to carry away or to hide anything, except the plate, which had been stowed away in a hole made in one of the walls, so that, as he was very rich and had good taste, the large drawing-room, which opened into the dining-room, had looked like the gallery in a museum, before his precipitate flight.

Expensive oil-paintings, water-colors, and drawings hung upon the walls, while on the tables, on the hanging shelves, and in elegant glass cupboards, there were a thousand knickknacks : small vases, statuettes, groups in Dresden china, grotesque Chinese figures, old ivory, and Venetian glass, which filled the large room with their precious and fantastical array.

Scarcely anything was left now; not that the things had been stolen, for the major would not have allowed that, but Mademoiselle Fifi *would have a mine,* and on that occasion all the officers thoroughly enjoyed themselves for five minutes. The little marquis went into the drawing-room to get what he wanted, and he brought back a small, delicate china teapot, which he filled with gunpowder, and carefully introduced a piece of German tinder into it, through the spout. Then he lighted it, and took this infernal machine into the next room; but he came back immediately, and shut the door. The Germans all stood expectantly, their faces full of childish, smiling curiosity, and as soon as the explosion had shaken the château, they all rushed in at once.

Mademoiselle Fifi, who got in first, clapped his hands in delight at the sight of a terra-cotta Venus, whose head had been blown off, and each picked up pieces of porcelain, and wondered at the strange shape of the fragments, while the major was looking with a paternal eye at the large drawing-room which had been wrecked in such a Neronic fashion, and which was strewn with the fragments of works of art. He went out first, and said, with a smile: "He managed that very well!"

But there was such a cloud of smoke in the dining-room, mingled with the tobacco smoke, that they could not breathe, so the commandant opened the window, and all the officers, who had gone into the room for a glass of cognac, went up to it.

274

The moist air blew into the room, and brought a sort of spray with it, which powdered their beards. They looked at the tall trees which were dripping with the rain, at the broad valley which was covered with mist, and at the church spire in the distance, which rose up like a gray point in the beating rain.

The bells had not rung since their arrival. That was the only resistance which the invaders had met with in the neighborhood. The parish priest had not refused to take in and to feed the Prussian soldiers; he had several times even drunk a bottle of beer or claret with the hostile commandant, who often employed him as a benevolent intermediary; but it was no use to ask him for a single stroke of the bells; he would sooner have allowed himself to be shot. That was his way of protesting against the invasion, a peaceful and silent protest, the only one, he said, which was suitable to a priest, who was a man of mildness, and not of blood; and everyone, for twenty-five miles round, praised Abbé Chantavoine's firmness and heroism, in venturing to proclaim the public mourning by the obstinate silence of his church bells.

The whole village grew enthusiastic over his resistance, and was ready to back up their pastor and to risk anything, as they looked upon that silent protest as the safeguard of the national honor. It seemed to the peasants that thus they had deserved better of their country than Belfort and Strassburg, that they had set an equally valuable example, and that the name of their little village would become immortalized by that; but with that exception, they refused their Prussian conquerors nothing.

The commandant and his officers laughed among themselves at that inoffensive courage, and as the people in the whole country round showed themselves obliging and compliant toward them, they willingly tolerated their silent patriotism. Only little Count Wilhelm would have liked to have forced them to ring the bells. He was very angry at his superior's politic compliance with the priest's scruples, and every day he begged the commandant to allow him to sound "ding-dong, ding-dong," just once, only just once, just by way of a joke. And he asked it like a wheedling woman, in the tender voice of some mistress who wishes to obtain something, but the commandant would not yield, and to console *herself*, Mademoiselle Fifi made *a mine* in the château.

The five men stood there together for some minutes, inhaling the moist air, and at last, Lieutenant Fritz said, with a laugh: "The ladies will certainly not have fine weather for their drive." Then they separated, each to his own duties, while the captain had plenty to do in seeing about the dinner.

When they met again, as it was growing dark, they began to laugh at seeing each other as dandified and smart as on the day of a grand review. The commandant's hair did not look as gray as it did in the morning, and the captain had shaved — had only kept his mustache on, which made him look as if he had a streak of fire under his nose.

In spite of the rain, they left the window open, and one of them went to listen from time to time. At a quarter past six the baron said he heard a rumbling in the distance. They all rushed down, and soon the wagon drove up at a gallop with its four horses, splashed up to their backs, steaming and panting. Five women got out at the bottom of the steps, five handsome girls whom a comrade of the captain, to whom *Le Devoir* had taken his card, had selected with care.

They had not required much pressing, as they were sure of being well treated, for they had got to know the Prussians in the three months during which they had had to do with them. So they resigned themselves to the men as they did to the state of affairs. "It is part of our business, so it must be done," they said as they drove along; no doubt to allay some slight, secret scruples of conscience.

They went into the dining-room immediately, which looked still more dismal in its dilapidated state, when it was lighted up; while the table covered with choice dishes, the beautiful china and glass, and the plate, which had been found in the hole in the wall where its owner had hidden it, gave to the place the look of a bandits' resort, where they were supping after committing a robbery. The captain was radiant; he took hold of the women as if he were familiar with them; appraising them, kissing them, valuing them for what they were worth as *ladies of pleasure;* and when the three young men wanted to appropriate one each, he opposed them authoritatively, reserving to himself the right to apportion them justly, according to their several ranks, so as not to wound the hierarchy. Therefore, so as to avoid all discussion, jarring, and suspicion of partiality, he placed them all in a line according to height, and addressing the tallest, he said in a voice of command:

"What is your name?"

"Pamela," she replied, raising her voice.

Then he said: "Number One, called Pamela, is adjudged to the commandant."

Then, having kissed Blondina, the second, as a sign of proprietorship, he proffered stout Amanda to Lieutenant Otto, Eva, "the Tomato," to Sub-lieutenant Fritz, and Rachel, the shortest of them all, a very young, dark girl, with eyes as black as ink, a Jewess, whose snub nose confirmed by exception the rule which allots hooked noses to all her race, to the youngest officer, frail Count Wilhelm von Eyrick.

They were all pretty and plump, without any distinctive features, and all were very much alike in look and person, from their daily dissipation, and the life common to houses of public accommodation.

The three younger men wished to carry off their women immediately, under the pretext of finding them brushes and soap; but the captain wisely opposed this, for he said they were quite fit to sit down to dinner, and that those who went up would wish for a change when they came down, and so would disturb the other couples, and his experience in such matters carried the day. There were only many kisses; expectant kisses.

Suddenly Rachel choked, and began to cough until the tears came into her eyes, while smoke came through her nostrils. Under pretense of kissing her, the count had blown a whiff of tobacco into her mouth. She did not fly into a rage, and did not say a word, but she looked at her possessor with latent hatred in her dark eyes.

They sat down to dinner. The commandant seemed delighted; he made Pamela sit on his right, and Blondina on his left, and said, as he unfolded his table napkin: "That was a delightful idea of yours, captain."

Lieutenants Otto and Fritz, who were as polite as if they had been with fashionable ladies, rather intimidated their neighbors, but Baron von Kelweinstein gave the reins to all his vicious propensities, beamed, made doubtful remarks, and seemed on fire with his crown of red hair. He paid them compliments in French from the other side of the Rhine, and sputtered out gallant remarks, only fit for a low pothouse, from between his two broken teeth.

They did not understand him, however, and their intelligence did not seem to be awakened until he uttered nasty words and broad expressions, which were mangled by his accent. Then all began to laugh at once, like mad women, and fell against each other, repeating the words, which the baron then began to say all wrong, in order that he might have the pleasure of hearing them say doubtful things. They gave him as much of that stuff as he wanted, for they were drunk after the first bottle of wine, and, becoming themselves once more, and opening the door to their usual habits, they kissed the mustaches on the right and left of them, pinched their arms, uttered furious cries, drank out of every glass, and sang French couplets, and bits of German songs, which they had picked up in their daily intercourse with the enemy.

Soon the men themselves, intoxicated by that which was displayed to their sight and touch, grew

very amorous, shouted and broke the plates and
dishes, while the soldiers behind them waited on
them stolidly. The commandant was the only one
who put any restraint upon himself.

Mademoiselle Fifi had taken Rachel on to his
knees, and, getting excited, at one moment kissed
the little black curls on her neck, inhaling the pleasant warmth of her body, and all the savor of her
person, through the slight space there was between
her dress and her skin, and at another pinched her
furiously through the material, and made her scream,
for he was seized with a species of ferocity, and tormented by his desire to hurt her. He often held her
close to him, as if to make her part of himself, and
put his lips in a long kiss on the Jewess's rosy
mouth, until she lost her breath; and at last he bit
her until a stream of blood ran down her chin and
on to her bodice.

For the second time, she looked him full in the
face, and as she bathed the wound, she said: "You
will have to pay for that!"

But he merely laughed a hard laugh, and said: "I
will pay."

At dessert, champagne was served, and the commandant rose, and in the same voice in which he
would have drunk to the health of the Empress
Augusta, he drank: "To our ladies!" Then a series
of toasts began, toasts worthy of the lowest soldiers
and of drunkards, mingled with filthy jokes, which
were made still more brutal by their ignorance of the
language. They got up, one after the other, trying
to say something witty, forcing themselves to be
funny, and the women, who were so drunk that

they almost fell off their chairs, with vacant looks and clammy tongues, applauded madly each time.

The captain, who no doubt wished to impart an appearance of gallantry to the orgy, raised his glass again, and said: "To our victories over hearts!" Thereupon Lieutenant Otto, who was a species of bear from the Black Forest, jumped up, inflamed and saturated with drink, and seized by an access of alcoholic patriotism, cried: "To our victories over France!"

Drunk as they were, the women were silent, and Rachel turned round with a shudder, and said: "Look here, I know some Frenchmen, in whose presence you would not dare to say that." But the little count, still holding her on his knees, began to laugh, for the wine had made him very merry, and said: "Ha! ha! ha! I have never met any of them, myself. As soon as we show ourselves, they run away!"

The girl, who was in a terrible rage, shouted into his face: "You are lying, you dirty scoundrel!"

For a moment, he looked at her steadily, with his bright eyes upon her, as he had looked at the portrait before he destroyed it with revolver bullets, and then he began to laugh: "Ah! yes, talk about them, my dear! Should we be here now, if they were brave?" Then getting excited, he exclaimed: "We are the masters! France belongs to us!" She jumped off his knees with a bound, and threw herself into her chair, while he rose, held out his glass over the table, and repeated: "France and the French, the woods, the fields, and the houses of France belong to us!"

The others, who were quite drunk, and who were suddenly seized by military enthusiasm, the enthusiasm of brutes, seized their glasses, and shouting, "Long live Prussia!" emptied them at a draught.

The girls did not protest, for they were reduced to silence, and were afraid. Even Rachel did not say a word, as she had no reply to make, and then the little count put his champagne glass, which had just been refilled, on to the head of the Jewess, and exclaimed: "All the women in France belong to us, also!"

At that she got up so quickly that the glass upset, spilling the amber colored wine on to her black hair as if to baptize her, and broke into a hundred fragments as it fell on to the floor. With trembling lips, she defied the looks of the officer, who was still laughing, and she stammered out, in a voice choked with rage: "That—that—that—is not true,—for you shall certainly not have any French women."

He sat down again, so as to laugh at his ease, and trying ineffectually to speak in the Parisian accent, he said: "That is good, very good! Then what did you come here for, my dear?"

She was thunderstruck, and made no reply for a moment, for in her agitation she did not understand him at first; but as soon as she grasped his meaning, she said to him indignantly and vehemently: "I! I! I am not a woman; I am only a strumpet, and that is all that Prussians want."

Almost before she had finished, he slapped her full in her face; but as he was raising his hand again, as if he would strike her, she, almost mad with passion, took up a small dessert knife from the table, and stabbed him right in the neck, just above the breastbone. Something that he was going to say, was cut short in his throat, and he sat there, with his mouth half open, and a terrible look in his eyes.

All the officers shouted in horror, and leaped up tumultuously; but throwing her chair between Lieutenant Otto's legs, who fell down at full length, she ran to the window, opened it before they could seize her, and jumped out into the night and pouring rain.

In two minutes, Mademoiselle Fifi was dead. Fritz and Otto drew their swords and wanted to kill the women, who threw themselves at their feet and clung to their knees. With some difficulty the major stopped the slaughter, and had the four terrified girls locked up in a room under the care of two soldiers. Then he organized the pursuit of the fugitive, as carefully as if he were about to engage in a skirmish, feeling quite sure that she would be caught.

The table, which had been cleared immediately, now served as a bed on which to lay Fifi out, and the four officers made for the window, rigid and sobered, with the stern faces of soldiers on duty, and tried to pierce through the darkness of the night, amid the steady torrent of rain. Suddenly, a shot was heard, and then another, a long way off; and for four hours they heard from time to time near or distant reports and rallying cries, strange words uttered as a call, in guttural voices.

In the morning they all returned. Two soldiers had been killed and three others wounded by their comrades in the ardor of that chase, and in the confusion of such a nocturnal pursuit, but they had not caught Rachel.

Then the inhabitants of the district were terror-
ized, the houses were turned topsy-turvy, the country
was scoured and beaten up, over and over again, but
the Jewess did not seem to have left a single trace
of her passage behind her.

When the general was told of it, he gave orders
to hush up the affair, so as not to set a bad example
to the army, but he severely censured the commandant, who in turn punished his inferiors. The general
had said: "One does not go to war in order to
amuse oneself, and to caress prostitutes." And Graf
von Farlsberg, in his exasperation, made up his mind
to have his revenge on the district, but as he required
a pretext for showing severity, he sent for the priest,
and ordered him to have the bell tolled at the funeral
of Count von Eyrick.

Contrary to all expectation, the priest showed himself humble and most respectful, and when Mademoiselle Fifi's body left the Château d'Urville on its
way to the cemetery, carried by soldiers, preceded, surrounded, and followed by soldiers, who marched with
loaded rifles, for the first time the bell sounded its
funereal knell in a lively manner, as if a friendly hand
were caressing it. At night it sounded again, and
the next day, and every day; it rang as much as anyone could desire. Sometimes even, it would start at
night, and sound gently through the darkness, seized
by strange joy, awakened, one could not tell why.
All the peasants in the neighborhood declared that it
was bewitched, and nobody, except the priest and
the sacristan would now go near the church tower,
and they went because a poor girl was living there

in grief and solitude, secretly nourished by those two men.

She remained there until the German troops 'departed, and then one evening the priest borrowed the baker's cart, and himself drove his prisoner to Rouen. When they got there, he embraced her, and she quickly went back on foot to the establishment from which she had come, where the proprietress, who thought that she was dead, was very glad to see her.

A short time afterward, a patriot who had no prejudices, who liked her because of her bold deed, and who afterward loved her for herself, married her, and made a lady of her.

MOONLIGHT

ADAME JULIE ROUBÈRE was awaiting her elder sister, Madame Henriette Letore, who had just returned after a trip to Switzerland.

The Letore household had left nearly five weeks ago. Madame Henriette had allowed her husband to return alone to their estate in Calvados, where some matters of business required his attention, and came to spend a few days in Paris with her sister. Night came on. In the quiet parlor darkened by twilight shadows, Madame Roubère was reading in an absent-minded fashion, raising her eyes whenever she heard a sound.

At last she heard a ring at the door, and presently her sister appeared, wrapped in a traveling cloak. And immediately, without any formal greeting, they clasped each other ardently, only desisting for a moment to begin embracing each other over again. Then they talked, asking questions about each other's health, about their respective families, and a thousand other things, gossiping, jerking out hurried, broken

286

sentences, and rushing about while Madame Henriette was removing her hat and veil.

It was now quite dark. Madame Roubère rang for a lamp, and as soon as it was brought in, she scanned her sister's face, and was on the point of embracing her once more. But she held back, scared and astonished at the other's appearance. Around her temples, Madame Letore had two long locks of white hair. All the rest of her hair was of a glossy, raven-black hue; but there alone, at each side of her head, ran, as it were, two silvery streams which were immediately lost in the black mass surrounding them. She was, nevertheless, only twenty-four years old, and this change had come on suddenly since her departure for Switzerland.

Without moving, Madame Roubère gazed at her in amazement, tears rising to her eyes, as she thought that some mysterious and terrible calamity must have fallen on her sister. She asked:

"What is the matter with you, Henriette?"

Smiling with a sad smile, the smile of one who is heartsick, the other replied:

"Why, nothing, I assure you. Were you noticing my white hair?"

But Madame Roubère impetuously seized her by the shoulders, and with a searching glance at her, re-peated·

"What is the matter with you? Tell me what is the matter with you. And if you tell me a falsehood, I'll soon find it out."

They remained face to face, and Madame Henriette, who became so pale that she was near fainting, had two pearly tears at each corner of her drooping eyes.

Her sister went on asking:

"What has happened to you? What is the matter with you? Answer me!"

Then, in a subdued voice, the other murmured:

"I have—I have a lover."

And, hiding her forehead on the shoulder of her younger sister, she sobbed.

Then, when she had grown a little calmer, when the heaving of her breast had subsided, she commenced to unbosom herself, as if to cast forth this secret from herself, to empty this sorrow of hers into a sympathetic heart.

Thereupon, holding each other's hands tightly grasped, the two women went over to a sofa in a dark corner of the room, into which they sank, and the younger sister, passing her arm over the elder one's neck and drawing her close to her heart, listened.

* * * * * * *

"Oh! I recognize that there was no excuse for one; I do not understand myself, and since that day I feel as if I were mad. Be careful, my child, about yourself—be careful! If you only knew how weak we are, how quickly we yield, we fall! All it needs is a nothing, so little, so little, a moment of tenderness, one of those sudden fits of melancholy which steal into your soul, one of those longings to open your arms, to love, to embrace, which we all have at certain moments.

"You know my husband, and you know how fond of him I am; but he is mature and sensible, and cannot even comprehend the tender vibrations of a woman's heart. He is always, always the same, always good, always smiling, always kind, always perfect. Oh! how I sometimes have wished that he would roughly clasp me in his arms, that he would embrace me with those slow, sweet kisses which make two beings intermingle, which are like mute confidences! How I wished that he was self-abandoned and even weak, so that he should have need of me, of my caresses, of my tears!

"This all seems very silly; but we women are made like that. How can we help it?

"And yet the thought of deceiving never came near me. To-day, it has happened, without love, without reason, without anything, simply because the moon shone one night on the Lake of Lucerne.

"During the month when we were traveling together, my husband, with his calm indifference, paralyzed my enthusiasm, extinguished my poetic ardor. When we were descending the mountain paths at sunrise, when as the four horses galloped along with the diligence, we saw, in the transparent morning haze, valleys, woods, streams, and villages, I clasped my hands with delight, and said to him: 'What a beautiful scene, darling! Kiss me now!' he only answered, with a smile of chilling kindliness, 'There is no reason why we should kiss each other because you like the landscape.'

"And his words froze me to the heart. It seems to me that when people love each other, they ought to feel more moved by love than ever in the presence of beautiful scenes.

"Indeed, he prevented the effervescent poetry that bubbled up within me from gushing out. How can me. A man was intently gazing at me. When I turned my head round, he recognized me, and, advancing, said:

"'You are weeping, Madame?'

"It was a young barrister who was traveling with his mother, and whom we had often met. His eyes had frequently followed me.

"I was so much confused that I did not know what answer to give or what to think of the situation. I told him I felt ill.

"He walked on by my side in a natural and respectful fashion, and began talking to me about what we had seen during our trip. All that I had felt he translated into words; everything that made me thrill he understood perfectly, better even than I did myself. And all of a sudden he recited some verses of Alfred de Musset. I felt myself choking, seized with indescribable emotion. It seemed to me that the mountains themselves, the lake, the moonlight, were singing to me about things ineffably sweet.

"And it happened, I don't know how, I don't know why, in a sort of hallucination.

"As for him, I did not see him again till the morning of his departure.

"He gave me his card!"

* * * * * * *

And, sinking into her sister's arms, Madame Letore broke into groans—almost into shrieks.

Then Madame Roubère, with a self-contained and serious air, said very gently:

"You see, sister, very often it is not a man that we love, but love. And your real lover that night was the moonlight."

I express it? I was almost like a boiler, filled with steam, and hermetically sealed.

"One evening (we had been for four days staying in the Hotel de Fluelen), Robert, having got one of his sick headaches, went to bed immediately after dinner, and I went to take a walk all alone along the edge of the lake.

"It was a night such as one might read of in a fairy tale. The full moon showed itself in the middle of the sky; the tall mountains, with their snowy crests, seemed to wear silver crowns; the waters of the lake glittered with tiny rippling motions. The air was mild, with that kind of penetrating freshness which softens us till we seem to be swooning, to be deeply affected without any apparent cause. But how sensitive, how vibrating, the heart is at such moments! How quickly it leaps up, and how intense are its emotions!

"I sat down on the grass, and gazed at that vast lake so melancholy and so fascinating; and a strange thing passed into me; I became possessed with an insatiable need of love, a revolt against the gloomy dullness of my life. What! would it never be my fate to be clasped in the arms of a man whom I loved on a bank like this under the glowing moonlight? Was I never then, to feel on my lips those kisses so deep, delicious, and intoxicating which lovers exchange on nights that seem to have been made by God for passionate embraces? Was I never to know such ardent, feverish love in the moonlit shadows of a summer's night?

"And I burst out weeping like a woman who has lost her reason. I heard some person stirring behind

MISS HARRIET

THERE were seven of us in a four-in-hand, four women and three men, one of whom was on the box seat beside the coachman. We were following, at a foot pace, the broad highway which serpentines along the coast.

Setting out from Etretat at break of day, in order to visit the ruins of Tancarville, we were still asleep, chilled by the fresh air of the morning. The women, especially, who were but little accustomed to these early excursions, let their eyelids fall and rise every moment, nodding their heads or yawning, quite insensible to the glory of the dawn.

It was autumn. On both sides of the road the bare fields stretched out, yellowed by the corn and wheat stubble which covered the soil like a bristling growth of beard. The spongy earth seemed to smoke. Larks were singing high up in the air, while other birds piped in the bushes.

At length the sun rose in front of us, a bright red on the plane of the horizon; and as it ascended, growing clearer from minute to minute, the country seemed to awake, to smile, to shake and stretch itself, like a young girl who is leaving her bed in her white airy chemise. The Count d'Etraille, who was seated on the box, cried:

"Look! look! a hare!" and he pointed toward the left, indicating a piece of hedge. The leveret threaded its way along, almost concealed by the field, only its large ears visible. Then it swerved across a deep rut, stopped, again pursued its easy course, changed its direction, stopped anew, disturbed, spying out every danger, and undecided as to the route it should take. Suddenly it began to run, with great bounds from its hind legs, disappearing finally in a large patch of beet-root. All the men had woke up to watch the course of the beast.

René Lemanoir then exclaimed:

"We are not at all gallant this morning," and looking at his neighbor, the little Baroness of Sérennes, who was struggling with drowsiness, he said to her in a subdued voice: "You are thinking of your husband, Baroness. Reassure yourself; he will not return before Saturday, so you have still four days."

She responded to him with a sleepy smile:

"How rude you are." Then, shaking off her torpor, she added: "Now, let somebody say something that will make us all laugh. You, Monsieur Chenal, who have the reputation of possessing a larger fortune than the Duke of Richelieu, tell us a love story in which you have been mixed up, anything you like."

293

Léon Chenal, an old painter, who had once been very handsome, very strong, who was very proud of his physique and very amiable, took his long white beard in his hand and smiled; then, after a few moments' reflection, he became suddenly grave.

"Ladies, it will not be an amusing tale; for I am going to relate to you the most lamentable love affair of my life, and I sincerely hope that none of my friends has ever passed through a similar experience.

I.

"At that time I was twenty-five years old, and was making daubs along the coast of Normandy. I call 'making daubs' that wandering about, with a bag on one's back, from mountain to mountain, under the pretext of studying and of sketching nature. I know nothing more enjoyable than that happy-go-lucky wandering life, in which you are perfectly free, without shackles of any kind, without care, without pre-occupation, without thought even of to-morrow. You go in any direction you please, without any guide save your fancy, without any counselor save your eyes. You pull up, because a running brook seduces you, or because you are attracted, in front of an inn, by the smell of potatoes frying. Sometimes it is the perfume of clematis which decides you in your choice, or the naïve glance of the servant at an inn. Do not despise me for my affection for these rustics. These girls have soul as well as feeling, not to mention firm cheeks and fresh lips; while their hearty and willing kisses have the flavor of wild fruit. Love always has

its price, come whence it may. A heart that beats
when you make your appearance, an eye that weeps
when you go away, these are things so rare, so
sweet, so precious, that they must never be despised.

"I have had rendezvous in ditches in which cattle
repose, and in barns among the straw, still steaming
from the heat of the day. I have recollections of
canvas spread on rude and creaky benches, and of
hearty, fresh, free kisses, more delicate, free from
affectation, and sincere than the subtle attractions of
charming and distinguished women.

"But what you love most amid all these varied
adventures are the country, the woods, the risings of
the sun, the twilight, the light of the moon. For
the painter these are honeymoon trips with Nature.
You are alone with her in that long and tranquil
rendezvous. You go to bed in the fields amid marguerites and wild poppies, and, with eyes wide open,
you watch the going down of the sun, and descry in
the distance the little village, with its pointed clock-
tower, which sounds the hour of midnight.

"You sit down by the side of a spring which
gushes out from the foot of an oak, amid a covering
of fragile herbs, growing and redolent of life. You
go down on your knees, bend forward, and drink
the cold and pellucid water, wetting your mustache
and nose; you drink it with a physical pleasure, as
though you were kissing the spring, lip to lip. Sometimes, when you encounter a deep hole, along the
course of these tiny brooks, you plunge into it, quite
naked, and on your skin, from head to foot, like an
icy and delicious caress, you feel the lovely and
gentle quivering of the current.

"You are gay on the hills, melancholy on the verge of pools, exalted when the sun is crowned in an ocean of blood-red shadows, and when it casts on the rivers its red reflection. And at night, under the moon, as it passes across the vault of heaven, you th·nk of things, singular things, which would never have occurred to your mind under the brilliant light of day.

"So, in wandering through the same country we are in this year, I came to the little village of Benouville, on the Falaise, between Yport and Etretat. I came from Fécamp, following the coast, a high coast, perpendicular as a wall, with projecting and rugged rocks falling sheer down into the sea. I had walked since the morning on the close clipped grass, as smooth and as yielding as a carpet. Singing lustily, I walked with long strides, looking sometimes at the slow and lazy flight of a gull, with its short, white wings, sailing in the blue heavens, sometimes at the green sea, or at the brown sails of a fishing bark. In short, I had passed a happy day, a day of listlessness and of liberty.

"I was shown a little farmhouse, where travelers were put up, a kind of inn, kept by a peasant, which stood in the center of a Norman court, surrounded by a double row of beeches.

"Quitting the Falaise, I gained the hamlet, which was hemmed in by great trees, and I presented myself at the house of Mother Lecacheur.

"She was an old, wrinkled, and austere rustic, who always seemed to yield to the pressure of new customs with a kind of contempt.

"It was the month of May: the spreading apple-trees covered the court with a whirling shower of blossoms which rained unceasingly both upon people and upon the grass.

"I said:

"'Well, Madame Lecacheur, have you a room for me?'

"Astonished to find that I knew her name, she answered:

"'That depends; everything is let; but, all the same, there will be no harm in looking.'

"In five minutes we were in perfect accord, and I deposited my bag upon the bare floor of a rustic room, furnished with a bed, two chairs, a table, and a washstand. The room opened into the large and smoky kitchen, where the lodgers took their meals with the people of the farm and with the farmer himself, who was a widower.

"I washed my hands, after which I went out. The old woman was fricasseeing a chicken for dinner in a large fireplace, in which hung the stew-pot, black with smoke.

"'You have travelers, then, at the present time?' said I to her.

"She answered in an offended tone of voice:

"'I have a lady, an English lady, who has attained to years of maturity. She is occupying my other room.'

"By means of an extra five sous a day, I obtained the privilege of dining out in the court when the weather was fine.

"My cover was then placed in front of the door, and I commenced to gnaw with hunger the lean members of the Normandy chicken, to drink the clear cider, and to munch the hunk of white bread, which, though four days old, was excellent.

"Suddenly, the wooden barrier which opened on to the highway was opened, and a strange person directed her steps toward the house. She was very slender, very tall, enveloped in a Scotch shawl with red borders. You would have believed that she had no arms, if you had not seen a long hand appear just above the hips, holding a white tourist umbrella. The face of a mummy, surrounded with sausage rolls of plaited gray hair, which bounded at every step she took, made me think, I know not why, of a sour herring adorned with curling papers. Lowering her eyes, she passed quickly in front of me, and entered the house.

"This singular apparition made me curious. She undoubtedly was my neighbor, the aged English lady of whom our hostess had spoken.

"I did not see her again that day. The next day, when I had begun to paint at the end of that beautiful valley, which you know extends as far as Etretat, lifting my eyes suddenly, I perceived something singularly attired standing on the crest of the declivity; it looked like a pole decked out with flags. It was she. On seeing me, she suddenly disappeared. I re-entered the house at midday for lunch, and took my seat at the common table, so as to make the acquaintance of this old and original creature. But she did not respond to my polite advances, was insensible even to my little attentions. I poured water out for her with great alacrity, I passed her the dishes with great eagerness. A slight, almost imperceptible movement of the head, and an English word, murmured so low that I did not understand it, were her only acknowledgments.

"I ceased occupying myself with her, although she had disturbed my thoughts. At the end of three days, I knew as much about her as did Madame Lecacheur herself.

"She was called Miss Harriet. Seeking out a secluded village in which to pass the summer, she had been attracted to Benouville, some six months before, and did not seem disposed to quit it. She never spoke at table, ate rapidly, reading all the while a small book, treating of some Protestant propaganda. She gave a copy of it to everybody. The curé himself had received no less than four copies, at the hands of an urchin to whom she had paid two sous' commission. She said sometimes to our hostess, abruptly, without preparing her in the least for the declaration:

"'I love the Saviour more than all; I worship him in all creation; I adore him in all nature; I carry him always in my heart.'

"And she would immediately present the old woman with one of her brochures which were destined to convert the universe.

"In the village she was not liked. In fact, the schoolmaster had declared that she was an atheist, and that a sort of reproach attached to her. The curé, who had been consulted by Madame Lecacheur, responded:

"'She is a heretic, but God does not wish the death of the sinner, and I believe her to be a person of pure morals.'

"These words, 'atheist,' 'heretic,' words which no one can precisely define, threw doubts into some minds. It was asserted, however, that this English-woman was rich, and that she had passed her life in traveling through every country in the world, because her family had thrown her off. Why had her family thrown her off? Because of her natural impiety?

"She was, in fact, one of those people of exalted principles, one of those opinionated puritans of whom England produces so many, one of those good and insupportable old women who haunt the *tables d'hôte* of every hotel in Europe, who spoil Italy, poison Switzerland, render the charming cities of the Mediterranean uninhabitable, carry everywhere their fantastic manias, their petrified vestal manners, their indescribable toilettes, and a certain odor of india-rubber, which makes one believe that at night they slip themselves into a case of that material. When I meet one of these people in a hotel, I act like birds which see a manikin in a field.

"This woman, however, appeared so singular that she did not displease me.

"Madame Lecacheur, hostile by instinct to every-thing that was not rustic, felt in her narrow soul a kind of hatred for the ecstatic extravagances of the old girl. She had found a phrase by which to describe her, I know not how, but a phrase assuredly contemptuous, which had sprung to her lips, invented probably by some confused and mysterious travail of soul. She said: 'That woman is a demoniac.' This phrase, as uttered by that austere and sentimental creature, seemed to me irresistibly comic. I, myself, never called her now anything else but 'the demoniac.' feeling a singular pleasure in pronouncing this word on seeing her.

"I would ask Mother Lecacheur: 'Well, what is our demoniac about to-day?' To which my rustic friend would respond, with an air of having been scandalized:

"'What do you think, sir? She has picked up a toad which has had its leg battered, and carried it to her room, and has put it in her washstand, and dressed it up like a man. If that is not profanation, I should like to know what is!'

"On another occasion, when walking along the Falaise, she had bought a large fish which had just been caught, simply to throw it back into the sea again. The sailor, from whom she had bought it, though paid handsomely, was greatly provoked at this act — more exasperated, indeed, than if she had put her hand into his pocket and taken his money. For a whole month he could not speak of the circumstance without getting into a fury and denouncing it as an outrage. Oh yes! She was indeed a demoniac, this Miss Harriet, and Mother Lecacheur must have had an inspiration of genius in thus christening her.

"The stable-boy, who was called Sapeur, because he had served in Africa in his youth, entertained other aversions. He said, with a roguish air: 'She is an old hag who has lived her days.' If the poor woman had but known!

"Little kind-hearted Céleste did not wait upon her willingly, but I was never able to understand why. Probably her only reason was that she was a stranger, of another race, of a different tongue, and of another religion. She was in good truth a demoniac!

"She passed her time wandering about the country, adoring and searching for God in nature. I found her one evening on her knees in a cluster of bushes. Having discovered something red through the leaves, I brushed aside the branches, and Miss Harriet at once rose to her feet, confused at having been found thus, looking at me with eyes as terrible as those of a wild cat surprised in open day.

"Sometimes, when I was working among the rocks, I would suddenly descry her on the banks of the Falaise standing like a semaphore signal. She gazed passionately at the vast sea, glittering in the sunlight, and the boundless sky empurpled with fire. Sometimes I would distinguish her at the bottom of a valley, walking quickly, with her elastic English step; and I would go toward her, attracted by I know not what, simply to see her illuminated visage, her dried-up features, which seemed to glow with an ineffable, inward, and profound happiness.

"Often I would encounter her in the corner of a field sitting on the grass, under the shadow of an apple-tree, with her little Bible lying open on her knee, while she looked meditatively into the distance.

"I could no longer tear myself away from that quiet country neighborhood, bound to it as I was by a thousand links of love for its soft and sweeping landscapes. At this farm I was out of the world, far removed from everything, but in close proximity to the soil, the good, healthy, beautiful green soil. And, must I avow it, there was something besides curiosity which retained me at the residence of Mother Lecacheur. I wished to become acquainted a little with this strange Miss Harriet, and to learn what passes in the solitary souls of those wandering old, English dames.

302

II.

"We became acquainted in a rather singular manner. I had just finished a study which appeared to me to display genius and power; as it must have, since it was sold for ten thousand francs, fifteen years later. It was as simple, however, as that two and two make four, and had nothing to do with academic rules. The whole of the right side of my canvas represented a rock, an enormous rock, covered with sea-wrack, brown, yellow, and red, across which the sun poured like a stream of oil. The light, without which one could see the stars concealed in the background, fell upon the stone, and gilded it as if with fire. That was all. A first stupid attempt at dealing with light, with burning rays, with the sublime.

"On the left was the sea, not the blue sea, the slate-colored sea, but a sea of jade, as greenish, milky, and thick as the overcast sky.

"I was so pleased with my work that I danced from sheer delight as I carried it back to the inn. I wished that the whole world could have seen it at one and the same moment. I can remember that I showed it to a cow, which was browsing by the wayside, exclaiming, at the same time: 'Look at that, my old beauty; you will not often see its like again.'

"When I had reached the front of the house, I immediately called out to Mother Lecacheur, shouting with all my might:

"'Ohé! Ohé! my mistress, come here and look at this.'

"The rustic advanced and looked at my work with stupid eyes, which distinguished nothing, and did not even recognize whether the picture was the representation of an ox or a house.

"Miss Harriet came into the house, and passed in rear of me just at the moment when, holding out my canvas at arm's length, I was exhibiting it to the female innkeeper. The 'demoniac' could not help but see it, for I took care to exhibit the thing in such a way that it could not escape her notice. She stopped abruptly and stood motionless, stupefied. It was her rock which was depicted, the one which she usually climbed to dream away her time undisturbed.

"She uttered a British 'Oh,' which was at once so accentuated and so flattering, that I turned round to her, smiling, and said:

"'This is my last work, Mademoiselle.'

"She murmured ecstatically, comically, and tenderly:

"'Oh! Monsieur, you must understand what it is to have a palpitation.'

"I colored up, of course, and was more excited by that compliment than if it had come from a queen. I was seduced, conquered, vanquished. I could have embraced her — upon my honor.

"I took my seat at the table beside her, as I had always done. For the first time, she spoke, drawling out in a loud voice:

"'Oh! I love nature so much.'

"I offered her some bread, some water, some wine. She now accepted these with the vacant smile of a mummy. I then began to converse with her about the scenery.

"After the meal, we rose from the table together and walked leisurely across the court; then, attracted by the fiery glow which the setting sun cast over the surface of the sea, I opened the outside gate which faced in the direction of the Falaise, and we walked on side by side, as satisfied as any two persons could be who have just learned to understand and penetrate each other's motives and feelings.

"It was a misty, relaxing evening, one of those enjoyable evenings which impart happiness to mind and body alike. All is joy, all is charm. The luscious and balmy air, loaded with the perfumes of herbs, with the perfumes of grass-wrack, with the odor of the wild flowers, caresses the soul with a penetrating sweetness. We were going to the brink of the abyss which overlooked the vast sea and rolled past us at the distance of less than a hundred meters.

"We drank with open mouth and expanded chest, that fresh breeze from the ocean which glides slowly over the skin, salted as it is by long contact with the waves.

"Wrapped up in her square shawl, inspired by the balmy air and with teeth firmly set, the Englishwoman gazed fixedly at the great sun-ball, as it descended toward the sea. Soon its rim touched the waters, just in rear of a ship which had appeared on the horizon, until, by degrees, it was swallowed up by the ocean. We watched it plunge, diminish, and finally disappear.

"Miss Harriet contemplated with passionate regard the last glimmer of the flaming orb of day.

"She muttered: 'Oh! I love—I love—' I saw a tear start in her eye. She continued: 'I wish I were a little bird, so that I could mount up into the firmament.'

"She remained standing as I had often before seen her, perched on the river bank, her face as red as her flaming shawl. I should have liked to have sketched her in my album. It would have been an ecstatic caricature. I turned my face away from her so as to be able to laugh.

"I then spoke to her of painting, as I would have done to a fellow-artist, using the technical terms common among the devotees of the profession. She listened attentively to me, eagerly seeking to divine the sense of the obscure words, so as to penetrate my thoughts. From time to time, she would exclaim: 'Oh! I understand, I understand. This is very interesting.' We returned home.

"The next day, on seeing me, she approached me eagerly, holding out her hand; and we became firm friends immediately.

"She was a brave creature, with an elastic sort of a soul, which became enthusiastic at a bound. She lacked equilibrium, like all women who are spinsters at the age of fifty. She seemed to be pickled in vinegary innocence, though her heart still retained something of youth and of girlish effervescence. She loved both nature and animals with a fervent ardor, a love like old wine, mellow through age, with a sensual love that she had never bestowed on men.

"One thing is certain: a mare roaming in a meadow with a foal at its side, a bird's nest full of young ones, squeaking, with their open mouths and enormous heads, made her quiver with the most violent emotion.

"Poor solitary beings! Sad wanderers from *table d'hôte* to *table d'hôte*, poor beings, ridiculous and lamentable, I love you ever since I became acquainted with Miss Harriet!

"I soon discovered that she had something she would like to tell me, but dared not, and I was amused at her timidity. When I started out in the morning with my box on my back, she would accompany me as far as the end of the village, silent, but evidently struggling inwardly to find words with which to begin a conversation. Then she would leave me abruptly, and, with jaunty step, walk away quickly.

"One day, however, she plucked up courage:

"'I would like to see how you paint pictures? Will you show me? I have been very curious.'

"And she colored up as though she had given utterance to words extremely audacious.

"I conducted her to the bottom of the Petit-Val, where I had commenced a large picture.

"She remained standing near me, following all my gestures with concentrated attention. Then, suddenly, fearing, perhaps, that she was disturbing me, she said to me: 'Thank you,' and walked away.

"But in a short time she became more familiar, and accompanied me every day, her countenance exhibiting visible pleasure. She carried her folding stool under her arm, would not consent to my carrying it, and she sat always by my side. She would remain there for hours immovable and mute, following with her eye the point of my brush in its every movement. When I would obtain, by a large splatch of color spread on with a knife, a striking and unexpected effect, she would, in spite of herself, give vent to a half-suppressed 'Oh!' of astonishment, of joy, of admiration. She had the most tender respect for my canvases, an almost religious respect for that human reproduction of a part of nature's work divine. My studies appeared to her to be pictures of sanctity, and sometimes she spoke to me of God, with the idea of converting me.

"Oh! He was a queer good-natured being, this God of hers. He was a sort of village philosopher without any great resources, and without great power; for she always figured him to herself as a being quivering over injustices committed under his eyes, and helpless to prevent them.

"She was, however, on excellent terms with him, affecting even to be the confidant of his secrets and of his whims. She said:

"'God wills, or God does not will,' just like a sergeant announcing to a recruit: 'The colonel has commanded.'

"At the bottom of her heart she deplored my ignorance of the intentions of the Eternal, which she strove, nay, felt herself compelled, to impart to me.

"Almost every day, I found in my pockets, in my hat when I lifted it from the ground, in my box of colors, in my polished shoes, standing in the mornings in front of my door, those little pious brochures, which she, no doubt, received directly from Paradise.

"I treated her as one would an old friend, with unaffected cordiality. But I soon perceived that she had changed somewhat in her manner; but, for a while, I paid little attention to it.

"When I walked about, whether to the bottom of the valley, or through some country lanes, I would see her suddenly appear, as though she were returning from a rapid walk. She would then sit down abruptly, out of breath, as though she had been running or overcome by some profound emotion. Her face would be red, that English red which is denied to the people of all other countries; then, without any reason, she would grow pale, become the color of the ground, and seem ready to faint away. Gradually, however, I would see her regain her ordinary color, whereupon she would begin to speak.

"Then, without warning, she would break off in the middle of a sentence, spring up from her seat, and march off so rapidly and so strangely, that it would, sometimes, put me to my wits' end to try and discover whether I had done or said anything to displease or offend her.

"I finally came to the conclusion that this arose from her early habits and training, somewhat modified, no doubt, in honor of me, since the first days of our acquaintanceship.

"When she returned to the farm, after walking for hours on the wind-beaten coast, her long curled hair would be shaken out and hanging loose, as though it had broken away from its bearings. It was seldom that this gave her any concern; though sometimes she looked as though she had been dining *sans cérémonie;* her locks having become disheveled by the breezes.

"She would then go up to her room in order to adjust what I called her glass lamps. When I would say to her, in familiar gallantry, which, however, always offended her:

"'You are as beautiful as a planet to-day, Miss Harriet,' a little blood would immediately mount into her cheeks, the blood of a young maiden, the blood of sweet fifteen.

"Then she would become abruptly savage and cease coming to watch me paint. But I always thought:

"'This is only a fit of temper she is passing through.'

"But it did not always pass away. When I spoke to her sometimes, she would answer me, either with an air of affected indifference, or in sullen anger; and she became by turns rude, impatient, and nervous. For a time I never saw her except at meals, and we spoke but little. I concluded, at length, that I must have offended her in something: and, accordingly, I said to her one evening:

"'Miss Harriet, why is it that you do not act toward me as formerly? What have I done to displease you? You are causing me much pain!'

"She responded, in an angry tone, in a manner altogether *sui generis:*

"'I am always with you the same as formerly. It is not true, not true,' and she ran upstairs and shut herself up in her room.

"At times she would look upon me with strange eyes. Since that time I have often said to myself that those condemned to death must look thus when informed that their last day has come. In her eye there lurked a species of folly, a folly at once mysterious and violent — even more, a fever, an exasperated desire, impatient, at once incapable of being realized and unrealizable!

"Nay, it seemed to me that there was also going on within her a combat, in which her heart struggled against an unknown force that she wished to overcome — perhaps, even, something else. But what could I know? What could I know?

III.

"This was indeed a singular revelation.

"For some time I had commenced to work, as soon as daylight appeared, on a picture, the subject of which was as follows:

"A deep ravine, steep banks dominated by two declivities, lined with brambles and long rows of trees, hidden, drowned in milky vapor, clad in that misty robe which sometimes floats over valleys at break of day. At the extreme end of that thick and transparent fog, you see coming, or rather already come, a human couple, a stripling and a maiden embraced, interlaced, she, with head leaning on him, he, inclined toward her, and lip to lip.

"A ray of the sun, glistening through the branches, has traversed the fog of dawn and illuminated it with a rosy reflection, just behind the rustic lovers, whose vague shadows are reflected on it in clear silver. It was well done, yes, indeed, well done.

"I was working on the declivity which led to the Val d'Etretat. This particular morning, I had, by chance, the sort of floating vapor which was necessary for my purpose. Suddenly, an object appeared in front of me, a kind of phantom; it was Miss Harriet. On seeing me, she took to flight. But I called after her saying: 'Come here, come here, Mademoiselle, I have a nice little picture for you.'

"She came forward, though with seeming reluctance. I handed her my sketch. She said nothing, but stood for a long time motionless, looking at it. Suddenly she burst into tears. She wept spasmodically, like men who have been struggling hard against shedding tears, but who can do so no longer, and abandon themselves to grief, though unwillingly. I got up, trembling, moved myself by the sight of a sorrow I did not comprehend, and I took her by the hand with a gesture of brusque affection, a true French impulse which impels one quicker than one thinks.

"She let her hands rest in mine for a few seconds, and I felt them quiver, as if her whole nervous system was twisting and turning. Then she withdrew her hands abruptly, or, rather, tore them out of mine.

"I recognized that shiver as soon as I had felt it; I was deceived in nothing. Ah! the love shudder of a woman, whether she is fifteen or fifty years of age, whether she is one of the people or one of the *monde*, goes so straight to my heart that I never had any difficulty in understanding it!

"Her whole frail being trembled, vibrated, yielded. I knew it. She walked away before I had time to say a word, leaving me as surprised as if I had witnessed a miracle, and as troubled as if I had committed a crime.

"I did not go in to breakfast. I took a walk on the banks of the Falaise, feeling that I could just as soon weep as laugh, looking on the adventure as both comic and deplorable, and my position as ridiculous, fain to believe that I had lost my head.

"I asked myself what I ought to do. I debated whether I ought not to take my leave of the place and almost immediately my resolution was formed.

"Somewhat sad and perplexed, I wandered about until dinner time, and entered the farmhouse just when the soup had been served up.

"I sat down at the table, as usual. Miss Harriet was there, munching away solemnly, without speaking to anyone, without even lifting her eyes. She wore, however, her usual expression, both of countenance and manner.

"I waited, patiently, till the meal had been finished. Then, turning toward the landlady, I said: 'Madame Lecacheur, it will not be long now before I shall have to take my leave of you.'

"The good woman, at once surprised and troubled, replied in a quivering voice: 'My dear sir, what is it I have just heard you say? Are you going to leave us, after I have become so much accustomed to you?'

"I looked at Miss Harriet from the corner of my eye. Her countenance did not change in the least; but the under-servant came toward me with eyes wide open. She was a fat girl, of about eighteen years of age, rosy, fresh, strong as a horse, yet possessing a rare attribute in one in her position—she

313

was very neat and clean. I had kissed her at odd times, in out of the way corners, in the manner of a mountain guide, nothing more.

"The dinner being over, I went to smoke my pipe under the apple-trees, walking up and down at my ease, from one end of the court to the other. All the reflections which I had made during the day, the strange discovery of the morning, that grotesque and passionate attachment for me, the recollections which that revelation had suddenly called up, recollections at once charming and perplexing, perhaps, also, that look which the servant had cast on me at the announcement of my departure — all these things, mixed up and combined, put me now in an excited bodily state, with the tickling sensation of kisses on my lips, and in my veins something which urged me on to commit some folly.

"Night having come on, casting its dark shadows under the trees, I descried Céleste, who had gone to shut the hen-coops, at the other end of the inclosure. I darted toward her, running so noiselessly that she heard nothing, and as she got up from closing the small traps by which the chickens went in and out, I clasped her in my arms and rained on her coarse, fat face a shower of kisses. She made a struggle, laughing all the same, as she was accustomed to do in such circumstances. What made me suddenly loose my grip of her? Why did I at once experience a shock? What was it that I heard behind me?

"It was Miss Harriet who had come upon us, who had seen us, and who stood in front of us, as motionless as a specter. Then she disappeared in the darkness.

314

"I was ashamed, embarrassed, more annoyed at having been surprised by her than if she had caught me committing some criminal act.

"I slept badly that night; I was worried and haunted by sad thoughts. I seemed to hear loud weeping; but in this I was no doubt deceived. Moreover, I thought several times that I heard some one walking up and down in the house, and that some one opened my door from the outside.

"Toward morning, I was overcome by fatigue, and sleep seized on me. I got up late and did not go downstairs until breakfast time, being still in a bewildered state, not knowing what kind of face to put on.

"No one had seen Miss Harriet. We waited for her at table, but she did not appear. At length, Mother Lecacheur went to her room. The English-woman had gone out. She must have set out at break of day, as she was wont to do, in order to see the sun rise.

"Nobody seemed astonished at this and we began to eat in silence.

"The weather was hot, very hot, one of those still sultry days when not a leaf stirs. The table had been placed out of doors, under an apple-tree; and from time to time Sapeur had gone to the cellar to draw a jug of cider, everybody was so thirsty. Céleste brought the dishes from the kitchen, a ragout of mutton with potatoes, a cold rabbit, and a salad. Afterward she placed before us a dish of strawberries, the first of the season.

"As I wanted to wash and freshen these, I begged the servant to go and bring a pitcher of cold water.

315

"In about five minutes she returned, declaring that the well was dry. She had lowered the pitcher to the full extent of the cord, and had touched the bottom, but on drawing the pitcher up again, it was empty. Mother Lecacheur, anxious to examine the thing for herself, went and looked down the hole. She returned announcing that one could see clearly something in the well, something altogether unusual. But this, no doubt, was pottles of straw, which, out of spite, had been cast down it by a neighbor.

"I wished also to look down the well, hoping to clear up the mystery, and perched myself close to its brink. I perceived, indistinctly, a white object. What could it be? I then conceived the idea of lowering a lantern at the end of a cord. When I did so, the yellow flame danced on the layers of stone and gradually became clearer. All four of us were leaning over the opening, Sapeur and Céleste having now joined us. The lantern rested on a black and white, indistinct mass, singular, incomprehensible. Sapeur exclaimed:

"'It is a horse. I see the hoofs. It must have escaped from the meadow, during the night, and fallen in headlong.'

"But, suddenly, a cold shiver attacked my spine, I first recognized a foot, then a clothed limb; the body was entire, but the other limb had disappeared under the water.

"I groaned and trembled so violently that the light of the lamp danced hither and thither over the object, discovering a slipper.

"'It is a woman! who — who — can it be? It is Miss Harriet.'

316

"Sapeur alone did not manifest horror. He had witnessed many such scenes in Africa.

"Mother Lecacheur and Céleste began to scream and to shriek, and ran away.

"But it was necessary to recover the corpse of the dead. I attached the boy securely by the loins to the end of the pulley-rope; then I lowered him slowly, and watched him disappear in the darkness. In the one hand he had a lantern, and held on to the rope with the other. Soon I recognized his voice, which seemed to come from the center of the earth, crying:

"'Stop.'

"I then saw him fish something out of the water. It was the other limb. He bound the two feet together, and shouted anew:

"'Haul up.'

"I commenced to wind him up, but I felt my arms strain, my muscles twitch, and was in terror lest I should let the boy fall to the bottom. When his head appeared over the brink, I asked:

"'What is it?' as though I only expected that he would tell me what he had discovered at the bottom.

"We both got on to the stone slab at the edge of the well, and, face to face, hoisted the body.

"Mother Lecacheur and Céleste watched us from a distance, concealed behind the wall of the house. When they saw, issuing from the well, the black slippers and white stockings of the drowned person, they disappeared.

"Sapeur seized the ankles of the poor chaste woman, and we drew it up, inclined, as it was, in the most immodest posture. The head was in a shocking state, bruised and black; and the long, gray hair, hanging down, was tangled and disordered.

"'In the name of all that is holy, how lean she is!' exclaimed Sapeur, in a contemptuous tone.

"We carried her into the room, and as the women did not put in an appearance, I, with the assistance of the lad, dressed the corpse for burial.

"I washed her disfigured face. By the touch of my hand an eye was slightly opened; it seemed to scan me with that pale stare, with that cold, that terrible look which corpses have, a look which seems to come from the beyond. I plaited up, as well as I could, her disheveled hair, and I adjusted on her forehead a novel and singularly formed lock. Then I took off her dripping wet garments, baring, not without a feeling of shame, as though I had been guilty of some profanation, her shoulders and her chest, and her long arms, slim as the twigs of branches.

"I next went to fetch some flowers, corn poppies, blue beetles, marguerites, and fresh and perfumed herbs, with which to strew her funeral couch.

"Being the only person near her, it was necessary for me to perform the usual ceremonies. In a letter found in her pocket, written at the last moment, she asked that her body be buried in the village in which she had passed the last days of her life. A frightful thought then oppressed my heart. Was it not on my account that she wished to be laid at rest in this place?

"Toward the evening, all the female gossips of the locality came to view the remains of the defunct; but I would not allow a single person to enter; I wanted to be alone; and I watched by the corpse the whole night.

"By the flickering light of the candles, I looked at the body of this miserable woman, wholly unknown, who had died so lamentably and so far away from home. Had she left no friends, no relatives behind her? What had her infancy been? What had been her life? Whence had she come thither, all alone, a wanderer, like a dog driven from home? What secrets of suffering and of despair were sealed up in that disagreeable body, in that spent and withered body, that impenetrable hiding place of a mystery which had driven her far away from affection and from love?

"How many unhappy beings there are! I felt that upon that human creature weighed the eternal injustice of implacable nature! Life was over with her, without her ever having experienced, perhaps, that which sustains the most miserable of us all—to wit, the hope of being once loved! Otherwise, why should she thus have concealed herself, have fled from the face of others? Why did she love everything so tenderly and so passionately, everything living that was not a man?

"I recognized, also, that she believed in a God, and that she hoped for compensation from him for the miseries she had endured. She had now begun to decompose, and to become, in turn, a plant. She who had blossomed in the sun was now to be eaten up by the cattle, carried away in herbs, and in the flesh of beasts, again to become human flesh. But that which is called the soul had been extinguished at the bottom of the dark well. She suffered no longer. She had changed her life for that of others yet to be born.

"Hours passed away in this silent and sinister communion with the dead. A pale light at length announced the dawn of a new day, and a bright ray glistened on the bed, shedding a dash of fire on the bedclothes and on her hands. This was the hour she had so much loved, when the waking birds began to sing in the trees.

"I opened the window to its fullest extent, I drew back the curtains, so that the whole heavens might look in upon us. Then bending toward the glassy corpse, I took in my hands the mutilated head, and slowly, without terror or disgust, imprinted a long, long kiss upon those lips which had never before received the salute of love."

*   *   *   *   *   *   *

Léon Chenal remained silent. The women wept. We heard on the box seat Count d'Etraille blow his nose, from time to time. The coachman alone had gone to sleep. The horses, which felt no longer the sting of the whip, had slackened their pace and dragged softly along. And the four-in-hand, hardly moving at all, became suddenly torpid, as if laden with sorrow.

TOINE

EVERYBODY for ten leagues round knew Toine, fat Toine, "Toine-my-Fine," Antoine Mâcheblé, the landlord of Tournevent.

He had made famous this village, buried in the depths of the valley which descended to the sea. It was a poor peasant hamlet, composed of a dozen Norman houses surrounded by ditches and encircled by trees. The houses were huddled together in this shrub-covered ravine, behind the curve of the hill, which had caused the village to be called Tournevent. As birds conceal themselves in the furrows during a storm, they seemed to have sought a shelter in this hollow, a shelter against the fierce salt winds of the sea, which gnawed and burned like fire and withered and destroyed like the blasts of winter.

The whole hamlet seemed to be the property of Antoine Mâcheblé, who was besides often called Toine, and Toine-my-Fine, on account of a manner

321

of speech of which he constantly availed himself. "My Fine is the best in France," he would say. His *fine* was his cognac, be it understood. For twenty years he had watered the country with his cognac, and in serving his customers he was in the habit of saying: "It warms the stomach and clears the head; there is nothing better for your health, my son." He called everybody "my son," although he had never had a son of his own.

Ah, yes, everyone knew old Toine, the biggest man in the canton, or even in the *arrondissement*. His little house seemed too ridiculously small to contain him, and when he was seen standing in his doorway, where he spent the greater part of every day, one wondered how he could enter his dwelling. But he did enter each time a customer presented himself, for Toine-my-Fine was invited by right to levy a little glass on all who drank in his house.

His *café* bore on its sign the legend "The Rendezvous of Friends," and old Toine was truly the friend of all the country round. People came from Fécamp and Montivilliers to see him and tipple with him and to hear his stories — for this great, good-natured man could make a tombstone laugh. He could joke without giving offense, wink an eye to express what he dare not utter, and punch one's ribs in a fit of gaiety, so as to force a laugh in spite of oneself. And then it was a curiosity just to see him drink. He drank all that was offered him by everybody, with a joy in his wicked eye, a joy which came from a double pleasure: the pleasure of regaling himself first, and the pleasure of heaping

322

up money at the expense of his friends afterward. The blackguards of the community wondered why Toine had no children, and one day asked him as much. With a wicked wink he replied: "My wife is not attractive enough for such a fine fellow as I am."

The quarrels of Toine and his homely wife were as much enjoyed by the tipplers as was their favorite cognac, for they had squabbled through the whole thirty years of their married life. Only Toine was good-natured over it, while his wife was furious. She was a tall peasant woman who walked with long stilt-like strides and carried on her thin, flat body the head of an ugly screech owl. She spent her whole time in rearing poultry in the little yard behind the public-house, and was renowned for the success with which she fattened her fowls.

When any of the great ladies of Fécamp gave a feast to the people of quality, it was necessary to the success of the repast that it should be garnished with the celebrated fowls from mother Toine's poultry-yard.

But she was born with a vile temper and had continued to be dissatisfied with everything. Angry with everybody, she was particularly so with her husband. She jeered at his gaiety, his popularity, his good health, and his *embonpoint;* she treated him with the utmost contempt because he got his money without working for it, and because, as she said, he ate and drank as much as ten ordinary men. She declared every day that he was only fit to be littered in the stable with the naked swine, whom he resembled, and that he was only a mass of fat that made her sick at her stomach. "Wait a little, wait a little," she would shriek in his face, "we shall soon see what is going to happen! This great wind-bag will burst like a sack of grain!"

Toine laughed till he shook like a bowl of jelly and, tapping his enormous belly, replied: "Ah, my old hen, let us see you try to make your chickens as fat as this."

And rolling up his sleeve he showed his brawny arm. "Do you not see the feathers growing already?" he cried. And the customers would strike their fists on the table and fairly writhe with joy, and would stamp their feet and spit upon the floor in a delirium of delight.

The old woman grew more furious than ever, and shouted at the top of her lungs: "Just wait a bit, we shall see what will happen. Your Toine-my-Fine will burst like a sack of grain."

And she rushed out, maddened with rage at the laughter of the crowd of drinkers.

Toine, in fact, was a wonder to see, so fat and red and short of breath had he grown. He was one of those enormous creatures with whom Death seems to amuse himself by tricks, gaieties, and fatal buffooneries, making irresistibly comic the slow work of destruction. Instead of showing himself, as toward others, in white hairs, shrunken limbs, wrinkles, and general feebleness which made one say with a shiver: "Heavens, how he has changed!" he took pleasure in fattening Toine; in making a droll monster of him, in reddening his face and giving him the appearance of superhuman health; and the deformities which he inflicted on other beings became in Toine's case laughable and diverting instead of sinister and pitiable.

"Wait a little, wait a little," muttered mother Toine, as she scattered the grain about her poultry-yard, "we are going to see what will happen!"

II.

IT HAPPENED that Toine had a seizure, and fell smitten with a paralytic stroke. They carried the giant to the little chamber partitioned off at the rear of the *café* in order that he might hear what was going on on the other side of the wall, and converse with his friends, for his brain remained clear while his enormous body was prone and helpless. They hoped for a time that his mighty limbs would recover some of their energy, but this hope disappeared very soon, and Toine-my-Fine was forced to pass his days and nights in his bed, which was made up but once a week, with the help of four friends who lifted him by his four limbs while his mattress was turned. He continued cheerful, but with a different kind of gaiety; more timid, more humble, and with the pathetic fear of a little child in the presence of his wife, who scolded and raged all the day long. "There he lies, the great glutton, the good-for-nothing idler, the nasty thing!" she cried. Toine replied nothing, only winking his eye behind the old woman's back, and turned over in the bed, the only movement he was able to make. He called this change "making a move to the north, or a move to the south." His only entertainment now was to listen to the conversation in the *café* and to join in the talk across the wall, and when he recognized the voice of a friend he would cry: "Hello, my son; is it thou, Célestin?"

And Célestin Maloisel would reply: "It is me, father Toine. How do you gallop to-day, my great rabbit?"

"I cannot gallop yet, Célestin," Toine would answer, "but I am not growing thin, either. The shell is good." Soon he invited his intimates into his chamber for company, because it pained him to see them drinking without him. He told them it grieved him not to be able to take his cognac with them. "I can stand everything else," he said; "but not to drink with you makes me sad, my sons."

Then the screech-owl's head of mother Toine would appear at the window, and she would cry: "Look, look at him! this great hulking idler, who must be fed and washed and scoured like a pig!"

And when she disappeared a red-plumaged rooster sometimes perched on the window-sill, and, looking about with his round and curious eye, gave forth a shrill crow. And sometimes two or three hens flew in and scratched and pecked about the floor, attracted by the crumbs which fell from father Toine's plate.

The friends of Toine-my-Fine very soon deserted the *café* for his chamber, and every afternoon they gossiped around the bed of the big man. Bedridden as he was, this rascal of a Toine still amused them; he would have made the devil himself laugh, the jolly fellow! There were three friends who came

326

every day: Célestin Maloisel, a tall, spare man with
a body twisted like the trunk of an apple-tree; Prosper Horslaville, a little dried-up old man with a nose
like a ferret, malicious and sly as a fox; and Césaire
Paumelle, who never uttered a word, but who enjoyed
himself all the same. These men brought in a board
from the yard which they placed across the bed and
on which they played dominoes from two o'clock in
the afternoon until six. But mother Toine soon inter-
fered: she could not endure that her husband should
amuse himself by playing dominoes in his bed, and,
each time she saw the play begin, she bounded into
the room in a rage, overturned the board, seized the
dominoes, and carried them into the *café*, declaring
that it was enough to feed this great lump of tallow
without seeing him divert himself at the expense of
hard-working people. Célestin Maloisel bent his head
before the storm, but Prosper Horslaville tried to further excite the old woman, whose rages amused him.
Seeing her one day more exasperated than usual, he
said: "Hello, mother Toine! Do you know what I
would do if I were in your place?"

She waited for an explanation, fixing her owl-like
eyes upon him. He continued:

"Your husband, who never leaves his bed, is as
hot as an oven. I should set him to hatching out
eggs."

She remained stupefied, thinking he was jesting,
watching the meager and sly face of the peasant, who
continued:

"I would put five eggs under each arm the same
day that I set the yellow hen; they would all hatch
out at the same time; and when they were out of

their shells, I would put your husband's chicks under the hen for her to bring up. That would bring you some poultry, mother Toine."

The old woman was amazed. "Can that be?" she asked.

Prosper continued: "Why can't it? Since they put eggs in a warm box to hatch, one might as well put them in a warm bed."

She was greatly impressed with this reasoning, and went out composed and thoughtful.

Eight days later she came into Toine's chamber with her apron full of eggs, and said: "I have just put the yellow hen to set with ten eggs under her; here are ten for you! Be careful not to break them!"

Toine was astonished. "What do you mean?" he cried.

"I mean that you shall hatch them, good-for-nothing."

Toine laughed at first, then as she insisted he grew angry, he resisted and obstinately refused to allow her to put the eggs under his great arms, that his warmth might hatch them. But the baffled old woman grew furious and declared: "You shall have not a bite to eat so long as you refuse to take them —there, we'll see what will happen!"

Toine was uneasy, but he said nothing till he heard the clock strike twelve; then he called to his wife, who bawled from the kitchen: "There is no dinner for you to-day, you great idler!"

He thought at first she was joking, but when he found she was in earnest he begged and prayed and swore by fits; turned himself to the north and the south, and, growing desperate under the pangs of hunger and the smell of the viands, he pounded on the wall with his great fists, until at last, worn out and almost famished, he allowed his wife to introduce the eggs into his bed and place them under his arms. After that he had his soup.

When his friends arrived as usual, they believed Toine to be very ill; he seemed constrained and in pain.

Then they began to play dominoes as formerly, but Toine appeared to take no pleasure in the game, and put forth his hand so gingerly and with such evident precaution that they suspected at once something was wrong.

"Hast thou thy arm tied?" demanded Horslaville.

Toine feebly responded: "I have a feeling of heaviness in my shoulder."

Suddenly some one entered the *café*, and the players paused to listen. It was the mayor and his assistant, who called for two glasses of cognac and then began to talk of the affairs of the country. As they spoke in low tones, Toine tried to press his ear against the wall; and forgetting his eggs, he gave a sudden lunge "to the north," which made an omelet of them in short order. At the oath he uttered, mother Toine came running in, and divining the disaster she uncovered him with a jerk. She stood a moment too enraged and breathless to speak, at the sight of the yellow poultice pasted on the flank of her husband. Then, trembling with fury, she flung herself on the paralytic and began to pound him with great force on the body, as though she were pound-

ing her dirty linen on the banks of the river. She
showered her blows upon him with the force and
rapidity of a drummer beating his drum.

The friends of Toine were choking with laughter,
coughing, sneezing, uttering exclamations, while the
frightened man parried the attacks of his wife with
due precaution in order not to break the five eggs he
still had on the other side.

III.

TOINE was conquered. He was compelled to hatch
eggs. He had to renounce the innocent pleasure of
dominoes, to give up any effort to move to the north
or south, for his wife deprived him of all nourishment every time he broke an egg. He lay on his
back, with his eyes fixed on the ceiling, his arms
extended like wings, warming against his immense
body the incipient chicks in their white shells. He
spoke only in low tones as if he feared a noise as
much as a movement, and he asked often about the
yellow hen in the poultry-yard, who was engaged in
the same task as himself. The old woman went from
the hen to her husband, and from her husband to the
hen, possessed and preoccupied with the little broods
which were maturing in the bed and in the nest.
The country people, who soon learned the story,
came in, curious and serious, to get the news of
Toine. They entered on tiptoe as one enters a sick-
chamber, and inquired with concern:

"How goes it, Toine?"

"It has to go," he answered; "but it is so long, I am tired of waiting. I get excited and feel cold shivers galloping all over my skin."

One morning his wife came in very much elated and exclaimed: "The yellow hen has hatched seven chicks; there were but three bad eggs!"

Toine felt his heart beat. How many would he have?

"Will it be soon?" he asked, with the anguish of a woman who is about to become a mother.

The old woman, who was tortured by the fear of failure, answered angrily:

"It is to be hoped so!"

They waited.

The friends, seeing that Toine's time was approaching, became very uneasy themselves. They gossiped about it in the house, and kept all the neighbors informed of the progress of affairs. Toward three o'clock Toine grew drowsy. He slept now half the time. He was suddenly awakened by an unusual tickling under his left arm. He put his hand carefully to the place and seized a little beast covered with yellow down, which struggled between his fingers. His emotion was so great that he cried out and let go the chick, which ran across his breast. The *café* was full of people. The customers rushed into the room and circled around the bed, while mother Toine, who had arrived at the first sound, carefully caught the fledgeling as it nestled in her husband's beard. No one uttered a word. It was a warm April day; one could hear through the open window the clucking of the yellow hen calling to her new born. Toine, who perspired with emotion and agony, murmured: "I feel another one under my left arm."

His wife plunged her great, gaunt hand under the bedclothes and drew forth a second chick with all the precautions of a midwife.

The neighbors wished to see it and passed it from hand to hand, regarding it with awe as though it were a phenomenon. For the space of twenty minutes no more were hatched, then four chicks came out of their shells at the same time. This caused a great excitement among the watchers.

Toine smiled, happy at his success, and began to feel proud of this singular paternity. Such a sight had never been seen before. This was a droll man, truly! "That makes six," cried Toine. "*Sacre bleu,* what a christening there will be!" and a great laugh rang out from the public. Other people now crowded into the *café* and filled the doorway, with outstretched necks and curious eyes.

"How many has he?" they inquired.

"There are six."

Mother Toine ran with the new fledgelings to the hen, who, clucking distractedly, erected her feathers and spread wide her wings to shelter her increasing flock of little ones.

"Here comes another one!" cried Toine. He was mistaken — there were three of them. This was a triumph! The last one chipped its shell at seven o'clock in the evening. All Toine's eggs were good! He was delivered, and delirious with joy, he seized and kissed the frail little creature on the back. He could have smothered it with caresses. He wished to keep this little one in his bed until the next day, moved by the tenderness of a mother for this being to whom he had given life; but the old woman carried it away, as she had done the others, without listening to the supplications of her husband.

The friends of Toine went home delighted, conversing of the event by the way.

Horslaville remained after the others had gone, and approaching the ear of Toine whispered: "You will invite me to the first fricassee, will you not?"

At the idea of a fricassee, the visage of Toine brightened and he answered:

"Certainly I will invite thee, my son."

THE STRING

A LONG all the roads around Goderville the peasants and their wives
were coming toward the burgh
because it was market day. The men
were proceeding with slow steps, the
whole body bent forward at each
movement of their long twisted
legs, deformed by their hard work,
by the weight on the plow which,
at the same time, raised the left
shoulder and swerved the figure, by
the reaping of the wheat which made
the knees spread to make a firm "pur-
chase," by all the slow and painful
labors of the country. Their blouses,
blue, "stiff-starched," shining as if varnished, orna-
mented with a little design in white at the neck and
wrists, puffed about their bony bodies, seemed like
balloons ready to carry them off. From each of
them a head, two arms, and two feet protruded.

Some led a cow or a calf by a cord, and their
wives, walking behind the animal, whipped its
haunches with a leafy branch to hasten its progress.

334

They carried large baskets on their arms from which, in some cases, chickens and, in others, ducks thrust out their heads. And they walked with a quicker, livelier step than their husbands. Their spare straight figures were wrapped in a scanty little shawl, pinned over their flat bosoms, and their heads were enveloped in a white cloth glued to the hair and surmounted by a cap.

Then a wagon passed at the jerky trot of a nag, shaking strangely, two men seated side by side and a woman in the bottom of the vehicle, the latter holding on to the sides to lessen the hard jolts.

In the public square of Goderville there was a crowd, a throng of human beings and animals mixed together. The horns of the cattle, the tall hats with long nap of the rich peasant, and the headgear of the peasant women rose above the surface of the assembly. And the clamorous, shrill, screaming voices made a continuous and savage din which sometimes was dominated by the robust lungs of some countryman's laugh, or the long lowing of a cow tied to the wall of a house.

All that smacked of the stable, the dairy and the dirt heap, hay and sweat, giving forth that unpleasant odor, human and animal, peculiar to the people of the field.

Maître Hauchecome, of Breaute, had just arrived at Goderville, and he was directing his steps toward the public square, when he perceived upon the ground a little piece of string. Maître Hauchecome, economical like a true Norman, thought that everything useful ought to be picked up, and he bent painfully, for he suffered from rheumatism. He took the bit of thin cord from the ground and began to roll it carefully when he noticed Maître Malandain, the harness-maker, on the threshold of his door, looking at him. They had heretofore had business together on the subject of a halter, and they were on bad terms, being both good haters. Maître Hauchecome was seized with a sort of shame to be seen thus by his enemy, picking a bit of string out of the dirt. He concealed his "find" quickly under his blouse, then in his trousers' pocket; then he pretended to be still looking on the ground for something which he did not find, and he went toward the market, his head forward, bent double by his pains.

He was soon lost in the noisy and slowly moving crowd, which was busy with interminable bargainings. The peasants milked, went and came, perplexed, always in fear of being cheated, not daring to decide, watching the vender's eye, ever trying to find the trick in the man and the flaw in the beast.

The women, having placed their great baskets at their feet, had taken out the poultry which lay upon the ground, tied together by the feet, with terrified eyes and scarlet crests.

They heard offers, stated their prices with a dry air and impassive face, or perhaps, suddenly deciding on some proposed reduction, shouted to the customer who was slowly going away: "All right, Maître Authirne, I'll give it to you for that."

Then little by little the square was deserted, and the Angelus ringing at noon, those who had stayed too long, scattered to their shops.

At Jourdain's the great room was full of people eating, as the big court was full of vehicles of all

kinds, carts, gigs, wagons, dump carts, yellow with
dirt, mended and patched, raising their shafts to the
sky like two arms, or perhaps with their shafts in
the ground and their backs in the air.

Just opposite the diners seated at the table, the
immense fireplace, filled with bright flames, cast a
lively heat on the backs of the row on the right.
Three spits were turning on which were chickens,
pigeons, and legs of mutton; and an appetizing odor
of roast beef and gravy dripping over the nicely
browned skin rose from the hearth, increased the
jovialness, and made everybody's mouth water.

All the aristocracy of the plow ate there, at Maître
Jourdain's, tavern keeper and horse dealer, a rascal
who had money.

The dishes were passed and emptied, as were the
jugs of yellow cider. Everyone told his affairs, his
purchases, and sales. They discussed the crops. The
weather was favorable for the green things but not
for the wheat.

Suddenly the drum beat in the court, before the
house. Everybody rose except a few indifferent persons, and ran to the door, or to the windows, their
mouths still full and napkins in their hands.

After the public crier had ceased his drum-beating,
he called out in a jerky voice, speaking his phrases
irregularly:

"It is hereby made known to the inhabitants of
Goderville, and in general to all persons present at
the market, that there was lost this morning, on the
road to Benzeville, between nine and ten o'clock, a
black leather pocketbook containing five hundred
francs and some business papers. The finder is re-

quested to return same with all haste to the mayor's office or to Maître Fortune Houlbreque of Manneville, there will be twenty francs reward."

Then the man went away. The heavy roll of the drum and the crier's voice were again heard at a distance.

Then they began to talk of this event discussing the chances that Maître Houlbreque had of finding or not finding his pocketbook.

And the meal concluded. They were finishing their coffee when a chief of the gendarmes appeared upon the threshold.

He inquired:

"Is Maître Hauchecome, of Breaute, here?"

Maître Hauchecome, seated at the other end of the table, replied:

"Here I am."

And the officer resumed:

"Maître Hauchecome, will you have the goodness to accompany me to the mayor's office? The mayor would like to talk to you."

The peasant, surprised and disturbed, swallowed at a draught his tiny glass of brandy, rose, and, even more bent than in the morning, for the first steps after each rest were specially difficult, set out, repeating: "Here I am, here I am."

The mayor was awaiting him, seated on an armchair. He was the notary of the vicinity, a stout, serious man, with pompous phrases.

"Maître Hauchecome," said he, "you were seen this morning to pick up, on the road to Benzeville, the pocketbook lost by Maître Houlbreque, of Manneville."

338

The countryman, astounded, looked at the mayor, already terrified, by this suspicion resting on him without his knowing why.

"Me? Me? Me pick up the pocketbook?"

"Yes, you, yourself."

"Word of honor, I never heard of it."

"But you were seen."

"I was seen, me? Who says he saw me?"

"Monsieur Malandain, the harness-maker."

The old man remembered, understood, and flushed with anger.

"Ah, he saw me, the clodhopper, he saw me pick up this string, here, M'sieu' the Mayor." And rummaging in his pocket he drew out the little piece of string.

But the mayor, incredulous, shook his head.

"You will not make me believe, Maître Hauchecome, that Monsieur Malandain, who is a man worthy of credence, mistook this cord for a pocketbook."

The peasant, furious, lifted his hand, spat at one side to attest his honor, repeating:

"It is nevertheless the truth of the good God, the sacred truth, M'sieu' the Mayor. I repeat it on my soul and my salvation."

The mayor resumed:

"After picking up the object, you stood like a stilt, looking a long while in the mud to see if any piece of money had fallen out."

The good, old man choked with indignation and fear.

"How anyone can tell—how anyone can tell—such lies to take away an honest man's reputation! How can anyone—"

There was no use in his protesting, nobody believed him. He was confronted with Monsieur Malandain, who repeated and maintained his affirmation. They abused each other for an hour. At his own request, Maître Hauchecome was searched, nothing was found on him.

Finally the mayor, very much perplexed, discharged him with the warning that he would consult the public prosecutor and ask for further orders.

The news had spread. As he left the mayor's office, the old man was surrounded and questioned with a serious or bantering curiosity, in which there was no indignation. He began to tell the story of the string. No one believed him. They laughed at him.

He went along, stopping his friends, beginning endlessly his statement and his protestations, showing his pockets turned inside out, to prove that he had nothing.

They said:

"Old rascal, get out!"

And he grew angry, becoming exasperated, hot, and distressed at not being believed, not knowing what to do and always repeating himself.

Night came. He must depart. He started on his way with three neighbors to whom he pointed out the place where he had picked up the bit of string; and all along the road he spoke of his adventure.

In the evening he took a turn in the village of Breaute, in order to tell it to everybody. He only met with incredulity.

It made him ill at night.

The next day about one o'clock in the afternoon, Marius Paumelle, a hired man in the employ of Maître Breton, husbandman at Ymanville, returned the pocketbook and its contents to Maître Houlbreque of Manneville.

This man claimed to have found the object in the road; but not knowing how to read, he had carried it to the house and given it to his employer.

The news spread through the neighborhood. Maître Hauchecome was informed of it. He immediately went the circuit and began to recount his story completed by the happy climax. He was in triumph.

"What grieved me so much was not the thing itself, as the lying. There is nothing so shameful as to be placed under a cloud on account of a lie."

He talked of his adventure all day long, he told it on the highway to people who were passing by, in the wine-shop to people who were drinking there, and to persons coming out of church the following Sunday. He stopped strangers to tell them about it. He was calm now, and yet something disturbed him without his knowing exactly what it was. People had the air of joking while they listened. They did not seem convinced. He seemed to feel that remarks were being made behind his back.

On Tuesday of the next week he went to the market at Goderville, urged solely by the necessity he felt of discussing the case.

Malandain, standing at his door, began to laugh on seeing him pass. Why?

He approached a farmer from Crequetot, who did not let him finish, and giving him a thump in the stomach said to his face:

"You big rascal."

Then he turned his back on him.

Maître Hauchecome was confused, why was he called a big rascal?

When he was seated at the table, in Jourdain's tavern he commenced to explain "the affair."

A horse dealer from Monvilliers called to him:

"Come, come, old sharper, that's an old trick; I know all about your piece of string!"

Hauchecome stammered:

"But since the pocketbook was found."

But the other man replied:

"Shut up, papa, there is one that finds, and there is one that reports. At any rate you are mixed with it."

The peasant stood choking. He understood. They accused him of having had the pocketbook returned by a confederate, by an accomplice.

He tried to protest. All the table began to laugh.

He could not finish his dinner and went away, in the midst of jeers.

He went home ashamed and indignant, choking with anger and confusion, the more dejected that he was capable with his Norman cunning of doing what they had accused him of, and ever boasting of it as of a good turn. His innocence to him, in a confused way, was impossible to prove, as his sharpness was known. And he was stricken to the heart by the injustice of the suspicion.

Then he began to recount the adventures again, prolonging his history every day, adding each time, new reasons, more energetic protestations, more solemn oaths which he imagined and prepared in his hours of solitude, his whole mind given up to the story of the string. He was believed so much the less as his defense was more complicated and his arguing more subtile.

"Those are lying excuses," they said behind his back.

He felt it, consumed his heart over it, and wore himself out with useless efforts. He wasted away before their very eyes.

The wags now made him tell about the string to amuse them, as they make a soldier who has been on a campaign tell about his battles. His mind, touched to the depth, began to weaken.

Toward the end of December he took to his bed.

He died in the first days of January, and in the delirium of his death struggles he kept claiming his innocence, reiterating.

"A piece of string, a piece of string,—look—here it is, M'sieu' the Mayor."

A MÉSALLIANCE

It is a generally acknowledged truth that the prerogatives of the nobility are only maintained at the present time through the weakness of the middle classes. Many of these, who have established themselves and their families by their intellect, industry, and struggles, fall into a state of bliss, which reminds those who see it of intoxication, as soon as they are permitted to enter aristocratic circles, or can be seen in public with barons and counts, and above all, when these treat them in a friendly manner, no matter from what motive, or when they see a prospect of a daughter of theirs driving in a carriage with armorial bearings on the panels.

Many women and girls of the citizen class would not hesitate for a moment to refuse an honorable, good-looking man of their own class, in order to go to the altar with the oldest, ugliest, and stupidest dotard among the aristocracy.

I shall never forget saying in joke, shortly before her marriage, to a young, well-educated girl of a

wealthy, middle-class family, who had the figure and
the bearing of a queen, not to forget an ermine cloak
in her trousseau.

"I know it would suit me capitally," she replied
in all seriousness, "and I should certainly have worn
one, if I had married Baron R——, which I was nearly
doing, as you know, but it is not suitable for the wife
of a government official."

When a girl of the middle classes wanders from
the paths of virtue, her fall may, as a rule, be rightly
ascribed to her hankering after the nobility.

In a small German town there lived, some years
ago, a tailor whom we will call Löwenfuss, a man who,
like all knights of the shears, was equally full of
aspirations after culture and liberty. After working
for one master for some time as a poor journeyman,
he married his daughter, and after his father-in-law's
death succeeded to the business. As he was indus-
trious, lucky, and managed it well, he soon grew very
well off, and was in a position to give his daughters
an education which many a nobleman's children might
have envied. They learned not only French and
music, but also acquired many more solid branches
of knowledge, and as they were both pretty and
charming girls, they soon became much thought of
and sought after.

Fanny, the elder, was especially her father's pride
and a favorite in society. She was of middle height,
slim, with a thoroughly maidenly figure, and with an
almost Italian face, in which two large, dark eyes
seemed to ask for love and submission at the same
time. Yet this girl with her plentiful, black hair was
not in the least intended to command, for she was

one of those romantic women who will give themselves, or even throw themselves, away, but who can
never be subjugated. A young physician fell in love
with her, and wished to marry her; Fanny returned
his love, and her parents gladly accepted him as a
son-in-law. But she made it a condition that he
should visit her freely and frequently for two years,
before she would consent to become his wife, and
she declared that she would not go to the altar with
him until she was convinced that not only their
hearts but also that their characters harmonized. He
agreed to her wish, and became a regular visitor at
the house of the educated tailor; they were happy
hours for the lovers; they played, sang, and read together, and he told the girl some of his medical experiences which excited and moved her.

Just then, an officer went one day to the tailor's
shop to order some civilian's clothes. This was not
an unusual event in itself, but it was soon to be the
cause of one; for accidentally the daughter of *the
artist in clothes* came into the shop, just as the officer
was leaving it. On seeing her, he paused and asked
the tailor who the young lady was.

"My daughter," the tailor said, proudly.

"May I beg you to introduce me to the young
lady, Herr Löwenfuss?" said the hussar.

"I feel flattered at the honor you are doing me,"
the tailor replied, with evident pleasure.

"Fanny, the captain wishes to make your acquaintance; this is my daughter Fanny, Captain—"

"Captain Count Kasimir W——," the hussar interrupted him, as he went up to the pretty girl, and
paid her a compliment or two. They were very

346

commonplace, stale, everyday phrases, but in spite of this they pleased the girl, intelligent as she was, because it was a cavalry officer and a Count to boot who addressed them to her. And when at last the captain, in the most friendly manner, asked the tailor's permission to be allowed to visit at his house, both father and daughter granted it to him most readily.

The very next day Count W——paid his visit, in full-dress uniform, and when Frau Löwenfuss made some observations about it, how handsome it was, and how well it became him, he told them that he should not wear it much longer, as he intended to quit the service soon, and to look for a wife in whom birth and wealth were matters of secondary consideration, while a good education and a knowledge of domestic matters were of paramount importance; adding that as soon as he had found one, he meant to retire to his estates.

From that moment, papa and mamma Löwenfuss looked upon the Count as their daughter's suitor. It is certain that he was madly in love with Fanny; he used to go to their house every evening, and made himself so liked by all of them that the young doctor soon felt himself to be superfluous, and so his visits became rarer and rarer. The Count confessed his love to Fanny on a moonlight night, while they were sitting in an arbor covered with honeysuckle, which formed nearly the whole of Herr Löwenfuss's garden. He swore that he loved, that he adored her, and when at last she lay trembling in his arms he tried to take her by storm. But that bold cavalry exploit did not succeed, and the good-looking hussar found out for the first time in his life that a woman can at the same time be romantic, passionately in love, and virtuous.

The next morning the tailor called on the Count, and begged him very humbly to state what his intentions with regard to Fanny were. The enamored hussar declared that he was determined to make the tailor's little daughter Countess W——. Herr Löwenfuss was so much overcome by his feelings, that he showed great inclination to embrace his future son-in-law. The Count, however, laid down certain conditions. The whole matter must be kept a profound secret, for he had every prospect of inheriting half-a-million of florins,* on the death of an aunt who was already eighty years old, which he should risk by a *mésalliance.*

When they heard this, the girl's parents certainly hesitated for a time to give their consent to the marriage, but the handsome hussar, whose ardent passion carried Fanny away, at last gained the victory. The doctor received a pretty little note from the tailor's daughter, in which she told him that she gave him back his promise, as she had not found her ideal in him. Fanny then signed a deed, by which she formally renounced all claims to her father's property, in favor of her sister, and left her home and her father's house with the Count under cover of the night, in order to accompany him to Poland, where the marriage was to take place in his castle.

Of course malicious tongues declared that the hussar had abducted Fanny. But her parents smiled at such reports, for they knew better, and the moment

when their daughter would return as Countess W——
would amply recompense them for everything.

Meanwhile the Polish Count and the romantic
German girl were being carried by the train through
the dreary plains of Masovia.* They stopped in a
large town to make some purchases, and the Count,
who was very wealthy and liberal, provided his future
wife with everything that befitted a Countess and a
girl could fancy, and then they continued their journey.
The country grew more picturesque but more melancholy as they went further east; the somber Carpathians rose from the snow-covered plains, and villages,
surrounded by white glistening walls, and stunted
willows stood by the side of the roads, ravens sailed
through the white sky, and here and there a small
peasants' sledge shot by, drawn by two thin horses.

At last they reached the station. There the Count's
steward was waiting for them with a carriage and
four, which brought them to their destination almost
as swiftly as the iron steed.

The numerous servants were drawn up in the
yard of the ancient castle to receive their master
and mistress, and gave loud cheers for her, for which
she thanked them smilingly. When she went into
the dim, arched passages, and the large rooms, for a
moment she felt a strange feeling of fear, but she
quickly checked it, for was not her most ardent wish
to be fulfilled in a couple of hours?

She put on her bridal attire, in which a half-
comical, half-sinister looking old woman with a tooth-
less mouth and a nose like an owl's assisted her.

---

* A division of Poland, of which Warsaw is the capital.

Just as she was fixing the myrtle wreath on to her dark curls, the bell began to ring, which summoned her to her wedding. The Count himself, in full uniform, led her to the chapel of the castle, where the priest, with the steward and the castellan as witnesses, and the footmen in grand liveries, were awaiting the handsome young couple.

After the wedding, the marriage certificate was signed in the vestry, and a groom was sent to the station, where he dispatched a telegram to her parents, to the effect that the hussar had kept his word, and that Fanny Löwenfuss had become Countess Faniska W ——.

Then the newly-married couple sat down to a beautiful little dinner in company with the chaplain, the steward, and the castellan. The champagne made them all very cheerful, and at last the Count knelt down before his young and beautiful wife, boldly took her white satin slipper off her foot, filled it with wine, and emptied it to her health.

At length night came, a thorough, Polish wedding-night, and Faniska, who had just assumed a demi-toilette, was looking at herself with proud satisfaction in the great mirror that was fastened into the wall, from top to bottom. A white satin train flowed down behind her like rays from the moon, a half-open jacket of bright green velvet, trimmed with valuable ermine, covered her voluptuous, virgin bust and her classic arms, only to show them all the more seductively at the slightest motion, while the wealth of her dark hair, in which diamonds hung here and there like glittering dewdrops, fell down her neck and mingled with the white fur. The Count entered in a red velvet dressing-gown trimmed with sable; at a sign from him, the old woman who was waiting on his divinity left the room, and the next moment he was lying like a slave at the feet of his lovely young wife, who raised him up and was pressing him to her heaving bosom, when a noise which she had never heard before, a wild howling, startled the loving woman in the midst of her bliss.

"What was that?" she asked, trembling.

The Count went to the window without speaking, and she with him, her arms round him. She looked half timidly, half curiously out into the darkness, where large bright spots were moving about in pairs, in the park at her feet.

"Are they will-o'-the-wisps?" she whispered.

"No, my child, they are wolves," the Count replied, fetching his double-barreled gun, which he loaded. Then he went out on the snow-covered balcony, while she drew the fur more closely over her bosom, and followed him.

"Will you shoot?" the Count asked her in a whisper, and when she nodded, he said: "Aim straight at the first pair of bright spots that you see; they are the eyes of those amiable brutes."

Then he handed her the gun and pointed it for her. "That is the way—are you pointing straight?"

"Yes."

"Then fire."

A flash, a report, which the echo from the hills repeated four times, and two of the unpleasant looking lights had vanished.

Then the Count fired, and by that time their people were all awake; they drove away the wolves with torches and shouts, and laid the two large animals, the spoils of a Polish wedding-night, at the feet of their young mistress.

The days that followed resembled that night. The Count showed himself a most attentive husband, his wife's knight and slave, and she felt quite at home in that dull castle. She rode, drove, smoked, read French novels, and beat her servants as well as any Polish Countess could have done. In the course of a few years, she presented the Count with two children, and although he appeared very happy at that, yet, like most husbands, he grew continually cooler, more indolent, and neglectful of her. From time to time he left the castle to see after his affairs in the capital, and the intervals between those journeys became continually shorter. Faniska felt that her husband was tired of her, and much as it grieved her, she did not let him notice it; she was always the same.

But at last the Count remained away altogether. At first he used to write, but at last the poor, weeping woman did not even receive letters to comfort her in her unhappy solitude, and his lawyer sent the money that she and the children required.

She conjectured, hoped, doubted, suffered, and wept for more than a year; then she suddenly went to the capital and appeared unexpectedly in his apartments. Painful explanations followed, until at last the Count told her that he no longer loved her, and would not live with her for the future. When she wished to make him do so by legal means, and intrusted her case to a celebrated lawyer, *the Count denied that she was his wife*. She produced her marriage certificate, and lo! the most infamous fraud came to light. A confidential servant of the Count had acted the part of the priest, so that the tailor's beautiful daughter had, as a matter of fact, merely been the Count's mistress, and her children therefore were bastards.

The virtuous woman then saw, when it was too late, that it was *she* who had formed a *mésalliance*. Her parents would have nothing to do with her, and at last it came out that the Count was married long before he knew her, but that he did not live with his wife.

Then Fanny applied to the police magistrates; she wanted to appeal to justice, but was dissuaded from taking criminal proceedings; for although they would certainly lead to the punishment of her daring seducer, they would also bring about her own ruin.

At last, however, her lawyer effected a settlement between them, which was favorable to Fanny, and which she accepted for the sake of her children. The Count paid her a considerable sum down, and gave her the gloomy castle to live in. Thither she returned with a broken heart, and from that time lived alone, a sullen misanthrope, a fierce despot.

From time to time, you may meet wandering through the Carpathians a pale woman of almost unearthly beauty, wearing a magnificent sable-skin jacket and carrying a gun over her shoulder, in the forest, or in the winter in a sledge, driving her foaming horses until they nearly drop from fatigue, while the harness bells utter a melancholy sound, and at last die away in the distance, like the weeping of a solitary, deserted human heart.

THE UMBRELLA

MME. OREILLE was a very economical woman; she thoroughly knew the value of a half-penny, and possessed a whole storehouse of strict principles with regard to the multiplication of money, so that her cook found the greatest difficulty in making what the servants call their "market-penny," while her husband was hardly allowed any pocket-money at all. They were, however, very comfortably off, and had no children. It really pained Mme. Oreille to see any money spent; it was like tearing at her heartstrings when she had to take any of those nice crownpieces out of her pocket; and whenever she had to spend anything, no matter how necessary it was, she slept badly the next night.

Oreille was continually saying to his wife:

"You really might be more liberal, as we have no children and never spend our income."

"You don't know what may happen," she used to reply. "It is better to have too much than too little."

She was a little woman of about forty, very active, rather hasty, wrinkled, very neat and tidy, and with a very short temper. Her husband very often used to complain of all the privations she made him endure; some of them were particularly painful to him, as they touched his vanity.

He was one of the upper clerks in the War Office, and only stayed there in obedience to his wife's wish, so as to increase their income, which they did not nearly spend.

For two years he had always come to the office with the same old patched umbrella, to the great amusement of his fellow-clerks. At last he got tired of their jokes, and insisted upon his wife buying him a new one. She bought one for eight francs and a-half, one of those cheap things which large houses sell as an advertisement. When the others in the office saw the article, which was being sold in Paris by the thousand, they began their jokes again, and Oreille had a dreadful time of it with them. They even made a song about it, which he heard from morning till night all over the immense building.

Oreille was very angry, and peremptorily told his wife to get him a new one, a good silk one, for twenty francs, and to bring him the bill, so that he might see that it was all right.

She bought him one for eighteen francs, and said, getting red with anger as she gave it to her husband: "This will last you for five years at least."

Oreille felt quite triumphant, and obtained a small ovation at the office with his new acquisition. When he went home in the evening, his wife said to him, looking at the umbrella uneasily:

"You should not leave it fastened up with the elastic; it will very likely cut the silk. You must take care of it, for I shall not buy you a new one in a hurry."

She took it, unfastened it, and then remained dumfounded with astonishment and rage. In the middle of the silk there was a hole as big as a sixpenny-piece, as if made with the end of a cigar.

"What is that?" she screamed.

Her husband replied quietly, without looking at it:

"What is it? What do you mean?"

She was choking with rage and could hardly get out a word.

"You—you—have burned—your umbrella! Why—you must be—mad! Do you wish to ruin us outright?"

He turned round hastily, as if frightened.

"What are you talking about?"

"I say that you have burned your umbrella. Just look here—"

And rushing at him, as if she were going to beat him, she violently thrust the little circular burned hole under his nose.

He was so utterly struck dumb at the sight of it that he could only stammer out:

"What—what is it? How should I know? I have done nothing, I will swear. I don't know what is the matter with the umbrella."

"You have been playing tricks with it at the office; you have been playing the fool and opening it, to show it off!" she screamed.

"I only opened it once, to let them see what a nice one it was, that is all, I declare."

But she shook with rage, and got up one of those conjugal scenes which make a peaceable man dread the domestic hearth more than a battlefield where bullets are raining.

She mended it with a piece of silk cut out of the old umbrella, which was of a different color, and the next day Oreille went off very humbly with the mended article in his hand. He put it into a cupboard, and thought no more of it than of some unpleasant recollection.

But he had scarcely got home that evening when his wife took the umbrella from him, opened it, and nearly had a fit when she saw what had befallen it, for the disaster was now irreparable. It was covered with small holes, which evidently, proceeded from burns, just as if some one had emptied the ashes from a lighted pipe on to it. It was done for utterly, irreparably.

She looked at it without a word, in too great a passion to be able to say anything. He also, when he saw the damage, remained almost dumb, in a state of frightened consternation.

They looked at each other; then he looked on to the floor. The next moment she threw the useless article at his head, screaming out in a transport of the most violent rage, for she had now recovered her voice:

"Oh! you brute! you brute! You did it on purpose, but I will pay you out for it. You shall not have another."

And then the scene began again. After the storm had raged for an hour, he, at last, was enabled to explain himself. He declared that he could not under-

stand it at all, and that it could only proceed from
malice or from vengeance.

A ring at the bell saved him; it was a friend whom
they were expecting to dinner.

Mme. Oreille submitted the case to him. As for
buying a new umbrella, that was out of the question;
her husband should not have another. The friend
very sensibly said that in that case his clothes would
be spoiled, and they were certainly worth more than
the umbrella. But the little woman, who was still in
a rage, replied:

"Very well, then, when it rains he may have the
kitchen umbrella, for I will not give him a new silk
one."

Oreille utterly rebelled at such an idea.

"All right," he said; "then I shall resign my post.
I am not going to the office with the kitchen umbrella."

The friend interposed:

"Have this one recovered; it will not cost much."

But Mme. Oreille, being in the temper that she
was, said:

"It will cost at least eight francs to recover it.
Eight and eighteen are twenty-six. Just fancy, twenty-
six francs for an umbrella! It is utter madness!"

The friend, who was only a poor man of the middle classes, had an inspiration:

"Make your fire insurance pay for it. The com-
panies pay for all articles that are burned, as long as
the damage has been done in your own house."

On hearing this advice the little woman calmed
down immediately, and then, after a moment's reflection, she said to her husband:

"To-morrow, before going to your office, you will go to the Maternelle Insurance Company, show them the state your umbrella is in, and make them pay for the damage."

M. Oreille fairly jumped, he was so startled at the proposal.

"I would not do it for my life! It is eighteen francs lost, that is all. It will not ruin us."

The next morning he took a walking-stick when he went out, for, luckily, it was a fine day.

Left at home alone, Mme. Oreille could not get over the loss of her eighteen francs by any means. She had put the umbrella on the dining-room table, and she looked at it without being able to come to any determination.

Every moment she thought of the insurance company, but she did not dare to encounter the quizzical looks of the gentlemen who might receive her, for she was very timid before people, and grew red at a mere nothing, feeling embarrassed when she had to speak to strangers.

But regret at the loss of the eighteen francs pained her as if she had been wounded. She tried not to think of it any more, and yet every moment the recollection of the loss struck her painfully. What was she to do, however? Time went on, and she could not decide; but suddenly, like all cowards, she made up her mind.

"I will go, and we will see what will happen."

But first of all she was obliged to prepare the umbrella so that the disaster might be complete, and the reason of it quite evident. She took a match from the mantelpiece, and between the ribs she burned a hole as big as the palm of her hand. Then she rolled it up carefully, fastened it with the elastic band, put on her bonnet and shawl, and went quickly toward the Rue de Rivoli, where the insurance office was.

But the nearer she got the slower she walked. What was she going to say, and what reply would she get?

She looked at the numbers of the houses; there were still twenty-eight. That was all right, she had time to consider, and she walked slower and slower. Suddenly she saw a door on which was a large brass plate with "La Maternelle Fire Insurance Office" engraved on it. Already! She waited for a moment, for she felt nervous and almost ashamed; then she went past, came back, went past again, and came back again.

At last she said to herself:

"I must go in, however, so I may as well do it now as later."

She could not help noticing, however, how her heart beat as she entered. She went into an enormous room with grated wicket openings all round, and a man behind each of them, and as a gentleman, carrying a number of papers, passed her, she stopped him and said, timidly:

"I beg your pardon, Monsieur, but can you tell me where I must apply for payment for anything that has been accidentally burned?"

He replied in a sonorous voice:

"The first door on the left; that is the department you want."

This frightened her still more, and she felt inclined to run away, to make no claim, to sacrifice her eighteen francs. But the idea of that sum revived her courage, and she went upstairs, out of breath, stopping at almost every other step.

She knocked at a door which she saw on the first landing, and a clear voice said, in answer:

"Come in!"

She obeyed mechanically, and found herself in a large room where three solemn gentlemen, each with a decoration in his buttonhole, were standing talking.

One of them asked her: "What do you want, Madame?"

She could hardly get out her words, but stammered: "I have come—I have come on account of an accident, something—"

He very politely pointed out a seat to her.

"If you will kindly sit down I will attend to you in a moment."

And, returning to the other two, he went on with the conversation.

"The company, gentlemen, does not consider that it is under any obligation to you for more than four hundred thousand francs, and we can pay no attention to your claim to the further sum of a hundred thousand, which you wish to make us pay. Besides that, the surveyor's valuation—"

One of the others interrupted him:

"That is quite enough, Monsieur; the law-courts will decide between us, and we have nothing further to do than to take our leave." And they went out after mutual ceremonious bows.

Oh! if she could only have gone away with them, how gladly she would have done it; she would have run away and given up everything. But it was too late, for the gentleman came back, and said, bowing:

"What can I do for you, Madame?"

She could scarcely speak, but at last she managed to say:

"I have come—for this."

The manager looked at the object which she held out to him in mute astonishment. With trembling fingers she tried to undo the elastic, and succeeded, after several attempts, and hastily opened the damaged remains of the umbrella.

"It looks to me to be in a very bad state of health," he said, compassionately.

"It cost me twenty francs," she said, with some hesitation.

He seemed astonished. "Really! As much as that?"

"Yes, it was a capital article, and I wanted you to see the state it is in."

"Very well, I see; very well. But I really do not understand what it can have to do with me."

She began to feel uncomfortable; perhaps this company did not pay for such small articles, and she said:

"But—it is burned."

He could not deny it.

"I see that very well," he replied.

She remained open-mouthed, not knowing what to say next; then suddenly forgetting that she had left out the main thing, she said hastily:

"I am Mme. Oreille; we are assured in La Maternelle, and I have come to claim the value of this damage. I only want you to have it recovered," she added quickly, fearing a positive refusal.

The manager was rather embarrassed, and said:

"But, really, Madame, we do not sell umbrellas; we cannot undertake such kinds of repairs."

The little woman felt her courage reviving; she was not going to give up without a struggle; she was not even afraid now, so she said:

"I only want you to pay me the cost of repairing it; I can quite well get it done myself."

The gentleman seemed rather confused.

"Really, Madame, it is such a very small matter! We are never asked to give compensation for such trivial losses. You must allow that we cannot make good pocket-handkerchiefs, gloves, brooms, slippers, all the small articles which are every day exposed to the chances of being burned."

She got red, and felt inclined to fly into a rage.

"But, Monsieur, last December one of our chimneys caught fire, and caused at least five hundred francs' damage. M. Oreille made no claim on the company, and so it is only just that it should pay for my umbrella now."

The manager, guessing that she was telling a lie, said, with a smile:

"You must acknowledge, Madame, that it is very surprising that M. Oreille should have asked no compensation for damages amounting to five hundred francs, and should now claim five or six francs for mending an umbrella."

She was not the least put out, and replied:

"I beg your pardon, Monsieur, the five hundred francs affected M. Oreille's pocket, whereas this damage, amounting to eighteen francs, concerns Mme. Oreille's pocket only. which is a totally different matter."

As he saw that he had no chance of getting rid of her, and that he would only be wasting his time, he said, resignedly:

"Will you kindly tell me how the damage was done?"

She felt that she had won the victory, and said:

"This is how it happened, Monsieur: In our hall there is a bronze stick- and umbrella-stand, and the other day, when I came in, I put my umbrella into it. I must tell you that just above there is a shelf for the candlesticks and matches. I put out my hand, took three or four matches, and struck one, but it missed fire, so I struck another, which ignited, but went out immediately, and a third did the same."

The manager interrupted her, to make a joke.

"I suppose they were Government matches, then?"

She did not understand him, and went on:

"Very likely. At any rate, the fourth caught fire, and I lit my candle, and went into my room to go to bed; but in a quarter-of-an-hour I fancied that I smelled something burning, and I have always been terribly afraid of fire. If ever we have an accident it will not be my fault, I assure you. I am terribly nervous since our chimney was on fire, as I told you; so I got up, and hunted about everywhere, sniffing like a dog after game, and at last I noticed that my umbrella was burning. Most likely a match had fallen between the folds and burned it. You can see how it has damaged it."

The manager had taken his clue, and asked her:

"What do you estimate the damage at?"

She did not know what to say, as she was not certain what amount to put on it, but at last she replied:

"Perhaps you had better get it done yourself. I will leave it to you."

He, however, naturally refused.

"No, Madame, I cannot do that. Tell me the amount of your claim, that is all I want to know."

"Well!—I think that— Look here, Monsieur, I do not want to make any money out of you, so I will tell you what we will do. I will take my umbrella to the maker, who will recover it in good, durable silk, and I will bring the bill to you. Will that suit you, Monsieur?"

"Perfectly, Madame; we will settle it on that basis. Here is a note for the cashier, who will repay you whatever it costs you."

He gave Mme. Oreille a slip of paper. She took it, got up, and went out, thanking him, for she was in a hurry to escape lest he should change his mind.

She went briskly through the streets, looking out for a really good umbrella-maker, and when she found a shop which appeared to be a first-class one, she went in, and said, confidently:

"I want this umbrella recovered in silk, good silk. Use the very best and strongest you have; I don't mind what it costs."

*This book
was printed on wood free paper
and bound by
Hazell Watson & Viney Ltd,
Aylesbury, Bucks*

Printed and bound in England